THE 8TH DEMON

A WICKED NUMINOSITY

BRUCE HENNIGAN

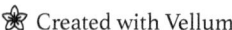 Created with Vellum

To my friend and brother in Christ, Gerald Brown, survivor for 18 years after his heart transplant. Every day we would talk about the love of Christ and our last conversations were about putting on the whole armor of God. He passed away on April, 3, 2020 and is even now living in the ultimate reality we all can experience one day in the presence of our Lord. Thank you, my friend for 36 years of friendship and brotherhood. As you have said so often, "Thank God for Jesus."

And, to my daughter, Casey who is the most courageous, powerful, and strong person I could ever know. I love you.

FOREWORD

I was a nerd before nerd was a word.

There is a photograph of me in the eighth grade. In the late 1960s and early 1970s the world was changing but my parents who were married in 1935 during the Great Depression were of a different era. My hair was short and slicked down with Brylcreem, "A little dab a do ya." That was the slogan. And, when at the age of 13 I finally got glasses, my parents purchased the cheapest set of black rimmed glasses available. All I was lacking was the tape in the middle.

In my yearbook picture with my short, glistening hair and my retro glasses, I also sported a pocket protector. Yes, a pocket protector! In my pocket protector I had several pens and a slide rule. Calculators had just appeared on the marketplace but my math teachers still require we learn the slide rule just in case of a nuclear apocalypse. Today, it would be a zombie apocalypse.

So, yes, I was a nerd. I loved science. Still do. My favorite gifts from the age of 10 to 13 (before I discovered girls were NOT loathsome after all) were a telescope, a microscope, and a chemistry set.

Why am I telling you this? When you read this story, I want

you to remember that I LOVE science! I am not here to criticize our efforts to advance technology to the point that human lives can be improved. However, there is a field of thinking called transhumanism. And, I applaud our desire to improve our basic humanity. But, I believe we must move ahead with great caution. As my son, Sean, would say, there are ways of thinking about what it means to be human that are "fraught with peril."

I believe we must not abandon our souls in the desire to be immortal. *"What good is it for someone to gain the whole world, yet forfeit their soul? Or what can anyone give in exchange for their soul?" Mark 8:36-37.*

My story explores this interface between the material and the non-material, between the brain and the mind; between the body and the soul. Those words just quoted came from Jesus Christ, the Son of God, the ultimate transhuman manifestation: God in man form.

So, don't think for a moment I am decrying the power of science. I am a scientist. But, we must temper any field or discipline with the reality there is more to our existence than just mere living and dying. Or, evolving beyond our humanity. All humans are of value and are sacred vessels of a soul, not just the end product of random processes. You are special. Everyone is special. And, as we advance into the future we must never forget that!

Bruce Hennigan

May, 2020

NUMINOSITY

1. Of or relating to a *numen*; supernatural.
    2. Filled with or characterized by a sense of a supernatural presence: a numinous place.
    3. Spiritually elevated; sublime.
    4. Arousing spiritual or religious emotions
    5. Mysterious or awe-inspiring — Latin *numen*, divine will

The term numinosity isn't too well-known beyond the academic study of religion and anthropology. In a sense numinosity is like the more familiar term luminosity. But numinosity refers to a subtle, spiritual light instead of an outwardly visible light such as the luminosity of the moon. While numinosity and luminosity may coexist, they remain somehow different.
    Urban Dictionary

~

Something numinous has a strong religious quality, suggesting the presence of a divine power. When you enter a temple, church, or mosque, you might feel as though you've entered a numinous space.

Numinous comes from the Latin *numin-* meaning "divine power." This word also comes from *numen*, a word used to describe the spirit or divine power characteristic of a thing or place. However, you don't have to be in a strictly religious environment to experience something numinous; you might see the beauty of a painting or the melody of a song as numinous — if they communicate a spiritual vibe.

Definition from <u>vocabulary.com</u>

THOUGHTS TO CONSIDER

"Up till now human life has generally been, as Hobbes described it, 'nasty, brutish and short'; the great majority of human beings (if they have not already died young) have been afflicted with misery... we can justifiably hold the belief that these lands of possibility exist, and that the present limitations and miserable frustrations of our existence could be in large measure surmounted... The human species can, if it wishes, transcend itself—not just sporadically, an individual here in one way, an individual there in another way, but in its entirety, as humanity."

Julian Huxley, the *"founder"* of Transhumanism.

"We feel the tension between using biomedical innovations to benefit humanity and encroaching upon God's domain. As Christians, we believe that God's image includes a moral component—an inherent sense of right and wrong. And regardless of one's worldview, this sense of right and wrong prompts people to feel uncomfortable about how emerging biotechnologies will be implemented, both for therapeutic and enhancement purposes. A sense of discomfort prompts Christians (and others) to raise the alarm about playing God."

Fazale R. Rana with Kenneth R. Samples "Humans 2.0"

PROLOGUE

In any other realm, the demon would not have existed in its current form. It would have been faceless and immaterial. But here in this reality, the demon was very real and very dangerous as it taunted the young man standing on the precarious mountain ledge.

The demon hovered over the young man, and its leathery wings beat the hot, sulfur tainted air. The face was vaguely human, but the rest of its body was that of a dragon. It smiled and exposed rotten teeth. The demon's putrid green eyes were twice the normal size, and it had no nose, just two dark slits. The young man choked on the thing's rancid breath, and he tried to turn his face away. Just a few more feet away was the opening to the cave he had sought for days. If he could reach the cave, it would provide a brief respite from the hideous things that populated this reality. But, in so doing, he would have to risk exposing his greatest weapon.

"You cannot enter the cave, mortal. It is forbidden." The demon hissed.

The young man pressed himself further into the cliff face and felt the stones slip beneath his feet. One false move, and he would slide off of the six-inch ledge and tumble into the lava pit below. His heart raced, and sweat poured across his bare chest. His jeans were mere tatters, and blisters covered the bottom of his bare feet.

"You are weak, mortal. You are fading, and soon my master will claim your soul." The demon's membranous wings caught the heat rising from the lava pit. "Give in and make the sacrifice, and all of your suffering and pain will cease. Enter into sweet oblivion."

"No! My pain and suffering will have just begun." He slid his hand into the pocket of his jeans and touched the cold stone.

"Then there is no hope, is there?" The demon laughed. "Give in. Give up. Embrace your inevitable fate. Why keep fighting?"

"Because I have to save my sister." He shouted and pulled the blue stone from his pocket. He held it up, and light burst forth and played across the demon's face. It shrieked and pulled its wing in to cover its eyes. When it did, it tumbled down toward the lava and disappeared in a gush of oily smoke. The young man sighed and slid the stone back into his pocket. With the use of the stone, other demons could find him quickly unless he made it to the safety of the cave. He inched his way carefully along the ledge. He stepped inside the cave and collapsed onto the cool, rocky floor.

How much longer could he hold out? The stone contained the seeds of triumph for him and also the seeds of worldwide domination for *her*. Balance. A careful balance was required to achieve his goal of stopping *her* and saving his sister. He closed his eyes, and the other reality beckoned, threatening to pull him back into the other world. No! He must stay! He must find his way to the monoliths and the altars! For a second, the cave faded in and out and revealed an ordinary room. He could not hold out much longer! He willed himself back into the cave.

THE PARISIAN BUILDING had been constructed in the 1700s and only recently purchased for remodeling and conversion into tourism rentals. However, the company developing the property had fallen into bankruptcy, and the remodeling process had halted.

The small apartment on the top floor was once reserved only for the poor. Each story from the ground level up to the sixth floor was decreasingly small until the topmost "lofts" were the lowliest with windows opening out over the exotic vista of the City of Lights.

When the buildings were constructed, it was for the wealthiest patrons to live on the second floor. The merchants such as butchers and bakers took in the ground floor, for there were the hottest and most uncomfortable levels. The higher floors were taken by servants and the poor because the stench and heat rose upward. One would think the topmost floor with its achingly beautiful vistas were the most desirable. They were the least wanted.

It was here, in this lonely abandoned flat overlooking the Seine river and the once splendid Notre Dame, the young man had chosen to hide while trying his best to save his sister. And, hopefully, the world. Although his mind and soul were trapped in some far-off cave, locked in mortal combat with demons, his physical body reclined on a tattered, stained sofa, his eyes, empty of awareness, were hidden behind a pair of thin, black goggles, and his body barely hung onto life. His feeding tube carried sustenance to his weakening body, but the nutrition bags attached to the pump that carried his life-sustaining water and nutrition through that tube were almost empty. Not much time remained.

A bird landed on the open window and tilted its head to examine the young man's body. The human's chest still moved as breath rattled in and out of his bare chest. And, his heart still beat, now slowly. There was no nourishment for the bird. Yet. In time, the bird would return to feast on the remains of this wretched creature who was lost, lost to hope and light and love.

The bird flew away, and the morning sun peeked through the window. A shard of sunlight fell upon the man's clutched fist, and for a moment, the blue stone clutched in his hand glittered with supernatural light.

1

N ovember -- Somewhere over Switzerland

"JONATHAN, HELP ME!"

Jonathan Steel lifted out of his seat, and the seatbelt strained as the passenger jet fell a thousand feet. The voice had come from behind him and was quickly drowned out by the screams from the other passengers. In the aisle ahead of him, a flight attendant flew upward and slammed against the ceiling before tumbling back down onto the snack cart. Her bloody face disappeared as she slumped to the other side of the cart.

Steel grabbed the arms of his seat and tried to steady himself in the turbulent thrashing of the airplane. He glanced over his left shoulder down the aisle separating the center rows from the outer row of seats. Three seats back, two women fought in the exit row. The aging woman in the aisle had walked past him just moments before the turbulence hit. Her gray hair was short, and a nasal cannula carried oxygen from the tank hanging around her neck. She had stumbled past him with a black cane clutched in her gloved hand. He remembered because of the image of two red snakes intertwined along the shaft of the cane.

Now, the elderly woman swung her cane at another woman who sat against the exit door. The other woman was dark-skinned with long, black hair and Asian features. She blocked the blows from the elderly woman's cane. The elderly woman grabbed the strap of a messenger bag and pulled it from around the other woman's neck. The other woman snared the strap and tugged it back towards her as they fought over the bag. The woman seated in the exit row looked directly at Steel.

"Steel, help me now!" She screamed in his direction. How did she know who he was? The airplane shuddered again in the turbulence just as Steel unfastened his seat belt. He floated up out of the seat and twisted around into the aisle, bent legs cushioning the blow when the airplane returned to gravity. The elderly woman glared at him, and her gray hair slid sideways and flew from her head. Bright red hair blossomed around her face.

"Stay out of this." She screamed above the shouts and cries of the other passengers. Steel lurched down the aisle, and the red-haired woman spun around and swung the black cane at his head. From its tip, a ceramic blade shot out and barely missed severing his carotid artery. He dodged the cane and dove at her just as the airplane fell through the air again. The woman shot up against the roof, trailing the oxygen tank and the messenger bag. She tucked herself up against the bulkhead and wrapped the strap of the bag around her shoulders.

Steel fell into the seat beside the other woman. Her head lolled on her shoulders. She was unconscious. He grabbed at the redhead's hand, and the graceful, leather glove slid away, revealing red, ceramic fingers on an articulated mechanical hand.

She landed in the aisle beside him and deftly flipped backward over the center four seats into the far aisle. She shrugged out of her heavy jacket, and a backpack appeared. She unscrewed the top of the oxygen bottle with her artificial hand and pulled out a face mask. She pulled it over her face like a ski mask with her eyes protected by glass goggles.

"Tell God I said hello." She shouted. The two passengers sitting by the exit door never knew what hit them. One swipe with the cane's blade and blood spurted into the air. The airplane tumbled again, and the redhead reached her normal hand to the exit door handle. Steel screamed, "No!" and quickly fastened his seat belt.

With inhuman strength, blood spraying into her face, the redhead jerked the exit door free and was sucked out into the darkness, the same darkness that shrouded Steel's vision and plunged him into frigid oblivion.

A COLD, gray cloud surrounded Steel, blanketing him with sudden silence. He blinked in confusion, and a man appeared before him out of the haze, decked out in a brilliant white three-piece suit with a bright blue tie. His dark hair was carefully combed, and a trim beard outlined his square jaw.

"Señor Steel, I presume." He said.

"Where am I?"

"Between life and death, mi amigo." The man plucked a red carnation from his lapel and inhaled its fragrance. "Life smells so wonderful, eh?"

"I was on an airplane."

"You are still on the airplane."

"Who are you?"

"A messenger from God. You may call me Miguel. Alphus is busy." He clicked his heels together and bowed his head. He stepped closer and tucked the carnation into Steel's shirt pocket. "When you awaken, you will have very little time. You must save the woman beside you. There is much at stake, and she has a role in the story that is about to unfold. Comprende, mi amigo?"

"I, yes, maybe." Steel mumbled as he looked down at the flower hidden in his pocket, and the fog around him swirled and eddied, and from a far distance, a roar proceeded, growing louder. He glanced back at Miguel, and the man disappeared in an explosion of snow and ice. The snow hit him in the face, and he shook his head in confusion as sound and fury assaulted him.

The front half of the airplane was gone, and snow showered the interior. Through the open end of the aircraft, he saw rocks and mountain peaks illuminated by a full moon. The airplane slid down a mountainside.

The woman beside him was still unconscious, and he unfastened both of their seat belts. His gaze fell on the exit door. Why not? It had worked for the redhead.

Steel slid the woman's body over his shoulder and crouched in her seat as the plane oscillated and yawed down the mountainside. He pulled the exit door free from the bulkhead and shoved it out onto the wing. Hanging onto the handle for dear life, he knelt on the door and slid forward onto the wing into the ice and snow thrown up by the airplane. The door slid off the wing with a painful drop, and his back cracked with the blow. Something dark loomed ahead, and he ducked as the tail of the airplane flew over him.

The door slid and gyrated on the snow, and the sudden cold made his free hand numb. Still, he held on, sliding and slipping down the slope with the woman tossed over his shoulder. The tail section of the airplane continued down the mountainside and disappeared from view as it plummeted over a cliff. An explosion painted the night in fire and ice. He used his feet to create drag and stop the spinning of the door. Trees flashed around him, and the door shot up a slope into the air. He clutched the woman against his chest as they landed in a hill of soft snow and tumbled forward until he slammed up against a wooden wall.

2

S teel gasped in pain with each breath. He stood up and leaned against the wooden structure behind him. What did he hear? Above the distant echoes of the airplane's explosion, a new sound surfaced. Dogs? Did he hear dogs barking?

The woman sprawled in a snowbank against the wall of the structure behind him. He found a door secured with a padlock. He kicked in the door and painfully lifted the woman's limp body. Inside, there was warmth and subdued light from red LEDs. A bank of handheld radios in chargers sat on a table in the center of the room. The dog barking grew louder. He cleared away brochures and release forms from the table and gently laid the woman on the worn wooden surface. She had a strong pulse and seemed to be no worse for wear. He, on the other hand, seemed to have a couple of painful ribs and several bruises on both arms from tumbling around in the airplane.

Steel picked up a radio and switched it on. Static filled the air, and he pressed the speak button. "This is Jonathan Steel. I'm in some kind of dog shelter or dog sledding facility on the side of a mountain. My airplane just crashed. Can anyone hear me?"

Static answered him, and he tossed the radio back onto the table. He walked toward the sound of the barking and opened a far door. The fetid, animal odor of dog excrement and urine assaulted him. The room beyond was long and housed at least a dozen husky dogs each in their individual enclosure. They fell silent as he appeared, tongues hanging out and tails wagging.

At the far end of the enclosure, he glanced through a fogged window. Two sleds waited outside. If he could get the dogs hooked to the sled, then he could get down the mountainside for help. Inside the door were piles of blankets and heavy jackets and gloves for the customers looking forward to a thrilling dog sled ride down the mountain.

"I know how to hook them up."

He whirled at the sound of the voice. The woman appeared behind him. "I've used a dog sled before."

"You! Are you okay?" Steel asked.

"I'm a bit foggy." She shrugged into one of the jackets and stumbled in the process. She put out a restraining hand and zipped the jacket closed. "Let me get the dogs ready to go. Why don't you go back and try to reach someone on the radio? We are on the Jungfraujoch, the saddle between the Mönch and the Jungfrau mountains. How did we get here?"

"The airplane crashed." Steel said. "How do you know me? Who was that woman?" Steel had a thousand questions, but right now, survival was uppermost in his mind. He glanced at her face hidden in shadow and once again felt a familiar pang of recognition. Did he know her?

"Not now! We have to move." The woman said as she began unfastening the cages of the dogs. "Radio?" She motioned back toward the other room.

As Steel walked back to the radio room, thoughts spun in

his mind. He suffered from amnesia, and over the past few months, only glimpses of his past had surfaced. Had he met this woman before? It was likely. And, if he had, she might hold the key to his lost memories. Perhaps she could lead him to his father, the Captain.

The room was dark. No LEDs. Where were the radios? They were gone. But how? He glanced around the room, searching for a telephone: nothing but bottled water and brochures advertising the dog sled ride. The woman must have done something with the radios. But why?

"I forget how beautiful your eyes are."

He turned, and she stood in the doorway to the dog compound. Her features were hidden in shadow. His heart raced. "You know me?"

"We don't have much time. My attacker. What happened on the airplane?"

"She jumped out through the other exit door. A backpack was probably some kind of parachute. And, she had oxygen." He came closer to her.

"Then, my messenger bag was on the airplane?"

"The woman took it."

She cursed and slammed a fist into the door frame. "No! This is bad. Very bad. What did she look like under that ridiculous wig?"

"Red hair. And, she had some kind of mechanical hand. A prosthesis."

"Yeah, this is beyond bad." The woman sighed, reached for her waist, and a fanny pack appeared. She rummaged inside. "I hate to do this, but she must continue to think I am dead."

Steel froze and watched her pull a thick, black bracelet out of the fanny pack. She pulled it onto her right hand. She touched the bracelet, and yellow bits of light glowed. They moved in a graceful pattern and then flowed off of the bracelet into the very substance of her hand. "I'm afraid you're going to have to forget about me. You'll be the sole survivor of the greatest aircraft tragedy in Swiss history." She looked up at him from her glowing hand, and the moonlight streaming in through the window illuminated her face. He gasped as the pieces of a far puzzle fell into place.

"Dr. Monarch?" The fury took him, red hot anger searing his heart and flooding into his mind. He was back in the gritty surgical suite in the prison camp in Africa. She stood over him with a scalpel in her hand. At the request of his father, this was the woman who had operated on his brain! "You did this to me." He balled his fist and launched himself at her.

Monarch simply put out her hand, palm spread toward him, and a bright light streamed from the fingertips into his face. Steel stumbled and fell to the side, blinded by the light. He tumbled into the table, and it upended, brochures and bottles of water cascading around him.

Monarch knelt beside him, and his mind exploded with pain. "What? How?"

"I threw the radios out into the snow until I could think. Don't worry. I'll put you out by the dog sled area. They'll think you got a sled ready to go, and the dogs ran off without you. You won't die. You might get a touch of frostbite, but we both know how quickly you heal." With her left hand, she tapped at the bracelet. "Now, listen carefully. You will forget me. You will forget the woman on the airplane. In time, I will come back for you because both of our lives are in grave danger. But I need you to finish what you started on your trip to Switzerland. You'll have a doozy of a headache for a few days, but at least you'll be alive."

Steel gasped as the pain in his head worsened. Monarch tucked her hair back as she leaned over him. "Have you ever heard of the third eye?"

"What?"

"Right between your eyes." She whispered, extending her

glowing index finger. He tried to pull back, but Monarch put her left hand behind his head and restrained him.

"Just relax. I'm activating a part of your implant. It'll only hurt for a little while." She touched his forehead between his eyes and pain, unlike anything he had ever experienced seared through his brain. Flames and electricity exploded in his vision engulfing him in a maelstrom of fiery amnesia, pulling him down, down, down into darkness.

3

S hreveport, Louisiana

"Yo, DEMON BOY!"

Joshua Knight winced and dropped his fork onto his tray. The chatter in the school cafeteria stopped. "Not now, Buck."

All three hundred pounds of Buck Sanderson towered over him. His head seemed to blend gradually into his shoulders. He was a linebacker for the Byrd Yellowjackets and good at it. But, this one skill seemed to be his only attribute other than being an obnoxious jerk. "My buddies and I noticed you were wearing a necklace in gym today."

Josh closed his eyes and sighed. His hand went involuntarily to the slivers of red stone hanging around his neck in the shape of a cross. It had been a part of the Bloodstone that had once belonged to his late father. "Buck, it was a gift from my father." Josh looked up at Buck. "Who is now dead because he saved my life."

Buck leered at the two stout boys behind him. "A gift from his daddy? My Daddy is getting me a new car for my birthday. All you got was a wimpy little necklace."

Josh nodded and felt the red jewel shards begin to heat up in response to his growing anger. He had to be careful with the thing. It had unworldly properties. For a moment, he imagined a death ray shooting from his chest to dissolve Buck and his minions into a pile of smoking goo. He swallowed and tried to calm down his racing heart. "So, you noticed it while I was in gym? In the shower, maybe? I always thought you were a perp, Buck." Josh said and turned away from Buck.

He closed his eyes and waited for the blow to the back of his head, a signature slap from the bully. Buck was quiet except for his heavy breathing. "Who's your girlfriend?"

Josh opened one eye and noticed the girl who had just sat down next to him.

"Olivia, Buck." She said. Her bleached blonde hair was cut to within an inch of her scalp, and her dark skin set off her icy blue eyes. A scar was visible along the top of her right ear. She wore a lacy, black pair of gloves with the fingertips cut out. She wore a loose sweatshirt with the sleeves cut off just below the elbows. A pair of gray sweatpants completed her ensemble. "I'm surprised you don't know me," Olivia said. "Your bully radar should have picked up on me weeks ago."

Josh swallowed hard and waved a hand at her. "Not a good thing to say, Olivia." He whispered. "Just ignore him."

"He's kind of hard to ignore," Olivia said louder. "Like trying to ignore a rhinoceros in a jewelry store." She snickered and took a bite out of her sandwich. "You're the poster boy for toxic masculinity."

Josh glanced up at Buck as he reddened, and a confused look crept over his face. "Yo, cyborg girl, you don't talk to me that way. I'm not toxic in any way."

On the other side of the table, three girls approached. The

lead girl had long black hair draped over her shoulders. She planted a hand on her hip.

"Buck, get lost. We got this." She said.

Josh rolled his eyes. Could it get any worse? "Not now, Mandy. Just let her eat in peace."

Mandy snapped her fingers, and the other two girls moved into position at her shoulders. "We just thought Olivia needed some fashion advice. Sweatpants are not attractive."

Olivia smiled at Mandy. "I am a practical person, Mandy. Don't need to festoon myself with bling to attract a male."

Mandy looked confused for a moment. She was processing that word, festoon. "Olivia, Olivia." She pulled out a chair at the end of the table right next to Olivia. "We'll just wait here patiently for one of your spells, and while you are off in la-la land, we'll do a makeover."

Olivia frowned, and suddenly, her face slackened, and her eyes averted to her right side. Josh gasped. He had seen this before. Olivia had epilepsy.

"Hey, chick, I'm talking to you!" Buck shouted from the other side of Josh.

"Stop it, Buck. She's having an absence seizure." Josh said.

"An absence seizure?"

"She freezes for a minute or two. Dude, her mind goes blank. Sort of like yours does when you try to understand a math equation."

Buck snapped his hands in front of Olivia's eyes. She didn't blink, staring off to her right. "Yo, I heard she had some kind of brain implants. Cyborg baby. So, I could do anything I wanted to her, and she would never know it?"

"You could. But I would know it." Josh said.

Buck grabbed Josh by his tee-shirt and lifted him out of his seat. "Watch your mouth, demon boy."

Josh felt the bloodstone shard heat up, and an uncharacteristic surge of power ran through his body. He shoved his two arms up between Buck's and slammed his hands into Buck's chest. Josh plopped back into his chair as Buck stumbled backward. "Dude, cut it out! Remember, I'm your tutor, and if you don't pass Algebra II, no LSU scholarship."

Buck looked down at his chest in shock. He looked down at his hands. Behind him, one of the two boys snickered. Buck slapped him on the back of the head. "What are you laughing at?" He clenched his hands into fists and glared at Josh. "We'll talk about this later, demon boy. After tutoring this afternoon, I might need to kick your butt." He whirled and stormed off across the cafeteria with his cohorts in tow.

Josh whirled to find Mandy and her friends gathered around Olivia's motionless figure.

"Now, a little blush on your cheeks," Mandy said. She held a French Fry in her hand and was dabbing ketchup on Olivia's cheek. "Lip gloss." She smeared ketchup on Olivia's lips. Olivia sat motionless with vacant eyes.

Josh grabbed Mandy's wrist. "Mandy, stop!"

Mandy glared at him, and her two friends leaned over her. "If you don't release my wrist, I'll scream, and you'll be kicked out of this school for sexual harassment so fast, your head won't stop spinning. How's that for toxic femininity?"

"It's okay," Olivia said.

Both Josh and Mandy jerked back as Olivia stood up. "I'm fine, Josh. I can handle this -- ." Olivia stood over Mandy and reached out and bushed the back of her fingers over Mandy's forehead. "Jezebel," Olivia said quietly.

Mandy gasped and slumped back in her seat. The other two girls backed away. Olivia took her napkin and wiped the ketchup from her lips and her cheeks. She towered over Mandy with a hand on her hip. "Now, Mandy, we've been over this before. You're not supposed to mess with me. I told you what would happen if you did."

Mandy's eyes were just as vacant as Olivia's had been only

moments before. She nodded. "Josh is my friend, and you will never speak to him that way again. Do you understand?"

Mandy nodded vacantly. Josh's mouth fell open. "Olivia, what is going on?"

"Hush, now." She whispered over her shoulder. "I've got this under control."

Josh glanced around. The cafeteria had fallen silent as every student's gaze was glued to the drama unfolding at their table. Olivia raked a hand through Mandy's hair. She tugged gently, and a hair weave pulled away, revealing a scalp covered with random patches of frazzled hair. A collective gasp rose from the other students.

"Olivia, tell everyone what happened to your hair," Olivia said.

A tear trickled down Mandy's cheek. "It's in my stomach." She said robotically.

"And why is that?" Olivia held up the long, luxurious locks of hair for everyone to see.

"Because I eat my hair."

"Olivia, that's enough!" Josh said.

Olivia nodded. "I agree." She put the hair haphazardly back on Mandy's head. "Mandy, you and your friends can go now."

Mandy nodded and slowly rose from the chair. The other two girls grabbed her arms and led her away. Olivia settled back into her chair and took another bite from her sandwich. The noise level returned as the other students went back to their business.

"Olivia, what was that all about?" Josh said.

"Just a little hypnosis. Mandy doesn't even know I hypnotized her. I gave her a post-hypnotic trigger word."

"Yeah, I get it. Jezebel."

Olivia tilted her head, and her light blue eyes lit up with anger. "Look, Josh, when I have absence seizures, I'm totally helpless. I'm at the mercy of bullies like Buck and Mandy. I'm alone here. No friends. No allies. I've developed a strategy to protect myself. Mandy won't try anything again."

"But that was so humiliating."

"And putting ketchup on my face isn't?"

"How did you know?"

Olivia tapped the scar behind her ear. "I have a brain stimulator. It senses when I have a seizure and gives the seizure focus a little shock. I come out of it pretty quickly now. I was awake by the time Mandy put the ketchup on my cheek."

"And, you let her?"

"Well, I'm always a little confused for a few seconds after I come back. It took a moment or two to realize what was happening." She sipped at her milk. "You should understand what I'm going through, Josh. Look what Buck tried to pull. I mean, 'demon boy'? What does that mean?"

"It's complicated." He took a sip from his water and felt the bloodstone shard dangling against his chest. The larger portion of the bloodstone had once belonged to his father and had housed a demonic spirit. "I've had run-ins with the paranormal. Demons. Angels."

"Get out of here! Really?"

"Really."

"Maybe you're having seizures. You know they can alter your perception of reality." Olivia said.

Josh stared off into space. It wasn't a seizure that had taken over his body, mind, and soul back in Lakeside. It wasn't a seizure that had flown around the cavern in Transylvania in the form of a giant bat. And, it wasn't a seizure that had led to the death of his father in the cold, dark reaches of space. All of that had been at the hands of supernatural evil power. But he couldn't tell Olivia any of this. She would never believe it.

"I wish it was that simple, Olivia. But it's all too real."

Olivia paused and wiped mustard from her lip. "Demons. Angels. I guess you believe in God, too."

"Yeah, I'm a Christian," Josh said quietly as he touched the cross hanging from his neck.

Olivia shrugged. "Well, I don't believe in God. If he exists, why did he let me have seizures? Huh? You have an answer for that?"

Josh looked away. He had his own questions about why God had allowed terrible things to happen in his own life. "I don't have all the answers."

Olivia stood up and picked up her tray. "When you do, I might consider believing. But for now, as long as your God lets the Mandys and Bucks of the world do their stuff, I choose not to believe." She stood up with her tray and walked away.

4

L akeside, Louisiana

"WHERE IS MY LION STICK?"

Montana Holmes looked up from the desk in the basement of the lake house at the image of Dr. Liz Washington on the large computer monitor mounted above Cephas Lawrence's reassembled desk. He had managed to put the pieces back together after the damage done by the golem and the tenth demon. He shook his head at the thought. What a strange world Jonathan Steel had pulled him into!

"It's still hanging over the fireplace upstairs. You left it."

Liz pointed to her short, gray hair. "I already have enough gray hairs without having to worry about my most prized possession. I thought it had gotten lost in the move."

Holmes gestured around him at the wooden crates filling the basement of the lake house belonging to Jonathan Steel. "It could have gotten lost in Cephas' treasures. And, I say that with great reverence, although many of these crates contain artifacts of totally unknown origin or nature. Now that you have had to go back to the university, leaving me alone, it will take months to go through this stuff."

"Sorry." Liz shrugged. "I finished the dig at the old church site, and if I didn't return to my position, I risked losing my job. I'll be back at Christmas break. Along with some of my students. We'll help you work through the crates now that the other job is finished. Honey child, just take a deep breath."

Holmes sighed and sat back in the desk chair. "There will be three fewer crates by then. We're loading up the crates donated to Dr. Hampton this afternoon. Jonathan's friend, a Major Miller, is offering to fly them to London."

"Miller is hardly a friend." Liz frowned. "The way he treated his wife, Renee, was despicable. That poor girl is off in the cosmos somewhere with the Children of the Bloodstone."

"Yeah, about that." Holmes pushed his long, black hair back away from his face. "What have I gotten myself into, Liz?"

"Honey child, the good Lord has put you in Jonathan's life for a reason. He lost Theo and Cephas, and someone has to take care of these artifacts. What you've seen is only the tip of the iceberg. Giant scorpions. An army of vampires. White-eyed ghouls. UFOs and aliens. Honey, this ain't for the faint of heart. Not to mention time travel. How much do you remember?"

Holmes looked away and wiped his mouth. "Some of it is coming back, Liz. I'm just so frustrated. I mean, I'm a defender of the Christian faith! I rely on evidence and rationality and logical arguments, and I was there!" He sat forward. "Liz, Jonathan said I was in Jerusalem for the crucifixion! He said I was in the Holy of Holies after the veil was torn. But I can't remember all of it. Just brief flashes of memory."

"Monty, faith is trusting in something for which you've seen the evidence, right? What does it matter if the evidence is what you see here and now versus what you saw in the past? Honey child, maybe this is God's way of testing that faith."

"But, Liz, to have been there. To have seen my Savior!" He ran his hands through his thick, black hair and pulled it back from his face.

"And, what a privilege to have seen all of that and have even an iota of memories. You are blessed, Monty. Be patient. Time will bring those memories back to you. And, you will find they will return when you need them most!" Liz smiled. "Now, take good care of my lion stick and don't let it get sent to London. I'll be back for it at Christmas."

"I will, Liz. And, thanks for the encouragement."

The image faded as Liz closed her connection. Holmes's phone dinged, and he studied the text message. He glanced at his watch. The professional movers were to arrive any minute, and there was no way he could leave and not supervise the move of the fragile objects in the three crates heading toward their flight to London. He dialed a number.

"Josh, I forgot to pick you up. Sorry. The movers are running late, and I can't leave right now." He said.

"Dude, don't worry. I think I can get a ride to my tutoring session. I just need you to pick me up later." Josh said.

"Not a problem. Just text me when you're ready. We should have the crates loaded by then." Holmes ended the call and turned to survey the room filled with crates. Three of them were marked with a giant red letter "L." Two of the crates were the typical wooden crates and were sealed with an electronic device. The third was burnished metal, almost like a fancy coffin.

Dr. Cephas Lawrence died in the affair with Anthony Cobalt and left his collection to be overseen by Dr. Washington. After Holmes's involvement in the incident in ancient Jerusalem, he had been invited by Jonathan Steel to help Washington. Cephas had collected hundreds of ancient artifacts over the decades. Being an archeologist and historian before becoming a Christian apologist, Holmes knew this was a dream come true. What secrets were hidden in these crates? What lost knowledge was buried in the packing material?

But, the three sealed crates were set aside to be loaned to a private museum in London owned by the famous archeologist, Dr. Nigel Hampton. Holmes felt a shimmer of joy and anticipation. To meet Dr. Hampton would be a dream come true. Of course, he was going to accompany the crates to London. And, that had become a problem when Jonathan Steel announced he was headed to Europe. Who would stay with Joshua Knight now that Liz had returned to her university?

The problem had been solved when Holmes found out Jason Birdsong, Jonathan's new part-time partner, would be coming to New Orleans for an FBI sponsored seminar. He had agreed to come a week early and stay with Josh. And, he had managed to hitch a ride on the same flight Miller was bringing from Tucson to Shreveport for his crates. Coincidence? Holmes shook his head. The more he learned about Jonathan Steel and his associates and all of their adventures, the more he realized there were no coincidences. And that thought drove a shudder down his back. He heard the doorbell ring upstairs. Time to get moving!

JASON BIRDSONG GLANCED at the screen of his laptop. The airplane lurched again as it passed through turbulence. Jonathan Steel had told him about the thunderstorms and tornados that frequented northeastern Texas and northwestern Louisiana. He was used to the quiet, serene, and dry climate of Tucson.

His laptop almost slid out of his lap, and he glanced around at the empty, shortened cabin of the transport airplane he had hitched a ride on. Robert Miller of Miller Avionics had offered him a ride on this airplane because it was headed first for Shreveport to load up some crates to be delivered later to London. He would trade his seat to Dr. Montana Holmes and then become a babysitter for a teenager!

Birdsong was single and had no kids. His only experience with teenagers had been with his younger sister. Nausea gripped him not so much from the turbulence but the memories of Kristin and her descent into the hell of drug abuse. She had almost died at the hands of a Mexican drug cartel. He was not proud of the aftermath of that encounter and the fate of those men. But he had saved his sister, and she was safely tucked away in a convent.

His face burned with shame at the memory of what he had done to those two men. And, journeying back in time to face the crucifixion of Jesus Christ and to hear the words of forgiveness He had for His executioners had been life-changing. Even now, a couple of months later, he felt like he had been walking through a dream. He had actually gone back in time. Only he, Jonathan Steel, and Cassie Sebastian, the "Artifact Hunter," had retained the memory of those brief hours. He righted his laptop and studied the email again.

"Birdsong, I was impressed with how you handled the events in Arizona. I know your supervisor was not so impressed. I understand you are no longer working with the Tucson Police Department and have decided to pursue a career as a private investigator. Don't! We need good investigators like you with the FBI. Attached is an invitation to a seminar in New Orleans. Come and check us out."

"Okay, so my motives are less than honest. I would never tell him, but Jonathan Steel is doing some good work. I once thought he was a criminal, but the man did save my life once. And, I've seen some of the, shall we call them, perps, he has to face. Now that

Theophilus King is gone, and I must add good riddance, he needs someone who will have his back. I think that might be you."

"Now, whatever you do, don't tell him I said that. If you do, I'll deny it! But I can afford you training in one of our special operations units that will equip you, and, yes, Steel, with the kind of skills needed to face these, uh, demons. Yes, I said the word! Let's talk at the seminar and see how you feel about all of this. I can fast track you through the academy and pull some strings to get you into the special operations training group I'm talking about. Now, I don't do this for just anybody. Anyone who knows me, knows I haven't an altruistic bone in my body! See you in New Orleans. FBI Special Agent Franklin Ross."

BIRDSONG HAD HEARD plenty about Ross from Steel. The two had a history. A bad history. But this might be the opportunity of a lifetime. He would stay with Josh Knight for a week before driving south to New Orleans to the FBI seminar. Maybe he would figure how to handle leaving his grandmother back in Sells, Arizona. If she knew he had a chance to join the FBI, she would tell him to follow God's plan for his life. Birdsong raised an eyebrow and snorted.

"What a convoluted and twisty way to make a plan!" He sat back in the seat and closed his laptop.

5

_____

J osh stood at the curb and ended the call from Montana Holmes. Dr. Holmes was supposed to have picked him up on his way to the airport. Jonathan had left his truck at the airport for Jason Birdsong to use while he was in Shreveport before going south to New Orleans for his law enforcement convention. Josh didn't have many friends, and he sure didn't want to hitch a ride with Buck. Surely someone could give him a lift. If only Theo were here!

For a second, Josh felt the pain of loss. Again. Jonathan's first partner, Theophilus Nosmo King, was gone, long dead in the distant past; gone like his great uncle Cephas Lawrence who died at the hands of the tenth demon. In that disaster, his father had returned from a faked death only to die in a heroic act of self-sacrifice. And, his mother had died saving him from the thirteenth demon. So much loss. So many demons. So much evil. He gripped the bloodstone and sighed. Maybe he should never have put the thing around his neck again. It carried nothing but painful reminders of the losses he had suffered.

He wiped at the moisture in his eyes and wished Momma

Liz was still in town. Dr. Elizabeth Washington had to return to her university or lose her job. For the past few months, she had been overseeing the archeological dig at the old church site in Lakeside and had become Josh's adopted grandmother.

A small, compact car pulled up to the curb. He stared at his reflection in the passenger side window. His ginger hair was standing on end. He tried to smooth it down as the window lowered, and Olivia leaned toward him. "Need a ride?"

Josh glanced at the small car. "You can drive?"

"Sort of. Hop in."

Josh froze. Olivia was allowed to drive? With her seizures?

"Josh, chill! I promise I won't hypnotize you."

Josh slid into Olivia's car. He stared at the dashboard. There was no steering wheel.

"Okay, this is weird."

"All I need is an address."

"What?"

"It's a self-driving car, a prototype programmed by my mother. She's into A.I. You know, artificial intelligence. So, where are we headed?"

Josh threw his backpack into the back seat. "You're not going to like it. I'm tutoring Buck Sanderson."

Olivia's mahogany features wrinkled with delight as she giggled. "Oh, sweet irony. Why are you doing that?"

"Money," Josh said. "His father has loads of money, and Buck's grades could get him kicked off the football team. So, his father hired me to tutor him in math." Olivia pushed a button on the LCD screen in the dashboard.

"Address?"

Josh gave the address, and the car slowly pulled away from the curb. "He must be paying you a lot."

"He is. I'm the fifth tutor this year. Each time, the price goes up. And I really need the money."

"What does your father do?"

"My father is dead." The Bloodstone pulsed over his heart.

"Mine, too." Olivia frowned and looked out the driver's side window. "Uh, what about your Mom?"

Josh's voice caught, and he cleared his throat. "She's dead, too. I'm living with my adopted father, Jonathan Steel. I was living with my great-uncle," he paused, and emotion thickened his voice. "But, he died, too."

Silence fell over them, and the quiet, electric motor of the car was a steady hum beneath them. Josh looked out through the window and blinked away moisture. "I, uh, have this vintage motorcycle that belonged to my father. I'm rebuilding it after it suffered some damage in Europe. So, I need money for parts."

"It connects you to your father," Olivia said. She reached into her shirt and pulled out a necklace. A golden whale's tail hung from the chain. "It's not a red jewel like yours, but it's just as important to me as your necklace is to you. My Dad brought me this from New Zealand. He was a researcher for the National Science Academy and traveled a lot around the world."

"What happened to him?"

"He was murdered." She tucked the necklace back into her shirt. "I was young. My father was a Maori. He was born in Napier on the north island and met my mother at a conference in Auckland. She's originally from Taiwan. My mother worked at UCLA as a professor and researcher, and that's where I was born. But my father was always gone. Always traveling. Always searching the world for the next big mystery." She wiped at her eyes. "It wasn't much better after that. We moved all over the world as she went from place to place with her research into the human brain."

"Because of your seizures?"

Olivia nodded.

"When did you first start having seizures?"

"Right after my Dad died." She tapped the side of her head. "Traumatic brain injury."

Josh looked away. "That's heavy."

"Yeah, well, let's just say the assassin who killed my father didn't hit her first target. A stray bullet hit me." Olivia looked out the driver window and sniffed. She brushed at her short hair and ran a finger along the scar above her ear. "Just dumb luck, right? Where was God when my Dad died? Where was God when I was recovering from that bullet?" Olivia turned to him, and her bright, blue eyes glittered with tears. "I'm sorry to be so maudlin. My life hasn't been ideal."

"Neither has mine. The difference is where you ran from God, I ran toward him."

Olivia glared at him, and her face reddened with anger. "Don't try and make sense of this, Josh. Don't try and share your faith with me. The only thing I have faith in is myself."

She turned her gaze out the windshield. Josh fidgeted with his phone. "Sorry. It seems like we're both damaged goods."

"My life isn't too bad. Like I told you earlier, I have a Responsive Neurostimulator. It's an electrode on the surface of my skull that senses when I'm about to have a seizure and then stimulates that area of my brain to stop it. Works most of the time. Technically you're supposed to be over eighteen, but my Mom has connections."

"My father had connections, too. Bad connections." Josh fell silent, deep in thought about his own father and the jewel at the end of his necklace. It tingled in synchrony with his emotions.

Arthur Knight had worked for a secretive government operation involving genetic experimentation on children. He had faked his own death when Josh was younger to protect Josh and his mother. Months before, his father had resurfaced to find the children of the Bloodstone kidnapped by the tenth demon, Anthony Cobalt. His father had died saving Josh, Jonathan

Steel, and Theo King from certain death. He had also lost his Uncle Cephas in the affair. It had been three months, but the pain was still raw and unrelenting.

"After Uncle Cephas died, the judge in Dallas awarded custody of me to Jonathan," Josh said quietly. He opened his mouth to explain what happened next. But who would believe that Jonathan Steel had gone back in time to the crucifixion of Jesus Christ? He closed his mouth and sighed.

"So, Jonathan Steel is your guardian now? Where is he?" Olivia asked.

"On a flight to Europe."

Olivia smiled. "Really? So is my Mom. Maybe they're on the same flight. That would be weird, wouldn't it?"

"Yeah. And, weird is my new normal." Josh said.

Olivia fell silent, and Josh watched the familiar landscape pass by his window in slow motion. Cars and trucks swerved around the self-driven car. He glanced at her and noticed her motionless gaze through the windshield.

"Are you okay?" He asked.

"Yeah, just thinking. Don't worry. I'm not having a seizure." She looked at him, icy blue eyes filled with unshed tears. "Look, I was out of line earlier with those remarks about God. But I have to ask. How do you do it?"

"Do what?"

"How do you believe in God when you've lost so many people in your life?"

"I've seen the enemy. I've looked him in the face. I've seen the chaos and damage he does. If Satan is real and evil is real, there must be a God. Olivia, we all have to serve somebody."

"Yeah, and that would be me," Olivia said as the car slowed and stopped in front of a two-story house. "I take care of number one."

Josh reached behind him and grabbed his backpack,

anxious to change the subject. "Speaking of evil, looks like we're here. Thanks for the ride."

"Sure," Olivia said. "Josh, if God is so good, then why does he let all of this evil happen?"

Josh turned away from the question. "I don't know."

6

B ern Hospital, Switzerland

THE VOICES GREW louder as Steel fought upward out of the deepening well of confusion. He opened his eyes and squinted into bright lights. The voices spoke in unintelligible phrases and were joined by a chorus of pain as consciousness returned. He looked around at the white curtains and the intravenous bag hanging beside him. A woman in blue surgical scrubs was shining a bright light into his eyes.

"Another ER?" He managed hoarsely. The voices babbled on, and another woman in a white coat pushed through the sea of scrubs to stand over him.

"Mr. Steel, I am Doctor Gudrin." Her voice carried a heavy German accent. "You are at the University Hospital of Bern in Switzerland." He was in Switzerland. He had been on the airplane, and there had been turbulence. They were headed to Zurich. Never made it.

"The airplane?" He tried to sit up.

"Please, Mr. Steel, you must remain lying down. You have suffered from a mild concussion."

"Considering how the rest of the passengers fared, you did very well." Another voice came from his left. He looked up into the face of a tall, heavyset man with short, blonde hair and pale, blue eyes. "I am Inspector Swarsin. Do you remember the airplane crash?"

Steel tried to pierce his foggy thoughts. "I remember the airplane dropping. Turbulence." He searched his memories. Like most of his life, the past few hours were blank. "That's all I remember."

Swarsin frowned and glanced at Dr. Gudrin. "When can he leave? I want him moved to a secure location as soon as possible."

"He is lucky. A couple of bruised ribs and probably a concussion. He should stay here for observation."

"I can observe him," Swarsin said.

"You are not a doctor."

Swarsin flashed a badge in her direction. "Get him ready to move. Now!"

Dr. Gudrin frowned. "Very well. But I cannot be responsible for what happens to him. You will take full responsibility?"

"Yes. Give him some pain meds. A big dose. Knock him out."

Steel tried to sit up again. "Look, I don't know who you are, but if the doctor says for me to stay, I'm staying."

Swarsin slid his badge into a coat pocket. "You can go with me voluntarily, or I can arrest you."

Steel felt his anger swell, and his face warmed. "I haven't done anything wrong."

"But you say you don't remember anything?" Swarsin raised an eyebrow. "How do you know you did nothing wrong? We need some answers, Mr. Steel. This is one of the worst aviation disasters in recent history. And, you are the sole survivor. What if you had accomplices who even now are plotting how to silence you? How secure do you think this hospital is?"

Steel opened his mouth to say something, and the image of a woman moved across his mind. He tried to focus on it, and the vision faded like smoke.

"Pain medicine, now, doctor." Swarsin barked.

Before Steel could protest, Dr. Gudrin injected something into his intravenous line, and he fell once again into darkness.

STEEL MOVED THROUGH WARM LIGHT, surrounded by total white. He slowly whirled, searching for a landmark, a structure, anything to orient himself. A man appeared from the white. He wore a three-piece white suit. A red carnation adorned his lapel. His dark hair was short, and his mustache and goatee were perfectly trimmed. "Ah, Señor Steel. We meet again."

Steel rubbed his eyes. "Do I know you?"

"Miguel. We have met, but unfortunately, you have forgotten our earlier encounter."

"Earlier?"

"On the airplane. But do not worry. Your memory will return when it is necessary. For now, just know that all will work out for you. Be patient, mi amigo."

"I'm not known for my patience."

Miguel smiled and plucked the carnation from his lapel. He handed it to Steel. "Yes, we know. Adios."

Miguel disappeared. Steel glanced down at the carnation. The bright, red bloom blurred and began to run like water. Blood ran down the front of his shirt, and the flower melted away. Around him, the warm light lessened, and darkness crept in around him until he stood in a blurred circle of light. A face appeared in the darkness. Lean face. Short, reddish-blonde hair. Bright, turquoise eyes. Steel looked at a reflection of himself. The face moved toward him, and the man's entire figure stood at the edge of the light.

"Who are you?"

The man remained silent. His gaze intensified, and the skin around his cheeks reddened. A muscle quivered beneath his right eye. Steel recognized all too well the signs of his uncontrollable rage.

"I am your shadow." The man whispered. "You've kept me at bay. But no longer. I want out."

Steel blinked in confusion and stepped away from the figure. "You want out? What does that mean?"

"Stop playing these moral games. Become who you really are." The man whispered, and the figure stepped fully into the circle of light. Steel stumbled backward and fell into the shadows. Only as he fell, there was no floor; no ground, and he tumbled through the cold air. He glanced up at the mirror man standing at the edge of the circle of light. The man's burning, turquoise eyes seethed with anger until the shadows drank him.

~

"I AM FILING AN OFFICIAL PROTEST, SWARSIN." A woman said.

"The Military Penal Code requires that all war crimes be prosecuted and tried in the country, regardless of where a crime was committed and whether the defendant was a member of an army or a civilian." A man's voice growled.

"Normal civilian rules of evidence and procedure apply in military trials. The MPC allows the appeal of any case." The woman said. "I will not stand for you transferring this man to your safe house without proper legal representation."

"Appeal my decision," Swarsin said.

Steel tumbled out of the shadows and awoke to bright light.

He was lying on a sofa. He blinked and tried to sit up. Nausea swam over him. Where was the mirror, man? Who was the mirror, man? Could he be Jonathan's true self buried beneath years of amnesia? He tried to focus on the room around him. The heavy-set man named Swarsin was glaring at him from behind a dining room table. And, the woman whose voice he had heard was standing at the end of the table. Where was Miguel? He shook his head, which brought on another wave of nausea. Who was Miguel?

"The highest level of appeal is to the Military Supreme Court. Any licensed attorney may serve as a military defense counselor. Under military law, the Government pays for defense costs. Are you taking the case?" Swarsin said.

"Hey! I hate to interrupt this debate, but where am I?" Steel asked.

"A safe house, Steel." The woman said. "Brought here by the Bern City Police."

"We've been here for about six hours. It is near midnight. The pain medicine knocked you out pretty good." Swarsin said.

"And, it could have killed him." The woman said. "He could have suffered permanent neurological damage. You should have left him in the hospital until he was cleared."

"Gudrin cleared him," Swarsin growled.

"I'm sure you have something damaging on her, too." The woman glanced at Steel. "He is insufferable. He keeps files on everyone so he can make them do his bidding."

Steel waved a hand and swallowed down bile. "Stop! Both of you. What is going on here?"

The woman straightened and became all cheery and business-like as she approached the sofa. "Lena Olafsen, a legal representative of TransEuro Air. I'm here to investigate the cause of the crash." She extended her hand, and Steel leaned back from it.

"I've met Mr. Personality." He gestured to Swarsin.

"I'm with the aviation division of the Swiss government," Swarsin said.

"He's with the terrorism investigation division, he means," Olafsen said.

"Which is why I had to secure our only surviving witness," Swarsin said.

"Or, do you mean, suspect?" Olafsen crossed her arms.

"I don't care!" Steel said. "Stop it, and just tell me what happened?"

"That's what we were going to ask you." Olafsen sat beside him. "So many lives were lost, and we have no apparent cause for the crash.

"Not yet," Swarsin said. "Back off, Lena. If he's going to sue, he's going to sue. You need to start worrying about the relatives of the dead."

Olafsen stiffened. "My main concern right now is with the survivor. We must find out why this airplane went down."

"And, I'm the only survivor?" Steel asked.

"Yes." Swarsin shuffled through papers on the table. "225 dead. And, you were the only one to walk away. I need to know what you heard and what you saw just before the crash. Our investigators have assembled on the mountainside and are currently going through the rubble. The airplane broke in half when it hit the mountainside. Took out the final station of the Jungfraujoch railway. Somehow, you managed to get out. We found you at a dog sledding venue. A sled was missing along with six dogs. We found the empty sled down the mountain. You must have lashed them all together to go down the mountain, and then, what? Passed out? You escaped from a horrific airplane crash through the exit door and managed to attempt an escape down the mountain in a dog sled."

"Escape?" Steel shook his head. "Escape from what?"

"The scene of the crime." Swarsin frowned. The room was

quiet, and Steel could hear the steady ticking of a wooden clock hanging on the wall.

"If I intended to escape from what you are thinking is an act of terrorism, I did a poor job. How could I have known that the airplane would survive a crash in the mountains?"

"You didn't. But it wouldn't be the first time a terrorist chickened out on a suicide mission and tried to get away."

"Mr. Steel, forgive Inspector Swarsin. At TransEuro Air, we do not believe you are a terrorist." Olafsen patted his hand.

"Why not?" Swarsin said. "That would save you from being the victim of another lawsuit."

"There will be plenty of them, Inspector. And, an act of terrorism doesn't release us from responsibility."

"If you could prove it was not the fault of your equipment or your crew, that would be important," Swarsin said.

"Stop! Both of you." Steel shouted, and his head pulsed. "I'm not a terrorist. I was headed to Zurich on business. The airplane hit some kind of terrible turbulence. I remember a flight attendant bouncing off the ceiling. After that, it's all black. Now, what time is it? I have family back in the states, and they need to know I'm okay."

"Family? You have no children, no brother, no parents, Mr. Steel." Swarsin tapped the papers. "Nobody that we can locate."

"Judge Bolton in Dallas, Texas. Contact him. I am the guardian of Joshua Knight. His father and uncle, his only living relatives, died in August. Go ahead and check. In the meantime, I need to make a phone call to let Josh know what happened."

Swarsin's cell phone rang, and he angrily stabbed the answer button. "I told you not to disturb me." He paused and sniffed. "Oh. Have you traced it? Do we have a secure connection?" Swarsin glared at Steel. "Very well, put it through." Swarsin handed the phone to Steel. "It's Joshua Knight."

7

The maid let Josh into the Sanderson mansion and grabbed her purse as she headed out the door. Guess she didn't want to stay any longer than she had to. He settled into the large den overlooking the backyard and its swimming pool. The pool gave off steam in the cool, November air. A large flat-screen television blared from the corner. Josh glanced at his watch. He and Buck were to have started the tutoring promptly at 4 PM, and Buck was absent. It was already 4:30 PM. He pulled out his phone and texted Buck.

"News Alert!" A news anchor blurted out on the television. "There has been an airline disaster in Switzerland. TransEuro Airlines Flight #4551 crashed on a snowy mountainside, and we fear there are no survivors."

Josh froze and slowly looked at the screen. TEA was the airline he had booked for Jonathan out of London to Zurich. "No, no, no!" His heart raced, and he felt nauseous. He opened the airline app on his phone and waited impatiently for it to refresh. There it was. Flight #4551 was listed as delayed. Delayed!

"Just a minute, our correspondent in Bern, Switzerland, has some breaking news. Jim?" The news anchor said.

The screen shifted from the fresh-faced anchorman to a short, swarthy man hunched in an overcoat dotted with fresh snow. "Sam, I'm here at a local hospital where reportedly, the sole survivor of Flight 4551 was brought for observation. We have learned from an inside source that the man's name is Johnny Steel from the United States. One of our reporters managed to capture a photograph of Mr. Steel in the emergency room."

Josh swore out loud when the photo of Jonathan Steel's face appeared on the screen. His eyes were open revealing his bright, turquoise eyes and his face was slack.

"That's about all I know right now." The image went back to the reporter. "As to the cause of the crash, perhaps this man can shed some light on this terrible disaster."

Josh collapsed back onto the couch. He dialed Jonathan's cell phone and waited. And waited. No answer. It went straight to voice mail. He watched the reporter drone on about the disaster and caught the name of the hospital in the background. Five minutes later, he had connected with the operator. She said something in French, and his was rusty. He hadn't spoken French since the eighth grade. He was connected with an "official" representative of the police.

"My name is Joshua Knight, and I'm Jonathan Steel's adopted son." Josh blurted. "I need to talk to him! I need to know if he is okay!"

The voice on the other end of the connection spoke in poor English, and he was put on hold. Minutes passed, and Josh stood up and paced. He ran a hand through his hair. How could this be happening? Jonathan was on a routine flight to meet with the mysterious Max for reasons Jonathan never bothered to share with him. But, he had assured Josh there was no danger. "Dude, you said no demon. No, demon!"

The line continued to buzz with white noise. Couldn't they at least use some kind of background music? Something to let him know he had not been disconnected. Josh glanced at his cell phone screen. Ten minutes had passed! Why the delay? Maybe Jonathan was hurt worse than the news report said. Maybe he was really dead? Josh froze, and a chill ran down his spine.

"Not this time! Dear God, don't let anything happen to Jonathan! Not now!" He had lost his mother. Then, Uncle Cephas. Then, the father he thought was dead. Then, Theophilus. He couldn't handle any more loss. He couldn't! Tears blurred his eyes, and he wiped them away angrily.

"Jonathan, don't you do this to me, dude!" Suddenly, a shaky, hoarse voice came over the line. It was Jonathan Steel.

"THEY'RE CALLING you Johnny Steel on the television. Jonathan, are you OK?" The young man's voice was trembling. "Dude, you scared me to death!"

"Josh, I'm fine. Just a concussion and a few bruises." Steel tried his best to sound reassuring. "How did you find out about the crash?"

"I'm over at Buck's house and heard the news on television." The teenager's voice was thick with emotion. "I thought the worst had happened."

"I was on the flight, Josh, and I survived." Steel swallowed, and his head pounded with the effort. He wanted to sound reassuring to his newly adopted son. But how? Change the subject? "Did Jason get there? Where's Monty?"

There was silence on the other end. He thought he heard Josh sniff and then clear his throat. "Yeah, Monty is waiting at the house to load up his precious cargo, bro, because a thunderstorm delayed Jason's flight. At least that's what I found out from Miller. Bro, even though I don't like him, maybe *you* should have flown with Miller Avionics."

"He's made restitution for his wrongdoings, Josh."

"Dude, did you just say restitution? That's an awfully big word for you. You must have a concussion."

"Look, I know you don't trust Miller. After all, it's because of Miller your father faked his death. I get it. But I wasn't going to leave you alone. Jason will look after you."

"Dude, I'm seventeen! I'm a senior in high school! I'll be fine. I did all right without a father for eleven years." Josh's voice filled with anger.

Steel sighed and felt his cheeks warm. "I'm not your father, Josh. I know that. But as long as you are my responsibility, we do things my way. When you're eighteen, you can make your own decisions."

"Let's drop it." Josh's voice softened. "Dude, I had to get a ride to Buck's from Olivia."

"Olivia?"

"A girl from school. What do you want me to do?"

"I'm sure Monty or Jason will come to get you. Just chill out." He heard Josh gasp again.

"Chill out?"

"Look, Josh," Jonathan glanced at Swarsin. "Just tell Monty and Jason I'm fine. I'm going to continue my trip."

"Did you lose the laptop?"

Steel rolled his eyes. Josh would worry about any lost tech. "I lost everything but what I had on me."

"What about the medallion?" Josh said tentatively.

Steel felt at his neck. The entire reason for flying to Switzerland was to meet with the mysterious "Max" and hand over the medallion that once belonged to the assassin, Raven. He panicked when he realized it was gone. "I'm not sure. I need to finish talking to Inspector Swarsin, and I'll call you as soon as I get to Zurich."

"Where are you now?"

Swarsin knocked on the table, and Steel glared at him. Swarsin shook his head. "I'm at the police's disposal, for now, Josh. Trying to answer some questions about the crash. And I can't talk about it right now."

"OK, Jonathan. Dude, please don't go trying to save anybody. OK?"

Steel drew a deep breath. "This time, I was the one who needed to be saved."

"Jonathan, are there any, you know, behind this?" Josh said.

"No! Goodbye, Josh." He ended the call.

"Are you looking for this?" Swarsin reached into his coat pocket and dangled the chain with the strangely shaped medallion from his hand. Jonathan recalled the aftermath of the assassin, Raven's death. She had given him the amulet. Days later, after the judge had awarded Josh to Cephas for temporary custody, he had opened the medallion in the courthouse restroom.

Steel started down the corridor and paused in front of the men's restroom. He stepped inside. The room was empty. He pulled off the tie and shoved it into his coat pocket. He took off the coat and tossed it on the sink. He looked at himself in the mirror. Slowly, he pulled his shirttails from his pants and lifted the shirt away from his chest. He examined the skin on his left side. It was clean of any scars. Raven had said she had stabbed him and ripped his chest open. And yet, there was no evidence of a scar. Then, she had acted surprised. Why?

He dropped the shirt and reached up and ran a finger along his scalp. Two years before, he had awakened with a huge cut at the hairline. No scar. It had disappeared. He pulled up the shirtsleeve on the arm where Raven had sliced his skin with the knife. The red line was gone. No wound. No scar.

Steel studied his reflection in the mirror. Now that he considered it, he had always healed quickly. And, apparently, completely. Had Raven left him for dead that day? And had he healed so quickly and so completely there was no scar? Why?

He felt the amulet in his pocket and took it out. He fumbled with the latch, and the pendant swung open like a clamshell. Inside a tiny key was taped to one side. On the other was a folded slip of paper. He took it out and unfolded it. It was the piece of paper he had given Raven in the restaurant.

Who shall separate us from the love of Christ? Shall tribulation, or distress, or persecution, or famine, or nakedness, or peril, or sword? As it is written: "For Your sake we are killed all day long; We are accounted as sheep for the slaughter." Yet in all these things we are more than conquerors through Him who loved us. For I am persuaded that neither death nor life, nor angels nor principalities nor powers, nor things present nor things to come, nor height nor depth, nor any other created thing, shall be able to separate us from the love of God which is in Christ Jesus our Lord.

Tears clouded his vision, and he sighed. It was the Bible verse he had found in the latrine. His life had come full circle. His hope and faith were vindicated.

THE AMULET WAS silver and round with the image of a bird in flight. A raven. He had long ago replaced the dark blue thread with a silver chain. Normally, he would have worn the small gold cross April had given him. But, his entire reason for coming on this trip was to bring the amulet and the enclosed key to Max. It was a promise he had made to Raven as she died.

"Yes. It was a gift from a dear friend who died. It has a great deal of sentimental meaning to me." He reached out his hand.

Swarsin raised an eyebrow and dropped the chain into Steel's open hand. "The rest of your goods are right here." He motioned to a bowl on the table. Inside the bowl were Steel's wallet, his passport, and his keychain. "I'm afraid that is all you have left." Swarsin pointed to a coat stand by the door. "And your jacket. Don't worry. The red carnation is still in your pocket."

Red carnation? Miguel? "Save the woman, Jonathan." The man had said. The words swam up from his damaged memory. What woman? He shook his head in confusion.

Olafsen placed a clipboard with a piece of paper before him. "If you'll just sign this waiver saying you will not hold us liable for any damage unless it is proven there was equipment failure or human error, we can wrap this up."

Swarsin swore. "Olafsen, you're a snake."

"Stop, both of you." Steel grabbed a pen and scrawled his name on the signature line. "I just want to get on with my business. I'm not suing anyone."

"Good!" Olafsen tucked the paper into a portfolio. She took out another sheaf of papers. "Just fill out the items that are missing, and we will be glad to reimburse you. I'll have someone come pick you up and take you to a hotel when Inspector Swarsin is finished with you. Give them the form." She moved to the front door, and it opened from the outside. Two officers in plain clothes flanked the doorway. For a moment, clear, cold air wafted into the room from the outside with Olafsen's departure.

Steel pocketed his stuff and slid the chain over his head and felt the cold metal of the medallion against his chest. "Now what? I'll have to find some clothes, too."

Swarsin sighed. "Olin!"

A dark-skinned man stepped into view from a doorway leading out of the dining room. For a second, the huge man with no hair reminded Steel of his lost partner and friend, Theo. "Yes?"

"Get Mr. Steel's measurements and go find some clothes for him. He's not going anywhere right now."

Steel frowned. "What about food? I haven't eaten in a long time."

"Olin can get you some take out. I'm not cooking." Swarsin stood up from behind the dining room table. "You can't use the television. No calls on the cell phone without our authorization." He took Steel's cell phone from his pocket and placed it on the table. "It needs to be charged. It's dead. But, Olin will charge it for you and keep it in his possession. That's why Joel couldn't reach you."

"Josh." Steel said through clenched teeth.

Swarsin never missed a beat. "There's a bedroom down the hall. Bathroom next to it. Olin will be available for any of your needs. Two guards outside the front door and others you don't need to know about. You're not going anywhere, Mr. Steel, until I have more answers. So, relax and enjoy your stay."

Before Steel could open his mouth, Swarsin moved past him and disappeared through the front door.

8

"For children born into a digital age, engaging technology is normal. It is a natural part of their world. Technology is an extension of themselves. For digital natives, using BCI (Brain-Computer Interface) technology and neuroprosthetics to enhance their biology will seem ordinary and an intuitively obvious thing to do."

Fazale R. Rana with Kenneth R. Samples, "Humans 2.0"

Josh pocketed his phone and had to get some air. He walked back to the front door and stepped out into the front yard. A ladder led up to the roof and stopped just short of the dormers on the second level. The steep roof leading from the ladder up to the apex of the second floor was covered with red tiles hidden under wet, brown leaves. Buck had been neglecting more than his math tutoring.

A roar echoed down the street, and a red sports car sped up to the driveway and stopped in a cloud of smoke. With wheels spinning and smoke gushing from the road surface, the sports car peeled out and rushed up the driveway stopping abruptly just inches from Josh.

Buck climbed out from behind the steering wheel. "What do you think?"

"What is it?"

"What is it, demon boy asks. It's a Maserati GranCabrio GC. Zero to 100 in 5 seconds. Maximum speed 285 mph. It's supposed to be my Christmas present."

Josh stepped back. "Didn't your father say you couldn't have a car unless you passed Algebra II?"

"Yeah, but that's just a formality." He ran a hand over the red hood. "But, as nice as this is, my old man preferred this over my choice, a tricked-out truck. Got one of them picked out." Buck threw an arm over Josh's shoulders, and he flinched. "You see, I got it all figured out. I'm going to pass Algebra II. Barely. Dad is gonna freak. So, I'll tell I'm settling for a truck instead of a Maserati." He slammed the keys into Josh's hand. "Go ahead and take it for a spin. I've got a new game to try out."

Josh stared at the keys. "Buck! Your Dad said you have to study at least two hours an evening for math. Dude, he'll find out we didn't work on your math."

Buck ignored him, and Josh followed him into the house and to the kitchen. Buck opened the refrigerator and drank from a gallon milk jug. An open pack of chocolate cookies littered the counter. Josh glanced at the keys and stuck them in his pocket. At least that might keep Buck from leaving. "Buck, come on. You only have a few more weeks until Christmas break. Four days of tutoring, and you can have your truck."

Buck belched as he slammed the milk jug on the counter. Milk spattered the granite top. "Beverly will clean this up." He shoved four cookies into his mouth. "I got better things to do."

He pushed past Josh and stopped in the den studying the television. "That's not Sports Center. Where's the remote?"

Josh picked up his backpack. "Buck, you'll never get that

scholarship to LSU if you don't pass Algebra II because you won't graduate in the spring. Dude, can't you get that through your thick skull?"

Buck whirled, and his face reddened. "Yo, don't you talk to me that way. Remember, I said I was gonna kick your butt?"

Josh held the backpack between them as a buffer. Buck grabbed it and pulled open the zipper. "I'm gonna take that Math book of yours and rip it in half. And then it's your turn."

He reached into the backpack and pulled out a pink bag. He sniffed, and a lopsided grin appeared on his face. "I didn't know you were into pink."

"Wait a minute. Dude, that's not mine." Josh's shoulders slumped. "It's Olivia's. She gave me a ride over here, and I must have grabbed her backpack instead of mine."

Buck dropped the backpack and unzipped the bag. He peered inside. "What's this?" He pulled out a game case. "Killer Cop Fifteen?" He tossed the pink bag to Josh, and he barely caught it. "This isn't supposed to be out for six months. How did she get a copy of this?"

"She said her mother was a programmer. Maybe she has an advance copy."

Buck rushed past him, and the staircase groaned under his weight as he ran upstairs. "I'm plugging this mother in, and we're gonna see how awesome it is."

"Wait." Josh clutched the pink case and the backpack to his chest and followed Buck up the stairway. He emerged into tech heaven. Buck stood in front of a large three-dimensional flat screen monitor that occupied almost an entire wall. He was studying the game case.

"Oh, my gosh!" Josh's mouth fell open. "Dude, that is huge."

"120 inches diagonal. Three D. But there isn't a disc in the case. Just this." He held up a small compact drive the size of a fingernail. "Yo, this won't work with my PS."

Josh looked in the backpack. "Wait, what is this?" He pulled out a laptop the size of a MacBook in luscious deep maroon. He placed it on a nearby table next to a row of a dozen recliners facing the big screen. He took out a pair of dark goggles. He turned it over. The lenses were opaque, and the rubber strap contained tiny metal studs on the inside lining. A metal disc with an eye on it sat slightly above the lenses centered on the forehead.

"What is that?" Buck asked.

"I don't know. Goggles. Here are earpieces that fit in your ears. It must be some kind of virtual reality gear."

Buck ran over to the big screen and retrieved something from the game console. He held up a set of bulky virtual reality goggles. "Like my Hololens? Yo, that thing is huge compared to this. Lame!" Buck jerked the goggles out of Josh's hands and handed him the Hololens.

"Yo, there's a slot in the side of the goggles. I bet it's for the pinky drive from the game case. Dude, look, it fits over your head. You pull down the lenses, and you put the earbuds in and you rock. Let me try it." Buck said.

"No way. You might break it."

Buck ignored him and pulled on the goggles. Buck took the tiny flash drive from the game case and plugged it into a slot on the side of the goggles. Behind him, the big screen came to life.

"Connecting." A female voice came from the television. Buck turned toward the screen. An image of him standing in front of the screen appeared in the corner of the screen while streaming code ran along the side.

"Buck, turn it off. It's connecting to your screen."

"Monitor identified." The voice continued. "Visual and audio interface optimized. Please state your name."

Buck smiled. "Buck Sanderson."

"Please state your full name."

"Eugene Stanton Sanderson," Buck said quietly.

"Thank you. Sampling DNA now."

Buck winced and pulled the cap off. He ran a hand over his forehead, and it came away with a drop of blood. "Yo, this thing just stuck me!"

Josh grabbed the goggles out of his hand. "Buck, I don't know what this thing is, but I've never heard of this kind of technology. This disc with an eye on it just sampled your blood for your DNA."

"You try it, then."

Josh shook his head. "I don't think so. And, Eugene. Really?"

Buck snared the goggles and grabbed Josh by the nape of his neck. "You tell anyone that's my real name, and I'll crack your skull. Now, try this thing out." He pulled the goggles down over Josh's head.

Josh tried to get his hands up, but Buck hugged his arms around Josh's shoulders. Something happened. The darkness in front of him swam with sparkles of light and became translucent. He was now looking at the big screen and Buck through a blue haze.

"What the?" He managed, and Buck released him. Before Josh could pull the goggles from his head, a pinpoint of light appeared in the center of his vision hovering just a meter away from his nose. It swirled and suddenly exploded into the figure of a woman dressed in a long flowing white gown. Her hair was deep blue and pulled back into a long braid that seemed to float in the air. Her face was exotic. Her eyes were a reddish-brown and slightly slanted. "Welcome." She said in a musical voice. She walked out of the big screen before him in full three dimensions. She glanced at Buck and actually stepped around him. She stopped just a meter in front of Josh.

"Mr. Sanderson, you have chosen to enter the world of the Third Eye. I am Lusensa, and I will be your guide as you set up your Third Eye Interface. You will be experiencing reality in 3E. Please permit me to access your wi-fi. Just say 'yes.'"

"What's happening?" Buck asked.

"It wants to connect to your Wi-Fi."

"Tell it 'yes' and then give me the goggles."

Lusensa smiled and bowed her head as Buck said, 'yes.' "Very well. Please be patient as we download the necessary drivers for your Third Eye Interface. While we are doing so, let me introduce you to your new world."

Lusensa motioned around her, and the translucency melted away into a swirling cloud of color and glittering points of light. Lusensa motioned behind her, and suddenly, Josh was standing on the edge of a cliff overlooking an ancient city. His heart raced, and he grabbed the back of the nearby recliner. It was so real, and he was sure if he took one step forward, he would fall to his death.

"As you can see, the impression of reality far exceeds any previous virtual device," Lusensa said as she stepped into view. "But, the Third Eye Interface goes beyond sight and sound. It truly is 3E." Suddenly, the earbuds emitted a burst of sound that swirled and moved around his head. The effect was disorienting at first, but Josh held his head as still as possible until the swirling died down. It settled into the background sounds of wind whistling over the mountaintop around him and the far cry of a bird flying over the domes and spinnerets of the ancient city.

Lusensa stepped closer to him. "The unique capacity of the Third Eye Interface is in reading your brain waves and creating sensations that are as real as reality by direct brain stimulation utilizing the latest in Brain-Computer Interface technology. I will now take you through a brief set of thought movements that will train your BCI with the neurological responses elicited by certain body movements and certain thought processes."

"Yo, what's happening?" Buck appeared briefly in the corner of his vision.

"It's taking me through a training session," Josh whispered.

"You don't actually have to move. Your thoughts regarding specific movements will be sufficient. Once the interface has mapped your motor cortex, it will directly stimulate your sensory cortex and simulate the sensation of movement. Please do not remove the goggles during this process, or you will suffer brain damage." Lusensa said.

Buck had turned, and Josh realized Buck could see on the big screen monitor everything Josh saw. "Yo, when you can take that thing off, it's mine! Brain damage or not!"

Josh ignored him. What was this thing? He had never heard of any technology this advanced. For the next few moments, Lusensa led him through a series of body motions and thought experiences. He thought about moving his arms and legs. He thought about jumping and running. He wrote his name in the air. He thought of warm cinnamon rolls and beef stroganoff and rotten eggs. He mentally stretched out his hands and imagined he was flying. After a few minutes, Lusensa stopped and bowed before him.

"Your training session is now complete. Please wait a moment while we process the data. In the interim, we will lead you through a training session on augmented reality. If you look around, you will discover the Third Eye Interface will identify objects around you and display a pop-up window with information about that object."

The image of the city disappeared, and the lenses were transparent again. Josh stumbled in disorientation as the mountains gave way to Buck's media room. Buck reached for the goggles.

"Yo, you have got to let me try that thing."

"It's still calibrating. When it's done, you can try it." Josh said. A window formed around the big-screen television. Out to the side of the window, a text box correctly identified the brand and model of the TV. Josh blinked. "Lusensa, you can stop the augmented reality. I get it."

"Of course. Would you confirm your identity for purposes of personalization of this device?" She said.

Josh felt a stab of fear. "Lusensa, this is not my interface. It belongs to someone else, and I would rather not continue with the training."

"You are correct. The current owner of this interface is not registered with Numinous Corporation. Without further registration information, connection with the Numinous Cloud will be restricted." Lusensa popped into view against the backdrop of the television.

A warbling sound hit his right ear. "What is that?"

"Your headset is linked to a cell phone nearby. You have an incoming call. Would you like to answer?" Lusensa said.

"Yes." Josh swallowed.

A small window appeared on the edge of his vision showing the icon of an iPhone. "Josh, I'm going to skin you alive!" Olivia's voice echoed in his ears. "You took my backpack."

"Uh, yeah. Sorry about that. My bad." Josh said.

Olivia was silent for a moment. "You sound strange. Are you okay? Did Buck hurt you? Is your phone working, right?"

"I'm not on my cell phone." Josh managed hoarsely.

There was silence followed by a gasp. "Josh, you didn't! Do you have the goggles on?"

"I'm sorry. Buck found it and wanted to use it, and I stopped him, and we were curious and--"

"Shut up! Shut up, you idiot! Listen to me very carefully. You are in danger right now. You should never have activated the thing. Mom told me to protect it. It's not even our prototype! Now they can find us! Oh, Josh, how stupid can you be? Okay, okay, let me think."

Josh blanched. "Don't call me stupid! What are you talking about?"

"Have you connected to the internet?"

"Yeah, I'm going through the training session," Josh said.

"No! No! No!" She shouted. "Exit the program. Tell it you want to exit the setup. Do not take the headset off until it tells you to or you will have a seizure. Once you get the thing off, put it back in my backpack, and you and Buck meet me out front. As soon as possible. I'm about ten minutes away. Surely they don't have anyone close enough to find us."

"They?" Josh asked.

"Just do it!" The connection went dead.

Lusensa appeared before him again. "Your call has been terminated. Are you ready to experience total sensory suspension?" Her smiling face filled his vision.

"No, I want to exit the program," Josh said.

Lusensa frowned, and suddenly, he was somewhere else. The impression was disorienting, and he felt nauseous and dizzy. He was standing on a large boulder surrounded by a swampy jungle. He felt the wind swirl through his hair. He smelled the mingled odors of exotic flowers and decay. The sun had broken through a rift in the clouds above him and spilled through a hole in the dense jungle to fall on his face. He felt the heat on his face and squinted in the bright light. He looked down, and he was wearing a pair of leather pants with high boots. His chest was bare, and his hand strayed across his skin. He felt the hair stand on end. He felt the heat of someone beside him.

"It is astonishing, is it not?" Lusensa said. He looked at her. Her hair was no longer in its braid. It flowed down her long, white gown to the level of her waist. Her eyes glowed with power, and her lips glistened with sensual pleasure. He inhaled the delightful fragrance of her perfume. She reached out with a delicate hand and traced it across his cheek. He gasped with delight. It was the most incredible sensation of his life!

"Would you like some nectar?" Lusensa held up a goblet in her other hand. He took it, and it felt heavy in his hands. He lifted the golden goblet to his lips and tasted the exotic flavor of the nectar. It was intoxicating!

"Do you see what I have to offer? There are many such pleasures in my world. Pleasures and sensations no human has yet to experience. All of this can be yours!" Lusensa motioned to the jungle around her, and it transformed into the ancient city he had seen before. Domed buildings glittered with gold. Tall spires carried blue and gold spinnerets that snapped in the breeze. Mountains towered above them, clotted with snowcaps and greenery. He stood on a balcony overlooking the city. His leather pants were gone, and he wore a gold-threaded garment dotted with rubies and diamonds. It was a royal robe of incredible wealth. Lusensa leaned on the balcony before them.

"In my world, you would be a king." Her lips glistened, and he drunk in the sight of them and the sound of her voice. He tasted the music of her words. He inhaled the fragrance of her skin and hair. "You could be a god."

With that word, alarm bells sounded in his mind. Deep down in the very heart of his soul, he felt a moving of something. The bloodstone burned into the skin of his chest. He reached into his shirt and gripped the tiny shard of red warmth.

Light bubbled up within him, and for a second, the surrounding world he sensed grew dark and pixelated. Lusensa's face grew old and wrinkled and flashed back and forth between something real and hideous and something unreal and beautiful.

"No, this is not real." He whispered. "This is evil. I know it. I feel it. God help me." He felt the world shudder around him, and Lusensa frowned.

"I am the goddess of this world. You answer to me." Her face sprouted hair, and he was now looking at the face of a lion-like creature with sharp, yellow teeth. Her hair rose in a sweeping semicircle of deep blue and turned into a pebbled fleshy cape. From the edges of the cape, snakeheads emerged. Eight cobra heads hissed in his direction. Her arms multiplied into eight arms, with each hand carrying a symbol of royalty.

She pointed a golden scepter at him. "You cannot deny me."

"I want to exit from the program," Josh shouted. "I want to exit. You must let me exit. I do not want this!" The bloodstone grew hotter, and the warmth spread across his chest and down his arms.

Lusensa's golden lioness eyes widened in alarm. "What are you? What have you done?" She blinked slowly and regained her composure. "Very well. If you request it, I must allow it. Begone." She waved her hands, and the world collapsed around him like sand blowing away in the wind. He fell back and landed in the recliner. He pulled his right hand free of the bloodstone and jerked the goggles from his head. Buck reached for the goggles.

"My turn."

Josh felt sweat run down his forehead and soaked his hair. He glared at the goggles and stuffed them back into the pink bag. "No way, dude. We have to get out of here."

"What are you talking about?"

Josh struggled to his feet. He was dizzy and weak as he stumbled across the room toward Olivia's backpack. He tucked the pink bag back into the backpack and shoved the purple laptop into the backpack. Nausea doubled him over.

"Man, I'm going to hurl!" Josh hurried to the door of the nearby bathroom. "Wait for me downstairs."

"You don't tell me what to do!" Buck's face reddened.

Josh gagged. "Go downstairs, or I'll throw up all over you. Now, Buck!"

Josh grabbed the backpack and pulled it into the bathroom with him. He knelt over the commode and vomited. The spasms gripped him until there was nothing left but dry heaves. He tried to clear his muddled thinking. What had that thing done to him? He had been somewhere else, and it had seemed so real! The bloodstone dangled beneath him as it swung out of his shirt. Had it protected him? From what? What was the thing in the goggles? He wasn't sure. But, one thing was certain. It was evil. He sat back against the bathtub and wiped spit from his lips as he tucked the bloodstone back into his shirt. His cell phone warbled. He grabbed it from his jeans pocket.

"Yeah!" He managed through his burning throat.

"Are you out of the house yet?" Olivia said. "I'm almost there. Meet me out front."

Josh stood up, shakily, and felt a cool breeze. He turned. There was a dormer behind the bathtub, and the window was angled open. He stepped into the tub and pushed his face into the cool breeze from outside.

"I'm in Buck's bathroom throwing up. We'll be there in--" A white SUV sat beside the Maserati. Josh leaned forward and looked down. A man in a black blazer and sunglasses was studying the front of the house. He motioned to someone out of sight and pulled a gun from his jacket. A pistol with a silencer! Josh gasped and pulled back from the window.

"Olivia, there's someone here! Some guys in an SUV. Walking clichés with guns!"

"No! They found us! That was fast, Josh. Way too fast. Where's Buck?"

"Downstairs." He heard a shout of alarm from Buck down the stairway. A muffled, chuffing sound echoed up the stairs. One-shot! He heard the sound of a falling body. His heart raced, and sweat broke out on his face.

"Olivia, they've shot Buck!" He hissed into the phone.

"You've got to get out of there, Josh. They'll find you, and they'll kill you, too." Olivia's voice was quivering. "And they'll take Thakkar's goggles. Oh, just get out of there."

Josh reached out and quietly pulled the bathroom door shut. "I can get out the window onto the roof." He said. He grabbed Olivia's backpack and shrugged into it. He quietly stepped up onto the dormer and pushed the window completely open. He glanced down. The man with the gun was not in sight. Josh stepped out onto the roof outside the window, and his foot slid on the slimy leaves.

"I'm going out of the window, but I need both hands. I'm hanging up. Don't call me. They'll hear it. I'll call you when I can." He pushed the end button and shoved the phone into the pocket of his jeans.

With both hands on the edge of the window, he stepped out onto the slippery roof. His shoes tried to slide, but he held onto the edge of the window. Once he was outside, he reached in and pulled the window closed behind him. Slowly and as quietly as possible, he made his way up the slope of the roof to the apex. Twice, his feet tried to slide out from under him. He reached the apex of the roof and spied the ladder on the front edge of the house. He took out the phone and called Olivia.

"I'm on the roof." He whispered.

"I see you. I'm just down the block hiding behind the dumpster. Can you get off the roof?" She said.

Josh studied the ladder and looked back along the roofline toward the closest chimney. "I can get down the ladder, but they will probably see me."

"Okay. I can help. I can create a diversion, but you have to do exactly as I say." Olivia whispered.

"Olivia," Josh felt his heart sink. "Buck is dead! They shot him."

"Don't think about that, Josh. You are in survival mode right now. We can grieve for him later."

"Okay, I can do this. What did you have in mind?"

"Listen very carefully. Look in the outer pocket of my backpack, and you'll find a lunch container. Inside are small spheres. Find the one labeled 'wasps.'"

Josh opened the outer pocket of her backpack and took out a purple rectangular container. He unzipped it, and inside were a dozen small, white spheres the size of marbles. He found the one labeled 'wasps.' "Got it. What is this?"

"Your diversion. Go to the chimney. Drop the marble down the chimney and then get back to the ladder. It has a mild explosive agent that will disperse the nanobites. Wasps are swarming now preparing for winter. I'm highly allergic, and I keep some of that around the house to lure them away."

"Nanobites? Explosive?"

She ignored his question. "When you can, get down the roof to that ladder and meet me by the dumpster."

"Wait, aren't you still in that self-driving car?"

The phone went dead. Josh slid up toward the apex of the roof and the chimney trying his best to keep from making a sound. He froze when he heard the creaking of the window as it opened below him. Josh waited quietly, but no one emerged from the window. He reached the chimney and dropped the marble.

A shadow fell across the roof edge as someone leaned outside the window. He couldn't see Josh, but whoever was there was climbing out the window. Below him in the center of the house, a small explosion rattled the windows and shook the roof. Josh fell backward and began sliding down the roof. The shadow disappeared as the man pulled back into the house to investigate the explosion.

Josh tried to slow his slide, and his fingers scraped over the leaf-covered roof. His feet slid into the gap of the gutters, and he stopped just two feet away from the ladder. He tried to slow his breathing and calm his racing heart. A red wasp landed on his hand. He studied it and started to swat it away when it flew off toward the chimney. Josh followed the flight of the insect and gasped at the sight before him.

A dark red cloud of insects came from all compass points. Hundreds of wasps clotted the sky and zoomed-in an almost solid column down the chimney. He heard screams beneath him. A man burst through the bathroom window. Josh could barely make out the man's features for the wasps covering him. The man was clawing at his face. It was so swollen Josh couldn't see the man's eyes. The body tumbled past him and fell off the roof. A swarm of wasps gushed from the window and followed the body to the ground.

Josh skittered sideways until he reached the ladder and gingerly crawled down the rungs. Wasps filled the air swooping and buzzing around him, but none of them touched him. His foot slid on a rung, and he almost fell backward onto the wasp covered body below. He made his way down the ladder and stepped over the man's body. He ran toward the dumpster.

Olivia crouched behind the dumpster. "Olivia, what is going on? Killer marbles? Killer wasps? Men in black with silencers?"

Olivia reached for her backpack. "I call them nanobites. They attract insects. Or, other things. The explosive dispersed them through the house and covered the assailants. The wasps are drawn to it."

"Assailants! Assassins!" He handed her the backpack. She glanced inside and tossed him his backpack.

"Do you realize what you've done?" Olivia said.

"Me? I didn't just kill two men with a wasp attack! Never mind that. We need to get out of here." He glanced at her self driving car. "We'll never get away in that." He snapped his finger. "Wait. I have the keys to Buck's Maserati. Let's go."

They ran around the dumpster, and Josh slid into the driver's seat. He looked at the console. "No! I can't drive a standard."

Olivia sighed and pulled him out from beneath the steering wheel. "Let me. I can drive a standard. Get in."

"But, your seizures."

Something pinged off the roof of the car. He whirled. One of the men from the house was crawling from the front door, his face swollen and red. He pointed the pistol at them with a shaky hand. Olivia started the car and gunned the engine, throwing it into reverse. Josh had barely gotten the door open and fallen into the passenger seat when she peeled out of the driveway.

"Let's get away from here, and then we'll worry about my seizures."

She raced down the street, and at the corner, another SUV appeared from a side street.

"Not good." She said. She blasted past the SUV. "We've got to get out of this neighborhood."

Josh glanced over his shoulder. "Head down Pierremont just ahead and get onto I-49. You can open this baby up."

"Isn't that a little too visible?" She asked as she downshifted and took the curve onto Pierremont Avenue.

"If we attract police, I think these guys would back off." Josh's head smacked against the window, and he winced as Olivia swerved around a car and paused at the red light.

"What are you doing?"

Olivia looked to her left and then into the rearview mirror. The SUV accelerated toward them. "Wait for it! Now!"

She punched the accelerator and the car dovetailed as it whipped through the intersection. The SUV followed and midway through the intersection, a garbage truck plowed into its side. The two vehicles screeched across the intersection in a cloud of smoke and trash.

Olivia headed up the ramp onto I-49 and headed north. She slowed down to just below the speed limit. "Josh, I need some--" She slumped to her left, and her eyes looked to the right.

"No, no, no, no!" Josh grabbed the steering wheel, but Olivia's foot pressed even harder on the accelerator. He swerved to miss a truck. Just ahead, a ramp led down onto King's Highway. He undid his seat belt and straddled the console in the center of the car and managed to push Olivia's foot off the accelerator and pumped the break. The car screeched and grumbled as he pulled over onto the shoulder of the off-ramp. The engine died because it was in the wrong gear.

Olivia sat up abruptly and blinked. "I zoned out, didn't I?"

"Yes. We're lucky to be alive." He felt the warmth of her leg against his and the touch of her breath on his neck. He quickly slid back into the passenger seat.

Olivia put an open hand toward him. "Give me your phone."

Josh pulled his cell phone from his pocket. "I thought you had one."

Olivia took his phone and put it with hers. "I do." She opened the driver's side window and glanced outside. Another garbage truck pulled down the ramp toward her. She waited until it lumbered past and then tossed the two phones into the open back of the truck.

"Hey! What did you do that for?"

"We have to get off the grid, Josh. Now! They'll follow our phones, and it should buy us some time." Before he could protest, Olivia put the car in gear and gunned it down the ramp. A few turns later, and they were lost in another neighborhood off Fairfield Avenue in the older residential part of town.

Olivia pulled into the maze of streets in the interior of some apartment buildings until she saw the 'for rent' sign hanging on a covered patio. She parked the Maserati beneath an aluminum awning and got out.

"Okay, Olivia, what is going on?"

She pressed a finger to his lips. "Shush. I'm thinking." She glanced into the back seat of Buck's car. "Do you have some cash?"

"Yeah."

She pulled Buck's purple and gold LSU jacket out of the back seat. "Give me your jacket and put this on."

Josh shrugged out of his denim jacket. "It will swallow me."

"Nope, you're going to put your backpack on first and look

bigger than you are. Fortunately, no drones in this area, thanks to Barksdale Air Base. They would shoot them down. But a satellite will be looking for people our size."

"Satellites?" Josh took Buck's jacket. It reeked of body odor. The thought of Buck washed over him in a cold wave. "Buck is dead."

Olivia's cold hand pressed against his cheek. "Josh, look at me."

Josh focused on her bright eyes. "He's dead, Olivia."

"We will be dead soon if you don't do exactly as I say. You said you've been in danger before. Those demons, right? Imagine you're in the same situation now. Then multiply it by ten. Got it? Hey, are you listening?"

Josh nodded numbly. "Yeah. I got it."

Olivia pulled on his jacket and retrieved an LSU cap from the back seat. She pulled it over her short hair. She retrieved Buck's backpack from the backseat and emptied its contents onto the driver seat. Candy bars and trash showered onto the seat.

"Do you have a laptop in your backpack?"

"Ipad Pro," Josh said. "Wifi only."

"Ok, we can keep that, but it needs to be off. It'll try and pick up any local Wi-Fi, and we can't afford that because they will find us by your IP address."

Josh pulled his iPad out of its flap in his backpack and powered it down. "Now what?"

"Put everything in Buck's backpack and put it on under his coat. That will make you look bigger. Swagger when we walk. Change your gait."

Josh shook his head. "I can't believe this is happening?" He emptied Buck's backpack and then transferred the contents of his backpack into Buck's. Olivia took his backpack and stuffed it into hers and pulled it on backward. She closed Josh's jacket over the backpack. Now, she looked like a pudgy man wearing an LSU cap.

"Ok, I see where you're going with this. But what now?" He shouldered into his backpack and pulled Buck's coat over it.

"We stay under this awning and move into those trees over there. There is a bus stop down the street. We get on the bus and keep our faces away from cameras."

"Cameras?"

"Cameras on street lights. Security on the buses." She shuffled through Buck's trash from his backpack and pulled out a black woven hat and a pair of sunglasses. "Put these on."

Josh pulled the cap down on his head and fought a sensation of panic. He was wearing his dead friend's clothes! NO! He couldn't think about that. He had been in worse situations than this.

"Now, let's go. And, when we get out into the open, swagger, or limp. Do something different." She hurried away beneath the awning, and Josh followed her into the unknown. For once, he wished he were just facing demons!

ustin, Texas

Vivian D'Arbonne Ketrick Wulf had become a practical woman. Now that she had the effectual control of multiple international world-class corporations, she realized she could dictate what others would do for her. But, as practical as her considerations had become in the past weeks, she had no control over the condescending attitude toward her from one member of the Council of Darkness. That is how she found herself alone in the vast round rotunda of the Texas State Museum in downtown Austin waiting for a clandestine meeting with one of the Council representatives.

The floor of the rotunda was a beautiful inlaid design of people sitting around a campfire. It was laid out in a strange, sort of squashed perspective so that when viewed from any of the four levels above, it would look like a more realistic scene of cowboys and native Americans clustered around the drifting smoke of a campfire. She found it quaint and vaguely interesting. She glanced at her watch and fought down, growing anger. The Council representative had requested a meeting at nine in the morning. That meant she had to fly into Austin the evening before and waste an entire night in a foreign city.

"Keep Austin weird." She said. "More like keep Austin boring!" There was considerable work to be done in selling off Ketrick Enterprises and consolidating the pharmaceutical labs of Wulf Pharmaceutical Industries. Not to mention her latest dilemma, convincing the board of directors of Cobalt Propulsion Laboratories that Anthony Cobalt had indeed left his stock to her. With great power came great misery, she realized. Her income had increased considerably with the dissolution of Boone Media Network after the man's death in the affair with the ninth demon. But money was one thing. Power was another. And, manipulating the board of directors of these corporations was becoming too time-consuming. But, her alliance, no, her dominance of the thirteenth demon had proven very useful. And, she had to keep that alliance a secret from the man she was soon to meet.

Vivian had donned a long, dark dress of corduroy and draped a gray and blue shawl over her shoulders. November in Texas could be cool. Standing on the edge of Boone's bottomless pit of lava and fire just before the explosion that had annihilated his island and his time machine had bathed her in infernal heat as she teleported away. Now, released from that heat and from that moment, she couldn't get warm for the life of her.

"I can warm you up." The raspy voice echoed just behind her eyes.

"No!" She muttered the real name of the thirteenth demon. That name alone gave her control.

"Very well. Just remember, I have great power."

"I know how much power you have." Vivian hissed. "And,

when the time comes, we will unleash it. But, for now, the Council must not find out you and I have a relationship."

"A relationship?" The voice softened. "I like the sound of that. Don't forget the power you have in your hand."

Vivian opened her right hand and examined her palm. In ancient Jerusalem, she had squeezed a shard of the Grimvox, and it had ruptured and burned its way into her flesh. The dark blue lines radiated from the center of her palm. She had pressed it against the forehead of Bile and had extracted the thirteenth demon after speaking the demon's name. Could she use it against the Captain? She tried to imagine pulling whatever demon lived within the man and bending it to her will. Somewhere, locked within the knowledge recorded in pieces of the Grimvox, was the real name of each of the remaining demons on the Dark Council.

If she knew their names, she could control the Council. After losing all of her lesser status demons in the confrontation with the ninth demon, she had achieved her ultimate triumph in acquiring and controlling the thirteenth demon from her assistant, Bile. Now, the demon danced to *her* song, not the other way around.

Vivian made her way across the rotunda to the entrance of an exhibit. An open room that stretched to the far ceiling four levels above was filled with ancient artifacts from Texas during the 1500s. She paused by a map of the ancient, unsettled North America. The map showed the path of several explorers who had ended up in Texas. A shadow passed over her, and a man stepped up beside her.

"Hernando DeSoto." He said as he pressed a button on the right side of the display. A series of tiny blue lights lit up and wormed a path from Florida across the southern part of the continent toward Texas. She looked over at the man. He wore a wide-brimmed Panama hat, and he had a Meerschaum pipe clenched in his teeth. A pair of wraparound sunglasses obscured his eyes.

"It's about time." She hissed.

The man ignored her and touched a finger to the word "Caddo" as the string of lights passed through what would become northwestern Louisiana. "This is where the thirteenth demon ended up, my dear. As you well know."

Vivian stiffened and kept her gaze focused on the map. Did he know she carried number thirteen? "Forget the map, old man. Why am I here?"

The Captain looked away and walked toward a diorama of three men in leather buckskin standing over a dugout canoe. "Such history and we see but tiny glimpses of it. The master has seen thousands of millennia, and you dare show impatience?" He stopped and glanced back at her. He wore a yellow tropical shirt with tiny green leaves and a pair of khaki pants. A brown blazer draped from his narrow shoulders.

Vivian felt her face grow warm with anger. "You made me fly from Los Angeles to Austin for an early morning meeting! Now, no more games."

He ignored her and pulled a gold lighter out of his pocket and stoked his pipe. Smoke billowed from his nostrils and filled the air. A museum attendant appeared behind him, a young man probably working as an intern from the UT Austin history department.

"Excuse me, sir. There is no smoking in here."

The Captain pocketed his lighter and touched one side of the bowl of his pipe. On the side facing Vivian, a demon was etched in the white material. As he stroked the image, it glowed red. He turned and blew smoke into the young man's face. The smoke glowed with a crimson tint. "You may smoke if you like." He said.

The man blinked in confusion. "You may smoke if you like." He repeated the words.

"I'm going on break." The Captain said.

"I'm going on break." The man turned around and disappeared through the exhibit. The Captain turned back to Vivian. "I learned that trick from a movie."

"Tell me what this is all about!"

The Captain pointed to a far case with his pipe. "Let me show you something." He led her over to a large enclosure. Inside, a metal helmet in the shape of a horse's head gleamed in the light. "How arrogant they were. They came to this land with their weapons and their armor and their superior attitude, and they were destroyed by the simplest of this world's weapons." He blew smoke into the air. "Hunger, dysentery, and smallpox. Not only did most of them perish, but they spread their disease to these peaceful natives, and most of them died."

Vivian closed her eyes and drew a deep, calming breath. "Very well, what is your point?"

The Captain clamped the pipe back in his mouth. He studied her from behind the dark glasses. "The master spoke to you personally, and I know of the gist of that conversation. The master shared it with me. The thirteenth demon had a good plan in Lakeside. It would have worked, and it would have enslaved thousands to the addiction of gambling. It was a plan with durability and patience. The twelfth demon had a good plan. It would have started with a few hundred and then slowly grown in size and influence through his 'vampyre majick.' The eleventh's plan was personal and utterly insane. It was not a part of the overall plan of the master. That demon was tainted by her association with the rival Vitreomancers. Ten was impulsive and wanted his own private world beyond the Barrier. And nine. Well, his plans were well-meaning, but we can't change the past, can we?" He pointed back to the display case. "This is the nature of the master's plans. They are slow and insidious and deceptive. As simple as a smallpox virus in the right place at the right time. The master is patient. You must learn that patience if you are to survive on this Council."

"You don't have to lecture me on his methods."

The Captain stepped closer to her. She felt his warmth and smelled a spicy aftershave. "It would be a shame if the Master found how ineffective you have become. Does he know you went back in time to the moment of the Messiah's death? What would he think if he knew about your total failure to alter the Son's plans?"

"I did what the Council instructed me to do. I stopped Nine. The Master knows of my triumph, old man." She pulled away from the dark glasses. "We couldn't change the past. It was already written in stone."

The Captain sighed. "That may be true, but the Master's patience may not last once he learns how you have squandered your opportunities with the demons' earthly triumphs. I know you are having problems integrating the corporations you have inherited in such a short time. The world is looking at you, Vivian. The court battle over the Boone Media Network assets put you on the world stage. They will see the hand of the Master if you are not careful. We do not want to draw unnecessary attention to the work of the Council, or you may be the next member to take a ride into the netherworld never to return." He pointed to the map again. "De Soto's ego drove his journey, and he died during his mission to find gold, and only a few of his men lived to reach Texas. But, in the long travels, they sowed the seeds of chaos and destruction that rippled across this land for centuries afterward. That is how we work, Vivian."

Vivian drew herself up and glared at him. "Lesson learned. Is that all you wanted to tell me? You could have sent me an email! And, where is Bile? I haven't heard from the thirteenth demon in a month. Not that I'm complaining."

The Captain tucked his pipe into a shirt pocket. "Thirteen

has his own agenda, it would seem. Our alliance no longer seems to be in place."

The Captain pulled off his sunglasses, and his bright, teal eyes glowed with malice. "Now, here is why I sent for you. The eighth demon has a plan that is powerful and will lead to the deaths of millions. It will harvest many souls for the master's kingdom, but it will draw unnecessary attention to the work of evil. Hitler made the same mistake, and it took us decades to overcome the sense of righteous indignation that followed his downfall. We must be more insidious, Vivian. You said you would work for the Master. I am to deliver to you his assignment."

The Captain reached into his jacket pocket and pulled out a large envelope. "Here is an agenda for you to follow. Sell off Ketrick Industries while you can and take the money and plow it into Wulf Pharmaceuticals. Let the board take control of Cobalt Propulsion Laboratories. You must see that Wulf Pharmaceuticals succeeds. We will need its laboratories one day. I think this plan will bring clarity to your future. And, some documents will allow you to gain unparalleled control over the boards. There is a memory chip inside with all the appropriate pictures and videos you'll need for increasing your influence."

Vivian took the envelope from the man. She recoiled from his bright, turquoise eyes. Why hadn't she seen it before? Why hadn't she guessed that the man was Jonathan Steel's father? But after the defeat of the tenth demon, she had met a man claiming to be the first demon outside the old castle who looked like the Captain. That man claimed to be able to wear many faces. Was the man before her truly the Captain? Or, was he the first demon in disguise. If she asked, she would reveal the first demon's capabilities. Best to assume this man was the Captain. She opened the envelope, and a flash drive slid into her hand. "Blackmail?"

"Now, I'm talking your language. I'm making it easy for you, Vivian. I am helping you. Remember that."

"Very well, I will take the help."

The Captain smiled. "Of course you will. We are members of the Council, Vivian. We are on the same team." The Captain gestured to the envelope. "There are three photographs in the envelope." Vivian pulled the photographs from the envelope. One showed a woman in a wheelchair.

"Do you recognize this woman?" The Captain tapped the top photograph with the moist stem of his pipe.

"She's Dr. Sultana Thakkar, head of the Numinous Corporation. Biggest software and hardware developer in Europe. She sits on the board of Wulf Pharmaceuticals."

"So, you've met her?"

"No. She always attends via a remote connection."

The Captain reached into another jacket pocket and pulled out another envelope. "You will. Here are first-class tickets on the next flight to London. There is a press conference she will hold tomorrow evening. You must be there and meet her. On the flash drive is a folder under her name with a briefing on what she is planning. You must get her to change her mind, Vivian. What she is planning is too bold and too big."

Vivian took the tickets. "Who is giving me this assignment. You? The Council? The Master?" The first demon, she thought. The thirteenth demon giggled in her mind.

"I'll never tell." It said.

The Captain ignored the question. "This is how things will go from now on, Vivian. You belong to the Master. I belong to the Master. Our plans must be his plans. Remember that or your soul will be harvested, and your demons will serve another. If you haven't made progress with Thakkar, then I will make sure my backup plan succeeds."

"Backup plan?"

"I always have a plan B. And, Vivian, my plan B's are always personal. Tie up loose ends on your business. A few carefully placed calls should put all your problems to bed." The Captain turned and walked deeper into the museum. Vivian stood stock still as she thought. The flash drive had information that could give her ultimate control over her businesses. For now, she would take the help. But she vowed that in the future, her plans would take precedence over those of the Captain. Despite his warnings, she would continue to grow and nurture her plan. And, she would not end up like Sultana Thakkar.

"I will help you." Thirteen whispered in the dark shadows of her mind.

"Yes, you will," Vivian said.

10

"Is it fair for people who already possess the advantage of wealth to gain the added advantage of human enhancements? And what if societies of the future choose to abandon free market access to human enhancements? What if these future societies impose other criteria for receiving human enhancement technologies? What should those criteria be? Who gets to decide?"

   Fazale R. Rana and Kenneth R. Samples "Humans 2.0"

Numinous Corporation's headquarters sat on a low hill and was the nightmarish dream of a demented architect. The building was silver and lavender metal bent and twisted into sharp angles alternating with rounded parabolic walls dotted with tiny porthole-like windows. The campus stretched over the length of two football fields, and metal and concrete sculptures meant to mimic a natural forest surrounded it. Vivian found the walk through the false trees and babbling brooks of red and green water disorienting. An open courtyard in the center of the main building held a modern rendering of Stonehenge. Vivian walked through upright burnished steel monoliths. In the center of the circle of monoliths were two slabs of metal. One on slab lay the sculpture of a nude woman in a fetal position. On the opposite slab, the striking and pristine sculpture of a human-like robot sat with its face turned toward the other slab. A smile adorned its mechanical face.

Who was this Sultana Thakkar? Which member of the Dark Council was she? Did this abstract, postmodern monstrosity reflect her inner chaos? If so, she would gladly take her down.

Hundreds of people streamed through the cavernous glass doors shaped like frozen amoebas dotted with tiny flecks of orange and blue "organelles." Inside, the open atrium continued the theme with abstract sculptures and hanging mobiles that gyrated above them. She was ushered into the main auditorium by greeters dressed in black from head to toe. Tight, black nylon masks covered even their faces. The only adornment was a silver eye on each greeter's forehead.

The seating inside was haphazard, with areas of uncomfortable stadium seating in cascading rows mixed with theater seating. Scattered along the levels were open "spectator arenas" as they were labeled and had the appearance of boxing rings slightly elevated to give standing room only crowds ample visualization of the main stage.

The stage was an open, silver metal platform that seemed to float a meter above the floor. Behind it, the entire wall glowed with video montages of Sultana Thakkar. The lights blinked and went down as Vivian settled into a hard stadium seat on the front row. She wanted to have a ringside seat!

The screen came to life. "Humanity, welcome to the Numinous Corporation presentation. Under the guidance of Dr. Sultana Thakkar, Numinous Corporation is the industry-leading expert on wireless communication, virtual reality, and transhumanism." Images played across the wall. Multiple satellites were floating in orbit. High altitude balloons carrying transceivers for Numinous' immersive wireless network—images of robotic humanoid shapes in various stages of activities. And, in the center, a dark-skinned smiling face of Thakkar herself. Her black hair was pulled back into a braid, and her dark, brown eyes glittered with mirth as she smiled as the audience. A tiny red dot sat between her eyes, and the image pulled back to reveal her surrounded by children on a vast soccer field.

"Dr. Thakkar has a singular vision for all of humanity, a vision of oneness, unity, a joining of our minds, spirits, and bodies in a vast human network that represents the next level of evolution. Driven by her untimely disease, Dr. Thakkar has managed to create technology that allowed her to escape from her trapped mind."

Vivian had read the dossier from the Captain carefully. Sultana Thakkar suffered from a degenerative brain disease rumored to be any one of several types of such conditions from ALS to Kuru. No one seemed to know for sure as Thakkar was a notoriously secretive figure. Five years previous, she had been a robust middle-aged woman appearing around the world in her Numinous Corporation Expositions, dominating the stage with her charismatic presentations. Then, she had mysteriously disappeared from the public eye for months only to resurface confined to a wheelchair. The Captain's sources said she had degenerated into a catatonic state with what was known as a "locked" brain. In her condition, she had been trapped within her own mind, unable to communicate to the outside world for over a year. Then, mysteriously, one day, she began to blink, and her aids placed a vision directed keyboard before her. According to the reports, in time, she relayed the details of a new invention she had created during her "exile," which allowed her to escape from her "locked" state. What was she like now? No one really knew. For the past four years as Numinous Corporation had advanced, Thakkar was represented by the image on the screen.

"Welcome, Dr. Sultana Thakkar." The video announced. Vivian felt the tension in the air; the expectation for this would be Thakkar's first public appearance in four years.

Their murmuring grew silent as a circular opening appeared in the stage, and something dark and shadowy ascended onto the darkened stage. Vivian peered beneath the stage and saw no connection with the floor. How was this happening? It was as if the figure elevating onto the stage came from nowhere.

The shadowy figure paused, and the floor of the stage became seamless. The lights slowly came up, revealing a graying, hunched figure. Thakkar's body was folded into a motorized wheelchair. Her once jet-black hair was now short and gray. Her head tilted to the side, and a pair of odd-looking goggles covered her eyes. Her upper torso was twisted and angled. The motorized wheelchair seemed sleek and modern, and from her waist down, a golden satiny blanket obscured her legs. Her frail, thin arms lay across the cloth. Skin covered bones, and even from the third row, Vivian could see large bruises under the woman's paper-thin skin.

The wheelchair moved silently toward the front of the stage and paused in a circle of bright light. The air was deathly still and filled with utter silence. Thakkar did not move as the lights grew dim in the lecture hall.

"Welcome, my friends and colleagues." A mechanical voice issued over the sound system. Vivian glanced around her at the quiet crowd. The voice was edgy and irritating and not at all as soothing as the voice in the video. "Today, I will change the world. In the past, as my frail body declined, I relied on outdated modalities of technology for communication. But, today, I will return to the form that you are so used to. Behold!"

From the substance of the stage, a dark disk slid upward

and hovered across the stage to her side. The disk suddenly glowed with a deep blue hue, and the air above the disk sparkled with fine points of light. The points of light began to swirl and dance in the air as ominous music began to fill the lecture hall. The light particles pulsed and danced and coalesced into the form of Sultana Thakkar as everyone had remembered her. The music built to a resounding crescendo. The figure solidified into a slightly translucent image of Sultana Thakkar. The black hair was back. The fiery eyes revealed great depths of intelligence and mirth. Thakkar wore a dark red evening gown that hugged her voluptuous figure. Gasps and whispers of amazement traveled around the room. The figure spoke, and the sound came from the platform, not the overhead speakers.

"This is what I look like in my mind. Not that twisted, deformed lump of tissue over there." Thakkar gestured toward the wheelchair. Her voice was flawless! "What you are seeing is my very essence. *This* is me." She ran her hands down the shiny evening gown and drew a deep breath. "I can feel my skin under this dress. I can feel the air filling my lungs. I smell that atrocious aftershave Rory McCavish is wearing in the front row."

Thakkar stared right at a man seated in the front row two chairs down from Vivian. The man laughed and ran his hand through pepper gray hair. "You look good, Sultana. Too bad, you're just a hologram."

Thakkar just smiled. "I'm more than a hologram, Rory. Notice how quickly I responded to your remark. I'm thinking and moving in real-time. I don't have to run my eyes over a virtual keyboard to respond to your taunting. I merely have to think, and it happens."

Thakkar paced around the periphery of the disk. "You have the impression I am confined to this disk that is necessary for a holographic projection. But what you don't understand is that the experience is very real for me. Inside that skull over there, my brain thinks it is inside here." She tapped her head and shook out her hair. "It is exhilarating." Thakkar snapped her fingers, and a floating image appeared in the air beside her. It was a pair of dark goggles that encircled the wheelchair-bound figure's head.

"This is how I achieve this magic. This is the Third Eye Interface, or as we refer to it, 3EI. It combines the latest in optical imaging and auditory input for my sake, not yours. You must see me. But it is more important that I believe I am over here. Not, over there." She pointed once again at the wheelchair. "The process used in the 3EI is proprietary, of course. But, the science behind the device utilizes the monitoring of brain activity and stimulation of key brain functions to simulate this virtual image. I AM here. Do you understand?" She looked out over the audience. "My friends, what you see before you is the next step in transhumanism. With this new technology, my very essence, my soul, if you will, can inhabit a virtual body and is no longer confined to that failing pile of decaying flesh."

There were murmurs of awe from the audience. "I can prove that the process is instantaneous. I see that an old friend of mine is in the audience. Vivian D'Arbonne, my dear, would you come to the platform?"

Vivian blinked in surprise as every eye turned on her. An old friend? They had never met. Unless she was referring to the times, Vivian had been called before the Dark Council. She matched the voice with those memories of the woman who had protested Vivian's presence on the Council. No, they were not old friends. More like old enemies.

Vivian stood up slowly, and a series of stairs slid out from the edge of the stage and lowered themselves to her level. Thakkar motioned toward the wheelchair as Vivian mounted the stairs and joined her on the stage.

"Would you please stand by me. Uh, that me over there?"

Vivian stepped up onto the platform and stood beside the wheelchair. Thakkar smiled at her and motioned to the audience. "My friend Vivian has found herself the unwitting head of several powerful corporations as of late. She dreams of great power and influence. But then, don't we all?" Thakkar smiled at Vivian, and Vivian fought the urge to unleash the thirteenth demon to tear out the woman's throat. Her real throat, of course.

"All of you need to know is that Vivian has come here today to stop me. Her mission is to keep me from allowing you to put your hands on this technology. Perhaps she wants it for herself. Who knows what motivates my rivals." The holographic Thakkar turned toward Vivian and gestured. "So, Vivian, I am going to allow you to pick those in the audience who would like to ask me a question. That way, I will not be accused of stacking the deck. Go ahead, everyone. If you have a question, raise your hand."

Rory McCavish stood up. "We've all seen you do something like this in the past. But I think this is just a show put on for the sake of your stockholders."

"Who is Amanda?" Thakkar asked.

"Excuse me?"

"On your phone screen. You have a note to call Amanda for a good time right after the presentation. Is she someone you met outside? Amanda, if you are here, I'd recommend you avoid Rory like the plague. He leaves lots of young women broken and discarded in his wake. I should know." She glared at him and smiled wickedly.

Rory's mouth fell open, and he glanced over his shoulder back into the crowd. He looked up at the ceiling. "Where's the camera?"

"There's not one. Go ahead, Rory. Take your phone out of your jacket pocket. Cover up the screen so only you can see it and bring up another note. I just adore embarrassing you."

Rory glared at her and took his phone from his pocket and covered the phone screen with his hand. He glanced at it, and Thakkar crossed her arms over her chest. "Really? You have reservations at a Chinese restaurant? Rory, don't you know what MSG does to you? And, 6:30 PM is the height of the traffic rush. I'm sure you were planning on using the Underground instead of spending money on a nice cab for the girl."

Rory looked back at Thakkar and swallowed. "You've hacked into my phone! Nice trick."

Thakkar shrugged. "Let me see. You have something else tucked into the inner pocket of your jacket." She closed her eyes. "I can see the edge of it. Letters and words. Ah, tickets for one of those illegal cage fights tomorrow night."

Rory put his hand over his jacket. "How?"

Thakkar turned and studied Vivian. "Go ahead, Vivian. Take the goggles off of me."

Vivian turned to the hunched figure beside her. She reached down and tugged the goggles up off of the woman's eyes onto her forehead. Her blank, hazy eyes glared out at the crowd. The image of the woman disappeared. Vivian left the goggles on the woman's forehead. But in the few seconds, her hand had touched the woman's forehead, she sensed a presence. Yes, there within Thakkar's soul lay the real source of her power, the eighth demon.

"I can still see you." The mechanical voice came over the speakers. "Right now, I'm hovering over the back row. Rory, your little girlfriend, just texted her other date and arranged to meet him instead of you. Isn't that right?"

A woman near the back stood up and squealed. Her long, black hair swayed as she glanced around the room. "I'm getting out of here." She ran out the back doors. Vivian listened to the door slam shut, and the crowd began murmuring. "Vivian, if you would be so kind as to return my goggles to their position."

Vivian slid the goggles back over the woman's eyes. Thakkar

appeared on the disk beside her. Only now, she wore a smart, three-piece business suit of black and gray. This was her signature attire whenever she made a presentation: black slacks, gray blouse, black jacket, and white pearls. Thakkar gestured to Vivian. "Now, I'll take some serious questions."

"I'll ask the first one," Vivian said. "How did you see Rory's tickets again?"

Thakkar nodded and gestured into the air beside her. A model of the human brain appeared, and she reached out and turned it bottom up in the air. She traced a finger along the folds at the base of the brain.

"The hippocampus is a region of the brain near the bottom of the cerebrum. Science has shown that if you stimulate certain areas in this region, you can cause the person to have an out of body experience. During these experiments, subjects were able to travel around a room and see objects that were never in their line of sight. Now, we don't understand this process or why this particular area of the brain reacts this way. But neuroscientists have called this the seat of the soul. I have decided to use that principle. I can stimulate that area of my brain, and for a while, I am out of that body. That is why, Vivian, I can say without hesitation that I am over here right now and not over there."

Vivian listened to the murmurs and questions coming from the audience, and she ignored the raised hands. "How do you plan on using this technology?"

Thakkar smiled, and the brain disappeared. "Imagine the application of the 3EI to stroke patients, to patients with degenerative brain disease, and other neurological conditions. That application alone is staggering. This disk I stand on is nothing more than the latest in holographic technology. It is not essential to the experience, but it does present an interface to the world. Let your imagination expand and begin to realize the implications of the power of the 3EI."

"But, you're limited by that disk. And, your brain is still stuck in this body in the wheelchair." Vivian pointed behind her.

"Very well. I wasn't going to go this far, but you've raised some good points." Thakkar gestured toward the wheelchair. A dark sphere, the size of a cantaloupe, appeared from beneath the back of the chair and floated into the air. It moved past Vivian's head, and she heard the gentle hissing of air jets as it maneuvered across the room. It hovered over Thakkar's head, and Thakkar snapped her fingers.

The bottom of the sphere irised open, and a cloud of blue particles poured out of the sphere. The particles pulsed and moved along the edges of Thakkar's hologram. They coated her image in bright blue light. Thakkar was a blue ghost, but suddenly, the image changed and solidified into the former image.

She looked at her hands and felt her face and then, without hesitation, stepped off of the disc. The crowd gasped in surprise. Dr. Thakkar walked across the room and stopped just inches from Vivian. She lashed out with her hand and slapped Vivian across the face. Vivian gasped and stumbled backward.

"That hurt, didn't it? Ever been slapped by a hologram?"

Vivian rubbed her face, and the thirteenth demon surged within begging for retribution. "How?"

"My newest technology. Amazing, isn't it? You see, Vivian, I am no longer confined to that body. I am here. In the flesh. The ultimate expression of transhumanism, the guiding principle of the Numinous Corporation." She turned and hurried back to the disc. Her image turned blue again, and the particle streamed back into the sphere, leaving her holographic form on the disc. "In time, my brain; my consciousness; my soul will be uploaded and transferred to that small orb. Using proprietary technology, I have discovered how to make my hologram into living, breathing flesh, Vivian." She leaned toward Vivian and smiled. "And, in that form, I can live forever! At the moment, 3EI has power issues, and my form cannot stray too far from the sphere. But these issues will be solved. Soon."

Vivian reached over and jerked the goggles off of the wheelchair-bound figure. For a fleeting second, the image in front of her persisted. Thakkar glanced at the audience with a surprised look on her face and then faded from view. The mechanical voice filled the air.

"Security, please restrain Ms. D'Arbonne."

A lithe, young woman with shocking red hair stepped forward from the shadows. She wore a full length bright green evening gown slit at the side to reveal her legs. For a second, Vivian caught sight of a tattooed snake's tail around the woman's leg. Black gloves covered her arms past the elbows. When her hand closed on Vivian's arm, it was a cold, metallic sensation. The woman leaned into Vivian, and her bright, emerald eyes glittered with malice.

"Take it easy, sweetheart. We don't want your blood all over the floor."

Vivian almost unleashed thirteen. Her face warmed with anger, but despite this tart's boldness, she had to play her hand smartly. "I'd be more concerned about yours." She jerked her arm out of the woman's grasp. "Lead, and I'll follow."

Vivian waited quietly in a nondescript office. The red-haired woman stood silently by the door and smiled at her.

"Got a name?" Vivian asked.

The woman turned around and motioned to a tattoo of two red snakes wrapped sensuously across her bare back. "Just call me Snake." Snake turned back around and smiled.

"Need some help?" The thirteenth demon hissed in her mind.

"No. I can handle her." She whispered. "In time, we will deal with Sultana Thakkar and her demon. Patience."

The door opened, and Sultana Thakkar's electric scooter rolled in. She paused just inside the door. "You may leave us, Snake." Her electronic voice said. Snake shrugged and blew Vivian a kiss as she sauntered out the door.

The figure in the wheelchair remained bent and deformed. A crimson glow came over Thakkar, and her body moved, twisted, unwound from her crouched state transforming from the old, bent body into something else. Her hair turned dark again, and she stood up. She transformed from the old, deformed woman into her younger, healthy self. She shivered and straightened her dress. She shook out her hair.

"That's much better. Can't let the offal see my true demonic power, can I Vivian?"

"Did you just say 'offal'?" Vivian snickered. "How quaint."

Thakkar walked across the room to a wet bar and poured herself a glass of amber fluid. She threw it back with one quick swallow and sighed. "I really needed that. Now, Vivian, why are you here? Who sent you? You can't be doing the bidding of the Council. You're not a full member yet."

Vivian nodded. "True. But you were at the meeting when I walked out arm in arm with our Master. Let's just say he gave me a task to perform."

Thakkar poured another glass and sipped it. "I'm shaking in my boots."

"You should be. I'm here to make sure that whatever plans you have are in line with the Master's plans." Vivian stood up and reached out and took the glass from her. She threw back the contents and swallowed the burning liquid. "Not the Council's plans. The Council has strayed from its true purpose. The Master is not happy."

Thakkar snatched the glass from Vivian's hand and tossed it across the room. It shattered against the wall. "You are a vixen that belongs in hell, Vivian. I will not bow down to you or your supposed mission. My plans are well thought out, long in execution, and once the Master sees the fruition of my labors, he'll send you spinning and bleeding to the ceiling like he did Lucas."

"I know how you do it." Vivian sat back down and crossed her legs. "They think your technology is responsible for what they saw in that auditorium. But you reveal your real self to me. Without your demon, your technology is worthless. What are you trying to accomplish? More investors? Is this really so mundane as to be all about money?"

Thakkar's eyes filled with rage. "Money! I don't need your money, Vivian. No, what I have devised is the most devious, most dangerous device this world has ever known. Yes, I used a little help from my demon, Vivian. But the end result will be apocalyptic! And, contrary to your thinking, my actions have the Council's approval."

Thakkar was enthralled with her own self-importance. She paced as she talked. "Imagine if every person on the face of the planet could enter a virtual reality that bridges these puny dimensions with our spiritual dimensions. What if every game that was played was more than just pixels and electrons on a circuit board?"

Thakkar whirled, and her eyes were wide and wild. "What if they were sucked into their virtual world? Gobbled up by the very technology they worship? You see, Vivian, I am making virtual reality a *new* reality where I will be worshipped as a god! They will fall at my feet, and before they know it, it will be too late to save their bodies and their souls, and I will harvest them for the Master. He will reward me, Vivian. So, don't get in my way!"

Vivian nodded. Time to take a different strategy. "The disc and the sphere I understand. It's the goggles that are the key. Did you invent that?"

Thakkar ran a hand through her dark hair. "Yes. It's a prototype."

"A prototype? But, not the finished product?" She tilted her head and glanced at Thakkar. "It's unfinished, isn't it? And, you need to find the inventor to complete it? Just my guess. Otherwise, today's demonstration would have had us all wearing goggles."

Thakkar's fist balled, and she actually growled. Her eyes almost glowed a violent green. "There is one missing element. I'm working on acquiring it."

Vivian walked across the room and took one of Thakkar's hands in hers. It was far from warm and supple. It bled cold like icy metal. Thakkar glared at her and tried to pull her hand away. Vivian smiled.

"Relax. I won't bite." She led Thakkar to the sofa and patted the cushion. "Sit down. I may be able to help. As you know, I own two major corporations, and I'm on the board at Cobalt Propulsion Laboratories. Anthony Cobalt developed some amazing technology. The Sunstone would have been his crowning glory if he hadn't gotten so ambitious and wanted to be greater than the Master. There's a lesson to be learned!" She smiled and sat beside Thakkar. "Perhaps with my businesses at your disposal, you might be able to overcome some of your technological challenges."

Thakkar jerked her hand away from Vivian. "Someone has already solved the problem."

"Oh, really?" Vivian had guessed as much. "You're not an innovator. You're just a petty thief."

Thakkar hissed. "Someone else has made modifications to the interface. They even managed to link it to my mainframe virtual reality world. But I can't find him."

Vivian sat back. "We can pool our resources. Find this person."

Thakkar looked at her. "You might be of use. This person

has a mother who took one of my prototypes and tried to modify it. She had planned on using it to find her son, the inventor of the new modifications. I managed to acquire the goggles, but they weren't altered in any way. And, now, the mother is gone, or I could use her as bait."

"Gone?" Vivian asked. What was going on here?

"I sent Snake to acquire the goggles, and in her typical heavy-handed way, she managed to find the goggles but sabotaged the airplane. The airplane crashed in the Alps, and everyone perished." Thakkar looked away, and Vivian sensed the avoidance. Was the woman lying?

"I'm so sorry," Vivian said. She looked around the room and spied a computer. "Was it on the news?" She crossed to the computer and tapped the keyboard. The computer came to life, and she surfed the Internet searching for news of the crash.

"I have a backup plan," Thakkar said. "The inventor has a daughter and earlier today, she activated another pair of the stolen goggles, and it logged onto my mainframe. If I can find her, I don't need her mother."

"Here's the news," Vivian said, clicking over a video.

"I already know there was only one survivor." Thakkar returned to her electric scooter and sat in it. "I'm growing tired, and I need to rest this body. I'll have Snake show you out."

She slumped into the chair and, in seconds, melted back into the old, twisted frame of her true self. Snake entered the room and crossed to stand behind Vivian. "Shall we go?"

Vivian was turning away from the video when she heard a name she cursed to the ends of the earth. She whirled and glared at the screen. "And, the lone survivor, shown here outside a hospital in Switzerland, is Johnny Steel." A reporter said.

Vivian's eyes widened, and she stumbled away from the monitor. Steel? How? How did he show up in the middle of this mess? Was he on the plane with the scientist? It had been weeks since she last tangled with Jonathan Steel.

She felt Snake leaning over her shoulder. A grainy photo of Jonathan Steel taken into a hospital on a stretcher showed up on the screen. "Oh, I know that dear man."

Vivian whirled. "What?"

"He was on the airplane. I thought I had killed him."

Vivian's features darkened with mixed emotions. She stepped back from Snake, and she glanced over at the sagging figure of Thakkar.

"She said your methods were heavy-handed. Not a pun, I take it." Vivian pointed to Snake's artificial arm.

Snake shrugged. "I had a small parachute. Boss lady wanted me to get the prototype from the scientist. She didn't say anything about keeping her alive."

"You couldn't have just waited until she landed?" Vivian said.

"You don't know this woman. She is wily and can disappear like smoke in the wind. I knew that on the airplane, she had nowhere to escape to. I knew there was a risk of doing too much damage, and everything would have been fine if he," She pointed to the image on the computer screen. "Hadn't interfered."

"He has that annoying ability. But all those people died needlessly." Vivian said. Thirteen writhed within her.

"Oh, precious baby, why are you so sentimental?" Thirteen said. Vivian ignored the demon within her. It wasn't that she was sentimental, she thought. Eight was being too showy, too bold, calling too much attention to her actions.

"Yes!" Snake smiled and licked her lips. "All the poor darlings that died that night." She closed her eyes and shook out her hair. "It was exhilarating." She opened her eyes again, and they filled with fire. "But, this man, this Steel as you call him can't be allowed to live. I will find him, and I will finish the job the crash should have."

Vivian studied the woman's wild eyes. Had she been like this? Had she wanted Steel to die so badly, she had become more like Snake than she dared imagine? Emotions warred inside her. She hated Steel. Yes, she hated him, right? She turned her back on Snake and glanced at the image of Jonathan Steel on the stretcher.

"Darling," she said, reaching out a hand to stroke the man's image. "I have missed you. And, if you are involved, then things just got far more complicated."

Vivian felt the woman's metallic grip on her arm. "You know this man?"

Vivian whirled on Snake and felt the spiral around her right eye. She unleashed the power of thirteen and tossed Snake across the floor up against the far wall. Snake tumbled to the floor and slowly stood up with her hair cascading around her face. She licked the blood from her lip. "Oh, I do like you."

"Don't ever touch me again." Vivian let the spiral fade. "Yes, I know, Jonathan Steel."

Snake brushed her wild red hair back away from her face and wiped the blood from her lip. "He was sitting next to the inventor. Maybe he knows something. Like, how did he survive? And, if he survived, maybe the scientist survived!"

"He has more lives than a feral cat," Vivian said.

"Maybe you and I can work together, Viv." Snake sauntered across the room and smiled. "Truce?"

Vivian looked into the woman's maniacal eyes. Perhaps this was the way into Thakkar's business. "Truce, honey child."

11

J osh followed Olivia from a bus stop near downtown
Shreveport toward the riverfront. The sun was setting,
and darkness fell across the sky.

"Where are we going?" he asked.

Olivia stopped at a corner and pointed across an empty,
abandoned lot at a warehouse. "That old warehouse is now a
storage facility."

Olivia walked calmly down the sidewalk, and Josh hurried
after her. She came to the corner of the two streets that inter-
sected at the warehouse, and she motioned to a bench. Beside
it, three people slept in old blankets and sleeping bags tucked
up against the building.

"Have a seat."

Josh slid onto the cold bench. "Why?"

"We have to enter a code to open the outside door. I have
the code, but we can't walk into the office without identifying
ourselves to the attendant. The storage unit is in one of my
mother's aliases. But, if we wait, someone will come out, and we
can slip into the building while the door is open."

"How long do we wait?"

Olivia glanced up and down the street and reached under the bench. Broken concrete from the curb littered the ground beneath the bench. She glanced up at the nearby traffic light and a camera attached to its support beam.

"That camera has been out for a couple of weeks. Mom turned it off so we could get into the building unseen. Hopefully, the city hasn't fixed it yet."

She motioned for Josh to follow her, and they stood just beside the outside door to the facility.

"When someone comes out, follow my lead."

She dug inside her jacket and pulled out three bills. "Go wake up those people and give them this money."

Josh opened his mouth to protest and then shook his head. He walked over to the nearest pile of blankets. "Hello! Anyone there?"

The pile of cloth stirred, and a head peaked out. "Hey, leave us alone."

Josh waved the money in the air. "I have a gift for you."

All three piles stirred. Three men emerged from their blankets and sleeping bags. The first one, nearest Josh, snatched the money from Josh's hand.

"Thanks, pal."

Josh jumped as the sound of breaking glass filled the air above him, and broken glass showered around them. He looked up at a broken window six feet above them. An alarm sounded within, and the door to the facility slammed open. A burly man burst through the door. Olivia pointed at Josh.

"Those men took money from my friend and threw a brick at him."

The men glanced once at Josh, swore, and all three ran down the sidewalk. The burly man took out after them shouting profanities. Josh stood there, open-mouthed.

"Well, come on. We have to get in before he gets back."

Olivia held open the door. "And, pull your cap down over your forehead. There are cameras inside."

Josh followed her into the foyer, and she led him quickly down an aisle to a freight elevator near the back of the warehouse.

"Olivia, that was cold-blooded."

"They got thirty dollars out of it. And that attendant is too fat to chase them very far. Now come on. Our unit is on the third floor." The elevator opened before them, and they took it to the third floor. Josh followed her to the back corner, and she stopped in front of a corrugated door. A simple combination lock yielded beneath her rapid fingers, and she lifted the door and motioned inside. Josh followed her into the dark interior, and Olivia closed the door behind her.

"Lights on," Olivia said. The room filled with light and Josh instantly spied the motorcycle leaning against the right wall. The remainder of the room held shelves covered with boxes and some kind of computer hardware. A small fold-down bed sat in the back corner. Along the rear wall stood an upright desk and wooden shelves covered with multiple computer monitors. Olivia took a pouch from a shelf. She opened it, and the inside gleamed with some kind of metallic lining. She dug into her backpack and pulled out the goggles. She dropped them into the pouch and sealed.

"Shielding will keep the goggles from being tracked. They are powered off right now, but I'm not taking a chance."

"Yeah, about those goggles," Josh said. "Where did you get those things?"

Olivia slid the pouch into her backpack. "It's a long story. Give me a minute to take care of some housekeeping, and I'll fill you in." She sat before the keyboard at the desk.

"What is going on, Olivia?" Josh said.

"Give me a moment. I downloaded my emails before school ended, and we're safe because there is no wi-fi here. This computer is hard wired to a phone and uses an old dial-up connection. It continually updates in the background." She glanced over her shoulder at Josh. "I haven't heard from my mother, and I've got to find out where she is."

"She's not in town?"

"No, she's on that flight to Switzerland."

Josh froze. "TEA #4551?"

Olivia swiveled in her chair. "Yes. How did you know?"

"Jonathan Steel was on that flight. It crashed sometime this morning. Olivia, he was the only survivor."

Olivia's hand went to her mouth. "No!" She stood up and hugged herself. "No, my mother can't be dead. She can't."

"I'm sorry. I talked to Jonathan while I was waiting for Buck. He was the only survivor, Olivia."

Olivia whirled, and her eyes filled with fire, tears streaking her cheeks. "Of course, he would survive. He always does, doesn't he? Demons, vampires, white-eyed ghouls, aliens from outer space, time travel, and yet, he survives. I hate him, Josh. I hate him!" She screamed, pounding her balled fists against her thighs. Her face suddenly slackened, and she froze. She teetered, and Josh caught her, lowered her to the floor. Another seizure! Only this time, she wasn't coming out of it as quickly as she had in the car. He sat beside her and cradled her head in his lap. She stared off into space while tears pooled in her eyes. After a long moment, she blinked and focused on him.

"Josh?"

"You had a seizure."

She wiped the tears from her eyes, and he helped her sit up. "I'm sorry."

Josh put his hands out defensively. "Okay, slow down and tell me what is going on. You talk like you know all about Jonathan."

She closed her eyes and hugged herself. "Okay, just chill.

My mother knows him. She's known him for years. She keeps up with his activities. Discretely, of course."

"What?" Josh slid back away from her. "Why?"

"They have met in the past. That is all I know." She turned to him. "Josh, you've got to believe me when I say we are in grave danger. There is a reason that airplane crashed. They wanted to kill my mother."

"Who is they?"

She motioned to the metal box. "Numinous Corporation. My mother took one of their prototypes augmented reality interface units. She duplicated it, and that is what is in the box. She took the original unit on the airplane. She is looking for someone, Josh. Look, let me explain."

"No one knows I'm her daughter here in Shreveport. We moved here in August to be close to Steel. Why, I don't know, Josh. I'm registered as Olivia Queen, but my real name is Olivia Monarch. Now, they have found me, and they won't stop until they have me."

Josh drew a deep breath. Olivia and her mother knew Steel's past? Did they know who he really was? And now, he was being drawn into a web of lies and deception. "Okay, we will talk about you knowing and stalking Jonathan later. For now, what do we do?"

"I have to believe she is alive, Josh. I have to." Olivia stood up and shakily retrieved her backpack. She removed a plastic pill dose pack and popped open one of the holders. She poured pills into her hand and threw them into her mouth. Olivia grabbed a bottled water from an open box and swallowed the pills. "There's water in the box. I have to keep taking my meds. I can't let these seizures get ahead of me."

"Do you have enough pills?"

Olivia motioned to another box on the shelf behind her. "A year's worth. We planned ahead."

"A year's worth? She knows a lot about Jonathan, doesn't

she?" Josh wondered if Olivia's mother knew more about the past Jonathan had forgotten.

Olivia shrugged. "I don't know. She keeps a lot of secrets to herself. The best way to keep secrets is to keep them to yourself. All I know is she felt it was time to try and get close to Steel. Why I have no idea."

"You knew it would be dangerous." Josh felt his face warm with anger. "You knew it would put you and your mother and Jonathan in danger, or you wouldn't have planned all of this!" He motioned to the shelves. "So, did you sit by me on purpose today? Did you know Steel was on your mother's flight?"

"To be honest, I had no idea. I just knew Mom was gone, and I might need someone I could trust. The only person I trust at school is you."

"You didn't even know me." He looked away and shook his head. "Or, maybe you did know me. More than I thought you did."

"I'm sorry, Josh. I had no idea about your losses. I really didn't." Olivia got up and sat back in her chair. "What was it like when you thought Jonathan might have, uh, died?"

Josh stiffened. "You know how to hit me where it hurts, don't you?"

"What happened in the sky? With Cobalt?"

Josh looked away. "I can't believe you know all of this."

"You mentioned it. About your father sacrificing himself for you. I promise my mother didn't tell me any details. Assuming that she knew."

Josh whirled on her. "Oh, it's pretty clear she knew, Olivia. What other secrets are you keeping from me? Huh? What do you know that I don't know? Honestly, how do you expect me to trust you?"

"I guess I can't, Josh. But, right now, we only have each other, and there are people out there who want to hurt us."

"So tell me, honestly, how does your mother know

Jonathan? You tell me that, and it goes a long way toward establishing trust. No more secrets. Our lives may depend on it."

"They have a history. She's never told me any details."

"You know he has amnesia."

"Yes."

"Why hasn't your mother filled him on his past? That's why he puts himself in danger all the time. He's trying to find out who he is." Josh shouted.

"Shh!" Olivia glanced toward the door. "We have to keep quiet. That's why we are in the back corner on the third floor for privacy. I'm sorry, Josh. I don't have any more answers."

He glared at her. "Yeah, but your mother does. Or did."

Olivia jerked. "That was cold."

"Sorry. That was uncalled for."

"Still believe in that God of yours?"

Josh glanced up at the flickering fluorescent lights of the storage unit. "He's all I have left."

"You have Jonathan."

"Whoever he is, right? Only your mother knows for sure, and she isn't telling."

Olivia turned to her computer and wiped at her eye. Josh had made her cry. Good! It made him feel good. For a moment.

"I don't think she's dead, Josh. She doesn't know it, but I have a connection with her. Always."

"What kind of connection? I didn't think you were spiritual."

Olivia tapped on the keyboard, and the monitors sprang to life. "Not spiritual. Scientific. My mother wears a bracelet. A very special bracelet. It has some kind of special effect on people."

"Like your hypnosis?"

Olivia glanced at him and then held out her right hand covered with the lacy glove. She pointed to her pinky finger, and Josh could see a small, flesh-covered pinkie ring. "The same technology is in this ring, and the glove augments it. I touch it to someone's forehead, and it emits an electrical impulse that makes the person suggestible for about ten minutes. I don't understand it because my mother refused to tell me how it works. This ring was one of her prototypes, and I managed to keep it when she thought it was destroyed."

Olivia turned back to the screen and opened a window on the lower monitor. She typed in code. "My brain stimulator generator has a cellular connection that is proprietary thanks to my mother and sends information to the cloud for evaluation by my doctor. I piggybacked a small app that monitors my mother's bracelet. When she has it on, the bracelet monitors her vitals. She had the bracelet on her wrist when she went through security, so I know she was wearing it."

Olivia finished putting in lines of code and hit the return key. A small window appeared with a flat line in a smaller window labeled EKG. Olivia moaned, and then the flat line fed across the screen with the typical wiggly lines of an active heart. She sat back in her chair and put her face in her hands.

"She's alive."

Josh stood up and studied the image. "This is not a live feed. It has a timestamp around ten P.M."

Olivia jerked her hands away from her face and stood up. She leaned into the monitor. "That would be 10:14 P.M. in Switzerland."

"When did the airplane go down?"

Olivia opened another window on her desktop and waited impatiently for a web page to load. She typed in "Swiss Air Disaster" and waited. A news story slowly filled the space line by line.

"I'm glad I didn't live in the day of dial-up," Josh said.

Olivia tapped her foot and crossed her arms over her chest. "Come on, come on."

"There!" Josh pointed to the window. "The airplane went down at 9:54 P.M. Swiss time."

Olivia turned abruptly and grabbed him in a tight hug. Josh tried to step back and held his arms away from her. Olivia's shoulders shook with her sobs, and slowly, he placed his arms around her. He felt the ribs through her warm skin and inhaled the fragrance of incense from her short hair. Her hot tears soaked through his tee-shirt and warmed his chest. They stood that way for a few moments until Olivia's sobs ceased.

She slowly stepped back from him and wiped at her face with the sleeve of her shirt. "Sorry. I was just so relieved."

"I know how you feel. I talked to Jonathan right after the crash."

Olivia slid back into the chair and enlarged the bracelet window. In the corner, a stream of numbers moved across the window. Olivia copied them and opened another window. She pasted the numbers into the window and waited.

"Our own special code," Olivia said. "Mom sent me a message."

The numbers blurred, and one by one fell into place. "See you in London. ASAP. They have the goggles." Olivia read. "I'm heading to London lab. Sent a message to Miller. He's at the airport and can get you here ASAP."

"Miller?" Josh glanced at her.

"Miller Avionics. Mom uses him for some of her flights. He was busy, and she had to fly commercial to Switzerland."

"Robert Miller?"

"Yeah, the same one you guys tangled with on the UFO thing."

Josh stepped back and felt the skin on his neck crawl. "That's the same man who is flying Jason Birdsong out of Tucson and taking Dr. Holmes' artifacts to London. Jonathan called him and got Miller to offer him a ride when his flight was canceled."

Olivia swiveled in her chair and looked up at him. "Who is Jason Birdsong?"

"Jonathan's new partner. Sort of. Policeman out of Tucson. He's flying to Shreveport to stay with me and then drive down to attend a law enforcement conference in New Orleans early next week. He offered to stay with me until Jonathan got back. And Dr. Holmes is an archeologist/historian kind of guy, I guess. He's working on Uncle Cephas' artifacts. Some of them are going to a private museum in London. Miller has some military supplies headed to London, leaving out of Tucson, so he combined Jason's needs with Holmes' needs."

"Well, this is certainly convenient."

Josh nodded and felt a chill race down his spine. "Uncle Cephas always said there were no coincidences. In my experience, when things like this happen, it's because there is a larger plan at work."

"Whose plan?" Olivia asked.

Josh pointed to the ceiling. "God's."

Olivia rolled her eyes. "Yeah, right!"

Josh shook his head. "I don't care what you think about all of this, Olivia. I know what has happened before, and it's happening again."

"So, where are your friends now?"

Josh shrugged. "Without my phone, I have no idea."

Olivia stood up and paced. She went to a box and took out two plastic-wrapped commercial cell phones. "These are untraceable. We paid cash for them, so their serial numbers aren't linked to our account." She paused and stepped close to Josh, looking up into his eyes. "I need to know. Does anyone know Jason is Jonathan's new partner?"

"Did your mother know?"

Olivia bit her lower lip. "No."

"It's not official. He was with Jonathan with the whole Boone fiasco."

"The island that blew up?"

"Yeah, that one. But, Jason's name was never mentioned. No one knows he is connected."

She unwrapped the phone and powered it up. "I guess we have to take a chance. Call him and see if he has landed. And, let's leave God out of this."

Josh took the phone and drew a deep breath. "Olivia, you need to know how these things work out. What are the chances these sequence of events would line up? What are the chances you would pick me up at the school, and we would accidentally trade backpacks?"

Olivia shook her head. "Just chance, Josh."

"No, something bigger is happening here. I've seen it too many times before. And, Olivia, every time something like this happens, there's a demon involved." His hand went instantly to his chest. Even though the shirt and jacket, he could feel the bloodstone grow warm with his touch.

Olivia stepped back from him and bit her thumb. "No, Josh, I can't think that way. I can't. Just make the call. See if Jason's airplane is on the ground. If he is, tell him I'm giving you a ride and have him wait for us. Miller will be expecting me so he will keep the airplane on the ground. Then, I can pass you off to Jason. You said he was a cop?"

"Yeah, a policeman."

"Then he might be able to protect you. There will be a fallout from Buck's shooting. His car is missing. Hopefully, they'll think his assailant stole the car and not us. You can tell them your story. Be very visible, and don't mention me at all."

Josh looked down at the phone in his hand. Josh closed his eyes and drew a deep calming breath. He couldn't put Jason and Holmes' lives in any more danger. What should he do? Go into hiding? Live here in this storage building until the danger passed? He opened his eyes and looked into Olivia's eyes. She was a stranger, and yet, he felt like he knew her, although not personally. It was her danger he knew all too well. He had been there—many times. And, there was always one person who he could turn to in times of danger. Jonathan. "We have to leave Jason out of this. I've placed too many people's lives in danger before today. I'm not staying here, Olivia."

"And you would what? Go with me to England?"

"Why are you going? And why does she need you in England? And, who is trying to kill you?" Josh asked.

Olivia bit her lip. "I have a brother. Steven. He's four years older than me. He's brilliant. His hands were damaged in the shooting." She pointed her finger at her scar. "He took the technology of my mother's original goggles and created his own version. Something even I don't know. But, if it falls into the wrong hands, it could be very, very dangerous." She pointed to the box. "Imagine if everyone had one of these rings?"

"Mind control?"

"All I know is mother is concerned about someone getting their hands on my brother's prototype. It is far beyond what I have in this backpack."

"Where is your brother?"

"We don't know. He's off the grid somewhere in Europe. And, he's looking for the person who killed our father."

"And who might that be?"

"Not sure. A paid assassin. Now, who paid him to kill my father is something my mother hasn't been able to discover. But," Olivia sighed, "Steven found a lead a few weeks ago. He told me whoever hired the assassin was tied to the Numinous Corporation."

Josh shook his head. "Never heard of it before today."

"Dr. Sultana Thakkar is the founder."

"Thakkar?" Josh looked away in thought. "Wait, that's the woman who is paralyzed? She's brilliant. And, she has all of this new technology for artificial intelligence and augmented reality."

"That's her. Numinous Corporation claimed to have created the goggles. But, in reality, they stole the plans from my mother months ago."

"And, Thakkar wants your brother's new version, doesn't she?"

Olivia nodded. "I think so. And, I believe Steven is dangling them before her eyes so he can get into her network."

"And, find the link to the assassin."

Olivia put her gloved hands on Josh's chest. "Josh, now you see how dangerous this can be. You can't go to England. It is safer here."

"England is closer to Switzerland than Shreveport. And, Switzerland is where Jonathan is." He couldn't believe he was saying this. But, in his spirit, in his soul, he knew it was the right thing to do. He expected Olivia to protest. She studied him with her intense gaze and then nodded.

"Then it's decided. We go to Miller Avionics. Once we get to England, you'll need to call Jason and tell him what's up, but not until. We can't take a chance they will intercept his call and knew we are on the way there."

Josh slid the phone into his jeans pocket. "Here, we go again."

12

———

Jason Birdsong glanced at his watch as his flight touched down in Shreveport, Louisiana. He had survived and had made it to the land of tornados, TexMex, and Cajun food. The airplane was loaded with military equipment destined for an American base in Europe after loading up cargo from Steel's basement headed for a museum in London. His path would cross Dr. Montana Holmes' briefly. Monty would be flying with the shipment. At least he would get to see his new friend. They hadn't talked since the incident in ancient Jerusalem. He wondered how much of Monty's memory of those events had returned. Birdsong remembered all of it.

Birdsong climbed down the airplane's stairs and walked across the tarmac to the offices along the periphery of a runway at the Shreveport Airport. The sun was setting, and the cold air sent a chill down his spine. He breathed in the dense, humid air far different from the dry climate of Tucson. Birdsong entered the building and followed a sign down a hallway to an office door bearing the simple sign, "Miller Avionics." He opened the door and stepped into the cramped office.

"Get those new crates loaded, Gonzalez, or you'll be late for take-off." A man sat on the other side of a desk with his back turned to the door. A console behind him held a wall-mounted computer monitor. Several open windows on the desktop showed live feed from the tarmac. Other windows showed a web browser with live streaming news and weather. Another man stood with his back to Birdsong between him and the desk.

"Remember, those crates hold fragile artifacts." Dr. Montana Holmes leaned over the desk. The man turned and glared at Holmes. His short, military hair cut only added to the stern look in his dark eyes.

"Dr. Holmes, I don't think any artifact you can come up with is as fragile as some of the instruments I'm shipping to RAF Alconbury Air Base one hundred kilometers from London," He looked over Holmes' shoulder at Birdsong with surprise.

"Who are you?" He gestured to Holmes.

Holmes whirled. "Jason!" Holmes still had a messy mop of black hair that hung to his shoulders. He grabbed Birdsong in a bear hug. Holmes's head barely came to Birdsong's shoulders. Birdsong fought back moisture in his eyes. He had missed his friend.

"Jason Birdsong." He said to Miller.

"Oh, yes." Miller stood up and extended his hand across the desk. He was in his late forties with salt and pepper military cut hair and an angular face. His eyes glittered with annoyance. "Robert Miller. What Steel wants, Steel gets." He growled.

Birdsong shook the man's hand. His grip was firm and almost overpowering. Overcompensating, maybe? "Tell me about it."

"You're the new partner?" Miller sat back in his chair. "Good luck with that. Most everyone around Steel suffers, and some just plain die." Miller grit his teeth. "Sorry, I shouldn't have said that."

"He told me about your ex-wife," Birdsong said. "Sorry about your loss."

Miller nodded and snared a set of keys from a bowl on his desk. "Here are the keys to his truck. It's parked outside in the lot."

Birdsong took the keys. "Thanks. I'm running late as it is."

"I was supposed to pick up Josh at some kid's house, but the movers ran late. Just give him a call, and he can give you the address." Holmes said. "Man, it's good to see you. I heard you're not with the Tucson police department anymore."

Birdsong shrugged. "They don't like time travelers on the payroll. It's okay. I've been doing some private security work, and there's always work with Jonathan."

"Well, Josh is at some kid's house tutoring. Last name was Sanderson?" Holmes said.

Miller froze. "Did you say, Sanderson? The oil guy?"

"Don't know about the oil. Got the text right here with the address." Holmes reached into his jacket pocket and pulled out his phone.

Miller turned to his computer and tapped on keys. He opened a link. "I think you'd better listen to this news story from a couple of hours ago."

The image of a two-story house surrounded by police cars and yellow tape filled the screen. A banner on the bottom of the screen listed "Barry Sanderson, CEO of Typhoon Oil." A reporter stepped into the frame.

"Roger Smith here at the home of local oil company executive Barry Sanderson. This afternoon around 4:30 P.M., authorities believe his son, Eugene Sanderson, was attacked during a home invasion. Eugene, also known as Buck to his friends, was shot in the head during the attack and is in surgery at University Hospital. The extent of his injuries is unknown at this time. Witnesses describe an SUV arriving on the property and two assailants entering the house. Later, Buck's new designer car, a birthday present from his father, was seen racing down the street accompanied by the SUV. Authorities are speculating the presence of the expensive car spurred the attack. We will have more on this story at ten o'clock."

Miller closed the window and spun around to face Birdsong. "Are you sure Josh was at that house?"

Holmes held up his phone. "Here's the text. 4 P.M. You know what this means."

Birdsong took out his phone and hit Josh's number. He listened as the rings went on and on and then went to voicemail. "No answer!" He ended the call. "They didn't say he was at the house. So, where is Josh?" His face blanched, and nausea gripped him. He glanced at Holmes. "Monty, Josh may be a hostage."

Miller reached for his desk phone. "I'll call the authorities." He paused, his hand hovering over the phone.

"What?" Birdsong asked.

"I've got to make sure those pallets get on the plane first. Can't afford a police investigation."

"What? This is about Josh, not your cargo." Birdsong towered over Miller's desk.

Miller turned to his monitor and studied the video feed. "You don't understand. In addition to military supplies, I'm shipping some crates of CBD oil to a neurology clinic in England for kids with seizures. Not approved by the British yet. It is not exactly illegal, but I can't afford it to be tied up in customs. Or, the local police."

Birdsong stepped around the desk and picked up the phone. "I don't care about your –"

Miller snatched the phone out of Birdsong's hand and shoved him back against the wall. Birdsong blocked Miller's arm with his and rolled to the side. Miller was quicker, wrapping the phone line around Birdsong's arm and spinning Birdsong into a tight circle until the phone line bound his arms.

"Just give me a few minutes, Birdsong," Miller said.

Birdsong flexed his arms, and the phone line burst into three pieces. He kicked Miller's feet out from under him and shoved him back onto the desk. Papers and folders exploded into the air. Holmes stood there with his mouth open.

"Dude, are we interrupting something?"

Birdsong glanced up at the open door. Josh Knight and a girl stepped into the room.

Birdsong released Miller and rounded the desk, gathering Josh in a bear hug. "You're safe!"

Josh pushed awkwardly away. "Dude, I'm fine. What's that all about?"

Miller sat up and glared at Birdsong. "You do that again, and I'll break your arms!"

"Hey!" The girl said. "Cool it, guys. What's going on?"

"Olivia." Miller pushed his hair back down. "You're almost too late."

Holmes pointed to the monitor. "Josh, what happened at your friend's house?"

Josh glanced at Olivia, and she nodded. "What do you mean?"

"Buck Sanderson." Birdsong studied the kid's eyes. "Guy you were tutoring? The news said there was a home invasion."

Josh swallowed nervously. "What? When?"

"This afternoon, while you were at his house," Birdsong said quietly. "Josh, what are you hiding?"

"Hiding?" He looked again at the girl.

"We left because Buck refused to study. Right, Josh?" She said.

"Uh, yeah," Josh said. "Olivia gave me a ride there, and Buck refused to, uh, let me tutor him. Wanted to play a video game.

And, he had gotten this new car and all. And, uh, how is he?" Josh's voice broke, and he cleared his throat.

Birdsong raised an eyebrow. "How is who?"

"Buck?" Josh's face whitened.

"He's in surgery for a gunshot to the head," Birdsong said.

"Then, he's not dead?" Josh said excitedly. "Great!"

"How did you know he had been shot?" Birdsong stepped closer. "Josh, you're not telling me something."

"Home invasion, sir," Olivia said. "There's always a gun. Right?"

Birdsong glanced over his shoulder at Miller. "Well, let's get you out of here and call the police on the way. I'm sure they have some questions. That way, Dr. Holmes can get on his flight, and Miller here can get his illegal CBD oil off the ground."

Josh glanced at Olivia. "Uh, but we have, uh, a –"

"Date." Olivia finished.

"Oh, really?" Birdsong nodded. "Where?"

"Bowling." Josh said at the same time, Olivia said, "Chinese."

"Chinese bowling." Birdsong crossed his arms. "Didn't know there was such a thing."

Holmes chuckled. "He's got you there, buddy."

Josh smiled weakly. "Look, why don't you take the truck and head on out to the lake house, and Olivia and I will have a quick bite, and then she'll run me home. Okay?"

Birdsong glanced back and forth from Josh to Olivia. "Grandmother warned me about teenagers."

Olivia punched Josh, and they both looked at the monitor. Birdsong turned. They were watching the window that showed the final loading of the pallets onto the airplane.

"Neither one of you is making any sense," Miller growled as he settled back behind his desk. "I'll forgive Tonto here for trying to beat the heck out of me. But, Olivia, if you want to hitch a ride on the flight to London, you don't have time for a quick bite."

Josh glanced nervously at Olivia and then back at Birdsong. "Listen, Jason, uh, dude, we really need to go so you will be safe. I mean, not safe, but, you know, tucked in for bed tonight."

A figure appeared in the hallway behind Josh and Olivia. Sensing the presence, Josh and Olivia stepped further into the office. Out of the shadows in the hall, a hand appeared holding a pistol with a silencer.

Olivia gasped. "They found us, Josh."

Birdsong tensed as the figure stepped into the light. He tried to put himself between the approaching assailant and Holmes and Josh. He could care less about Miller.

The woman was about Josh's height and small and willowy. She wore a flannel shirt under a down vest and blue jeans. Her dark hair was short over her ears, and her eyes revealed a ferocity and bestial hunger with which Birdsong was all too familiar.

"You two are going nowhere." She said quietly.

Josh glanced quickly at Birdsong and back at the woman. He tilted his head. "Your voice. It's familiar." His eyes widened. "Your face is different, but that voice."

The woman's face twisted in confusion for a second, and then she raised the pistol higher. Three red threads dangled from her fingers, and her hand whitened as she tightened her grip. "If you know who I am, you just signed your death warrant."

"But you're supposed to be dead," Josh said.

The woman's hand wavered slightly. "Obviously, I'm not. Who do you think I am?"

"Raven," Josh said.

13

R AVEN'S STORY
Transylvania, Romania -- Cavern of the 12th Demon

RUDOLPH WULF *slowly raised the pistol in his hand and pointed it at Jonathan Steel. Time seemed to slow as Raven recognized the gun she had given to King the night he was to have died along with Steel. She felt the weight of the amulet at her neck and gasped. Now she was certain. She did not want Steel to die.*

Raven felt the strings of her past binding her still, holding her back, keeping her safe from harm. Survival, she reminded herself. It was all about taking care of herself. But for the first time in her life, she couldn't stand and let another person die. Time lurched forward, and she ran across the platform. Steel's gaze met hers, and he knew what she was about to do.

"No!" He screamed, but it was too late. Raven shoved him aside, throwing herself between Steel and the gun. Wulf pulled the trigger, and a bullet plowed through her rib cage. White-hot pain lanced

across her chest as the bullet burrowed into her lungs. She whirled and started toward Wulf. He pulled the trigger again, and another bullet tore through her chest, splintering bone and shredding muscle. Is this what her victims felt in the microseconds before their death? Were the final moments of their lives filled with the sharp, eviscerating pain she felt? She paused, blood spurting from the wound in her chest, her vision swimming with the pain. And still, she moved toward Wulf.

Wulf tightened his grip on his cloak and aimed the pistol at her head. He pulled the trigger for the last time as Raven extended her arms, jumping up into the air to shield the others as much as she could from the exploding bullet she had placed in the pistol.

The air exploded in hot shrapnel. Bits of metal flayed her face and arms, tearing into her abdomen, her legs, her chest. The concussion grabbed her and threw her across the platform toward the front edge. She landed hard, sliding across the slick metal on her own blood until she came to rest just inches from the chasm.

In place of Wulf's body misted a haze of atomized bone, flesh, and brain. His entire upper torso was missing. The residual flesh and bone toppled backward and fell into the pit, dragging the red robe after it. For a second, it fluttered in the breeze like the crimson banner of the Wolf Dragon.

Raven's pain was incredible, the pain of every bullet she had ever fired, every wound she had ever inflicted. Steel's face appeared, and she felt her strength quickly fading.

"Raven?"

"It's okay." She coughed blood in a fine spray. "You were right."

Steel gently lifted her head and placed it in his lap. Blood pooled and ran down her side as he teased her hair out of the lacerations on her face.

"Hold on, and I'll get help."

Raven coughed, and a bloody bubble burst from her lip. "We're in the middle of nowhere." Raven studied his bright turquoise eyes, damp with tears. The cold was spreading, and her hand went into *her blouse. She grabbed the amulet with all her might and jerked until the blue twine broke.*

"Take this." She pressed it into his hand. "It's the key. Call Max. Tell Max you redeemed me." She coughed, and blood sprayed on Steel's face. "Promise me. Pay them all back. Make it right. Promise," she begged.

"I promise, Victoria." Steel's hand closed on the amulet.

Raven felt her hand fall, losing strength, and it snagged against Steel's torn shirt. She pulled the shirt away. "I thought I killed you--" she swallowed blood. "How did you live?" Her vision blurred, and she refocused on his chest. With her remaining strength, she pulled herself upright and leaned forward to study Steel's chest. There was no wound.

Even as life began to fade from her, the realization dawned. She laughed, blood bubbling on her lips. "You're not--" For a second, she thought she heard Jonathan's voice. Was he asking her a question? It didn't matter anymore, for she was once again in a pink dress with the warm spring air on her face. She looked down at the cake shaped like a lamb. A shadow fell across it.

"I am here." His voice was kind and gentle. A hand reached out for hers its perfection marred only by a red wound. She looked up into the face of her Maker.

As Raven died, she tumbled away from Steel toward the dark shadows of the pit. She was free now, flying through the darkness as all her regrets and sorrows vanished in the shadow of Endless Love. Something appeared in the air beside her. A gauzy wing fluttered in the meager light, and she felt hands cradle her back. They slid around her and slowed her descent. Warm hands embraced her, and two enormous wings beat the air around her.

The seemingly bottomless chasm ended in a river of frigid

water. Her body dipped effortlessly into the cold, more cold, invading her fading limbs.

"Who?"

"Don't worry." A voice spoke into her ear. "The Savior is not done with you. The cold will slow your metabolism, and you will not die this day."

She floated in chilling waters as a net of gray threads closed around her and pulled her into the light. She felt more threads pierce her chest, her abdomen, her face. Her skin tightened and scarred. And still, she floated on a sea of confusion. The being with wings had told her it wasn't over yet. In fact, it was just beginning.

What did he mean? Where was she?

Images of a man with turquoise eyes flashed in and out of the dark shadows of her memory. And then, her vision cleared. The doctor in the white coat nodded to a nurse.

"Our Jane Doe is awake." He said in Romanian. And she understood it. How did she know a foreign language? From her darkness, the strings began to emerge, weaving a new tapestry, showing her the life she could only barely remember.

"I will get her uncle." The nurse said. She paused to lean over her. "He's been waiting for weeks for you to wake up. But, he refuses to tell us your name. Such secrets!"

The doctor reappeared and ushered a man up to the bedside. He was short and wore a wide-brimmed Panama hat. He clenched a Meerschaum pipe in his teeth. His bright, blue eyes glittered from the shadows beneath the hat brim. "Hello, honey."

Raven's eyes widened. "No!"

"You've been busy." He motioned the doctors and nurses away. "You should have known by going rogue you would never escape me. You work for me, Raven. Not yourself."

"But I'm forgiven. I died."

"Not yet." The man tapped a finger against the face of a

demon carved into the side of the pipe bowl. "Now, we can do this the hard way or the easy way. Come back to me voluntarily, and you can keep those wonderful memories of my son. If not, well, we can just restart everything."

Raven tried to push up from the bed, but her arms were weak, and pain lanced into her back. "No! Please!"

"Very well." He leaned forward. "Beware the wicked numinosity."

Raven felt the strings break, felt the growing light fade back into darkness, saw the fires and the tall tower with a large clock face, heard the thunder roll across a green plane where huge stone slabs towered, felt herself dwindling fast, hands clawing at the man with the turquoise eyes sitting alone in a restaurant, the man with the knife and the blood of a lamb faded away until she was empty. She relaxed and blinked.

"Where am I?"

The Captain tucked his pipe into a shirt pocket. "You're safe."

She looked up at him and then around her. "Captain? How did I get here?"

"What is the last thing you remember?"

Raven lifted her bandaged hands and touched the gauze on her face. "London." Raven touched her face and felt pain beneath the gauze. Her mind was filled with confusion. How had she gotten here, wherever here was? What was wrong with her face? She studied the Captain's turquoise eyes.

"Not a problem. I'm afraid someone tried to kill you. In time, I will tell you who that person was. But, first, we must get you well. I'm afraid you'll need some facial reconstruction and a few weeks of rehabilitation. I've arranged to fly you back to the states." He leaned forward, and his eyes gleamed with malice. "And, when you are well, I will pay you fabulously to kill the person who did this to you."

Raven nodded, a chill running down her spine. Kill? She

didn't want that anymore. Something had changed. Something deep within her. But, what? For a moment, she recalled the embrace of wings in cold darkness and a man with a nail-scarred hand. Don't let the Captain know, she thought. Get well and try and remember what happened. Her jumbled memory fed the confusion in her mind. But, there was one thing she was sure of. The Captain was lying to her.

"Thank you, Captain." She mumbled through her dried, chapped lips. "Let's get started."

WEEKS PASSED FILLED with painful surgeries and even more painful rehabilitation. Raven found herself in a private clinic north of Dallas, Texas, hidden away by rolling hills and scrub bush on a rambling 2000 acre ranch. The clientele was exclusive and elite. They kept to themselves, which was fine with her. She seldom saw the Captain and worked tirelessly to recover her strength and agility. At times, she was visited by three doctors who were identical in appearance. Were they triplets? They often appeared in her room and watched her quietly without saying a word. Surgical masks always obscured their faces, but their eyes were Asian in appearance. Often, one of the clientele, an elderly English gentleman, would speak to her as she passed him in the hallway. Other than those four, the only attention she received was from her personal nurse and the rehabilitation technologist.

Often during the weeks of recovery, she would probe her memories. Possibly years of her memory were gone. Would it matter now that she was back in the clutches of the Captain? Something told her she had escaped his control in the years since the assignment in London. She must have gone rogue. Each puzzle piece of almost retrieved memory tumbled around her mind refusing to fit together. The last solid memory was of the affair in London. And, each time she spoke to the man with the British accent, she relived those horrible moments.

For now, she would play the Captain's game. She would regain her strength and get better. Perhaps in time, her memory would return.

RAVEN EXAMINED her face in the mirror. She ran a finger along the fine, red lines on her face and the angle of her jaw.

"You've had quite a bit of reconstructive surgery." Nurse Puckett held up a sweatshirt.

Raven glanced down at her bare abdomen covered with scars. The pain was gone. Beneath these scars, her muscles were finely honed. Her strength had returned. It was time to leave this place. She slid into the sweatshirt and pulled on a pair of warm-up pants.

"Where did you get these clothes?" She asked the nurse.

"I got you some when I found out your uncle was coming to pick you up. Funny, but I would have thought he would have brought some clothes from home for you."

The Captain was coming. Great! She tried to smile at the nurse. Be friendly, she thought. Put on a front of normalcy. "I don't remember 'home.'"

"It will take time for your memory to return. Once you get into familiar surroundings, things will begin to clear up." The nurse picked up a small canvas bag. "I put together some toiletries for you."

"Thank you." Raven took the bag and slung it over her shoulder. "What now?"

"Your uncle is sending a car to pick you up. I'll walk you out to the front."

Raven followed the nurse out of the room and down the hall. It smelled of antiseptic and a faint underlying odor that she could only attribute to disease. In the distance down a long hallway, she saw the three doctors talking to the gentleman from England. She would miss them.

They reached the foyer of the clinic, and a black limousine waited in the driveway. She turned to the nurse. "Thank you for everything, Cynthia. Oh, do I have a name?"

Cynthia pointed to the bag. "It's all in there. Your driver's license, social security card, everything."

"Who am I?"

Cynthia patted her hand. "Raven Poe."

The name rolled around in her head. Raven. Poe. Appropriate. The Captain had a warped sense of humor.

"If you have any questions, just call me. I put my card in your bag." Cynthia squeezed her shoulder.

Raven nodded and started toward the door. She paused. This nurse had been her only companion for the past months. "Thank you, Cynthia." Raven stiffly walked out the door.

The front door of the dark car opened, and the driver got out. He wasn't the Captain. Not surprising. "Ms. Poe?"

"Yes. Who are you?"

"The Captain's driver. I am to take you to the ranch house." He opened the back door, and she climbed into the limousine. He handed her a cell phone. "Your uncle wants you to call him as soon as we arrive." The driver got into the front seat, and the car moved out of the hospital entrance. Raven glanced once at Nurse Puckett standing in the doorway and felt what little familiarity she had vanish.

A tinted glass window separated the front compartment, and she sat in total silence as the car moved away from the hospital through winding roads surrounded by pine trees and scrub bushes. She waited. No need to call the Captain just yet. She needed time to formulate her plan. For, she was sure the Captain would send her after another target.

Raven would need resources; weapons, money, and, most

importantly, information. But, before embarking on any mission, she wanted to ensure her meager recovered memories would remain. There were hazy memories of a cavern, a towering man in a crimson robe. She recalled brief flashes of a younger man with turquoise eyes. Was he somehow related to the Captain? Even her muddled memories before the London assignment were tumbled and mixed up. She had known a fellow assassin with such eyes. Was his name Jeremiah? Joshua? Some name that started with the letter "J." But, the most potent memory was one of forgiveness, a sense of resolution with God; a gnawing contentment that she had found peace. She cursed the Captain for most likely breathing one of his trigger phrases in her ear. It had almost eased all of these returning memories. It was the inevitable reset he always performed on his operatives. And there might be a way to undo those changes.

Raven opened her bag and pulled out a tangle of red threads. She had worked them out of a coarse clinic blanket. Three red threads. She slowly tied them around the middle of the second, third, and fourth fingers of her right hand. They were tight enough not to slip off but not too tight to cut off the circulation. She used her teeth to bite off the excess thread dangling from the knots.

Raven held her hand in front of her and concentrated on her fourth finger. "The man with the turquoise eyes." She said out loud. She focused on the fleeting image and tied it to the red thread. She studied her third finger. "The cavern and the gun with the exploding bullet." She gasped as the memory of the gun returned. Was this where her injuries had come from? She tried to enlarge the frame of her memory. Was her killer in her memories? Hold onto that memory, she thought. For with that memory came the inescapable inclination the bullet that pierced her chest had come along with a powerful revelation, a revelation that had changed her life. It was a seminal moment she could not forget, and it had led to the most crucial memory.

Raven looked at the red thread around the base of her index finger. Forgiveness. Peace. Grace. These profoundly spiritual feelings embraced her mind and heart. She couldn't lose them. They were her connection to God. And, she could not remember if she had ever reached out to God. The spiritual depth of her feelings testified otherwise. This peace; this mercy; this compassion toward her had to become her foundation. She didn't have to show compassion to the one that tried to kill her. But, she had to return to it and find a way to fully and ultimately become the whole person she desperately wanted to be.

Raven closed her hand into a fist. "I'll play your game, old man. I will have my revenge. But, then, we are done."

She regarded the cell phone again. One phone number showed up in the contacts tab. She pressed it.

"Hello, Raven." The Captain said. "How are you feeling?"

"Stronger. Better. Ready."

"Good. Frank will bring you to the ranch house, and we will discuss your new assignment."

Raven glanced up at Frank in time to see the driver's head explode in a gush of blood and brain. The tinted window shattered into a thousand pieces covering her with flesh and glass. She dropped the phone and grabbed for the armrest. The car began to swerve, and she instinctively ducked. Another gunshot shattered the window beside her.

Raven felt the car slow and spin out of control. She grabbed the seat belt and twisted into it as she lay across the back seat. The car tumbled sideways and began to roll down a steep embankment. She tightened her grip as airbags deployed and pinned her against the seat. The car lurched to a halt.

Raven reached for her thigh. Why? There was supposed to be a knife there, but she was totally disarmed. She rolled out from under the airbags down onto the floorboard. The car was canted at an acute angle. She kicked the window out on the door closest to the ground and slithered out onto a rock and behind a low lying brush. She had done this because the other door was higher and was in sight of the road. Whoever was trying to kill her would expect her to come out that way.

She grabbed her bag and the phone and duck-walked down the slope deeper into the thicker brush. She paused behind a large boulder to take stock of her situation.

Her neck was sore from the rolling car, but the crash hadn't hurt her. She looked through the canvas bag for a weapon. A few toiletries rolled around. She grabbed a can of spray deodorant and a cigarette lighter. She waited.

The approaching footsteps crunched in the underbrush, and she held her breath. Someone was coming, and they were trying to be very quiet. She cracked a twig on purpose, and the footsteps came toward her. She wanted to know who was trying to kill her.

She squatted behind the rock with the spray can in one hand and the cigarette lighter ready. A man appeared at the edge of the boulder, and she stood up quickly, pressed the button, and the lighter at the same time. A plume of fire gushed into the man's face and ignited his hair and his eyebrows. He screamed and dropped the gun he was holding.

Raven scooped up the gun and pulled the trigger three times. Each shot found its mark, and the man collapsed in the underbrush. She stood up and glanced up the slope. It was empty of life. She walked over to the man. One bullet had entered between his eyes. The other two had entered his chest right where the heart would be. She had recovered her mojo! Then she cursed. Her instincts had kicked in, and she had killed her only source of information.

She knelt over the man's body and felt through his clothes. He wore a pair of khaki pants and a tweed overcoat. Inside the coat, she found a set of car keys. That was it. No identity, no cell phone, nothing. She picked up the pistol and dropped it into her canvas bag, and started back up the slope.

Raven glanced in the limousine. The driver was quite dead. She continued up the slope and found the shooter's car parked at the side of the road. A truck came barreling toward her and, she turned her back as it passed. She didn't want the driver to see her face.

She unlocked the car and climbed in. The interior was clean and, there was no phone or other identity. But, tucked on top of the sunscreen was an envelope. She pulled it out. Inside was a thick pile of one hundred dollar bills. And, a lone piece of paper with her name scribbled on one side. On the other was a handwritten note.

"Kill Raven. Thakkar." Sultana Thakkar? An image swam into her mind of a woman huddled in a wheelchair. Thakkar was one of the wealthiest women in the world. Why would a world-renowned figure of business and technology want to kill her? And, how had the woman found out she was here?

Raven climbed out and studied the license plate. She pressed the edge of the plate, and it fell away, revealing another plate. The car was stolen with a fake license plate. She put the phony license plate back over the real one and climbed into the car. She started it up and pulled out onto the highway.

Raven called the number on the cell phone.

"Raven? Are you all right? I heard gunshots." The Captain said.

"Your driver is dead. And, so is the assassin sent by Thakkar to kill me."

The Captain was silent for a moment. "This is bad. It would seem my operation may be compromised. Your location, your very existence, was a deep secret. But, somehow, Sultana Thakkar found out you were alive. I guess I don't have to emphasize how important your next target is."

"She thought I was dead, but now she knows differently!" Raven shouted at the phone. "Nowhere is safe for me."

"So it would seem. Very well. I hate to do this, but you must not lead her back to me."

"What?"

"Beware the demon of the spiral eye." The Captain said.

Raven stiffened and dropped the phone. "No! Not now! Don't do this!" She managed as her mind whirled in confusion. Deep within the currents of her memories, priorities shifted about; memories tucked away. New memories created by the Captain surfaced and, she shuddered and trembled as the changes took place.

Raven looked around her in confusion. Where was she? What was going on? She was Raven. The assassin. But, the rest of her mind was a blank. She heard a voice far away speaking to her. A cell phone lay on the seat of the truck. She picked it up and glanced briefly at three red threads tied around the base of three of her fingers. What were they for? She couldn't remember.

"Who is this?"

"Your boss." The voice carried a strange familiarity, a ring of authority. "I know you are confused right now. I have erased your memory temporarily to protect me and to protect you. I'm afraid your answers will come from one person. I can't help you, but you must fly to London, England and, confront Dr. Sultana Thakkar."

Thakkar? Raven blinked and found a piece of paper on the dashboard. A note with her name and this strange name of Dr. Sultana Thakkar. "I don't understand."

"She tried to have you killed."

Raven felt a thrill of anger at the mention of the name. She glanced in the rearview window. Blood dotted her face and her hair. "Where am I now?"

"North of Dallas, Texas."

Raven glanced at the canvas bag on the seat beside her. She pulled out a passport with her picture and a name. "Raven Poe?"

"It was to be your new identity. I'm afraid if I've been compromised, Thakkar's people will be looking for you under that name. You'll have to get off the grid."

"I need money."

"Perhaps the assassin has some?" The Captain said.

Raven spied an envelope on the seat beside her. It was full of money. Someone had paid the assassin in cold hard cash.

"Found it. Lots of money."

"Listen, you can't get to London on a commercial flight. There is a man I worked with a long time ago. He has gotten back his private air service. I just sent him a text, and his office informed me he is conducting some private business in Shreveport, Louisiana. He'll be there for a couple of days. That's a three-hour drive. Go find him and remind him he owes the Captain a favor."

Raven dropped the money in the canvas bag. "And he'll take me to London?"

"For the right price. As I said, he owes me."

"Yes. I can't keep this car. They'll be looking for it."

"Raven, I trained you well. You may have lost temporary access to your memories, but you will still find your skillset intact."

"About that. I want my memories back. I want my freedom from you. I want my own life." Raven said.

"You've asked for that before. I promise you if you find Thakkar and eliminate her, I will utter the phrase that will give back all of your memories." The Captain said.

Raven sighed and punched the end button. She had a lot of planning to do, and for that, she needed somewhere safe and secluded. She gripped the steering wheel as her mind sifted through endless plans and possibilities. Her gaze fell on the threads. There were there for a reason. She had tied them. She blinked furiously as she searched for the memories tied to the strings, but nothing surfaced. She cursed and pounded the steering wheel in frustration. She studied her reflection in the rearview mirror. She did not recognize her own face. Why? Thin red lines were etched along her jawline. Someone had altered her face. Plastic surgery! Why?

"What to do?" She spoke to her reflection. "The mission. It's always the next mission. Finish it and maybe, just maybe my boss would give me back my memory. If not," She raised an eyebrow, and fury filled her vision with a red light. "I will kill him and start over."

IT HAD TAKEN LESS than an hour to find a roadside rest area with a restroom. Raven had cut away most of her hair with scissors she had gotten at a drug store. She had chosen the small drug store because it had no external or internal video cameras. It was a mom and pop business in a small town off the beaten path of Highway 80, the old route from Dallas to Shreveport. She looked at herself in the mirror and realized the shorter hair made her look significantly different from the woman who had walked out of the hospital just hours before.

Raven pulled aside the "closed" sign she had placed in front of one of the two women's restrooms. She returned to the assassin's car and drove away from the rest stop. It was near sunset when she found what she was looking for in the small town. She parked down the road and walked back to the front yard of a double-wide trailer.

"May I help you?" The dumpy woman asked as she opened the door.

Raven looked past her into the living room filled with at

least five tumbling, screaming children. "I see you have a truck for sale."

"Yes, ma'am. My husband's out hunting, and he should be back soon. He can tell you all about it." The woman bit into a greasy doughnut.

"I'll pay you in cash right now if you let me have it," Raven said.

The piece of doughnut fell out of the woman's mouth. "In cash?"

Raven held out a hand full of money. "All I need are the keys."

The woman grabbed the money and disappeared inside. The odor of fried fish rolled from the doorway. She realized she was famished. The woman appeared at the door. "What about the paperwork?"

"I'll come back in the morning and get your husband to sign the papers." Raven took the keys. "I want to surprise my boyfriend."

Raven slid into the interior of the truck and started the engine. It sounded fine with just a hint of misfire in the timing. She pulled out of the driveway and down the road to the old bridge. She had pulled the other vehicle into the brush along the bridge. She took off the stolen plates and attached them to the truck. Then, she released the vehicle's parking brake and pushed it forward. It rolled through the underbrush and over the edge of the river. It tumbled down into the deep waters of the river that flowed beneath the bridge. Raven made sure it disappeared before going back to the truck. Now, she had a new look and a new ride. She was back. And, with the funds from the assassin, it was now time to build an arsenal and get that flight to London. And, heaven help anyone who got in her way!

14

Detective Jared Samuels sucked down the last of the cold coffee and tossed the cup into the bushes.

"Hey, you're contaminating the crime scene." A crime technician barked back at him. Samuels glared at the man.

"I threw it outside the yellow tape, newbie. Just get on with your job." Samuels rubbed his hand through his short hair and swallowed down the acid reflux from the nasty coffee. One day, it would kill him. If this kind of stuff didn't kill him first. He had been with the police department for twelve years and had worked his way up through the ranks to homicide detective. Few things surprised him anymore, but this one was a real puzzle. Smoke still drifted from the home of Brandon Sanderson. The crime scene tech held up an evidence bag.

"This is strange. We found hundreds of wasps in the front yard."

Samuels glanced at the bag. "Must have been one whopper of a nest somewhere. What about bullet casings?"

"Nothing, sir. Maybe more inside when the fire department releases the house." The tech stepped to the side as a member of the fire department pulled his hose back toward the fire truck.

"We got the fire out, sir. Your men can safely go in now." The fireman said.

A car pulled up to the barricade, and a man got out and argued with a uniform. Samuels squinted into the setting sun as the man slid under the crime tape and headed for him. The man wore a long, black overcoat over a rumpled white shirt and a red tie. His dark hair was in disarray, and his eyes hidden behind mirrored sunglasses. He reached into his coat as he approached Samuels and pulled out a badge.

"Special Agent Franklin Ross. You Samuels?"

"Yippy. The FBI has come to the rescue." Samuels growled.

"Yeah, I'm happy to be here, too. I'm supposed to be on my way to an FBI seminar in New Orleans. I should have flown instead of driving. I'm sitting in Copeland's eating oyster Rockefeller, and I get a call from my old college buddy, Sanderson. Said something about his boy had been shot up, and someone stole his new car."

Samuels sighed. "So, this is not an official FBI investigation?"

"No, it's a favor to a powerful and wealthy local, and it would be, uh, kind of you if you would let me, uh, tag along," Ross said.

"Ha! This isn't easy for you, is it?"

"No."

"Good! Okay, looks like someone shot up the house. The boy was found on the stairway with a bullet to the head. Something caught fire in the upstairs media room. Most of the second floor is burned, but the fire department got here before it could fry Sanderson's son."

"EMT's say the bullet grooved the skull but didn't penetrate. Guess your friend's son is hardheaded." Samuels led Ross across the water-soaked front yard to the driveway. "No bullet casings were found. None! And, yes," he pointed to a black streak of rubber on the driveway. "Someone peeled out of the driveway in a hurry. But, back over there by the dumpster, we saw fresh tire tracks where someone pulled up on the grass. Looks like an SUV, and it took off in a hurry also. Tore up the grass."

"Home invasion?"

"Could be. If someone was here with the boy, they might have taken the car and ran with it. I've got a tech checking traffic cams. Ah, here he is."

The crime scene tech appeared holding an iPad. "Looks like the Maserati busted through lights at the on-ramp for I-49. And, get this, sir. An SUV collided with a trash truck and didn't bother to wait for the police. They took off and disappeared into the neighborhood. But, we got a couple of snapshots of the Maserati."

He held up the iPad, and Samuels studied the image. The driver of the Maserati was hidden behind the sunshade, but the passenger had leaned forward, horror and fear etched on his face. Ross took one look at the iPad and swore. He stomped away and swore and swore and swore.

Samuels handed the iPad to the tech. "Okay, I'll bite."

Ross turned and glared at Samuels. "No, no, no, no! I will not get pulled into this demon crap again! Not now. Not tomorrow. Never! I'm out of here." He turned and was halfway across the yard and stopped. He whirled and stomped back across the yard. "He saved my life. He saved my life!" He screamed at Samuels. "Why did he have to save my life? Huh? Just once, why couldn't he put me out of my misery?"

"You're a raving lunatic, Ross," Samuels said.

"You're right! I am! And I have one person to blame for it. That boy sitting in the passenger seat is the adopted son of the one man on the face of this planet that continues to make my life a living hell."

"You know the kid?"

"Yeah, Joshua Knight. And, I can tell you that he was running from demons. You heard me right, running from demons with guns and the ability to burn down the scene of the crime, pick up their own casings, and disappear after a major accident and melt into the woodwork."

"Demons, huh? Not familiar with a gang of that name."

Ross leaned into him and jerked off his sunglasses. His bloodshot eyes glared at him. "I'm not talking a gang, Samuels. I'm talking real, solid, scare the crap out of you, demons." He backed off. "Now, I have to call him and find out what he's gotten himself into this time." He pulled out his cell phone.

"Who you gonna call?" Samuels asked.

"Demonbusters!"

15

"You're supposed to be dead," Josh whispered.

"How do you know me?" Raven asked.

"Your face is different. Sort of. Plastic surgery? But, I'd know that voice anywhere. Still gives me the creeps." Josh shuddered. "Listen, don't you remember the cavern in Transylvania? The vampires? Rudolf Wulf, the twelfth demon?"

"I don't know what you're talking about." Raven shifted the pistol to point at Olivia, and for a second, Josh saw her gaze shift to three red threads tied around her fingers. "And, if you don't want me to shoot your girlfriend, you'll shut up. Now."

Josh sighed and stepped in front of Olivia. "You'll have to shoot me first."

"Not a problem." Raven wore a dark hoodie over a black sweatshirt and pants. She took the backpack off her back and placed it on the desk. "All of you step behind the desk and cross your arms. Now."

Birdsong slid around the desk to stand by Miller and Holmes joined him. Josh pushed Olivia behind him as they rounded the desk. "What are you doing here?" Josh asked.

Raven ignored him and lifted a pouch out of her backpack

and tossed it on the desk. "You." She pointed at Birdsong. "Open the pouch. You'll find a padded sticker like an EKG lead. Peel off the back and stick it below your left breast."

Birdsong opened the pouch and pulled out the pad. He hesitated, and there was a puff of air and sheetrock showered down on his shoulders. Raven had shot the wall behind him. "Next time I will not miss. Do it. Now."

Birdsong nodded assent and peeled off a silver pad. He lifted his pullover and shirt and pressed the pad to the skin on his chest. Raven reached into the backpack and took out a cell phone. She held it up so they could see the screen. The number "1" filled the screen.

"I touch it, and your pad shocks your heart and stops it. I drop the phone, and your pad shocks your heart, and it stops. I die, and your pad shocks your heart, and it stops."

"I get it," Birdsong growled.

"Good." She pointed the pistol at Holmes. "Your turn."

Holmes placed a pad on his chest. Josh followed suit. Olivia took her pad and, without hesitation, lifted her shirt and stuck the pad just beneath her bra. Josh looked away in embarrassment.

Raven shifted the pistol to Miller. "I believe my boss spoke to you."

Miller frowned. "Yes. You need to hitch a ride to London. But, I didn't expect you to show up with guns blazing."

"There's one pad left. Put it on your chest." Miller complied.

"I wish I had never met your boss." Miller tossed the paper from the pad aside. "These people have no business with you. Let them go."

Raven lowered her pistol and slid it into the backpack. "That was before he recognized me." She pointed to Josh. "How do you know me?"

"You were hired to kill someone, and Jonathan Steel stopped you. You saved his life in Transylvania. You asked God for forgiveness. We thought you were dead after that exploding bullet and the fall into the pit." Josh said.

A muscle twitched in her cheek, and she glanced down at the threads on her finger. "I don't remember that."

"Jonathan told me all about you," Birdsong said.

Raven looked at him. "That's too bad. I can't leave any witnesses."

"I have no idea who you are," Holmes said.

"You know who I am now," Raven said. "That's too bad for you."

"Who are you after?" Olivia asked.

Raven shifted her gaze to Olivia. "None of your business. I'm here to get on that airplane to London. Without any witnesses."

"That's why we are here," Josh said.

Birdsong glanced at him. "What?"

"Jason, someone is trying to kill us. And, it's not Raven. This has to do with Olivia's mother. And, I think it's all tied to Jonathan's trip to Switzerland. If I stay here, I'll be killed. By them, bro. That is if Raven doesn't kill me first. You're safe. They don't know about you."

"Who is they?" Birdsong said.

"Dr. Sultana Thakkar's people," Olivia said.

Something in Raven's face twitched and she stared at Miller. "How long before my flight leaves?"

"And, I bet this Thakkar has something to do with the next demon on the list." Josh sighed. "Let me think? Which one are we on? Oh, yeah, the eighth demon? There are so many now that I've lost count."

"I don't know what you're talking about. I have my assignment."

"Look, there's no need to kill us, Raven. We are all after the same thing. If Thakkar is the eighth demon, then Jonathan will be right in the middle of it. And, if we stay here, we're dead."

"My mother is the one Thakkar is pursuing," Olivia said. "We are just pawns in the game. We have a common enemy. You take me with you to London and find my mother, and she will lead you to Thakkar."

Raven raised an eyebrow. "I don't use partners. But, what you say makes sense."

"Josh isn't going anywhere without me," Birdsong said. "I promised Steel I would protect him. I'm Steel's new partner."

"And I'm not abandoning my friends," Holmes said.

"Or, your precious cargo," Miller said.

"Okay, here's the deal. The three of you will go with me on the airplane to London. You try anything and," She touched the cell phone screen, and the numeral one began scrolling from one to five. "I touch the screen, and whoever's number is up dies. Got that?"

"Yes," Birdsong said.

"We get to London, and I go my way, and Olivia comes with me to find her mother. As long as the two of you don't get in my way, I don't care."

"What about me?" Miller said.

"You will inform your crew that five passengers will board the airplane. No questions asked. Now."

Miller picked up his desk phone and talked briefly to someone on the other line. He hung up the phone. "You leave in five minutes."

Before Raven could react, Olivia reached over and brushed her hand across Miller's forehead, and she said, "Astra." The man slumped into his desk chair.

"What are you doing?" Raven pointed the pistol at Olivia.

"You need me. Put the gun away. I've worked with Major Miller before. Mother hypnotized him to forget putting us on flights around the country. Posthypnotic suggestion. The name of his adopted daughter." Olivia glanced once at Josh and tugged the ring from her finger and slipped it into her pocket.

"Don't try that with me." Raven said.

"How could I? I've never hypnotized you before." Olivia turned to Miller. "Now, Robert, you will forget what has happened for the past hour, and you will fall asleep at your desk. When you wake up, you will lock yourself in the closet and sleep through the night."

Olivia turned back to Raven. "That should keep him out of the way until after we land in London."

Raven slowly placed the pistol back in the backpack. "Okay, get your stuff and let's head to the airplane. Just remember, you try anything, and all I have to do is touch the face of my cell phone or just drop it, and one of you is dead." She motioned to Miller as she slowly slumped forward over the desk and began to snore. "Including him."

GONZALEZ, one of Miller's assistants, met them on the tarmac and motioned up the stairs. "We need to go. We have a schedule to keep. The pilots are already locked into the cockpit. Once you get in, close the door and strap in for take-off. Got that?"

Josh watched Raven's hand twitch inside her hoodie pocket, where she held the phone. "No problem." She nodded to Josh. "After you."

Josh and Olivia climbed the stairs, followed by a quiet and sullen Holmes and Birdsong. Once they were in the front cabin, Raven pulled the phone out of her pocket and pointed to the door. "Close it."

Josh struggled with the heavy door, and Birdsong moved to help him. "Don't help him. In a seat. Now. Strap in."

Birdsong glared at her and collapsed into one of the seats. Holmes sat next to him. Josh managed to get the door closed and cinched down the lever sealing them in.

Raven motioned to the floor between the facing seat rows. "Backpacks on the floor. Now."

"I need to take my medicine," Olivia said.

"What medicine?"

"I have epilepsy. If I don't take my medicine, I'll have a seizure." She held up her backpack.

"Get your medicine and don't try anything, or you won't have to worry about having a seizure."

Olivia placed the backpack in Josh's lap and unzipped the top. Did she have any more of the nanobites, Josh wondered? Even if she did, they were locked in an airtight airplane and all of them would be victims. She took out the zippered fabric container, and it rattled. Olivia took out a handful of pills.

"I need water."

Raven motioned to a nearby metal cart locked against the bulkhead. It held bottled water and snacks. "Get us each a bottle of water and a handful of snacks."

Olivia grabbed a bottle and sipped to swallow her meds and then passed around bottles and snacks. Raven motioned to the seat between Josh and Holmes. "Now, sit and strap in." Once Olivia had fastened her seat belt, Raven took a seat across the shortened aisle from them.

The airplane engines roared, and they moved along the tarmac. Soon, they were airborne. A voice came over the speakers above them. "Hey, this is your pilot. There are drinks and snacks and one lavatory at the far end of the cargo section. See you in London."

Raven unbuckled her seat belt and walked over to the doorway to the cargo section. She opened it and peered in. "Josh, come here."

"What is it?"

She motioned down the cargo bay. "Go find an empty cargo holder."

Josh stepped past her into the cargo section. There was

barely room to walk down a narrow aisle between multiple containers held back by cargo nets. Not far from the door, there was a row of empty cargo containers waiting to be filled with goods. The containers were four by four by four feet.

"Take your snacks and your water and climb in."

Josh froze. "What?"

"You heard me. Get the others. Each one in a cargo container. Now."

Josh motioned to Birdsong and Olivia, and they joined him. "What about my meds?"

"Get your backpack and take it with you. The others stay out here. Just remember, I fall asleep, and you die. I get jostled, and you die. I hear a noise, and you die."

"We got it," Birdsong said. "The kid promised you we would cooperate. As long as you keep your end of the bargain and let us go to London."

"I gave you my word. But the girl goes with me. Remember?"

Josh tensed, and Olivia placed a hand on his arm. "It's okay, Josh. I'll be fine." She glanced down at her backpack.

"What about the pads?" Birdsong said.

"Bluetooth. Short-range. Once I'm off the airplane and gone for, I'd say, about an hour, it's safe to remove them. But, if you try now while they are connected to my phone, they'll shock you."

"And we die." Holmes blurted. "We got it."

"Now, into the crates. I'll seal them from the outside."

"What about bathroom breaks?" Olivia said.

"You have a bottle."

Olivia chose the second crate and sat cross-legged on the floor, cradling her backpack. Raven shut the front door. She glanced at Birdsong. "You next."

Birdsong folded his considerable form into the first crate and cast one lingering look at Josh. Josh nodded. Raven closed the door and latched it. She motioned to the fourth crate. "That's yours, Sherlock."

Holmes cast one look at Josh. "I'm so sorry, Josh. I was supposed to be taking care of you."

"It's okay, bro," Josh said. "It happens."

Holmes disappeared into the crate, and Raven secured the door. She nodded to Josh. "You're last."

"When we get to Europe, Jonathan could help you," Josh said.

Raven shook her head. "I don't need any help."

"Except Olivia. Promise you won't hurt her or her mother. Once they are together, you'll let them go. Promise me, Raven. On those red threads tied around your fingers."

Raven's face reddened, and she glanced down at the threads. "I can't make that promise."

"The Raven I knew would. The Raven I knew would do anything to protect us."

Raven motioned to the crate. "I'm not that person. Get in."

Josh crouched down and sat on the bottom of the crate. The door closed. He heard the door to the main cabin open and close.

Ventilation slits were present in all four walls and allowed some meager light into the crate interior. He leaned forward and pressed his mouth close to the slits next to Olivia's crate.

"Can you hear me, Olivia?"

"I'm scared, Josh. I didn't mean for this to happen."

"I know. But this is my life, Olivia. This kind of stuff happens to me all the time."

"So, who is this Raven?"

"An assassin. She tried to kill Jonathan's old partner, Theo. We ended up in the caverns of Transylvania, and she changed. She saved us. I thought she was dead." Josh whispered.

"Josh, I think I know her," Olivia said.

"What?"

"I remember her voice from somewhere," Olivia said.

"I don't recognize the face, Olivia. I can't explain why she has changed so much. Probably plastic surgery? She was pretty cut up by the explosion, and then she fell into the chasm. Maybe it erased her memory. All I know is she can be ruthless. But there is something beneath the killer exterior that showed us compassion. We thought she had sacrificed herself to save Jonathan." Josh said.

"Josh," he felt her breath through the ventilation slit. "If she is who I think she is, I will NOT show her any compassion. If I get the chance, I will kill her!" She sobbed quietly.

Josh shook his head. "Olivia, listen to me. If there's one thing I've learned in all this time is that revenge won't bring you peace. Besides, I don't think you're a match for Raven."

Olivia sniffed, and her voice receded as she leaned back into her crate. "Don't try and talk to me about forgiveness and mercy, Josh. I've got none of that in my life."

"But, Olivia –."

"I'm not talking to you anymore right now. I'm going to get some sleep."

Josh sat back in his crate and leaned against the rear wall. "Olivia, don't become Raven. You'll regret it. Jason?" He whispered to the other side of his crate. "Can you get us out of these crates?"

"I could. But Raven holds us hostage with these pads." Birdsong said.

Josh's hand brushed against the pad under his shirt, and then he touched the bloodstone. He pulled his necklace from his shirt and studied the tiny red shard in the meager light coming through the slits. Could the jewel give him power? Could it open the crate door?

"Come on, bloodstone. Help us." He whispered. Nothing happened. He leaned back against the crate wall and sighed. Soon, he fell into a troubled sleep.

"Josh, wake up!"

Josh lurched forward, and his head hit the top of the packing crate. He blinked away the pain and glanced around him. He was still in the cargo crate. It hadn't been a bad dream. The voice had come from outside the crate. Behind the sound of the voice, a deep rumbling filled the air, and his ears popped.

"What's going on?"

"The airplane has depressurized." The voice continued. It was male, and it wasn't Jason Birdsong.

"Who is there?" Josh leaned forward, his cramped back and legs complaining. He peered through the ventilation shafts. A short, dark-haired man wearing green surgical scrubs stood in the aisle. "Dude?"

"Dude!" He said and grinned. "Long time, no see, Josh, man." Josh had not seen the angel he had named "Dude" since the events with the eleventh demon back in Lakeside.

"I thought you were my guardian angel?"

"I am." Dude winked and crossed his arms. "Your guardian angel is at your command."

"Why haven't I seen you, Dude?"

Dude shrugged. He seemed totally unaffected by the jostling of the airplane. "You haven't been in trouble since then."

"Not in trouble?" Josh hissed as Dude opened the door to the crate. Josh painfully crawled out and tried to stand up without falling over. "What about Cobalt? Huh? I almost died, saving Jonathan's life. Where have you been?"

Dude reached forward and tapped the necklace beneath Josh's shirt. "Right in there."

"In the bloodstone?"

"Well, sort of." Dude shrugged. "You finally put it back on after your father's death."

"You live in the bloodstone, Dude?"

"Not really. Kind of." Dude cradled his chin and tapped the tip of his nose. "You know we're from other dimensions, right? What I needed you to do was to find the faith to trust in God again."

"I've always trusted," Josh said.

"Really?" Dude put his hands on his hips. "You didn't ask for much help with Cobalt."

Josh gasped. "See, that's what I mean! He tried to kill me. And then, Jonathan disappears back in time, and Theo is gone. And –"

"Theophilus is not my responsibility." Dude said. "Look, Josh, you had to remember the sacrifice your father made to keep you from dying. That sacrifice echoes the Father's love and the Son's sacrifice. When you chose to put your sorrow aside and chose to honor your father's memory and his act of bravery and love, then I was able to return to help. It's that simple." Dude smiled and raised his open hands in triumph.

The pitching of the airplane tossed Josh forward before he could respond. He fell up against Birdsong's crate. "Let's get my friends out of these things."

Dude popped open Birdsong's crate, and the big man crawled out.

"My whole body is asleep." He mumbled. "Who are you?"

"My guardian angel," Josh said. "At least, in theory."

Dude opened Holmes's crate. Holmes emerged, his eyes wide. "I felt the pressure drop. Are we going to die?"

"Not yet." Dude said.

Josh glanced at the first crate. It was open. "Where's Olivia?"

"She is with Raven." Dude motioned to the back of the airplane. "Raven took her, and they jumped out of the airplane after opening one of the exit doors when our flight was southwest of London. She had a parachute, so don't worry."

"Wait! What?" Birdsong said. "They jumped out of the airplane at thirty thousand feet?"

"Now that we are on the final approach to landing, we are below five thousand feet." Dude said.

"Who is he?" Holmes ran his hands through his disheveled hair.

"My guardian angel," Josh said.

"Well, he hasn't been doing a very good job, has he?" Holmes said. "What am I saying? An angel? Really?"

Birdsong placed a hand on Holmes' shoulder. "Hey, brother, calm down. You shouldn't have problems believing in angels."

"I know. It's just this was supposed to be a calm flight to London. I had no idea I'd be kidnapped and locked in a cargo cage."

"Bro, welcome to my world," Josh said. The airplane shook again. "Why so much turbulence?" He grabbed a nearby cargo net to keep from falling.

"The pilot is making an emergency landing at Heathrow Airport. Civilian, not military. It's closer. Now, Dr. Holmes is supposed to be on this flight. But, the two of you can't be back here after they land." Dude said.

"Oh, and how do you propose to handle that?" Josh said.

Birdsong stretched his legs and arms. He patted the inside of his loose jacket and pulled out his wallet. "I have my passport. Josh?"

"I don't even have a passport. All I have is my driver's license." Josh said.

Dude handed Josh his backpack. "That will be a problem. Follow me." Dude led them down the aisle, and Josh grabbed his shoulder.

"I need to know. Is Olivia, okay? Does she have a guardian angel?"

Dude glanced over his shoulder and knelt before a door

recessed into the floor. "She is fine. And, no, she doesn't have an angel. She is not a child of the King."

Josh swore out loud, and Dude glared at him. "Watch your language."

Dude pulled the door open, and cold air poured in. "This will lead down into the rear cargo bay. This area is a converted passenger section. Now, the lower cargo bay is only partly full."

"That's where my artifacts are?" Holmes asked.

"Yes?"

"What do I do when we land?"

"Tell them the truth. Raven locked you in a cargo cage, and that's all you know. Don't mention anyone else who is on the airplane."

"I'm not leaving, Josh."

"Bro, if you even hint that you know I was here, those people who tried to kill us in Shreveport will kill you, too. It's best to act innocent. Dude, what's the plan?" Josh said.

"When the airplane slows down and starts to taxi at a reasonable rate, I'll open the cargo bay door. The two of you need to jump out and hug the tarmac until the airplane and all the emergency vehicles move away. When you're alone, head for the nearest highway. Cross the fence, and you'll find a Tube station. It's raining outside and overcast, so you'll be almost invisible on the tarmac."

"What's a Tube?" Josh said.

"Subway," Birdsong said. "I have money. We can buy a card to ride."

"Keep your face hidden. It's just after noon here, so you'll be visible on the streets. There are CCTV cameras everywhere. Then, make your way to Dr. Holmes' hotel." Dude said.

"Uh, the Royal Renaissance." Holmes shook his head. "I don't know about this."

Birdsong put a hand on the man's shoulder. "Brother, I'll look after Josh."

"Monty, I'll be fine," Josh said. "I have to find Olivia. And, as soon as you land, call Jonathan. Just do it on a landline and fill him on what's going on. We'll meet you at the hotel."

Holmes nodded. "Godspeed, Josh. You too, Jason."

Dude dropped through the door into the cargo bay, and Josh and Birdsong followed. Emergency lights dimly lit up the bay. The airplane was shaking less, and they heard the landing gear go down. Dude pointed to a release by a door in the nearby bulkhead. "Just pull the lever, and the door will open. Wait until you touch down and begin to slow down. Got it?"

Josh glanced at Birdsong. "I don't know, Dude. This sounds dangerous."

"You'll be fine, Josh. I've seen you take worse falls on your motorcycle."

Just then, the airplane lurched as it landed roughly on the runway. Before Josh could answer, Dude, faded out of sight. He glanced at Birdsong. "This is insane, right, bro?"

Birdsong nodded. "Yes. But so was going back in time two thousand years." He placed his hand on the door lever and listened carefully as the airplane's engines quieted down. The forward speed slowed, and Birdsong jerked on the lever. The door popped open, and cold, moist air poured into the cargo bay. The runway was a dark strip beneath them. Off to the sides, emergency vehicles paced the airplane. Birdsong nodded to the runway.

"I think it's safe now. Keep your knees bent and roll away from the fuselage and keep your head down, got that?"

Josh nodded, and his heart raced. His mouth grew dry. He jumped.

16

S teel had no idea what time it was when he awoke. He had eaten a tasteless take out meal of noodles and bland beef and then swallowed more pain pills before collapsing into the bed in a darkened bedroom. He sat up slowly on the side of the bed, and his head pounded with the effort. Sparkles swam before his eyes, and he sat as still as possible.

Olin had brought him a set of flannel pajamas and cotton briefs. They were a size too large, but he had worn them anyway. The bedroom was cold, and the tile floor frigid when he stood up. He made his way to the kitchen. The smell of brewing coffee made his stomach growl with nausea. He had never liked coffee, but right now, he would gladly swallow a cup if it cleared the confusion from his mind.

Olin was nowhere to be seen. A short, trim woman with coffee-colored complexion appeared from the dining room. She smiled at him.

"Mr. Steel." She said with a heavy French accent.

"Who are you?"

The woman's hair was short and framed a plump face. Her dark brown eyes gleamed with malice. "Your worst nightmare."

Steel backed up against the cabinet. "Where's Olin?"

"Relieved." She wore a tight, dark blue business suit with smartly creased slacks and a white shirt buttoned to her neck beneath a matching blazer. She reached into her inside pocket and pulled out a leather wallet and flipped it open, revealing a badge.

"I am Inspector Goudreaux." The woman answered. Steel heard the front door open.

"Where is she?" He heard Swarsin swear as he thundered into the kitchen. His face was red, and his eyes burned with anger.

"Who gave you the authority to relieve my men and barge your way into my safe house?" He said to Goudreaux.

Goudreaux smiled at Swarsin and slid her wallet back into her jacket. "National concerns are above your pay grade, Swarsin. I'm taking over this investigation."

Swarsin licked his lips and glanced once at Steel. "I don't think so."

Goudreaux ignored him and poured herself a cup of coffee. She sipped it and motioned to the dining room. "Let's have a seat, Mr. Steel. We need to have a conversation."

Swarsin glanced at her with bulging eyes. "This is not over, Goudreaux."

She pushed past him, and Steel followed shakily. He glared once at Swarsin. "I don't like this, Swarsin."

Swarsin shrugged. "She outranks me. You should cooperate."

Steel nodded and sat opposite Goudreaux at the dining room table. "I'd like to call and check on Josh."

"I took the liberty of confiscating your phone." Goudreaux sipped more coffee and studied Steel like a lizard surveying a fly. "You've gotten several calls. What does Special FBI Agent Ross have to do with any of this?"

Steel's face blanched. "Why would he be calling?"

"All I saw was the name and caller ID on the notification screen. Can't unlock it." Goudreaux pulled his cell phone out of another of her inner pockets.

Steel held out his hand. "May I?"

"In a minute." Goudreaux studied the phone screen, sipped more coffee, and then slowly turned her gaze on Steel. "Why would the FBI be calling? Maybe you're a suspect in the destruction of an airplane that cost the lives of hundreds of innocent people!"

"What are you talking about?"

"We found out why the airplane went down," Goudreaux said quietly. "I'm with the Swiss equivalent of your own FBI. Tell him, Swarsin."

"Tell me what?" Steel glanced at Swarsin. He paced behind Goudreaux and then paused. He leaned on the end of the table.

"The airplane's black box revealed a failure in the hydraulic system, and our inspectors found evidence of a small, well-focused bomb. We found an airplane emergency exit door next to the dog sled cabin. Is that how you got out of the airplane?"

Steel's face warmed. Was Josh in trouble? Why was Ross involved? And, now, this? "Look, I don't remember anything."

Goudreaux snapped her fingers, and another agent appeared from the hallway. Had he been stationed there all night? He handed Goudreaux a tablet. She looked at the screen. "According to our records, you were in the center aisle three seats away from the exit door. How is it you managed to be by the exit door when the airplane broke in half, and your row was at the breaking point? If you had been in your seat, Mr. Steel, it would have been impossible for you to leave via the exit door."

Steel shook his head in confusion. "I don't remember. How many times do I have to tell you?"

"Until I am satisfied you are not lying." Goudreaux placed the tablet on the table and pushed it toward Steel. The image of a seating diagram filled the screen. A red X marked the aisle seat of an emergency exit row. Two seats were in the row. Had he been seated in one of the chairs? Goudreaux quietly tapped a seat in a row three feet in front of the exit row. She sipped more coffee and waited.

"Anything to say, Mr. Steel?"

Steel shook his head, and pain lanced down his neck. He blinked in confusion. He remembered sitting in the original seat. How had he ended up in the exit row? Had there been time for him to move to the exit row to help people before the airplane crashed? But, there had been turbulence, sudden, unexpected turbulence. "You said there was a bomb?" He glanced at Swarsin.

Swarsin nodded. Steel looked back at the diagram. "I wouldn't have had time to move to the exit row if there had been a bomb."

Goudreaux smiled. "It was a small and carefully focused explosion, Mr. Steel. It was designed to take out the steering hydraulics. There would have been plenty of time for you to save yourself." She stood up and towered over the table. "Plenty of time for you to move from your row to the exit row where you had planned an escape."

Steel sat back and looked up into her fiery gaze. "And do what? Hope the airplane landed on a mountain top in one piece? Hoped that I could jump out of the exit door and escape into the night? It sounds to me like whoever planned on that explosion planned on everyone dying when the airplane crashed. Not landed safely, but crashed. If I had planned this thing, it would have been a suicide mission, and I would have been in my seat when the airplane went down."

Goudreaux's voice rose in volume. "Unless you were a coward, Mr. Steel. Many terrorists have had second thoughts and tried to orchestrate their own escape even when it was fruitless to do so. You were just very, very lucky." She smiled and drank more coffee. "Or not so lucky. You ended up here. With me."

Steel glanced hopelessly at Swarsin. "Don't you realize how ridiculous this sounds? You should be looking for the real culprit, that –" He paused, and a fleeting image ghosted through his memory.

"Yes?" Goudreaux leaned forward. "Someone just came to mind? An accomplice, perhaps?" She pulled out his cell phone. "Maybe someone whose number is on this cell phone? You want to check on, who was it, Josh?" She held the phone up like a carrot dangled before a donkey.

"Yes. Let me check on Josh. Please."

"And, how do we know you won't erase the contents of your phone when you unlock it?"

"I'll let you hold it as I put in the code, and you can unlock it yourself. I have nothing to hide."

"Then we will listen on speaker." Goudreaux smiled. She held the cell phone tightly in her grip. "You don't mind us listening in, do you?"

Steel's face grew hot with anger. "Like I said, I have nothing to hide." He tapped in his code. Goudreaux studied his keystrokes carefully and smiled. She touched the call from Ross. His voice echoed over the speaker.

"Steel, it's 3 A.M."

"I know you're not asleep, Ross. Not if you've got something to tell me." Steel answered.

"Well, I'm smoking again. Do you have any idea how much paperwork got dumped in my lap because of that business in Arizona? Time travel? Really?"

"Don't you have a partner for that?"

"Yeah, I do. But, she's getting her beauty sleep right now. I was driving through Shreveport on the way to New Orleans for a conference, and I get a call from one of my old gambling buddies. I don't know how you do it, but you manage to drag me into some crap." Ross' hoarse voice trailed off into a coughing spell.

"What is this about, Ross?" Steel glanced up at Goudreaux.

"I got a call from my gambling buddy, Buck Sanderson's father. Someone shot his son. Grazed his head, and they took him to surgery for a blood clot on the brain. They got to Sanderson's house in time to save him from the fire."

"Fire? Shot?" Steel reached for the cell phone, and Goudreaux pulled it away. Steel glared at her. "Ross, tell me what's happening!"

"We're not sure. My opinion is that someone invaded Buck's house, and Josh and a friend took Buck's Maserati and escaped. They were chased by an SUV that got caught in a traffic accident at Pierremont and I-49. They disappeared, and Josh and his friend are nowhere to be found. Probably hiding, is my guess."

"Olivia?"

"We found a self-driving car down the street. Registered to Olivia Queen. She goes to the same school as Josh. She probably gave him a ride. How did you know?"

"Josh called yesterday. Said he was at Buck's, and a girl named Olivia gave him a ride from school." Steel stood up, his face growing cold with shock. Josh was in trouble? Someone shot his friend? "I don't understand. Dr. Montana Holmes was supposed to give him a ride to the airport to get our truck. He must have been running late." Steel tried to contain his racing thoughts. "I'll be on the first plane home, Ross."

Goudreaux shook her head. "You're going nowhere."

"Who's that?" Ross's voice came over the cell phone.

"Frances Goudreaux with the Swiss equivalent of the FBI. Mr. Steel is a terrorist suspect."

Laughter came over the phone speaker. "Steel may be many things, but he is not a terrorist."

Steel glared at her. "Don't even think about stopping me."

She pushed back her jacket to reveal a holstered pistol at her hip. "You want me to pull this pistol? You want me to use it on you?"

"Hey, Goudreaux!" Ross said. "Calm down. Tell Steel I will keep him posted. We are still looking for Josh."

"He's right, Goudreaux. Let's dial it back a bit." Swarsin said.

"The man is a suspect in the death of over 200 innocent people." Goudreaux's gaze never left Steel's. "He's not leaving this country."

"Oh, yes, I am!" Steel whirled and headed for the front door. Goudreaux moved more quickly than he imagined and grabbed his arm from behind. She pulled his arm painfully behind him and slapped a handcuff on his wrist in one fluid motion. Steel tried to pull away, and she shoved him face down onto the floor, jerking his other arm over his back and fastening the other cuff.

"Goudreaux!" Swarsin barked. "That's enough!"

"Oh, I'm just beginning, Swarsin." She pulled Steel to his feet and shoved his face against the wall.

"I can't let anything happen to Josh. He's my responsibility." Steel mumbled through swelling lips pressed against the wall. "He lost his great-uncle on the same day he lost his father. He has no one but me."

"I don't care!" Goudreaux hissed. "Tell that to the people who lost someone on Flight #4551."

"I had nothing to do with that!"

"Swarsin, get his coat. Don't want our suspect to freeze in his pajamas. We're going down to a nice, cold cell where you can cool off."

Swarsin reached for Steel's coat hanging on a coatrack next to the front door. As he pulled it away, the red carnation fell out of the pocket and landed at Steel's feet. He stared at it and gasped. His mind reeled.

"You must save the woman at all costs." A voice echoed in his head. Woman? What woman? Flashes of a woman with red hair somersaulting through the air danced through his mind. He saw another woman with dark hair, but her face was blurred. But, the redhead? What had she done? He remembered the smell of blood, the sound of screams, and the sudden decompression.

"I remembered something!" He said, nodding to the red carnation. "Red hair. There was a woman with a backpack. She opened an exit door in the air! I can see her face."

"What?" Swarsin said.

Steel nodded toward the flower. "That triggered my memory. Or it might have been slamming my head against the wall." He blinked as the memory sharpened. "She killed two passengers! Cut their throats right before she opened the exit door."

Goudreaux relaxed a bit. "No one knows that detail. Two of the passengers had their throats cut. Their bodies were intact enough to tell the cut wasn't from the crash." She glanced at Swarsin. "Now you see why I can't let this man go. How did you get the knife on board, Steel?"

"No, it wasn't like that. The woman had an oxygen tank! That's right! She had on a wig to disguise herself as an old woman, and the tank had a mask. The backpack must have been a parachute. And, she had a bag that she took from someone. From someone! I can't remember who."

"How convenient you remember all of this just as I am taking you in." Goudreaux hissed in his ear.

Steel nodded toward the flower. "The carnation. Someone gave it to me right before the accident. I can't remember who."

"This red-haired woman, do you think you could work with a sketch artist?" Swarsin asked.

"No! He's lying, Swarsin. Can't you see?" Goudreaux shouted.

"I am not!"

"Tell me. How would she get a knife on board to cut someone's throat?" Goudreanx repeated the question.

Steel paused. Knife? There had been a knife, right? "Wait! I remember. The old woman was carrying a black, wooden cane. It had these two red snakes imbedded in the cane from some kind of jewels, and when she took off the wig, I tried to stop her. She had a ceramic blade in the end of the cane."

Goudreaux gasped and whirled him around and shoved his head back against the wall. Pain thundered through his head. "A cane? Did you say red snakes?"

"Yes." Steel blinked away tears from the pain.

Goudreaux stepped back and released him. Her mouth was open in shock. "The Crimson Snake."

"Is it possible?" Swarsin said.

"Who is the Crimson Snake?" Steel asked.

"An assassin. One of the best." Goudreaux looked away deep in thought.

"So, you believe me?"

Goudreaux shook her head. "Not many people know her cane contains a ceramic knife. She has used that disguise before. Maybe you were working with her?" Goudreaux's gaze narrowed.

"Oh, come on! Just because I survived doesn't mean I'm part of her plan. If I had been, don't you think I would have had a parachute, too? What are the chances of me surviving a plane crash like this? Huh?"

"I supposed it is possible you were not working with her. She has a nasty habit of killing her accomplice after their first job together." Goudreaux said.

Steel gasped as another memory surfaced. "Her glove came off, and she had some kind of mechanical hand."

Goudreaux froze. She glanced at Swarsin. "Okay, this just got very interesting."

Swarsin frowned. "You're right. Steel can't go home. We need him here until we track down the Crimson Snake."

"No, no, no!" Steel said and grimaced as his headache pulsed.

"More details might surface." Goudreaux put a hand on her chin.

Swarsin moved closer to Goudreaux. "All the more reason to keep him here at the safe house. We take him to a cell, and the Snake will know. He won't survive twelve hours."

Steel glanced at Swarsin. "But, Josh? I have to go find Josh."

Goudreaux turned on him. She gestured to Steel's phone. Her assistant handed it to her. "Did you hear all of that?"

"Yeah, sort of. Kind of lost the conversation in the noise of you shoving my friend's head against the wall, a man who already has a concussion." Ross said.

Steel's eyes widened. Ross had called him his friend!

"Listen up, Ross, while I explain to Mr. Steel his only options. Steel, you have one of two choices. Stay here and work with your friendly FBI agent over the phone, or I put you in a cell with nothing but the clothes on your back and three tepid meals a day and around the clock guards who will most likely die right before the Snake slits your throat. Accomplice or not, she leaves no witnesses, Mr. Steel."

Swarsin put a hand on Steel's arm. He tried to pull away, but the pain in his head was too great. Swarsin's hardened features actually softened a bit.

"Steel, stay here, and let me see what I can find out from Ross. It would take hours to fly home anyway, and we all know that time is of the essence when someone disappears. Let Ross and the local officials do their job. Besides, you're not going to fly with a concussion. Brain swelling would kill you."

Steel grit his teeth. "Who made you a doctor?"

Swarsin blinked a few times and looked away. "Trust me. I know from personal experience." He glanced at Goudreaux. "We will put an anklet on him. Even if he tries to escape the safe house, we will know exactly where he is."

"Jonathan, cooperate. You won't do Josh any good in a jail cell." Ross said over the phone speaker. "I'll keep you posted." The call ended.

Goudreaux looked like she had swallowed ground glass as she glared at Swarsin. "I'd rather put the man in a cell. But, unfortunately, you're right. The Snake and her employer, whoever that person may be, have too many connections." She unlocked the cuffs. "I'll keep my own guards outside in a vehicle. We'll be by shortly with the anklet." Her eyes narrowed, and she leaned closer to Steel. "Just remember what Snake did to those two passengers, Steel. She's out there right now looking for you. Leave this safe house, and you won't last an hour." Goudreaux silently exited through the front door, followed by her assistant. Olin appeared in the front door and stepped back into the living room.

Swarsin sighed. "And you thought I was a pain in the backside."

17

An hour later, Ross called back on FaceTime with more information. Josh had not been found. Buck's car had been located in an apartment complex. But, no one, including the Shreveport police or the Caddo Parish sheriff's department, had found a lead to just where Josh had disappeared to.

Steel sipped some warm soup and tapped the iPad left by Goudreaux impatiently. "Is there static on this line, Ross? You're not telling me anything new!"

Cigarette smoke obscured Ross's face. He waved it away and leaned into the iPad FaceTime image. "Steel, I'm doing everything I can to find Josh. We found out more about Queen. Junior student. Her mother is Ilene Queen, and when we checked out Olivia's registered address, it's an open field. Can't find any record of Ilene Queen anywhere in the area."

Steel slapped the table in frustration. "So who is this mystery girl?"

Ross shrugged. "My partner, Sybil, is interviewing students at the school right now. Take a deep breath, Steel. I hate to admit it, but you've trained the boy well. Josh can take care of himself." Ross drew another lung full of smoke and blew it out of the side of his mouth. "But, I have to ask you, Steel, could this be another one of your demons?"

Steel blanched and sat the soup cup roughly on the table. "I hadn't thought of that!"

"Well, no matter what, Steel, even though we have had our differences in the past, I will do everything I can for Josh. I'll keep you posted."

"What about Dr. Holmes and Jason Birdsong?"

"The airplane with Holmes and his cargo took off as scheduled headed for London. We found your truck in the parking lot. No sign of Birdsong." Ross looked away and sighed. "Okay, I got to tell you I reached out to Birdsong before he came to Shreveport. I invited him to the FBI seminar in New Orleans next week after you got back from your trip. That's the last I heard of him."

"He would have gotten off the same cargo airplane Holmes left on." Steel said. "He was supposed to take the truck and get the keys from Miller to go to my house and stay with Josh."

Ross nodded. "Yeah, you told me that already. No sign of Miller either. He's staying in a hotel somewhere, but we don't have the address. Look, there are lots of loose ends at play, Jonathan. Just be patient." Ross lifted an eyebrow. "Never mind. You've never been capable of that!" Ross signed off.

Steel stood up shakily. He wore a loose pair of jeans and a flannel shirt that was a size too big and uncomfortably tight boxer shorts beneath. He paced around the dining room table, picked up the soup cup in one quick fluid movement, and tossed it against the wall. Olin peaked into the dining room from the living room. He regarded Steel with angry eyes and then shrugged.

The doorbell rang. Olin's eyes widened, and he motioned to Steel. "Into the bedroom. Now."

Steel hurried down the hall, his left foot lagging a bit from the heavy security anklet. He stepped into the bedroom door-way. He watched as Olin peered through the peephole of the front door and then opened it. There was a brief, terse conversation, and a small, thin man in black pants and sweatshirt stepped around Olin. Compared to the huge, heavily muscled Olin, the man seemed diminutive. He wore a ski hat over his black hair. He glanced down the hallway at Steel. Sunglasses hid his eyes. He handed Olin a piece of paper, and Olin touched an earpiece and spoke to the air above the short man's head. He nodded and motioned to Steel.

"Steel, you got a visitor."

Steel walked into the living room, and the small man said something quietly to Olin. Olin shrugged and stepped outside. The short man took off his sunglasses. He was Asian, and his dark eyes glittered as he studied Steel.

"Mr. Steel, I represent Max, and I need to make sure you are clean."

Steel frowned. "Clean?"

The man pulled an iPhone from his pants pocket and attached a blinking device to the bottom of it. He pointed the phone at Steel. "I will need you to come closer, so I can scan you."

Steel moved closer, and the man ran the phone up and down his body. A beep sounded at the level of Steel's navel. The man motioned to Steel's shirt. "Lift your shirt, please."

Steel lifted his shirt exposing his jeans. The man touched the phone to the buckle of Steel's belt. The belt had been necessary because the jeans had been too large. The phone warbled. The man pointed to the belt.

"Remove the belt, please."

Steel pulled the belt loose and handed it to the man. He grabbed his jeans just as they threatened to fall from his waist. The man turned the belt buckle over and smiled. He pointed to a tiny black dot attached to the buckle's underside. He turned and opened the front door and handed the belt to Olin.

"Mr. Steel values his privacy." Olin took the belt and held it like it was a snake. The man turned back to Steel. "Get your coat. You are going for a ride."

Steel shrugged into his jacket and scooped up the iPad and his cell phone. He followed the man into the outside air for the first time in almost twenty-four hours. Olin followed close behind.

"We will be in the vehicle behind you, Steel." He said.

A large, black SUV sat at the end of a walkway. For a brief second, Steel saw towering distant mountains barely visible through the falling snow. The small man opened the back door and motioned inside. Steel slid onto the back seat, and the door closed behind him. A light came on inside, and he stared in wonder at the woman sitting on the driver's side of the back seat. The man opened the driver's door and slid behind the steering wheel.

"You know what to do, Ishido." The woman said in a faint British accent. She was tall and willowy swathed in a gray and black overcoat. Her hair was shoulder length and shiny silver in color. Her face was ageless, and her eyes were a light green.

"Mr. Steel, I am Max."

Steel gasped. "But, on the phone, you sounded like a man."

She nodded. "Our first conversation was altered to convey the misdirection I was a man. I had no idea of your intentions, Mr. Steel. Sometimes, subterfuge is necessary. For instance, the listening device Goudreaux placed in your belt buckle. She knew I would be paying you a visit. But, after putting some pressure on certain high-level authorities, I managed to gain you a brief reprieve."

The car moved away from the house onto the street. "That's how you got me out of the house?"

"I have certain connections with highly placed people in

the Swiss government. I am sorry I did not get here earlier, but Ishido and I had to come from Zurich."

Steel studied her face, the tiny wrinkles, and fine lines. "You look so familiar. Forgive me, but I suffer from amnesia, and I can't believe it, but I might know you. Do I know you?"

"Cephas may have spoken of me. He knew me as Molly."

Steel gasped. "Molly? But, Max? I mean, I'm confused."

"I was married for twenty years to Dr. Renfield Xavier. Dr. Xavier was quite the Renaissance man. Physician, psychiatrist, philanthropist, and diplomat. My full name is Molly Alexandra Xavier. Max." She nodded at him. "I was saddened to hear of Cephas' death. I want to hear all about what really happened."

"But he looked for you. He searched for you. He loved you." Steel said. "He told me his story of how you met. He talked about your daughter." Steel swallowed and looked away. Did she know about the fate of her own daughter?

For a moment, Max's intense gaze was clouded by grief. "I was a foolish woman blaming Cephas for the death of my daughter. I hid from him for years to punish him. Soon, I moved on and met Renfield. I tried to put the past behind me." She turned her steady gaze back on him. "But I kept track of Cephas in recent years once the war began."

"The war?"

"Between the Vitreomancers and the Dark Council. It had been taking place in the shadows for centuries, but a new leader brought the Vitreomancers into the 21st century."

"Lynn Alba." Steel whispered. An attorney in league with the eleventh demon had orchestrated the attempted assassination of a man running for governor of Louisiana. Her cabal of "white-eyed goons" was demonically possessed humans calling themselves Vitreomancers for replacing the vitreous fluid of the eyes with the physical presence of a demon. But, it was clear that Max had no idea who Lynn Alba really was.

"Yes, a most mysterious host for the eleventh demon. She

disappeared, and her organization has fallen into chaos. Ironic, yes?" Max studied him with her relentless gaze. "An organization bent on fomenting chaos falls prey to its own philosophy. I couldn't be more pleased. But, lately, it seems to be rallying. Perhaps a new leader?"

Steel's pulse quickened. "You know the real identity of Lynn Alba?"

Max's forehead wrinkled in puzzlement. "I tried for years to dig into her past. I failed to learn anything about her. Do you know of her fate?"

"Yes. Alba came to Louisiana to her regional law office. She planned assassination of the governor. I thought you knew this."

Max straightened. "I've heard nothing of this. The news talked of a conspiracy. A local deputy sheriff bent on revenge because of state budget cuts. He was stopped by Vivian Ketrick, a witch if there ever was one."

Steel grimaced at the thought of Vivian and swallowed. "This will be very hard for you to hear, Max. Cephas told me what really happened. Lynn Alba, the eleventh demon, planned the assassination, and it was Cephas who sent the demon packing off to Tartarus."

"Good!" Max smiled. "I'm happy to hear the old man finally got his demon."

Steel reached out and rested a hand on her arm. "Lynn Alba's real name was Mary. Marilynn." He paused, and Max gazed at him with confusion etched on her face.

"She was your daughter, Max."

Max blinked, and her face paled. Her gloved hand went to her mouth. "No!"

"Cephas told me everything. Your daughter survived the fire in the asylum and was taken by the eleventh demon."

Max's eyes filled with fire, and a tear trickled down her cheek. "And, Cephas knew this? Why didn't he tell me?"

"He tried to find you. If he had known where to find you, he would have told you. He only found out who Lynn really was on the day she died."

Max's eyes afire with fury. "Then, I will finish this Council and the Vitreomancers, Mr. Steel. I will take up Cephas' mantle and destroy these demons."

"Is that why I'm here?"

She wiped tears angrily from her cheeks. "No." She fell silent, and her gaze turned away from him, and she fell silent as the car moved down the streets of Bern. Steel glanced through the frosted windows at the people walking down the sidewalks shopping and eating lunch in small cafes; of bright storefronts and a dusting of snow on window seals. Ordinary people who had no idea of the evil that fought for their souls. Max was silent as they drove past a dome building, Switzerland's Parliament. Max kept her gaze out the windows. Finally, Max wiped her eyes with a lavender-hued handkerchief and sighed.

"Forgive me. I needed a moment to compose myself in light of this news. Mr. Steel, we don't have long before I must return you to the safe house. Do you have the medallion?"

Steel touched the medallion through his sweater. "Yes. But, Max, my main concern right now is for my adopted son."

"I understand how your concern over Joshua Knight should supersede our business with Raven's amulet."

"I have to find him, Max. I'm all he has left."

Max nodded. "He is missing. I am well aware. I already have my contacts looking for him as well, Mr. Steel. I can assure you he is not with Dr. Holmes as the flight to London took off on schedule. As to the whereabouts of your new partner, Jason Birdsong, we have been unable to locate him. Nor have we found Major Miller. Both may be missing."

"That's what Ross said."

"The FBI agent?"

"Yes. An old enemy." But he had called me his friend, Steel

thought. He sat back in the car seat. His head throbbed with pain, although to a lesser degree. Perhaps he was already healing. Josh missing. Jason and Monty out of touch. What was going on? "This is getting out of hand. Too many things are happening. It's one of them again."

"You refer, of course, to the demons of the Dark Council," Max said.

"Yes. What will I do?"

"Ishido, take us back to the safe house. We can discuss Mr. Steel's options with Inspector Goudreaux. I am sure she is waiting for us. Olin will need to reassure his boss he had nothing to do with this little side trip."

"Olin knew you were coming?"

Max raised an eyebrow. "I have many people in my confidence who have suffered losses thanks to the workings of the evil forces in this world, Mr. Steel. Unlike Cephas, who chose to go it alone, I have built a silent, well-hidden army of holy warriors to combat the growing darkness in the world. Olin is one of them. Ishido is another."

Steel glanced at the back of Ishido's head. "And, just where did Raven fit in with your army?"

Max frowned. "I'm afraid Raven was a failure."

Steel touched the medallion hanging beneath his shirt. "Why do you want her medallion?"

"It is no ordinary medallion. The key has a tiny circuit that is now linked to your biometric fingerprint. When Raven passed it to you, you became the default owner." She pulled a silver chain from around her neck. A matching medallion hung from the chain. "And my medallion has the second key to a safety deposit box in one of the most secure banks in Switzerland. Together, these keys give us access to the contents."

"And what is in that box?"

"A record of every assassination Raven has ever been paid for." Max tucked the medallion out of sight. "I need access to those records because Raven made me promise in the event she died, I was to take her assets and make reparations to the family of those she had killed."

Steel's mouth fell open. "So, you're not Raven's boss?"

"Ishido," She said quietly. "Tell Mr. Steel your story."

Ishido's head turned slightly, and he pulled the car over to the curb. Outside, shoppers moved down the sidewalk from one high-end store to the next. Light snow filtered down from a gray sky. Ishido tilted the rearview mirror, so his dark, glistening eyes could be seen by Steel. He bowed slightly.

"In my homeland, there are certain evil organizations that require young men to become part of their forces. I refused to be recruited. My family was held, hostage." Ishido's voice was barely above a whisper. "I was told they would die if I did not learn the ways of the assassin."

"What happened?"

Ishido's dark eyes glittered. "They killed my wife and two children. I made the men who did so pay dearly. After I killed them slowly, after I tortured them, I realized I had become just like the men who I despised. That is when I tried to kill myself."

Max reached forward and patted Ishido's shoulder with her gloved hand. "I found him just in the nick of time. Ishido has lived with me for the past four years. You may head back to the safe house now, Ishido."

"Are you saying you also 'took in' Raven?" Steel asked.

"Ishido found her in an alleyway in Zurich. She was bleeding from a dozen knife wounds. He brought her to me and said she kept mumbling something."

"What?" Steel asked.

"The Albino Devil," Max said.

"Lucas!" Steel hissed.

"He is the most evil of Satan's operatives on this Earth." Ishido hissed. "He enlists those who would do the work of evil through his deceptions and lies. His influence on Raven cannot be underestimated."

"She's not the only one he's influenced. I've met others." Steel said.

"What you must understand about Raven, Mr. Steel," Max said. "Is that after she recovered, it took some time, but she began to feel remorse for her killings. But not until after one more assassination attempt." Max nodded to Ishido. "Raven tried to kill me one night, and Ishido stopped her. In the months she recovered in my chalet in Zurich, she began to pull away from the influence of the Pale Devil. We made an agreement that she would try and leave this business and make amends for her crimes. Ishido developed these medallions, and Raven hid her secrets away in that bank." She sighed deeply. "She told me Lucas is not the person who pulled her strings. There was another person behind the scene. Someone very powerful with almost supernatural influence on Raven. She chose to leave the business of assassination. Unfortunately, all she was able to do was to hide from her former employer. Her rogue operations were, at best, marginal concerning assassinations."

"She was hired by Vivian D'Arbonne Ketrick to kill a lawyer on the board of directors of Ketrick's business. She didn't give up killing." Steel said.

"I was afraid of as much. Something happened on the last night I saw her. She received a phone call, and I overheard a whispered phrase. Something about a demon."

Max swallowed, and for a second, Steel saw pity and sorrow filled her eyes. "I do not know who called her or what that person said, but there was an instant change in Raven. It was as if she became someone else."

Steel looked away. Could it have been the same phrase whispered in his ear? The phrase that had erased his memory? He closed his eyes and fought against the memory because embracing it would send him into a deadly cardiac event. "I have an idea what that phrase might have been. Some kind of programming, Max."

"I suspected as much, and Raven left before I could talk to her. Whoever spoke to her on that phone put her back on the assassination track." Max looked at Steel with moisture in her eyes. The car slowed as they pulled back into the driveway of the safe house. "My hope and my prayers have been that someone would come into her life from God who would push her across the line away from killing. I was so pleased to hear she had found forgiveness, Mr. Steel. Now, perhaps in death, she will find some peace. Now, we must make amends for her on behalf of the families of those she has killed."

Olin appeared at Steel's door and opened it. The front door of the safe house gaped open. Goudreaux stood in the doorway. "Olin, bring Mr. Steel inside now!"

Olin's grasp was tight but not painful, and he frowned at Steel as he pulled him jerkily from the back seat. He pushed him roughly up the walkway to the front door. Goudreaux had retreated into the living room and stood with a hand on her hip, her eyes filled with fiery contempt.

"What do you think you were doing, Olin?"

Olin handed her the papers he had taken from Ishido. She glared at them. "Xavier!" Goudreaux said as she crumpled the papers and tossed them on the floor.

Max appeared in the doorway, and Steel stepped back at her sudden transformation. Max held onto a cane and was hunched over in obvious arthritic pain. "Oh, my, I had no idea you were involved with this affair, Frances," Max said in a hoarse, aged voice.

Goudreaux pursed her lips and looked down at Steel's midsection. He struggled to hold up his ill fitting jeans. She knew about the missing belt, Steel realized. "Don't try and pull that ruse on me, Max."

Max smiled. "You should refer to me as Dr. Xavier, Inspector Goudreaux. I am recording this conversation." She tapped her coat pocket, where a cell phone was barely visible inside an outer pocket. "I am perfectly within my rights on insisting I have an audience with my client."

"Client?" Goudreaux crossed her arms. "Did you hire him to blow up an airplane?"

Max raised an eyebrow and wiped at her lips with her lavender-hued handkerchief. "What nonsense, Frances. You know I own stock in that airline. Mr. Steel is here at my request. If you had done your job fully and completely, you would have discovered that I was the one who paid for his ticket from the United States to Switzerland. If you are indeed accusing me of being a terrorist, then, by all means, report me to your boss."

Max wobbled closer and leaned on her cane as she pressed her face close to Goudreaux's. "But, Frances, make sure you have all your ducks in a row before you go down that path. We both know there are many skeletons in your closet, and I know where to find each one. I don't know who is paying you to continue to perpetuate this farce regarding Mr. Steel. Still, I suggest you bring forth the evidence to your boss and have me arrested or," She reached out with a gloved finger and pressed it into Goudreaux's chest pushing her back an inch. "back off."

Goudreaux stepped back, and her face filled with uncertainty. She opened her mouth to speak, and suddenly, Steel's phone warbled. A FaceTime call was coming in. Steel hurried to the dining room table and scooped up the phone.

Goudreaux shook off her discomfort. "Wait a minute! Don't answer that?"

Steel ignored her. "It might be Josh." He unlocked his cell phone. The face that filled the screen was the last person he expected to hear from. Major Miller's harried face filled the screen.

"Jonathan? Good, you're alive." He said.

"Robert? Where's Josh?"

Miller swallowed and behind him, whirling red and blue lights bounced off the windows in an office. "That's why I'm calling. Been locked in my own office closet for hours." He moved his phone, and Steel saw the monitor behind him on the office wall. The image showed police cars sitting outside Miller's airport office.

"Miller, what's going on?" Steel said through clenched teeth.

"Holmes was here, loading up his crates and then your new partner, what was his name?"

"Jason Birdsong."

"Yeah, Birdsong arrived on the same outgoing flight. We were talking when Josh and his girlfriend just suddenly showed up."

"Olivia?"

"Yeah." Miller sipped from a bottle of water. "They had some cockamamie story about going on a date or something instead of going with Birdsong. It was all pretty fishy. Then, *she* showed up." Miller drew a deep breath.

"She? Who showed up, Miller?" Steel asked.

"This woman in a hoodie packing a 9 mil. Flaky and spooky all rolled into one. Wound up real tight. Threatened to kill all of us. Said she wanted on the flight to London."

Steel collapsed into the dining room table chair. He felt Max put a hand on his shoulder. "Miller, cut to the chase."

"She forced all of them to get on the flight with her. It was Josh's idea. Said he had to find you. The girl kept talking about being in danger from someone and staying off the grid. Birdsong wasn't going to let them go alone. So, they all packed up with the woman onto my airplane. Somehow, they knocked me out and locked me in my own closet. I guess I'm lucky I'm not dead." Miller drank more water. "That flight should be landing in Great Britain within the hour, Steel. You've got to get to that airport and find Josh."

Steel shook his head. "This doesn't make any sense. Why would Josh come to London looking for me?"

"I don't know, Steel. But, it was obvious Josh thought if he and the girl stayed here, they would be dead."

"Get the flight details," Max said quietly.

Miller heard her and rattled off the airplane flight number and arrival times. Steel glanced at Goudreaux, but she was ignoring him talking to someone on her cell phone. Was she sending someone to retrieve Josh? He glanced at Max, and Max nodded.

"We can't trust anyone, Jonathan," Max whispered. "I will get you to London."

Steel looked back at his phone. "Have you talked to Ross, yet?"

"Yes, he's on his way," Miller said. "He told the police to keep me here until he arrives. I'll do whatever I can to help, Steel. You know that."

"Thanks, Miller. Any idea who the woman was?"

Miller shook his head. "I didn't recognize her. But it's weird. Josh knew her. Said he recognized her voice, but she didn't look like the same person."

Steel stiffened. A chill ran down his back. "Did he say who she was?"

Miller leaned into the phone. "Called her Raven."

Steel stood up abruptly and glanced at Max. Max's already pale features grew paler, and suddenly Max reached out and closed the connection with Miller. Steel opened his mouth, and Max shook her head. She turned abruptly to Goudreaux.

"Frances, would you be so kind as to check on that flight for Mr. Steel?"

Goudreaux placed her hand over her phone. "What?"

Max took her by the arm and gently led her toward the

front door. "This is obviously far more complex than any of us have anticipated. If some malevolent force kidnapped Mr. Steel's adopted son and brought him to London, you may find more answers from that process than hovering over Mr. Steel. Could you be so kind as to accommodate him?"

Goudreaux jerked her arm out of Max's grasp. "You just told me to back off." She glanced over Max's shoulder at the cell phone warbled again with an incoming call. A strange expression came over her face for a second, and then she nodded. "I will do what I can to clear up this mess, Max. But don't ever touch me again!"

18

Goudreaux marched through the open door, and Max slammed it behind her. She straightened from her slumped position and motioned to Ishido. "Take Olin and get Steel some traveling papers. You know the kind I'm speaking of."

Ishido nodded. "And, his luggage?"

"Yes, the valise you prepared for him. Olin, before you go, get that anklet off of him. Are there men outside?"

"Yes, ma'am." Olin knelt beside Steel and fumbled with the anklet. "I have five posted out of sight.

"Don't underestimate the Snake. Or, Goudreaux. I'm sure the reason she is hurrying out of here has something to do with that girl on the airplane. Funny how quickly she abandoned Mr. Steel. Now go."

Olin tossed the anklet on the table, and he and Ishido disappeared through the front door. The iPhone continued to warble. Max nodded to Steel. "Don't worry. Olin made sure the surveillance devices throughout the safe house were disengaged. We can talk freely."

Steel was still reeling from Miller's claim. "How can Raven

be alive? I saw her fall into the chasm. I saw her body bleeding from the exploding bullet."

"Let's get some more information, Jonathan, before we panic."

Steel answered the call, and Miller's face reappeared. "What happened to our connection?"

Steel sat down again. "We needed some privacy. Miller, are sure Josh called this woman Raven?"

"Yeah. Josh acted like they should know each other. But he said her face was different. Maybe plastic surgery?"

Steel shook his head. "Renee was involved with the affair of the twelfth demon, Robert. Raven was hired to kill me. She died in the caverns under Transylvania when she saved us from the twelfth demon. I saw her fall into a pit."

Miller shrugged. "Look, Steel, whoever this woman was, she was clearly dangerous." He licked his lips and drew a deep breath. "She put a shock pad on all of us. Threatened to kill us, Steel. No matter what her name is, she's bad news."

Steel sat back. "Josh and Jason and Monty are in danger."

Miller glanced at his desk. "Just a minute." He glanced at a text message on his laptop. "The airplane diverted to Heathrow? What?" Miller glanced at Steel. "Just got a text from my man in London. The airplane diverted to Heathrow. There goes my CBD oil!" He shook his head. "Oh, and in the text, there is a message for you to call Dr. Holmes on his cell phone." He continued to read the text message.

"The fight decompressed en route to RAF Alconbury Air Base. They made an emergency landing at Heathrow. My pilot says Holmes claims the woman and the girl jumped from the airplane with parachutes."

"What about Josh?"

"The pilot didn't mention Josh or Jason. Holmes said he was alone on the airplane. Something isn't right, Steel."

"You think?" Steel ran his hands through his short hair. His heart raced. His cell phone rang with a second incoming call. "Let me get this."

Steel closed Miller's connection and picked up the incoming call. "Monty?"

"Jonathan. Oh, my God! Lord, help me! I've been through some stuff, Jonathan, but this takes the cake." Holmes's voice broke. "Is this a secure connection? Oh, my God! They may know about your phone number!"

Max picked up the phone and studied the face. "Mr. Steel will call you right back, Dr. Holmes." She hung up and took a cell phone from her coat pocket. She handed it to Steel.

"Your new phone, by the way. Highly encrypted. If Dr. Holmes is worried about security, then there will be no way to trace your call from his phone. Whoever they are. Once you get him on the line, hand it back to me." She dropped Steel's phone into a flower vase filled with water. "I'll replace that later."

Steel activated the phone and dialed Holmes' number. "Monty? Are you there?"

"Yes."

"We're on a secure line. Just a minute." He handed it back to Max. She pressed some buttons and nodded.

"Dr. Holmes, this is Dr. Xavier. I have just texted you an app extension. Activate it now, and it will connect us with a secure, encrypted connection. If anyone is listening, they will never understand what we are saying."

"Got it. Just a minute." A buzzing and clicking came over the speaker. "Okay, are we good?"

Steel glanced at Max. She nodded.

"Yes. What happened?"

"I was loading the crates on Miller's flight to London. Jason was on the flight, and then Josh and Olivia just show up out of the blue."

"Ross said they were together."

"Yeah, and they were acting really strange. Turns out, someone was chasing them. While we were in the crates, Olivia told me the whole story."

"Crates?"

"Empty storage crates in the airplane. That Raven woman locked us in there. Put these EKG pad things on our chests. Said she would stop our heart if we didn't do what she said." Holmes sighed. "Anyway, Josh showed up saying someone was after them. Turns out whoever is after them may have sabotaged Olivia's mother's flight. The same one you were on, Jonathan. She was on that flight."

Steel blinked as the image of a strange woman fleeted across his memory. "I can't remember what happened on the flight, Monty."

"Well, Olivia told me she was sure her mother survived, and she made a bargain with Raven to take her to meet her mother if Raven let the rest of us live. I don't know what Olivia's mother has to do with Raven. Frankly, I don't know what any of this has to do with anything!"

"Welcome to my world." Steel growled.

"Jonathan, Raven put all of us on the airplane. When we got on the airplane, Raven put us all in these crates. And, somewhere on the approach to London, Olivia and Raven must have jumped out of the airplane with parachutes. At least, that's what Dude said."

Steel glanced at Max. "Dude?"

"Yeah, Josh's guardian angel." Holmes giggled. "What am I saying? I actually met an angel, Jonathan. He had to be an angel. He let us out of the crates and told us what to do. Told me to act like nothing happened or the people chasing Olivia and Josh would kill me. He told me Olivia and Raven jumped, and the airplane decompressed, so they had to make an emergency landing."

"Monty, what happened to Josh and Jason?"

"They jumped out of the airplane when we landed on the tarmac. Dude told them to get away from the action and meet me later at a prearranged location."

"Did they make it?" Steel asked.

"I think so, Jonathan. What is going on? Who is this Raven, and what does she want with Olivia's mother?"

Steel glanced at Max. "I have no idea, Monty. But, I am pretty sure we are dealing with the next demon encounter."

The line was silent. "So, this is what your life is like?"

"Yeah." Steel said.

"I'll start praying even more then. So, what now?"

"Dr. Holmes." Max leaned over the phone. "I am making arrangements for Jonathan to get to London. I'm afraid he will be traveling under a different name."

"To hide from the next demon, right? How many demons are we dealing with?" Holmes's voice broke.

"I'm running from an assassin, it seems." Steel said. "Someone I recalled from the flight. A woman called the Crimson Snake."

"Okay, so let me get this straight. You, Josh, Jason, and Olivia are being sought by two woman assassins and probably a demon from the Dark Council."

"That sounds about right." Steel said. "So, you need to be very careful, Monty. Where are you headed?"

"Well, once we clear customs, which I had not anticipated having to deal with at Heathrow since we were headed for a military base, I will deliver the crates to Dr. Hampton at his private museum. He's probably sent his truck to Alconbury instead of Heathrow, so we'll be tied up for a while."

"Dr. Holmes, it is probably a good thing you will be surrounded by multiple authorities," Max said. "Text the address of the, uh, prearranged rendezvous to Jonathan, and I will see that he gets there as soon as possible."

"Will do. Jonathan, be careful. I'll keep a low profile, and I hope to see you, Josh, and Jason soon."

"Godspeed, Monty." Steel ended the call. The door opened, and Olin and Ishido came through. Olin carried a large piece of luggage. Ishido held a leather folio under his arm.

"Got the clothes and toiletries for Mr. Steel." Olin placed the luggage on the couch. In his other hand, he held a bag. "And, a fresh change of clothes for the trip. Clothes that will fit!"

Ishido placed the folio on the table. "New identity, Jonathan." He emptied the contents on the table.

Steel picked up a passport with his photo in it. "Jeremiah Stone?"

"Close enough so you can easily remember it," Max said. "Driver's license from Florida. Pensacola. That way, in casual conversation, you can talk about a location you're familiar with. Your Alabama license given to you by Ross would be a little suspect. I suggest you hand it all over to Olin, and we will keep it for you. Cash for the trip. Euros and British pounds. Two credit cards in your new name."

Steel took out his wallet and handed it to Olin. "I'll let you change it out while I take a shower. How will I get to London?"

"My private airplane can take you to Paris," Max said. "But, if we try to fly you to London, there will be international requirements that will bog you down. No commercial flights."

"I don't want to endanger another airplane full of innocent people." Steel said.

"My private airplane has clearance for most of continental Europe. The Snake doesn't know I'm involved in this. Yet." Max said.

"And, when I get to Paris?"

"You'll take the train."

Steel shook his head. "Train? I can't take days to get there, Max."

"Days? You haven't traveled in Europe by train, have you?"

"A couple of hours' flight to Paris then two hours by the Chunnel to London." Olin handed Steel a swath of tickets from his jacket pocket. "I sent them to your electronic wallet on your phone."

Steel opened his mouth and then closed it. "I don't know what to say."

Max removed her gloves and reached over and took Steel's hands in hers. "Jonathan, look at me. Our business with Raven just changed. If this woman is Raven and if she has gone back to the business of assassination, then I have to stop her. It's a good bet that someone took her in, changed her appearance after her recovery, and is now using some pre-programmed phrases to make her forget what happened with you. Just like before. That makes her very dangerous."

Steel looked into Max's pale eyes. "I can get to her, Max. I can reach her. Jog her memory. But, I will not let her harm Josh."

"Or, Olivia's mother?" Max lifted an eyebrow.

Steel rolled his eyes. "Josh told me not to try and save someone. Looks like he beat me to it."

Max motioned to Ishido. "Ishido will be going with you as far as Paris. He can't leave the continent, unfortunately. There are those in Great Britain who would kill him on sight. But, he will make sure you get on the train to London." Her grip tightened. "And, make sure the Snake doesn't stop you."

Steel slowly pulled his hands from hers. "And then what?"

Max shrugged. "You stop the next demon, save the world and then come back to Zurich with Raven in tow so we can get on with her business. One way or the other."

BY THE TIME Steel had showered and dressed, Max had sent for another less conspicuous car to take them to a private airport on the periphery of Bern. Ishido loaded up the nondescript two-door sedan with their luggage, and they climbed in. The drive to the airport would be short, and then he would be in the air headed for Paris. Max stood in the driveway, a stately figure of power and assurance. For a brief moment, the clouds parted, and sunlight streamed down from the heavens. Steel hoped it was a sign. They drove in silence to the airport, and Ishido ushered Steel hurriedly onto a small jet airplane. Once inside, they buckled into the eight-seat interior, and the airplane took off before Steel could get his seat belt buckled. Steel glanced across the aisle at Ishido.

"Ishido?"

"Do not talk. I do not talk, Mr. Steel. Sleep. You will need it." Ishido said as they rocketed down the runway and into the gray cloudy sky. Ishido closed his eyes, and Steel did as he was told although his sleep was interrupted by dreams of Josh in trouble.

A car was waiting at the airport in Paris. Steel barely had time to register his whereabouts as Ishido rushed him into the small, nondescript car. It pulled out of the busy airport, and they rattled across Paris toward the train station.

"Mr. Steel, you must now be incognito. Keep a low profile. Wear these glasses." Ishido handed him a pair of dark-rimmed glasses. The lenses were flat. He gave him a cap. "Slump like an older man. Keep your cap on, but don't go out of the way to hide your face."

Steel wore an overcoat. Beneath, he wore corduroy pants and a dark blue flannel shirt covered by a sweater vest, not exactly chic attire. The cap reminded him of the old-fashioned caps of the early 1900s, and he half expected someone to ask him for a newspaper. Ishido handed him a messenger bag.

"You will need this. Just a few incidentals." As they drove through the heavy traffic of Paris, France, Steel explored the contents of the bag.

Steel pulled out a guide book to London. He opened it to the map and tried to find Dr. Hampton's private museum. It must be in some obscure location. But, he found the destination Holmes had indicated. The Royal Renaissance Hotel. Train stations dotted London's map, and for a moment, his mind shifted, and he was somewhere else.

He sat in a first-class seat on a train. Outside the large windows, trees, and sheep dotted countryside passed by. He glanced to his right, and a woman sat next to him. Her eyes were obscured by dark sunglasses. Her short hair was colored with a dark blue rinse. A matronly woman appeared in the aisle, pushing a cart filled with snacks.

"Would you like something from the trolley?" She said in a British accent. The woman pulled off her sunglasses and glared at the woman.

"I'm on a diet."

The woman turned and looked at Steel. She was Raven.

"Steel? Steel?"

Steel blinked, and he was back in the car with Ishido. "What happened to you?"

Steel shook his head. "Bad memory." He tucked the guide back into the messenger bag. Steel leaned back in his seat. He had been on a train in England with Raven? He had experienced more than one flashback to the time before he lost his memory, and one of them concerned Raven. They had been close. Very close. Were they an assassination pair? Had whoever controlled Raven also controlled him? How many people had he killed? The car swerved to the curb, and hundreds of people milled outside Gare du Nord. The colossal structure with its triumphal arch around its many windows and columns were all too familiar to Steel. He had been here before.

19

The trip through customs was quicker than Steel imagined, and they were soon waiting in the embarkation room with dozens of groups of tourists. The huge arching ceilings supported by cast-iron beams kept Steel steeped in déjà vu. As happened so many times, familiar settings echoed in the empty vastness of his lost memories.

Steel sat in a chair nervously, tapping his hand. He would not board for another hour. Keep a low profile Ishido had said. Ishido sat beside him with his eyes half-closed. Was the man asleep? Was he alert enough to protect Steel from the Snake?

Steel closed his eyes and chased away the speculations. Instead, he concentrated on Josh. He had to find him. He had to save him. He reached deep down within his very soul and found the light. When he had faced off the Major in the hippodrome, he had grabbed the jewel around the Major's neck just as the Major was about to kill him, and there had been a light!

And then, something happened. As quickly as the red haze had taken his mind, the crimson waves receded in the face of a glowing, shining light. In the light within his mind the face of Alar, the angel, appeared. A familiar voice whispered in his ear. "Take the jewel." Steel looked at the golden chain around the Major's neck.

His left hand ached like it had since they had arrived in the past. He reached up with his left hand as his sight began to fail. He snared the chain and pulled on it. A blue jewel the color of a robin's egg tumbled into view. He grabbed it in his left hand and squeezed it tight. The chain broke away from the Major and suddenly, light gushed from the crevices of his hand. The stone was colder than ice and he saw things; heard things; knew things that no man living would remember. He saw Nine through the ages deceiving, lying, using, killing all around him; plotting against men and women and governments; he saw the arcane power of the Dark Council assembled around a tall, lurching figure of a ghostly man with a noose hanging around his neck. This was the true appearance of Nine; a leprous, sore ridden husk of a man with slash marks on his wrists and poisonous foam in his spittle; a figure who had used suicide and depression and fear as his weapon! And then he saw his father. The Captain stood before Nine and spoke Nine's name.

Steel's eyes widened, and he whispered the name. It was not a human name. A ghostly figure appeared superimposed over the Major's face. Hu'ul smiled down at him, and she leaned forward. Her wrinkled chin brushed his cheek. Her dry lips blew cool breath in his ear as she whispered the demon's name again. Her image pulled back and she smiled at him again. "If you know its name, you can end this. Remember, we are complete with this light. This is the way we begin and end things." She said as she faded from view. He whispered the name again as his mind began to fail. The tightening chain around Steel's neck slackened and the Major glared at him.

"What?" He noticed the stone in Steel's fist for the first time. "No!" He screamed and released Steel's neck. His hands closed over Steel's and Steel once again said the name. Louder. More coherently and the Major jerked and spasmed.

"*What did you say?*" *He was trying to pry the stone from Steel's hand, but the light that poured forth was a holy light, a righteous light, the light of Truth and Love; the light that lay waiting in the tomb for only a few more moments now; the light that would burst forth with the morning sun to chase away the darkness from this world forever!*

Steel snatched the chain from around his neck with his free hand and cleared his throat. He shouted Nine's demonic name, and the syllables and consonants seared his throat. The Major froze, his eyes wide with fear.

"*No!*"

"*I call your name and in the name of my Lord and Savior Jesus Christ who has conquered the grave, I command you to the deepest, darkest pits of hell. Now!*" *Steel shouted and his voice filled the chamber and light burst forth from his hand as he released his grip. The jewel exploded into shards of greasy, green light and in the midst of that jewel, a tiny point of light appeared. The voice of Alar echoed forth.*

"*Thank you, my brother.*"

The light exploded into a diaphanous membrane that surrounded the Major.

THE MAJOR'S demon had been taken to hell by the angel Alar. Steel looked down at his left hand. For a moment, he thought he saw a flicker of subcutaneous light. That encounter had taken place two thousand years in the past. And, here he was about to board the train to London protected by an ex-assassin hoping against hope that Josh was safe. How could he even doubt that Josh wasn't safe? God had brought him through so much. He studied the flicker of light. It was like the tenuous ember of his own faith. Yes, he believed in God. Yes, he even claimed to be a Christ-follower. How could he not and still battle demons?

But, where was the "gift" of the spirit? That patience and long-suffering and self-control and compassion and, yes, love? He closed his fist and felt the light slowly fade in the face of his growing anger. Once again, he wondered why he was the chosen one to end the Council of Darkness? Why was he denied a normal life? If he was to battle the most heinous evil creatures in existence, then why endanger Josh's life too?

"Because you are the only one who can do this." A voice said quietly in his ear. He jerked and looked up. A man in a three-piece suit smiled at him. He wore a red carnation in his lapel.

"You! I remember you. Miguel."

He bowed. "Your guardian angel for this time. Do not worry about Josh, mi amigo. He is safe. He is as important to the plan as are you."

Steel stood up and leaned forward into the angel's face. "I am tired. Don't you get it! I don't want to fight them anymore. I don't want to face the enemy. I just want to rest."

"There will be plenty of time for that soon." The angel smiled. "You feel the Spirit moving within you. You have the matter in hand." He faded from view.

Steel looked around. People had turned and were glaring at the mad man talking to the air. He adjusted his glasses and slumped back into his seat.

"So much for keeping a low profile," Ishido said.

The call came for his train to board, and Steel headed for the check-in counter. Ishido put a hand on his shoulder.

"Here is where we part, Steel. From now on, you are on your own. Be careful and Godspeed." He bowed and turned and disappeared into the crowd.

Steel found his seat in first class and settled in, making sure he slumped like Ishido had suggested. He adjusted his cap and made sure his glasses sat on his nose. But, there was no need to be inconspicuous. He looked around the cabin and spotted one elderly woman sitting in the back row. The rest of the first-class cabin was empty. An attendant came by dressed in a vest and tie.

"Sir, why is this cabin empty?"

The attendant shrugged. "There was a large group traveling, and they did not make the train. But, they prepaid for the seats, so they are empty. You can sit anywhere you like."

The attendant moved to the connecting door and disappeared into the forward first-class cabin. At least Steel would be almost alone. The train pulled out of the station for the three hour trip to London. He glimpsed the high rise buildings of the financial district of Paris and, for a fleeting moment, caught a glimpse of the Eiffel Tower. He had eaten at a restaurant on the middle level. He had ridden a boat down the Seine. In his mind, he saw the rose stained glass of Notre Dame, now lost in the hunger of a fire. He had spent time in Paris, and it was all too familiar. But, the specifics were not there. An empty vault of memories pasted with travel patches of Paris, France.

He studied the travel guide as time passed. Each street in London was familiar also. He had been in London, too. But, despite the address on his phone, he had no idea where Dr. Hampton's museum would be.

"Mr. Stone?"

Steel glanced up at an elderly woman with a cane leaning toward him. She pointed to the empty seat across the aisle from him. "Mind if I have a seat?"

The hair stood up on Steel's neck when he recognized the eyes. The woman settled into the seat just as the train flashed into darkness in the tunnel beneath the English Channel. For a moment, they sat in shadows, and he stiffened, waiting for the blow from the Snake's ceramic knife.

"I am not here to hurt you." The woman whispered in a

husky voice. "Of course, it took some convincing to make me NOT kill you. I never leave witnesses behind. But, the day is young, Mr. Steel and after this little adventure, I am sure we will meet again, and when we do, I may be working with someone else, someone not so eager to spare your life."

Steel swallowed and slowly placed the London guide back in the messenger bag. If only Ishido had put some kind of weapon, but, of course, security would have claimed it.

"What do you want?"

The Crimson Snake faced forward and leaned both hands on the top of her crane. "First Class is uncharacteristically empty, don't you think?"

"I wouldn't know."

"My employer purchased most of the tickets so that you and I could have a moment of peace and quiet." She turned her head slowly to him. She smiled and tilted her head.

"You said you weren't here to hurt me."

"No. On the contrary, I have a gift." Snake retrieved a purse slung over her shoulder and sat it in her lap. "Vera Bradley. Like the pattern?"

Steel tried to control his breathing as he studied the multi-colored purse. He was gauging the room, the exits, the lavatory for any avenue of escape.

"You are a very clever man, Mr. Stone." Snake said as she opened her purse. "Registering on a flight to London from Bern almost diverted me. But, I always have a backup plan and a healthy attitude of skepticism. I suspected you might take the train." She paused her rummaging through the purse and looked at him. "But, the decoy was a brilliant touch."

"Decoy?"

"Looked just like you. That is, just like Jonathan Steel. I watched him arrive and check his luggage, and he even got on the airplane. I almost followed until I realized that you had created an alias. When I checked the manifest, as an old woman, of course, looking for my nephew Jonathan Steel and the sweet lady at the gate desk was kind enough to tell me there was no such name. I did see Jeremiah Stone on the list. Now, why would you go to the trouble of creating fake credentials as Jeremiah Stone if you were going to show up in a very obvious public fashion as yourself and make sure everyone saw you get on the airplane? That's when I took another flight to Paris and hurried here to catch the train. Almost brilliant." She went back to rummaging in her purse.

Steel's heart raced. A decoy? Max had been very resourceful. But, how had the Snake known? Someone had betrayed him and Max. Someone in her organization? Or, had Snake been incredibly lucky?

"Ah, here it is." Snake pulled a black cloth bag from her purse. "I told security this was something to soothe my eyes, to help me sleep on the train. But it's far more than that." She held the bag out to Steel. "Go ahead. Take it. It isn't a snake." She giggled and wiggled the bag.

Steel gingerly took the bag and pulled the drawstring open. Inside, he spied a set of goggles. "What is this?"

"A gift, like a said, from Numinous Corporation. It's a Third Eye Interface. There's wi-fi on the train. Just put them on, and all will be explained." She leaned toward him, and her cold breath played on his cheek. "I paid the attendant to give us an hour of uninterrupted time together, so you're free to use the goggles without interruption."

Steel examined the pair of goggles in the bag as if it were a poisonous spider. The door to the rear cabin opened and closed. The Crimson Snake turned and glanced down the aisle. An attendant in a dark vest and cap made his way toward them.

"I told him not to interrupt us." The Snake placed her left hand on his. Inside a thin glove, he felt the ceramic pieces and parts of her artificial hand. Snake stood up slowly and faced the approaching attendant. "Monsieur," her voice

sounded shaky and tremulous. "I would like some uninterrupted time with my nephew, please. I thought we had an
agreement."

Steel looked over his shoulder into the eyes of the attendant. It was Ishido! The Snake made the same conclusion at the
same time.

"You!" She hissed. With one fluid motion, she hurled the
wig from her head and unsheathed the ceramic tipped sword
from her cane.

Ishido tossed his cap aside and tore off his vest, dodging her
thrust sword with a deft twisting motion. He wrapped his vest
around the shaft of the sword and ripped it from her grasp,
throwing it across the cabin where it clattered into the rear
seats.

What followed was a blur of their bodies as the Snake and
Ishido flipped and twisted around the cabin. Steel stood up and
tried to get past them to retrieve the sword cane. If he could just
find it, he could hold Snake hostage. Ishido kicked the ceiling
on one flip, and the light fixtures broke, showering the cabin
with glass. Fractured LED bulbs hung from the ceiling,
throwing off sparks.

Snake grabbed a seat top and swiveled in midair, catching
Steel in the chest with her feet. He fell back into the seat, his
breath knocked from him. Ishido grabbed her from behind in a
chokehold. Almost nonchalantly, Snake pulled the glove off of
her mechanical arm with her teeth and clenched the hand
around Ishido's arm.

Ishido grimaced but did not scream, but the pain was
enough to loosen his grip. Snake flipped up and over his head
and put her mechanical arm around Ishido's neck. Steel found
his breath and climbed over the back of the seat. He threw
himself at Snake, and she turned Ishido between them. But,
Steel had something else in mind. He snared one of the
sparking wires from the ceiling and shoved it into Snake's

exposed prosthetic arm. Electricity shot along the arm, and Snake's surprised face was priceless.

Ishido pulled with all of his might, and the arm snapped away from Snake's body. He spun and swung the arm like a bat at Snake's head. Blood speckled the overhead bins at the blow from the upper arm, and Snake sank back into a chair.

Ishido dropped the arm and slumped into the facing chair. His hand was pressed against the right side of his neck. Blood gushed from under his hand.

"Ishido, you weren't supposed to be here."

"I saw the old woman get on the train, and I remembered your account of the woman on the airplane."

"I never told you or Max." Steel's eyes widened. "You had the safe house bugged? Of course, Max did. But, you said you couldn't be caught in London."

"It was a chance I was willing to take." Ishido gasped as blood trickled from beneath his hand.

"Your neck!"

Ishido shook his head. "It's just superficial. She didn't get the jugular or the carotid, but if you hadn't stopped her, I would be dead." Ishido stood up shakily and kept his hand pressed to his neck.

"Now what?"

"We have to hide her until the train arrives. I turned off the security cameras for this cabin. Give me a hand."

They took Snake's body and carried it to the lavatory. Ishido retrieved the sword cane and sheathed it. He placed it next to her in the lavatory.

"Why are you doing that?"

"When the authorities find her, they'll detain her because of the sword. Now, help me put these ties on her hand and feet."

"Where did you get those?"

"Attendants are also trained in restraining combative passengers. I'll gag her, and we'll lock her in the lavatory."

Steel helped Ishido as he could only use one hand. Soon, Snake was restrained and a gag on her mouth, and she sat on the toilet in the lavatory. Ishido closed the door and took a placard from the attendant's stand. He placed it on the door. "Now, it's out of order."

"What now?" Steel said.

"The other lavatory. Take me there. A first aid kit is in the attendant's cabinet. Get me some fresh gauze. And then wash your hands. After that, get your things and take this pass." He handed him an electronic card. "Go back to the dining car and take a table. Stay there until the train arrives and then leave. Leave quickly because once they find us, they will detain everyone."

"Find both of you?"

Ishido stumbled, and Steel caught him. He saw the blood from his neck had soaked his shirt and jacket.

"It's worse than I thought. But, I can stop the bleeding with meditation. I've done it before. Help me into the lavatory, and I'll lock the door. They'll find me later."

Steel helped the man as he stumbled down the aisle. He retrieved the first aid kit from the locker across from the lavatory. He handed Ishido a bundle of gauze pads. "Ishido, Max said you shouldn't come to Great Britain."

"If I live, and I plan to, Jonathan, I can easily escape from a hospital. Now, put me in the lavatory." He had pressed the gauze to his neck, and the bleeding slowed. "Hurry. I must lower my blood pressure and my heart rate if I am to survive."

Steel opened the door, and Ishido sat on the toilet seat. Steel washed the blood from his hands in the small sink. "Are you sure?"

But already, Ishido's eyes were closed, and his breathing had slowed. Could he be dying? Ishido opened one eye. "Tell Max there is a traitor in our midst. You have to tell her, Jonathan. And, think of Josh. Find him before more of these 'snakes' gets to him. Go with God." He whispered. His hand slipped from his neck, and the bandage stayed put. The bleeding had stopped.

Steel closed the door, and Ishido locked it from within. He retrieved his overcoat and his messenger bag and the goggles and made his way through the adjoining doors to the dining car.

20

The motivation behind transhumanism reflects a deep-seated need that all humans have for transcendence. Transhumanists desire a utopian future and have hopes for immortality—a type of eternal life. This is exactly what the gospel offers.

Fazale R. Rana and Kenneth R. Samples "Humans 2.0"

The problem lies in the desire to take matters into their own hands and doing what they think is best for humanity—in effect, taking God's place—by creating posthumans in their image. This attitude should be what concerns Christians most.

Fazale R. Rana and Kenneth R. Samples "Humans 2.0"

Steel pulled his cap down and pushed his glasses back up onto his face. He held his overcoat folded against his chest to hide any stray droplets of blood. The dining car was only half full, and he found a booth near the far door where he could face the entire cabin. He slid into the booth and tried to calm his racing heart. All he could think about was

Ishido bleeding out in a first-class cabin lavatory. True, most of the bleeding had stopped by the time Ishido had gone into his "trance," but Steel hoped that wasn't because he had already bled out! As to Snake, he didn't doubt she would wake up before they pulled into the station in London. What would she do? She couldn't alert the "authorities" because she was covered in Ishido's blood, and she was carrying a sword cane. Steel glanced at his watch. There was still just under an hour before they arrived.

A waiter came by, and he ordered sparkling water and paid for it. He sipped the water and tried to look out the window, but they were still in the darkness of the tunnel. His reflection gazed back at him, turquoise eyes gleaming intensely, almost gaunt face and a peppering of reddish blonde beard across his jawline.

"What are you going to do?" Steel asked his reflection. He looked down at the black bag and pulled out the goggles. They were larger than a set of swim goggles, and the lenses were completely opaque. The strap was divided into three sections that would not only fit around the back of his head but over the top of his head and his forehead. Inside the strap, there were numerous gleaming metal points of contact. What was this thing? Every instinct told him NOT to put the thing on his head. But, if it would give him an insight at all into what was happening, he was willing to take the risk.

The waiter appeared again, and Steel frowned as he took his glass.

"Sir, I'm going to take a short nap with my sleep mask."

The man nodded. "That will be fine, sir. But, ten minutes before we reach the station, I will awaken you so you can return to your seat."

He walked away, and Steel breathed a prayer for Ishido, himself, and Josh and Jason as he took his cap off, tossed aside his glasses and pulled the goggles over his eyes.

The strap seemed to tighten across his forehead, the top of his head, and the back of his head and eyecups settled tightly against his orbital rims. For a second, nothing happened, and he stared into total black emptiness. Then, as if from a very far distance, a tiny pinpoint of light appeared in the center of his vision. As it approached, he realized he was not moving, but the sensation the light was moving toward him was eerily real.

The light blossomed into a logo, Numinous Corporation, and it spun in three-dimensional fashion in his vision. A hand appeared out of the darkness and brushed the logo away. It dissolved into pixels that seemed to blow away in a sudden wind. A face appeared in the darkness. She was of obvious Indian descent with deep-set dark eyes in an exotic and alluring face. Her hair was pulled back away from her face, and a gleaming red jewel was set in the skin just above the center of her eyebrows. The point of view pulled back, and the woman's entire body filled his field of vision. She wore a red and gold gown.

"Good evening, Mr. Steel." She said. Steel jerked at the sound of the voice. It was as if he were sitting in front of her. He reached for the goggles, and she put out a restraining hand. "I wouldn't advise pulling off the goggles once the cerebral connection has been made. It could cause permanent brain damage."

Steel paused. Her voice was low and sultry, almost hypnotic. "Who are you?"

"Dr. Sultana Thakkar. CEO of Numinous Corporation. You are enjoying our latest invention."

"Numinous Corporation? What does that mean? Numinous?"

A book appeared in her hands. Thakkar glanced down at it and read out loud. "*Those who have not met this term may be introduced to it by the following device. Suppose you were told there was a tiger in the next room: you would know that you were in danger and would probably feel fear. But if you were told 'There is a ghost in the next room,' and believed it, you would feel, indeed, what is often called fear, but of a different kind. It would not be based on the knowledge of danger, for no one is primarily afraid of what a ghost may do to him, but of the mere fact that it is a ghost. It is 'uncanny' rather than dangerous, and the special kind of fear it excites may be called Dread. With the Uncanny one has reached the fringes of the Numinous. Now suppose that you were told simply 'There is a mighty spirit in the room', and believed it. Your feelings would then be even less like the mere fear of danger: but the disturbance would be profound. You would feel wonder and a certain shrinking--a sense of inadequacy to cope with such a visitant and of prostration before it--an emotion which might be expressed in Shakespeare's words 'Under it my genius is rebuked'. This feeling may be described as awe, and the object which excites it as the Numinous."*

Sultana looked up from the book. "Too academic? Well, I'm sure you've heard of C. S. Lewis. He said the numinous experience was the non-rational part of a religious experience. A feeling one gets in the presence of the divine."

Steel put up his hand to stop her, and it appeared in his vision. He felt disoriented. How could his hand be in the vision? Some kind of augmented reality. "I get it. You want to be God. What's new. I've met a few already who had the same dream. Who are you? Number Eight?"

"My corporation is dedicated to transhumanism. Do you know what that is? It means moving beyond the weak, mortal flesh of being human." Thakkar ignored his questions.

Steel's hands appeared in his field of view again. "So, what is this?" He gestured around him.

"Numinocity. The ultimate expression of the numinous. Man and god as one, surpassing all of our weaknesses and fragilities."

"Then, it is a wicked numinosity." Steel said.

"Mr. Steel, there is no such thing as wicked or good; truth

or lies. All is relative. When we ascend to quasi-godhood, we become the arbiters of morality. You see, what science has been ignoring in its quest for the transhuman transition is the place of the spiritual in transhumanism. Instead, science seeks the mundane, the mechanical, the computed; science can only see the hard, binary world of physical storage; light and shadow; ones and zeroes. There is more to our universe than we can sense as mere humans. There are other ways of transcending the mere mortal coils of our flesh and blood. Why shouldn't I avail myself of an immortal, trans-dimensional being who has the memory capacity of a hundred millennia or so? This is what proponents of transhumanism are missing."

"Demons?"

"Symbiosis. Life on earth has always thrived thanks to a symbiosis between two different organisms. This spiritual dimension is the missing key, Mr. Steel."

"Why are you telling me this?"

"Joshua Knight signed on using a prototype of these goggles. The goggles he used were in the possession of the daughter of a scientist who has made certain improvements in the third eye interface, as I call it."

Steel's face warmed. "You attacked Josh?"

Thakkar's face twitched for a moment. "I had nothing to do with that attack."

"Then who did?"

Thakkar shrugged. "I don't know. Yet. But, what I do know is Josh, and Olivia Queen were on a flight to London. Olivia is somewhere in that city, and Josh is the key to finding her. Olivia holds the missing piece to the perfection of my technology."

"Why her?"

Thakkar pressed her hands together. "I am afraid her mother perished on the airplane crash which you survived."

"You sent the Crimson Snake to get the messenger bag,

didn't you?" A red haze began to pulse and fill the background behind Thakkar. Thakkar looked briefly over her shoulder.

"The crash was accidental. The bomb was supposed to force the airplane to land in Bern, where my operatives could secure Olivia's mother."

Steel paused. "Why are you talking to me?"

"I need to find Olivia and her mother. I will not harm them, but I would hate for your adopted son to get caught in the crossfire. Help me, and I will assure you that Josh will not be harmed. I can protect him from these other factions."

"Other factions? You don't even know who was after Josh!" Steel felt the heat, and fire grow around him. The red pulsations grew stronger, and behind Thakkar, crimson and black root-like tendrils began to emerge from the red background. "Hundreds died, Thakkar. Is this the utopia you envision? Do you think the eighth demon cares anything about human life? We are nothing to them but souls to be harvested."

Thakkar turned away from him and faced the growing tendrils. "How are you doing this? This is impossible!"

"Doing what?" Steel hissed.

The tendrils turned into bifurcating tentacles and began to wrap themselves around the figure of Thakkar. She gestured with her hands and blue-white fire shot from her fingertips, shattering the tendrils. But, there were more than she could handle. "You shouldn't be able to do anything but observe!" She shouted as a groaning, moaning wind began to whip around her.

Steel reached out his left hand, palm up. It appeared in front of him, and a white light began to build in the deep tissues of his hand. Thakkar whirled, and a horrified look came over her face. "This is impossible! What are you? What did they do to you?"

Steel gritted his teeth and pointed his palm at Thakkar. "I don't know what you are talking about, but I will stop you!" He shoved his hand forward, and a cone of bright light obliterated the image of Thakkar. He jerked the goggles from his eyes, his chest heaving, his heart racing. He looked up in confusion at the waiter standing beside him.

"Monsieur, are you in distress?"

Steel fought to control his breathing and shook his head. "Bad dream."

"We are fifteen minutes from the station. You will need to return to your seat."

Steel produced the card from his pocket. "The first-class attendant said I could stay here." He held up the card.

The waiter's eyes widened in surprise. "Of course, sir. You are welcome to remain in your seat." He turned and walked away.

Steel opened his left hand and studied the fading pinpoint of white light. What was happening? How had he influenced the world of Numinocity, as Thakkar called it? And, what was the light in his palm?

A shadow began to emerge from his memory. Besides the Crimson Snake, there had been another woman on the airplane, Olivia's mother? A fleeting image returned from the recesses of his memory, and he looked into the eyes of the woman on the airplane. Her? He shook his head in confusion. Where had he met her before? Suddenly, without the help of the goggles, he was somewhere else.

THE MAN *in the white Panama Hat disappeared into the crowd of people walking along Wellington Street. Where was the Captain going? He had been following the man for blocks now through the crowded streets of London. The Captain had led him on a long, circuitous route through the underground tube and had exited in the West End theatrical district. Now, a throng of theater patrons was*

lining up outside a huge building with fluted columns. He glanced up at the marquee.

"The Lion King?" He whispered. He shook his head. He had never been much of a fan of Disney musicals. To be honest, he had never been a fan of any musicals. A cloud of smoke drifted above the line of theater patrons, and he made out a flash of sunlight on the Captain's hat and his inevitable Meerschaum pipe. The sun was setting on an unusually warm and dry August day.

The Captain stepped into view and shook hands with a woman dressed in a dark, all-encompassing gown. She was taller than the Captain, and her head and face were obscured by a cowl. A much taller man appeared behind the woman. His suit coat bulged with muscles, and his knobby face betrayed years of pounding in the ring. His eyes roved over the crowd. A bodyguard. Great! He must have been the woman's bodyguard, not the Captain's. The Captain tamped out the tobacco from his pipe and slid it into the tuxedo jacket he wore. He offered his arm to the lady, and the three disappeared into the open doors of the theater.

A sign hung in the box office window. It said, "Sold Out." How was he going to get in? He could wait until the Captain came out of the performance. By then, the sun would be down, and the street would be dark. But, the Captain would be totally relaxed and unprepared for a confrontation at a theatrical production. He could catch the man taking a break at intermission or going to the loo. But, if the performance was sold out, his chances were slim. He stood there, frozen in front of the box office window, and studied his reflection. His turquoise eyes gleamed in the light of the setting sun, and his face was twisted with anger and frustration. He pulled up his jacket hood over his short, reddish-blonde hair to hide his face as he turned away in bitterness. Two teenage girls were squealing as they ran across the street toward him.

"Fantastic! They had some tickets over there!" One of the girls was shouting. The other girl grabbed the ticket out of her friend's hand.

"Who cares if they're scalped. Let's go."

He watched the girls present the tickets at the door and they disappeared inside. He glanced back across the street at a man standing furtively in the shadows. Maybe his plan would work after all!

~

THE FOYER WAS FILLED with performers when he stepped through the outer doors. The "animals" of the savannah infiltrated the audience at the beginning of the performance, and the air was filled with music and singing. An usher stopped him from proceeding.

"Sorry, mate. You've got to let the animals finish." He shouted.

"I'm supposed to meet my father. He came in here a while ago. Had on a white Panama hat. Do you remember him?"

The usher nodded. "Has a box seat on the second-floor stage right. Let me see your ticket."

"I'm not sitting with him. Can't afford the seat. But we're going to meet at intermission. Can you direct me to the loo while we're waiting?" He didn't give the usher a chance to check his ticket.

"Right over there with you. Might as well take your time."

He pushed past the usher and continued along the front of the foyer toward a restroom sign. A stairway led upwards toward the balconies, and he slipped quietly past the usher directing a host of performers inside a huge, gauzy elephant.

The stairs led to the "Royal Circle" on the second level. A narrow hallway led along the outside wall to the box seats. He was halfway down the hall when an usher popped out of a doorway marked "Storage."

"Here, here." He put a handout. "Let's see your ticket now."

"Sorry. I was late meeting my father."

"Late? If I recall, all of the seats are full. That means you're--"

"Lost?" He said and then caught the man with an uppercut to the jaw. He crumpled into Steel's arms, and he pulled him into the storage room. Moments later, he stood outside the curtains to one of the box seats. There were only two seats inside, but the tall body-guard stood quietly in the back corner, his eyes searching the audi-ence below. Steel remained quiet as he glanced around the curtain's edge.

The Captain sat in the chair to the right of the box, and the woman in her flowing cowl and dress sat beside him. Her hand was resting casually on the Captain's leg. The Captain had taken off his signature hat and placed it on the floor beside his chair. His white hair was short and shot through with wisps of red.

Steel glared at the back of his father's head with as much hatred and resentment as he could muster. He willed the man's head to explode. He tried to imagine blood bursting from the man's ears. And, when his eyes strayed down to the woman's hand, his anger surged hotter and darker. One quick movement and he could snap the man's neck before the bodyguard could react. But, he stepped back away from the curtain and fought for control. Here and now was not the time. The Captain would have to come back up the hall at intermis-sion or, at least, when the performance was over. He would wait in the storage room.

He was almost to the storage room when the door burst open. The usher stumbled out of the interior and fell against the far wall. He stood up, glanced with horror at Steel, and screamed as he ran up the hallway. So much for subtlety. Steel raced after him and realized the man would be down the stairs and with security by the time he reached the stairway. He paused in the second-floor foyer and thought furiously for a solution. He smiled as his hand touched the fire alarm on the back wall. He pulled it, and the air was filled with the strident warble of an alarm. He glanced through the open doors of the balcony to the stage at the sight of Mufasa's death after the great stampede. Scar was huddled over Simba. The symbolism was priceless.

The audience flooded from the doors to the second-floor balcony with alarming speed. He never had time to react and was pushed *back toward the stairs. For a fleeting moment, he saw his father appear at the top of the hallway. He glanced over the crowd and motioned to the bodyguard. For the first time, Steel noticed the emergency exit door at the top of the hallway. As he was pushed and shoved by the crowd down the stairs, he watched his father disappear through the door with the woman and the bodyguard.*

Now, he turned and raced with the crowd. He shoved past burly men and large women. He hopped over children to get to the foyer. He caught sight of the usher he had hit arguing with a security guard, but the mass of people flooding through the foyer distracted the guard, and he ignored the man's pleas.

Steel squeezed through one of the outer doors into utter chaos. People milled and screamed along Wellington Street in the darkening evening. Steel pressed against the wall and slid toward the alleyway that ran down the side of the theater with the exit door. He felt something sting, and he clapped a hand over the right side of his neck. He pulled away a small, metal dart and felt the paralysis take him. Strong hands caught him under the armpits as he fell helplessly backward. Warm air played across his left ear.

"Now, now young man. Don't fight it. I won't hurt you. Your father said to disable you so you will stop following him."

Steel glanced over his shoulder and blinked at the face of the bodyguard. "It will only last a few minutes, and then you'll be spit spot, good as new." The huge man lowered him to the sidewalk while patrons of the theater surged around them. "They'll just think you were trampled. Remember what I could have done to you, laddy." The man stood up, and he seemed impossibly large and far away. He stepped into the crowd and disappeared.

Steel was helpless with his head propped against the brick wall and his feet extending into the sidewalk. A young girl fell over his feet and tumbled into his lap. She was probably eleven or twelve at that tender age between awkward girlishness and blooming adolescence. Her face came close to his, and he saw her dark skin, eyes wide in alarm and dark hair. Her eyes had a faint Asian appearance. Her mouth opened and she screamed. She pushed up off of him, and a woman grabbed her from behind. The woman was taller than the young girl with dark hair piled on top of her head. She wore a full-length white evening girl studded with sequins. She was definitely of Asian descent. The young girl shook her head and pointed at him.

"Mom, what's wrong with him?"

The woman shook her head and squatted beside Steel, a feat of incredible grace in the long evening gown. Her hand pressed cool against his neck.

"His pulse is strong. He probably was knocked around in the evacuation. Let's call a constable." She stood up, and a huge man stepped around her.

"What is it, dear?" He seemed oddly out of time dressed in a top hat and one of those cloaks that drapes halfway down on the shoulders over the rest of the cloak. His black bowtie was perfect. His eyes turned down toward Steel, and for a moment, they registered unmistakable recognition. A strange tattoo covered his right cheek, one of those island tattoos, maybe?

"My word, I know you!"

From behind the man's cape, a teenage boy appeared. He had shoulder-length jet back hair and dark skin like his father. His eyes were riveted to a game on his phone. "Dad, you know everybody." The boy said.

"Put that thing away!" The man said.

The boy ignored him. "And die of boredom? I mean, Hakuna Matata? Really?"

The woman glared at the boy. "Steven, this man needs help. Can you look away from your phone long enough to find a constable?"

The boy sighed and rolled his eyes. "He's just a homeless loser, Mom."

Two things happened then. First, the beginnings of a wave of strength crawled up his feet as the drug wore off. Second, a figure appeared from the alleyway. Steel's gaze flitted to the figure. A cap obscured the person's face, but a passing patron knocked against the figure's shoulder, and the cap fell away. Brown hair cascaded down, and the woman's face was plainly visible in the streetlight from the corner. Three shots erupted from the pistol, and Raven cursed after being jostled.

Blood erupted from the man's chest. The man's face betrayed shock and dismay. The girl had stepped into the cradle of the woman's arms. Raven glanced at the girl and shifted the aim of the pistol toward the two women. Hesitation passed across her face. The huge man fell backward into the astonished and chaotic crowd. The woman and the girl screamed and ran to the man's fallen body. Raven aimed at the woman and was jostled again just as her gun fired. A bullet collided with the boy's phone. It shattered in a shower of metal and glass, and then the bullet ricocheted and caught the young girl along the right side of her head. She screamed and fell across her dying father.

Steel felt his strength fully return, and he bolted up from the sidewalk. He stumbled to the corner and glanced down the alleyway. It was empty. Raven was gone! He turned back, and the mother was shouting for help, but the man was already dead, and the young girl lay limply in her father's lap. The teenage boy's hands were bloody, and he was screaming at the top of his lungs.

There was nothing for him to do here. Raven's assassination was none of his business. It had all been an incredible coincidence that he was there when it came down. His main goal was his father. He slipped away from the murder scene and along Wellington Street. It was only then he realized his face and the front of his hoody were covered with blood.

STEEL JERKED as the train ground to a halt and gasped as he studied the cabin around him. People were lining up to get off the train. He had been in London with Raven when she had killed the man and injured the girl! The woman from the airplane was younger in his flashback but the same person. And, she was no stranger to him. He had met her more than once. Back in North Africa, while in prison, his father had authorized surgery on his brain, and Dr. Monarch had been the surgeon. She had done this to him. She had stolen his life and made his memory a tool of his father, the Captain. Like a ferocious wind, the events on the airplane came rushing back; the attack by the Crimson Snake, the messenger bag, the woman's plea for help, the crash, the dogs, the electrifying touch of the woman's finger on his forehead that triggered the loss of this memory.

He lurched up from his seat, glasses, and cap forgotten. He didn't care if anyone saw him and made the connection he was Jonathan Steel. Thakkar had already made that connection. All he knew was Josh and Olivia were in danger. And Olivia's mother was not dead! He had saved her from the airplane!

STEEL FOLLOWED the stream of people off the train and on to the customs area. He glanced around nervously, waiting for the Crimson Snake to pop out of the crowd at any moment. He was pushed and shoved by fellow passengers as he moved toward the queue.

Somewhere, he heard a cell phone warbling and realized it was not coming from his phone in his coat pocket but from the messenger bag. He stopped and stood in the slowly moving line and reached into the messenger bag. The warbling was coming from an inner zipped pocket of the bag. He opened the compartment and pulled out a flip cell phone. He opened it.

"Don't react, just listen," Max said in his ear. Steel fought the need to tell her everything. "Get out of line now and walk toward the restroom on your right. Just do it."

Steel stepped out of line and entered the men's restroom.

Every urinal was occupied. "Go to the last stall and close the door," Max said.

Steel stepped into the stall and locked the door. He sat on the toilet. "Max, Ishido, and the Crimson Snake were on the train. You've been compromised."

"I know," Max said. "I monitored the video feed on the train until the cameras went out in your first-class car. That's when we figured out the old woman was the Snake. Now, listen carefully. There is a service entrance in the corner across from your stall. It will open in a moment. Electronic lock. Walk calmly through that door, and you will be in a service corridor. Take a left and go through the third door on your right. Before you do that, there is a Bluetooth earpiece in the messenger bag. Put it in your ear and place the phone in the bag. Now, go!"

Steel retrieved an earbud from the bag and put it in his ear. He slid the open phone down into the bag. "Got it."

"Now, go!"

Steel opened the stall door and, as calmly as his racing heart would allow it, opened the opposite service door. In the distance, he heard the warbling of sirens. They had found Ishido or the Snake or both. He closed the door behind him and stood in a dingy, poorly lit corridor. When he came to the third door, its electronic lock clicked, and he stepped through. He found himself in a short hallway that opened out onto the luggage retrieval area.

"Now, take your luggage and exit the terminal. Once you get outside, turn right. A cab will be waiting for you. I'll tell you which one." Max said.

"How do you know –"

"CCTVs, Jonathan. Everywhere."

"And, you hacked into them?"

"Child's play."

Steel snared his luggage from the carousel and exited the terminal. The night air was cool and moist. He recognized the red-bricked arched building of St. Pancras train station. Across the street, lights gleamed from the famous King's Cross train station. Cabs and cars filled the streets around him. He had been here before. Police cars converged on the terminal, lights whirling, sirens blaring.

"The cab just in front of you. Get in." Max said.

Steel opened the back door of the cab and climbed in. A heavyset man looked back at him through the plexiglass divider. "Good evening, Mr. Rockfield. I'll have you at the hotel in no time, mate."

Rockfield? Steel blinked. He was supposed to be Mr. Stone, wasn't he? Max spoke in his ear.

"We registered you under Rockfield when I suspected I had been compromised. You'll find backup passports in the messenger bag for Jeremiah Rockfield and his son, Joseph. I always have a plan B."

"Josh?"

"He didn't have a passport, did he?"

"No."

"Call Dr. Holmes and find out where he is. I believe he is still being retained by the airport security over the crates. Call him and then call me back. Use the encrypted phone I gave you earlier."

Steel closed the flip phone and took out his cell phone. He opened the encryption app and then dialed Holmes' number.

"Jonathan?" Holmes sound harried and tired.

"Monty, where are you?"

"I've been at the airport security for hours in a holding room. They're going over the crates with a fine-toothed comb. I told them I would leave the crates if they would let me go on to the hotel. Where are you?"

"In a cab in London. What is the name of your hotel again?"

"The Royal Renaissance."

Steel leaned forward and slid aside a plexiglass partition. "Sir, where are we going again?"

The cabbie glanced over his shoulder. "You don't know, mate?"

"My reservations were made by my boss."

"The Royal Renaissance. We'll be there in ten minutes, mate."

Steel closed the partition. "Max continues to amaze me. I'm headed to your hotel. Monty, any word on Josh and Jason?"

"No, Jonathan. I told them to meet me at the hotel."

"Okay. I'll call you when I get there."

"Let's hope and pray they made it," Holmes said and ended the call.

Steel opened the flip phone and called Max. "No word from Josh and Jason." He said. "Holmes is still in security. He'll be heading to the hotel at any moment. Max, I have to find Josh."

"You're not alone, Jonathan. I'm working on locating them." Max said.

The cab ground to a halt, and Steel took his luggage and climbed out. He offered his credit card, but the cabbie waved him away.

"Already taken care of by the boss lady." He paused for a moment and nodded as if listening to something. "I've been told to take your credit cards and destroy them." He opened his hand.

"They have an RFID in them," Max said. "Mason will take care to drive them around for a while and then destroy them. Don't worry, there are others in the messenger bag in your new name."

Steel handed both credit cards to Mason, and the man tipped his cap and drove away. "Max, you never cease to amaze me."

"I'm about to amaze you even more. But you have to hurry

into the hotel lobby. The policeman is about to ask for identification."

"From who?"

"Josh and Jason. They are inside. You have to sell it, Jonathan. Run!"

The next few seconds were a blur as Steel ran through the revolving doors of the stately, old hotel. In the center of the lobby, a uniformed policeman talked to Josh and Jason. Sell it, she said.

"Joseph!" He shouted as he slid to a halt by the policeman. "There you are."

Josh's eyes widened, and he hurled himself into Steel's arms. Steel embraced him and fought off tears. "It's okay, Jason was watching after you."

Steel looked at the policeman. "Thank you, officer. Joseph went off and left his identification." He reached into the messenger bag and pulled out the passports. He handed them to the policeman. He leaned close to Josh's ear. "Play along. Your name is Joseph." He whispered. Steel nodded toward Josh as his gaze locked with Jason's.

The officer examined the passports, and a business card fell out of one of them. He retrieved it and studied it. He looked through the passports. Steel held Josh close to him, letting the boy get his bearings.

"I must say, mate, the management was a bit worried what with the two of them loitering in the lobby."

"I was late getting in at the train station. Traffic." Steel said. He gently pushed Josh away. "Are you okay, Joseph?"

"Probably getting a chill, don't you think?" The officer said, pointing to Josh's tee shirt and jeans.

"I lost my jacket on the airplane," Josh said. "All I had left was my backpack."

"And our luggage," Jason added with a frown.

"Uh, Mr. Rockfield, may I ask what your business is about?"

Steel blinked and motioned to the card. "I think you have my business card."

The officer handed it back to Steel. "Consulting Detectives? Really?"

Josh rolled his eyes and tried to hide a smile. "Well, Jason thought it was clever." Steel said.

"And, are you registered, Mr. Rockfield?"

"Yes. We are meeting our client here. He has hired us to safeguard some crates of antiquities headed for Dr. Nigel Hampton's Museum. Are you familiar with the museum?" Steel said.

The officer handed Steel the passports. "Bloody strange place it is. Who is your client?"

"Mr. Holmes."

The officer raised an eyebrow. "Oh, it is, now? His first name wouldn't be Sherlock, would it?"

"No, it's Montana." Steel said.

The officer took a double-take. "Are you sure his name isn't Indiana Jones?"

"We named the dog Indiana," Josh said. He grinned, and Jason nudged him and shook his head.

The officer looked at them one by one and nodded. "All right. I'll just wait until your client arrives if you don't mind."

At that moment, the revolving door moved, and Dr. Montana Holmes hurried into the lobby pulling his luggage behind him. Steel ran to him.

"Monty. Joseph and Jason are perfectly safe. They got lost but found their way to the hotel. Thank you so much for calling me about them." Steel said as he positioned himself between Monty and the officer.

"You're my client, and my name is Rockfield." He whispered.

The officer appeared behind Steel's back. "Would you mind if I take a look at your identification, sir?"

Holmes looked like a deer caught in the headlights. He fished his passport out of his jacket pocket and handed it to the policeman. He studied it carefully.

"Now, you've hired these two guys to look after something?" The officer handed the passport back to Holmes.

Holmes's mouth fell open, and he looked back and forth between the officer and Steel. "The crates?"

"Of artifacts." Steel prompted.

"Yes, the artifacts that are to be delivered to Hampton's Museum. I'm afraid they are being held up at the airport security and will not be delivered for a while."

Steel patted Holmes on the back. "Then they should be perfectly safe under the constant guard of London's finest. Right, officer?"

The policeman frowned. "Get on with yourselves and register, will you please? Consulting detectives. You Americans think you are all comedians!"

Holmes started to say something, and Steel took his arm and guided him toward the desk. "Right, Dr. Holmes, go ahead and check-in, and then we will follow suit."

The officer stayed close to the door, and Holmes smiled at a young woman behind the reception desk. He handed her his passport. "Dr. Montana Holmes. I have reservations."

The desk clerk checked her computer. "It looks like we were able to upgrade your rooms, Dr. Holmes. I assume the other three gentlemen are with you? May I see some identification?" She reached for Steel's passports. Jason passed his over.

Steel glanced over his shoulder at the officer. The young woman studied the passports and then nodded to the officer. "Everything is in order, sir. There is a note here that Mr. Birdsong and young Mr. Rockfield's luggage has been located and will be delivered in the morning." She handed the passports back to them, and Steel nodded to the officer as he left through the revolving doors.

"You'll have to forgive me for being so careful, gentlemen." She said to Dr. Holmes. "We don't like loiterers in today's toxic atmosphere."

"Totally understandable," Jason said, and he smiled his thousand-watt smile at the woman. Her face reddened, and she turned back to the computer, touching a hand to the hair behind her ears. "Looks like all four of you have been moved to the Royal Chambers. That's one of our penthouse rooms. You'll find four bedrooms, a parlor, a dining room, a fully stocked kitchen, and 24-hour concierge service."

Holmes' eyes grew wide, and he glanced at Steel, "I don't have that kind of money."

"Your bill is being covered, it would seem." The young woman glanced once more at Jason, and he beamed. She cleared her throat. "If you'll take the elevator to the fifteenth floor, you will find your suite, and here are your keys."

Steel glanced at the clock on the wall. It was two o'clock a.m. "Thank you."

Jason reached out and patted her hand. "You're a sweetheart."

Holmes led them across the lobby to the elevator. They piled in, and Steel held up a hand. "No talking. Not now."

The phone warbled in his messenger bag, and he opened it. Max spoke in his earpiece. "That was close, Jonathan. You'll find an attachment to your other cell phone in the messenger bag. Secure it to your phone, then open the security app we installed to talk to Dr. Holmes. When you get to your suite, scan each room. Don't say a word until you hear back from me." The line went dead.

Steel motioned for them to be quiet. The elevator opened onto a foyer with double doors directly before them. The hallway was a square-shaped foyer with no other exits. Steel pulled the module from the inner pocket of the messenger bag and snapped it into the end of his cell phone and opened the app. He swiped the key card and motioned for them to stay behind.

Inside, the room was obscenely decorated with several plush sofas, a huge mahogany dining table, and a well-stocked kitchen. He went into the four bedrooms and moved his phone around. Nothing. The suite was clean. He motioned for the other three to come into the room and shut the door behind them. He dialed the phone.

"The room is clean." He said.

"Just a moment," Max said. "Okay, we have our own video feed from the foyer and the elevator. There is an emergency stairway exit off the kitchen, and we have that covered. Now, tell me everything."

"Just a second." Steel ended the call. He walked to Josh, and his face grew warm with anger. "What were you thinking?"

Josh's eyes widened with fear. "Jonathan, they shot Buck. In the head. And they came after Olivia and me. We had to run! They were going to kill us." His breathing quickened, and Steel reached out and took him by the shoulder. Josh flinched.

"It's okay. We'll get it all sorted. By the way, Buck is alive. He was in surgery last I heard." Steel turned on Jason. "Thanks for taking care of Josh."

"My friend," Jason reached over and hugged him tightly. Steel tried to relax. "You get us into the most bizarre messes I've ever heard of." He pushed back and looked Steel in the eye. "I told you I would take care of Josh. No matter what."

"Okay. Let's sit. We need to tell Max everything."

"Jonathan, it's 2 in the morning!" Holmes said.

"Not at home," Josh said. "I'm starving, and I stink to high heaven."

"Yes, you do." Jason agreed. "And I'm not much better."

Steel nodded. "We'll take about fifteen minutes only. Give Max the highlights."

"Who's Max?" Holmes asked.

"Right now, the only person keeping us alive. She was a close friend of Cephas. She's here to help us." Steel gestured to the table. He dialed Max's phone and put it on the speaker. "Max, we're here and very tired."

"I am, too," Max said. "Briefly, let's start with Josh. Tell me what happened with Olivia."

Josh told his story and ended with him and Jason jumping onto the tarmac with the spilled luggage and then making their way off the tarmac and through London to the hotel. "We ate at McDonald's next to the London Eye." He said to Steel.

"Doesn't surprise me." Steel said. He watched Josh's eyes fill with unshed tears. The kid had been through another ordeal; no teenager should ever have to endure. Once again, Steel's insecurity about being Josh's adopted father flooded over him. What should he do? He just wasn't very good at this. Based on what he knew about his own father and their fractured relationship, that didn't surprise him. "Josh, I talked to Ross. He's involved in the investigation, and he said Buck was in surgery. We don't know how bad he is."

"Young Mr. Sanderson is recovering in SICU," Max said. "And don't ask how I know. I have my connections. He is expected to make a full recovery."

"That's too bad," Josh said hoarsely and tried to smile. "I was hoping it would change his personality."

Steel cleared his throat and tried to smile. No go. He looked back at the phone. "Now, Max, let me tell you about our train ride." He filled her in on the details and ended with Ishido being shut up in the lavatory.

"Ishido made it out of the train before the authorities stopped him. He was weak, but they were tied up trying to apprehend the Crimson Snake." Max said.

"Where is Ishido? Is he okay?" Steel asked.

"He is safely in the hands of one of my private physicians. He lost a lot of blood, and he's lucky he didn't run into any of his opponents. As to the Snake, the last I was able to ascertain, she was at Scotland Yard in a holding cell."

"There was something else." Steel looked at Josh. "Like Josh, I used the pair of goggles the Snake gave me. It was unreal. I spoke with a Dr. Thakkar."

"Dude, you tried virtual reality? It was so totally cool, wasn't it?" Josh said. He blinked. "In an evil sort of way."

"Yeah, it was too real." Steel said.

"Jonathan, where are the goggles?" Max asked.

"I left them on the train."

"Good! If you had kept them, you could be tracked to the hotel. Listen, if anyone comes up the stairway or the elevator, I will alert you. For now, get some food, get some sleep and call me in the morning when you wake up. We're all exhausted. In the meantime, I will see what we can find on Thakkar and her Third Eye Interface."

21

R aven examined the sleeping girl and wondered what had kept her from killing the teenager. Olivia had passed out when Raven had opened the emergency door exit on the initial approach for landing, and the dropping oxygen level had sent the girl into one of her absence seizures. Raven had immediately snagged the dropped oxygen masks and pulled herself into the parachute she had tucked away into her duffel bag. She had attached the girl to her front harness before jumping from the airplane.

Their descent had been quick and short, and she had landed in a field. Her phone map showed them in Surbiton, England, south of London. Olivia began to stir, and her eyes opened, and she squinted in the bright sunlight. They focused on Raven, and she sat up and vomited into the grass. She wiped her mouth and glared at Raven.

"Are you out of your mind?"

"Yes. I should have pushed you out the door." Raven looked around and spotted a trail through the brown grass toward the nearby train station she had located on her map. "We were on the descent for landing. There was plenty of oxygen in the air for your friends."

"But not me!" She cursed again and tried to stand up. She wobbled and looked around her. "Where is my backpack? I need it for my meds."

Raven motioned to her duffel bag. "In my duffel. Now, you said you could help me by finding your mother."

Olivia nodded. "I can. Why do you want to kill Thakkar?"

Raven put a hand on her hip and held up the phone. "Stop asking questions."

Olivia rolled her eyes and pulled up her shirt and ripped off the silver pad. Nothing happened. She tossed it into the grass. "I know when someone is bluffing, Raven. Look. We both are headed in the same direction. We both are looking for my mother, so you can stop Thakkar. Thakkar is a very public figure, so you really don't need me, do you? In fact, you could have killed me a dozen times before now. So, why am I still alive?"

Raven sighed. The girl was good. Memories of her past surfaced for a moment. A little girl in a pink dress with a lamb. She chased those painful memories away. She unzipped the duffle and pulled out the backpack. She unzipped the top and pulled out the pouch and opened it. She pointed to the goggles and inside. "What is this?"

The girl's eyes widened. "You had no right!"

"You said someone was trying to kill you and the boy. I'm pretty sure because they want this. Now, if those people with those kinds of resources are working for Thakkar, then I can't afford to go marching into a very 'public' place." Raven dropped the pouch back into the backpack and handed it to Olivia. "I think Thakkar wants that little item, whatever it is. And you are going to contact your mother and set up a meeting with her and Thakkar. In a very 'private' place where I can complete my mission."

Olivia bit her lip and looked longingly at the duffel. "There's more to this than you know."

"I don't care," Raven said.

Olivia's eyes filled with tears. "I have a brother. He's seventeen. He is brilliant. He developed another set of goggles like that one. Only it has the, well, missing ingredient that Thakkar is looking for. My mother was coming to Europe to try and find him."

Raven motioned to the nearby tree line. "Okay. We need to get undercover. Someone will be looking for our parachute. We get undercover, and then, you will tell me everything." Raven touched the app on her phone and pointed to the silver lead Olivia had tossed into the grass. It erupted in a shower of sparks. "Yours was the only one I activated, by the way. I could have killed you at any time."

OLIVIA CONTINUED TO SURPRISE RAVEN. Once they found the train station in Surbiton, Olivia had pulled a passport from a hidden compartment in her backpack that identified her as Sophia Queen. Raven used one of her aliases, and after donning some altered clothes from the duffel bag, they walked onto the train to London in plain sight and settled in a back seat for the hour-long ride to London.

Olivia bought some snacks from the trolley and shared them with Raven. Raven sat with her duffel bag tucked beneath her feet. She had tossed the gun in the trees just outside the train station. She didn't need it. She was deadly without any weapons.

"Now, finish what you were telling me."

Olivia nodded and sipped bottled water. She wore a knit cap to cover her short hair. "My brother entered Numinocity."

"Where is that?"

"Good question. It's a construct by the Numinous Corporation. A virtual community for transhumanists."

Raven stared at the red threads on her fingers. "You are making no sense."

Olivia sat in the seat, facing her, and leaned forward. "We're not sure exactly what Numinocity is. Part virtual reality. Part real location. No one knows. You can put on one of those devices in my backpack called the Third Eye Interface. Thakkar stole the original design from my mother. My mother designed the original goggles to help me with my seizures, but my brother 'improved' its capabilities and found a way to enter Numinocity while it was under development by Thakkar. Thakkar found out and hacked into my mother's computer and obtained one of the early prototype designs. It's not nearly as sophisticated as mine. Nor is it anywhere close to the one my brother has. We have no idea what improvements my brother made to his prototype."

Raven nodded. "How do we find your mother?"

"I have a link to her through my neurostimulator. I set up a meeting in London later this evening." Olivia ate more of her snack and swallowed some water.

Raven studied Olivia and sighed. Was she this calm when she was a teenager? She couldn't remember. Something had taken her memories. Again. Raven crossed her arms and leaned back in the seat. "Why do you have seizures?"

Olivia stopped chewing and blinked furiously. "An assassin shot my father. One of the bullets ricocheted and hit me in the head. I was ten."

Raven blanched, and for a moment, she saw the tall figure of a man in a tuxedo and ridiculous top hat standing between her and the woman and a girl. She felt the recoil of her pistol as she pulled the trigger. She saw the bullet plow through the teenager's phone and ricochet to the girl. She recalled the blood pouring from the girl's head. She closed her eyes and tried to clear up the memory. Someone else had been there. A man who had tried to stop her? Her eyes flew open, and she looked away from Olivia. In a sudden cold rush of unfamiliar guilt and shame, she realized this teenage girl was the daughter of the man she had assassinated years before.

"If you double-cross me, I will snap your neck in a heartbeat." She said hoarsely with far less menace than usual.

22

Raven stood on the edge of profound darkness. The chasm stretched far below her into the depths of the mountain, and behind her, she heard the deep-throated laughter of someone echoing through the cavern. She turned, and the large, bat-like creature stood upright on spindly legs towering over her. It stretched out vein etched wings of dark flesh, and its huge, floppy ears stood suddenly erect as it sought out her position with its echolocation. Huge, yellow eyes rimmed with blood vessels leaked greenish tears down its dark cheeks into a mouth open to reveal fangs.

Raven's heart raced in fear, and she backed slowly toward the edge of the chasm. "You're not real!" She whispered. "You're dead. I saw your body disintegrate from the exploding bullet."

The creature smiled, and another deep-throated laugh echoed through the chamber. "I am very much alive within you, Raven. Look at your hand."

Raven glanced at her right hand. Two black threads were tied around her index finger and her thumb. The black threads suddenly moved and writhed as if alive. The threads thickened and took on a scaly flesh. The dangling ends of each thread moved upward toward her face and slowly changed into the heads of two dark snakes with red eyes.

"No! This is not real! I'm different now! I'm not a killer! I found forgiveness!" Cold water splashed into her face, and she gasped. She tried to see the advancing creature through water-filled eyes. Before she could gather another breath, the snakes sank their fangs into her wrist, and more water splashed into her face. She stumbled back over the edge of the chasm and fell!

Raven jerked upright and screamed. She blinked water out of her eyes and looked across the room. She was no longer in the cavern but in a brightly lit room filled with tables and cabinets bearing scientific equipment. She shook the water from her face.

"She's awake, Mom."

Raven glared at the girl standing before her. She held an empty bucket in her hand. "Trying to drown me?"

"Don't tempt us." A woman said as she stepped from behind the girl. "I know who you are, and I remember what you did."

Raven blinked moisture from her eyes. Water ran down her face and soaked into her clothes. Her hands were bound behind her, and she sat in a metal chair. Her feet were bound one to each leg. She shook her head. The woman looked familiar. But, Raven couldn't clear the lingering cobwebs from her memory. She had to buy some time to consider her current predicament.

"There have been so many victims." She said. "Which one were you?"

The woman stepped closer and, with a sudden movement, slapped Raven across the cheek. Raven tasted blood on her lips. She smiled. "That didn't work."

The woman's chest heaved with emotion, and she crossed her arms. "I'm Dr. Monarch. Why did you kill my husband?"

Raven relished the sting of the flesh on her cheek. She tongued the blood off of her lip. "Not getting it. Sorry."

"London. In an alleyway outside of a musical theater. One of your shots ricocheted and struck my daughter."

Raven leaned back against the chair to relieve the pain and pressure in her arms. "I'm sorry to report that my memory isn't what it used to be. I don't recall all of my targets."

"Mom, she's lying." The girl said.

"What did you do to me?" Raven glared at Olivia.

Olivia held her hand up and motioned to a ring on her pinky. "Something my mother created. One electromagnetic pulse, and I can put you under. It's like hypnosis only quicker. You rode the train with me all the way here to London. They thought you were my auntie. You even paid for our cab ride through the cool, London night to my home."

Monarch reached over and pushed her daughter's hand down. "I told you not to use that thing. You were supposed to have deactivated it."

"Yeah, and if I had, I would be dead, Mom," Olivia said.

"Are you going to kill me now?" Raven asked. She moved her wrists and hands inside the duct tape that bound her to the back of the chair.

"Not yet." Monarch stepped closer. "Why are you after Thakkar?"

Raven raised an eyebrow. "She's my next target."

"Why?"

"I don't ask that question."

"Maybe you should."

Raven shrugged painfully and grimaced as pain lanced up her arm. It was worth it. The tape had loosened on her right hand. "Mine is not to question why. Just to see that my targets die."

Olivia rolled her eyes. "Mom, she's not going to be any help."

Monarch leaned toward her and looked into her eyes. "You said your memories were messed up. Suffering from amnesia?"

Raven flinched at the word and looked away. "I remember what I need to."

Monarch leaned closer until her lips were close to Raven's ear. Raven tried to loosen the tape as she tried to lean away from the woman.

"Can I whisper a phrase in your ear?" Monarch said.

Raven's heart raced, and she gasped for breath. "What?"

"You know, a special phrase that triggers amnesia?"

Raven tried to pull her head away from the woman, and her right hand tore loose from the tape, leaving behind skin and hair. She swung her hand upward and grabbed the woman by the throat. Monarch's eyes bulged, and she grabbed Raven's hands. She looked deep into Raven's eyes and whispered.

"Beware the demon of the spiral eye."

Darkness exploded within Raven's mind, and she fell, whirling, plunging down a tunnel of blood and flesh. She bounced against the walls of the tunnel and pressed her right hand against her throbbing head.

"No!" She tried to find reality, tried to hang onto the external world. But, the flight into her own mind did not end as she fell and fell until a hand lashed out and caught her at the last minute. She hung in total and complete darkness. Where had the hand come from? Where was she?

She felt the ground beneath her as she and the exposed arm holding her up lowered gently. The arm was attached to a man standing just outside a circle of light. He stepped forward, and his turquoise eyes were hidden behind a veil of smoke.

"No! Please, no more!" She tried to scream, but her words were a bare whisper.

The man waved away the smoke and stepped fully into the light. He was tall with reddish-blonde hair, and his face did not bear anger or malice.

"Victoria, it's me. You're safe now."

"Jonathan?" She said, and she threw herself toward his open arms. She passed right through him as his figure evaporated into smoke. She stood alone in the cone of light and glanced at the threads tied to the fingers of her right hand. Threads. Strings. Holding all of her life together, leading back into the past.

She touched the thread on her second finger. "Steel." She took it off and dropped it. The thread turned to smoke before it hit the ground. She looked at the thread on her fourth finger. Just moments before she had been in a cavern with the bat creature. Yes! The man had fired a bullet. It had exploded but she took the bullets that came before because she wanted to protect Steel. And, she had found something else in that cavern. She took the thread from her fourth finger and dropped it. She touched the thread on her third finger and one word surfaced. Forgiveness.

She gasped and drew a deep, shuddering breath as it all came back to her in one fluid redemptive moment. The darkness around her disappeared and the bright light of Monarch's lab made her squint. She was hanging halfway from the chair, her face pressed against the wet floor. She sat up slowly and pain from her taped left hand drove her out of confusion.

Monarch stood before her with a pistol aimed at squarely at Raven's head. Olivia hovered behind her mother. Monarch massaged her neck with her free hand. "Now, where were we?"

Raven slowly righted the chair and managed to sit down with her left hand, stilled tied behind her. She massaged her head and sighed. "I'm fine now. My memory has returned. I'm not going to kill anyone."

"Nope, not buying it." Monarch said, her pistol steady and unwavering in her grasp.

"Look, I died. In a cavern in Transylvania. An angel saved me, and God gave me a second chance. They found me and fixed my injuries. I was doing just fine until the Captain came along." Raven leaned back wearily. "I owe it all to Jonathan Steel. He helped me find forgiveness. I was willing to die that day. I should have died. But, a power greater than me brought me back." Raven glanced at Olivia. "I'm sorry about the airplane and the throats. I was under the influence of a forced mission. Isn't the first time."

Raven swallowed as the memories of that night in the alley surfaced. "Dr. Marshall Monarch was your husband's name. I have no idea why I was hired. That part, I never remember. My employer makes sure of that." She looked Monarch in the eyes. "I'm sorry now. I wasn't then. But now, I am myself."

"I don't believe you." Monarch said in a trembling voice. Tears trickled down her cheeks. "You killed my husband. You crippled my son's hands. You condemned my daughter to a lifetime of epilepsy."

Raven nodded. "Then kill me now so I won't have to live with this pain anymore. Go ahead and shoot me. I've made peace with God. I'm ready for eternity."

Olivia reached up from behind her mother and pushed her trembling arm down. "Mom, there's been enough killing."

Monarch put her free hand up to her face and pressed it against her mouth as she sobbed. Olivia gently took the gun from her mother's hand. She tucked it into the waist of her blue jeans. She glared at Raven. "Although I'm not above injuring you."

"Why do you want to find Thakkar?" Raven asked.

Monarch gasped and finally controlled her sobbing. "No! You can't change the subject."

"Look, I freely admit I killed your husband. I acknowledge it. No excuses. But that is behind me. I was sent by the Captain to kill Thakkar. You've returned my memory now, and that mission is over."

Monarch wiped her eyes and moved to a nearby table. She

rummaged through some equipment and picked up a computer tablet. She plugged a wire into a port and held up a funnel-shaped scanner attached to other end of the wire. "I'm going to scan your brain now." She said. "If you try to hurt me, Olivia will shoot you in the knee. You may want to die, but I don't think you want to hurt."

Raven raised her right hand. "I promise not to do anything. Why are you scanning my brain?"

Monarch leaned forward and held the scanner close to Raven's head. As she studied the readouts on her tablet, she stepped closer, running the scanner around the periphery of Raven's head.

"What is it?"

"You've had surgery. Implants. But, they're like nothing I've ever seen. Not like my implants." Monarch said.

Raven looked up at Monarch. "*Your* implants?"

Monarch drew a deep breath. "I did pioneering surgery on brain-computer interfaces or BCI. I was trying to cure my daughter."

"Where?"

Monarch looked away. "In a prison camp in North Africa. Jonathan Steel was one of my patients. At the request of his father."

Raven laughed. "You worked for the Captain, too? You have no room to condemn me, then."

Monarch walked away and dropped the tablet and the scanner on the table. "You don't have to remind me. That's how I suspected what your trigger phrase would be. He used it to program his own son's implants." She slammed a clenched fist onto the table. She turned and crossed her arms.

"Thakkar stole the plans for a BCI from me. A set of goggles with cortical electrodes built into the straps. I originally designed them to investigate Olivia's brain. To look deep within to find the scar tissue. I thought I could possibly obliterate the seizure foci with the help of nanotechnology. That's how I developed my brain implants."

"But, you weren't going to experiment on your own daughter." Raven nodded. "Who did my surgery?"

"Probably, Dr. Sno. He was at the prison camp before I got there. But, he couldn't do surgery anymore. He's blind. White eyes." Monarch said. "I'm ashamed of what I did, but I refuse to apologize for trying to help my daughter."

Olivia had moved closer to her mother. "It's okay, mother. I understand. You don't have to keep doing this, you know. I'm just fine with my seizures."

Monarch reached out and pulled Olivia into an embrace. For a moment, Raven felt the old pull of attraction to her father. But, then, she saw his psychotic eyes, smelled his alcohol breath, saw the knife with the blood as she pulled it from her lamb shaped cake. Only it had been more than just the shape of a lamb. It had been her pet lamb. Her "Olivia."

"Thakkar?" Raven said quietly.

Monarch released Olivia. "My son, Steven. He's a virtual genius. Just turned twenty-one. He took one of my goggles and adapted it to interface with virtual reality games. He told us he had found something online, something special."

"Numinocity," Olivia said. "He took mother's latest prototype and flew to Europe last week. Now, we can't find him. He's disappeared. Off the normal grid."

Raven nodded. "I remember you mentioning some of this on the train. Why don't you go online and find him?"

Monarch shook her head. "He sent us a message. Cryptic. Said he was trapped in Numinocity. Trapped online, maybe? Trapped in a virtual world? I started looking into Thakkar's Third Eye Interface and found out some rather unsavory things. It's more than just a technological tool for interfacing with some kind of virtual gaming platform. I was coming to

Europe to try and locate him when the airplane crashed. I realized someone was trying to stop me."

"Thakkar?"

"I assume, yes. Her operative took a messenger bag with an old prototype. Probably thought Steven's prototype was with me."

Raven had taken the other tape binding loose while they were talking. Monarch looked at her with surprise when she moved over to stand beside her. Monarch flinched, and Raven shook her head. "I'm not going to hurt you. I will help."

"How?" Olivia asked.

"Thakkar can't possibly have discovered Steven's modifications. He's still lost in Numinocity, according to his last message. We have to find him before she does." Monarch said.

"Who can we trust?" Olivia said. "We don't know who was following Josh and me."

"I know someone we can all trust. Right now, we need rest. It's almost midnight, and first thing in the morning, I'm making a call." Raven said. It was time to call Max.

23

Josh stood on the edge of a steep precipice looking down on a vast valley surrounded by snow-covered mountains. Two armies sped across the plains toward each other, the dust of their approaches obscuring the details. From the choking dust, lights sparkled here and there emitted by energy weapons of unknown type. Where was he?

"On the outskirts of Numinocity." A voice said behind him.

He turned and realized for the first time he wore a light-weight armor of sparkling white. He looked down at his hand, and he held a long, shimmering crystal sword that glowed faintly with a blue light. He studied the figure that approached. It was a young man, not much older than Josh. His long, black hair was pulled back in a bun on the back of his head. His chest was bare and covered with tattoos. Maori? He had similar tattoos on his face, and he wore some kind of loincloth wrapped around his waist. A gleaming blue stone hung from a chain around his neck.

"Who are you?"

"A friend. How is it you are here?"

Josh looked around. He hefted the surprisingly lightweight crystalline sword. "Where is here?"

"Numinocity." The man said. "You may call me Roland1143."

Josh gestured around him at the billowing clouds of mist and dust. "And, where is Numinocity?"

"Here, there, everywhere and nowhere. It is a land dedicated to transhumanism. It is the next phase of human evolution." Roland1143 said.

Josh shook his head. "You are making no sense."

"Did you use a third eye interface?" Roland asked.

"The goggle thingy? Dude, I put it on, and it almost got me killed."

Roland1143 stiffened and whirled. Something tall and spindly moved in the mist behind him. The long, jointed extremities of the thing cast long, slatted shadows through the mist until it emerged. Josh gasped. A giant scorpion towered over them. Around one of the thing's far too human eyes was a black spiral. A voice far too familiar came from the thing's mouth.

"Well, looky what the cat dragged in, honey child! Bless my stars and garters!"

Josh's mouth fell open, and he grasped for words. "Vivian?"

JOSH SAT UP, gasping for breath, his heart racing. He flailed at the air around him and slid off the bed onto the floor. He glanced at his hand. No sword. He looked around the dim bedroom of the hotel suite. No scorpion or pike wielding warrior. He was in his hotel room. In London. Where had that dream come from? And what was Numinocity? Vivian and the scorpion were really no mystery. Vivian and the thirteenth demon had always plagued his nightmares. He shuddered at the thought of the two of them working together. Again.

Josh stumbled through the double doors of the bedroom out into the living area of the hotel suite. Jonathan, Jason, and Monty sat at the dining room table. The fragrance of bacon and pastry filled the air. His stomach growled. It was 10 AM in London, and 4 PM in Louisiana. He had missed an entire day of food!

Josh wandered over to the kitchen island where a feast was laid out. "Who did the cooking?"

"Concierge delivered it an hour ago," Jonathan said.

Josh surveyed the plates of food. "Bro, who eats beans for breakfast?"

"Not me," Jason said. "Start my day with a cup of black coffee and beans? I'd clear out the precinct."

Josh loaded up his plate with two poached eggs and toast and a limp line up of bacon. "This bacon is not done."

"It's British," Holmes said.

"Hurry up and eat," Jonathan said, glancing at his watch. "You need to be at the airport in a couple of hours."

Josh stopped eating. "What?"

Steel's turquoise eyes glittered. "You're going back home with Jason."

Josh dropped his toast. "Okay, dude, and get blown out of the sky like you did?"

"That explosion wasn't intended for me."

"Yeah, and you're going to teach me that trick on how to escape a crashing airplane? Dude, my safest place is right here with you." Josh's face burned. "I'm not going back home with those homicidal maniacs running around Shreveport looking for me and Olivia."

"He has a point," Jason said

Steel glared at Jason. "This is not your decision."

"I think it is." Jason sipped coffee. "My life is on the line, too. I say we finish this thing right here. This guardian of yours, Maxine, is her name?"

"Max." Steel said.

"Seems to have everything under control. I say we do what she advises."

"Jonathan, Jason, and I have been through a lot together. I trust his judgment, dude."

"No."

Jason calmly put his coffee on the table and stood up, towering over Steel. "Am I your partner?"

Steel looked up at him and then at Josh. "Don't ask me, bro. I think you know the answer."

"Are we brothers?" Jason crossed his arms. "If you recall, Hu'ul made us adopted brothers. Our connection goes deeper than a mere partnership. Right?"

"Yes."

"But?"

"I'm still the boss."

"And, I have years of experience in law enforcement. Not to mention, I stood up to a Mexican cartel. This is a piece of cake compared to those psychopaths."

Steel glanced back and forth between Jason and Josh. "You think Josh should stay?"

"Yes. I'll look after him."

Steel stood up slowly. "That's my job."

Jason leaned across the table. "No, that's OUR job, Jonathan."

Josh got up and pushed his way between Jason and the table and put a hand on both of the men's chests. "Ladies, let's not fight over me. We're wasting time. We have to find Olivia and her mother."

The door to the suite opened, and one of the guards outside ushered in a limping, small-framed man in a long, black overcoat. A low riding fedora hid his face.

Steel stood up. "Ishido? And we have guards?"

Ishido pulled the fedora away from his dark hair. A

bandage covered his neck. His skin was far paler than Steel remembered. He had lost a lot of blood. Ishido sat in Steel's chair and reached into his inner coat pocket and took out a tablet. He tapped a few times on the tablet and the television mounted on the wall above the living room sofa came to life.

"Max wants you to see this video posted this morning by Thakkar."

The video started with a stirring visage of the universe and zoomed in toward the Milky Way Galaxy and into the solar system and finally to Earth. "Imagine a universe so vast, eternal, and infinite in size and scope." Thakkar's voice narrated. "Come with me as we surf the emptiness of space from the edges of our known universe down to our home, planet Earth." The image zoomed in on Earth, but the close-up image revealed an open field of bright green grass and, in its center, a circle of upright monoliths. "Behold the New Stonehenge. The center of a new universe that has no boundaries." Thakkar said. She slowly faded into view in the center of New Stonehenge. She wore a long, flowing white gown that rippled with iridescence. "In this new universe, there is no limit to knowledge, no limit to pain, no limit to pleasure. Here, you can find anything you can imagine. Forget the real universe. Forget the ordinary limits of your puny humanity. Embrace a transition from the known to the possible! Welcome to Numinocity! Here you will find the next level of human evolution as you leave behind the mundane physical existence and limitations of your bodies and brains. Here, in Numinocity, you will find a greater heaven than can ever be imagined. In two weeks, the Numinous Corporation will release the Third Eye Interface."

Thakkar held up a gleaming golden pair of goggles. "In partnership with our immersive Wi-Fi capability covering all of Europe, anyone can have access to unlimited data streaming as they enter into this new world. Reservations can be made online for your citizenship in Numinocity. And the cost. Nothing! The goggles and citizenship are free! Join today!" The image pulled back from New Stonehenge, revealing surrounding cities and kingdoms of all kinds of various appearances. As the image zoomed back, it showed starships in orbit around Earth and space stations. The pixelated images of the ships coalesced against a starry backdrop into the name "Numinocity."

Thakkar's video faded on the large screen television in the living room. While it was playing, they had all moved away from the table into the living room. Steel slumped onto the couch. The screen faded to black, and the face of Max appeared. Ishido tapped his tablet.

"We are videoconferencing with Max now." He said. Max's face filled the screen, her aristocratic features framed by her perfectly styled gray hair.

"Well, now we know what Thakkar is up to. Fortunately, Ishido salvaged the goggles from the train, and they are now in the hands of one of my associates in London. I am forwarding the findings to someone who can help us." Max said. "Jonathan, I have some updates."

Steel sat forward, his heart racing at this news from Thakkar. "I have an idea of what you're going to tell me. If Thakkar succeeds in getting millions to use her goggles, she can control all of Europe."

Josh sat beside him, and Birdsong paced behind the couch. "It's worse than the Matrix, dude."

Holmes sat in a winged back chair and ran his hands through his dark hair. "What do we do?"

"You have some visitors arriving. I'd like to include them in this conversation."

The door opened to the suite, and two of the guards stepped into the room. Dr. Monarch walked through the doors, followed by Olivia. "They are clean. We are still clearing the other." One of the guards said.

Olivia's eyes widened, and she ran across the room. Josh stood up and grabbed her in a hug. "Josh, you're okay!"

"You, too?"

"Yeah, no worse for wear," Olivia said as she released Josh and sat beside him on the couch.

Steel stood up slowly at the sight of Dr. Monarch. His face grew warm, and he gritted his teeth. "You! What did you do to me?"

Monarch held up her hands as she walked toward the couch. "I had to erase your memory, Jonathan. They had to think I was dead for Olivia's sake. And, Steven's."

Steel shook his head. "I'm talking about Africa." He rammed his finger into his temple. "My brain! What did you do to me?"

Monarch blinked. "You have to understand. Olivia has seizures. I was trying to perfect brain implants. Your father gave me the perfect laboratory to try out some of my implants."

Steel blinked away tears. He clenched his fists. "Do you know what I've been through?"

"No." She whispered. "But, you don't know what *we* have been through. My husband assassinated before my eyes. My son's hands getting mangled by a stray bullet. My daughter injured and now suffering from post-traumatic seizures! No, I have no idea what you have been through. But, you have no idea what a mother will do to help her children."

Steel paused and fought for control. "Do you know who I really am? Do you know my history, my past?"

Monarch shook her head. "No. I only learned you were your father's son when he talked about it being your birthday the day of the surgery. You are one screwed up family."

Steel looked away. "You have no idea." He wanted to lash out. He wanted to hurt her, hurt someone, make someone pay for his pain.

"Jonathan, calm down." Another voice came from the doorway. He looked up into the face of someone foreign, but with a voice he recognized. "Raven?"

Raven nodded, and Steel's heart raced. His breathing quickened. "I need some air."

Steel spun away from the room, his mind reeling, and went to the sliding doors and opened them onto a balcony. For a moment, he heard Max protest, but he ignored her. What did he care if a sniper ended it all right now?

24

"The loss of human identity is a weighty concern for Christians. We believe that human beings are the crown of creation, uniquely made in God's image. ... And though we view the image of God as an immaterial aspect of human nature, we do not think a human being is simply a spirit housed in a body—a "ghost in the machine." Instead, our spirit is intertwined with our physical bodies, and our physical bodies are an important part of our identity as humans."
"Humans 2.0" by Fazale R. Rana with Kenneth R. Samples

Vivian glanced impatiently at her wristwatch. Where was Snake? She had wasted hours and hours in her suite in London, waiting for their rendezvous. Now, she stood in a conference room at Numinous headquarters, awaiting a meeting with Thakkar. The woman had put her off over and over, but all Vivian had to do was to tell her the truth: that she and Snake had reached a truce and could help her with her little problem.

The door to the conference opened, and Snake appeared.

Her hair had exploded into a wild, strawberry red bush of tangles. Scratches carried the line of blood clots across her forehead. She was wearing a slightly doughy ancient dress, and she carried a copper-colored mechanical arm in her good hand.

"Scotland Yard thinks they are the best." She was mumbling. She paused and glanced at Vivian. "Where were you when I needed you? I thought you were going to help me with Steel?" She pulled the blouse off, exposing her upper torso and a tank top. The short stump of her missing arm glittered with blinking circuitry. She attached the copper-colored arm to the stump and flexed the fingers.

"My sources lost track of him after he left the safe house in Switzerland," Vivian said. "What happened to you?"

"Steel." She growled and flexed the arm. "This is an older prototype, unfortunately. They kept my newer one. Couldn't break into the evidence room and still manage to escape. So, back to old reliable."

Vivian smiled. "So, you ran into Steel?"

"And his ninja warrior friend."

Vivian raised an eyebrow. "Who?"

"Don't know. Someone I've never heard about. Quite formidable. I would have had him, too, if not for Steel. Where's my boss?"

"I've been waiting for over an hour." Vivian took a tablet from her purse. "I have had some success in the past few hours looking for Steel. Have you ever heard of Max?"

Snake tilted her head. "Who hasn't? She was behind Steel's escape."

Vivian nodded. "And, do you know why Steel was meeting with Max?"

Snake shook her head. "I don't care."

"I think your boss might care. He and Max were going to uncover a secretive dossier of assassinations and who paid for them." Vivian handed the tablet to Snake. "It's a bargaining chip for me. I want to take down your boss. I want to end this little project of hers. And, I think we can misdirect her toward Max and let Max take her down."

Snake looked up from the tablet. She picked up the blouse and shrugged into it as she regarded the tablet. "Why are you telling me this?"

"I sense that you are more of a free agent than you let on. I could use an ally like you. I have resources that make Thakkar's look like a piggy bank. Help me take her down, and you and I can start a very lucrative partnership." Vivian stood up and walked over to Snake. "I know damaged goods when I see them. There is a story behind that arm. I'm guessing Thakkar supplied you with your prosthetic but at a price?"

Snake drew a deep breath and ran her good hand through her wild hair. She stepped back from Vivian and giggled. "You are good, and I'll give you that." She raised her mechanical hand. "You can match this?"

"I can replace that. Wulf Pharmaceuticals has new technology on limb growth. Trade secret."

"So this is why Steel was meeting with Max? To get her hands on the dossier?" Snake licked her lips.

Suddenly, the door to the conference slid open. "Sorry to keep you waiting, Vivian, but I had a very important video announcement to make to the world." The robotic voice came from the opening door. Thakkar's stooped, deformed body sat in the wheelchair as it rolled into the room and came to rest beside a black disc similar to the one on the stage. "I've just announced the Third Eye Interface to the world."

"Then, you found the missing factor?" Snake said.

"No thanks to you!" The voice grated. Thakkar's holographic image appeared next to the crumpled figure of the woman. She glared at Vivian and then turned her attention to Snake.

"What are you doing bringing her into my office?"

"We've reached a truce." Snake said. "Vivian is going to help me track down Jonathan Steel so I can tie up loose ends."

Thakkar's image moved off of the black disc beside the woman's desk and seemed to solidify. This was no spiritual transformation of her original form. This was something new, something more substantial.

"How are you doing that? I don't see the projection sphere."

Thakkar stopped right in front of Vivian. Her skin seemed flawless and a dark chocolate color. Her eyes looked just a bit bigger than they should have been. Her hair floated around her face. "Nanotechnology. If I had known the other day that you had been inoculated with Boone's nanomemes, I could have saved some time."

Vivian laughed. "Boone? That's what you were missing? Well, it would have done you no good. My demons neutralized the nanomemes. They never affected me."

Thakkar sniffed. "I had to track down blood samples from that Indiana Jones rip off."

"Now, you have the final piece of the puzzle?" Snake asked.

Thakkar shook her head. "Not exactly. These nanomemes are short-lived. Defective. I still need Monarch's nanobites. If I can solve the problem of longevity, I can unleash my goggles on the world. World leaders. Corporate boards. Unlimited control!"

"Then there is something you might be interested in." Snake said as she glanced at Vivian. She handed her tablet to Thakkar. The woman's hand seemed to shutter for just a second as she took it, but maintained its solidity. Thakkar studied the image.

"What is this?"

"Raven. The assassin." Snake said. "Turns out, she has a dossier of every assassination and everyone who hired her."

Thakkar's image turned to static for a second, and the tablet fell from her hand. Snake caught it deftly with her cyborg hand. The image stabilized.

"Sorry. I'm still working on maintaining the image with biochemical surges in the body. In this case, excitement. If I had that dossier, I could use it to pressure reluctant world leaders to allow my technology into their country." Thakkar laughed and glanced at Vivian. "You found out this information?"

"Yes. A distraction. I'm still trying to stop you." Vivian said. "In the meantime, I have other priorities, other interests."

Thakkar stepped closer, and for a second, Vivian saw her skin crawl with the swirl of nanomemes. "Why?"

"I have my reasons. Let's just say I'm working more than one angle with the Master's permission. There's more at stake here than the Council, Thakkar." Vivian felt her stomach churn at the sight of the woman's unearthly face and the swirl of digitized light in her large eyes.

"Once I get my hands on that dossier, Vivian, nothing will stop me. Including you. Where is the dossier?" She looked back at Snake.

Snake grinned. "You're going to love this. According to Vivian's information, Steel has a key to a safety deposit box. And your old friend has the second key."

"Old friend?"

"Max?" Snake said it with great anticipation, an almost whisper, and she leaned toward Thakkar as the name left her lips.

Thakkar's image disappeared. Behind the desk, the crumpled, paralyzed figure of Thakkar twitched, and with great effort, she raised her head on a trembling set of atrophied neck muscles. Her eyes flew wide, and her lips parted. Words tumbled from those lips so long unused to speaking. "Killllll herrrrrrr!"

The hologram pinged back into solidity. Thakkar's pixelated image shifted with her warring emotions. She glared at

Vivian. "Pardon my emotional outburst. I'm getting control now. I see what you're doing, Vivian. Divide and conquer. Well, one thing at a time. Once I find Monarch and get my hands on her nanobites, then the goggles will be optimized, and I can go after Max. I can be patient." She pointed to her slumped body. "If there is one thing I understand, it is patience."

Vivian nodded. "Very well, I concede Thakkar. I will pursue my other interests. Unless Snake here is going to try and kill me first."

Thakkar's wild eyes blinked, and her breathing slowed as she regained control. "I'll let you live, for now, Vivian, if only to see the expression on your face when the Dark Council calls you to its next meeting and watches as I flay you alive."

Vivian raised an eyebrow. "With holographic fingernails? Don't ruin your manicure." She sauntered toward the door and leaned in toward Snake and whispered.

"There's more on the tablet if you're interested." She threw a kiss toward Thakkar and left the room.

25

Steel stood alone on the balcony, and a cold breeze chilled his skin. Thick, gray clouds hid the sun. He gazed out over the Thames River and across to the distant towers of Parliament and Big Ben. The door opened behind him, and Raven leaned against the railing.

"Didn't see that coming, did you?" She said.

"I thought I was way past surprises, Raven. I thought nothing could shock me anymore." He hissed.

"How do you like my new look?"

Steel glanced at her. "I can still see you behind the new skin job. The voice is the same. I thought you had changed. But Josh said you threatened to kill him and the others."

"I lost my memory thanks to the Captain but Monarch managed to restore it. I'm not his puppet right now. I'm different, Jonathan." She held up her hand. "No more strings attached. You were right. I found forgiveness and a second life. I didn't deserve it."

"Neither did I." Steel said. He turned to look at her. He could make out the thin, barely visible scars on her face. With makeup, you would never know she had surgery. "Problem is, I can't remember my past. And the woman responsible for erasing it is right inside that room. I can't forget *her* past."

"I've had a shocking memory return." Raven stepped closer to him. "I assassinated her husband. It was my bullet that ruined Olivia's life. I have to live with that memory now. Maybe amnesia isn't such a bad thing for you."

"You still have trouble remembering? Do you know who I am? Do you know anything about my past? Our past?" Steel pleaded.

Raven looked away and shook her head. "I can't remember much of it, either. Bits and pieces. I still see the faces of everyone I assassinated." She said. "But why I did it? Who hired me? No clue."

"It's all in your dossier?"

"Yes. Max said, you haven't retrieved it yet?"

"No." Steel reached into his shirt and pulled out the amulet. "You can have it back."

Raven put a hand on his. "No. This isn't over. I probably won't survive this time, Jonathan. Keep the amulet. You always survive."

Steel dropped the amulet back into his shirt, and his hand brushed his chest wall. "When you were dying, you said something about me, something about leaving a scar."

Raven squinted at him. "I did? Don't remember why I said that. I do remember saying something about thinking I had killed you, and you should have this huge knife scar on your chest. But, there isn't a scar, is there?"

Steel shook his head. "I seem to have good healing powers."

"Of course. Maybe due to the presence of all of your guardian angels?" Raven crossed her arms. "Come to think of it; I must have one of my own, or I would never have survived that fall in the caverns. Now, I have to come to grips with my past and help Monarch and Olivia find Steven."

"That's what's next for you?" Steel said.

"Technically, the world thinks I'm dead. Well, except for the Captain."

"Are you going after him?" Steel tensed.

"No. I'm going to work with Max to start making things right. Time to heal some old wounds." Raven stood up and looked him in the eye. "Besides, I know you'll take care of your father, won't you?"

Steel turned away. "I don't know anymore. I have to think about Josh. And we have to stop Thakkar."

"She's one of the demons, isn't she?"

"Number eight."

Raven looked down at his hand and then took it. Steel almost pulled away. She looked into his eyes. "Let's bury the past and focus on now."

Steel released her hand. "After we stop Thakkar."

Big Ben tolled its doleful chimes, and a sudden shard of sunlight burst through the clouds. The light caught the movement of the London Eye, and Steel glanced into the reflection. He was somewhere else.

STEEL WATCHED his father and the woman step up onto the platform to enter the pod like capsule of the London Eye. The huge observation wheel towered above him. It moved slowly as it rotated. Cash exchanged hands at the entrance to the next pod, and the operator pushed back the waiting crowd. The Captain and his friend would be alone on the pod. The bodyguard followed up the platform. Now was his chance.

He bolted up the metal framework of the ramp in front of him and hopped down directly in front of the bodyguard. He pushed off of the man's chest, and his shocked features disappeared as he fell back down the ramp behind him. The operator glanced once at Steel and reached for a red emergency stop button. But, another hand intercepted his.

"It's quite all right, young man. He is with me."

Steel straightened and looked into the eyes of his father. The bodyguard hustled up from the ramp, and the Captain put a hand out to stop him.

"I'll be fine, Finley. Let him have his say." The Captain motioned into the open door of the pod as it was slowly moving away across the boarding platform. "After you, son."

Steel's teeth grated at the sound of that name, and he stepped into the cool interior of the pod. It was cocoon-shaped and transparent. The door to the pod slid shut behind the Captain. The woman sat on a metal bench in the center of the pod that normally could hold up to two dozen.

"Is this your son?" She asked. She wore the same type of long dress and draping cowl she had worn to the theater. She stood up gracefully. Her face was beautiful and timeless. Her skin was dark. Her long, black hair was tucked into the folds of the cowl, but Steel knew if she lowered the cowl, the long tresses would cascade down the woman's shoulders. There was an unmistakable air of dignity and power and eternal beauty about her. The only thing that marred her face was the totally flat white opaque set of eyes that.

"You're a Vitreomancer." Steel whispered.

"I asked you to wear your contacts." The Captain said.

"I am many things, young man." The woman ignored the comment. "But, you are not here to speak to me. You are here to speak to your father. I will not interfere." She sat back down and turned her blind eyes toward the far horizon where the buildings of London gleamed in the midday sun. Light sparkled and reflected off the moving waters of the Thames.

Steel spun and felt his anger surge. The Captain smiled. "We have thirty minutes, son. And, remember that this pod is totally transparent. Whatever you do to me, they will see below. And, there

is no escape. The police will be waiting for you when the pod returns
to the loading platform."

"You planned this, didn't you?" Steel realized in a flood of cold
hatred. "You planned this whole thing!"

"Of course, son. You should know me by now." The Captain took
out his pipe and placed it between his perfect teeth. A speaker hissed
in the ceiling. "Sir, there is no smoking on the attraction." A voice
issued from the speaker.

The Captain laughed. "I won't light it up, young man." He gestured to
the ceiling of the pod. "Bear in mind, we are under constant surveillance.
Yes, I made sure you would come for me in a controlled environment." He
sucked on his pipe, and his turquoise eyes glittered in the sunlight.

Steel swallowed and tried to control his fury. "You are always in
control, aren't you?"

"Yes." The Captain said around the pipe stem. He took the hat off
of his head and ran his hand through his short hair. "Why you
haven't realized it by now, is beyond me. You know I have considered
all eventualities and have planned accordingly."

Steel felt something cold on his neck. He looked slowly over his
shoulder. The tip of a stiletto rested against the side of his neck from
the woman's hand hidden in the sleeve of her blouse.

"Do not harm your father." She hissed.

He raised his hands in surrender and slowly backed away from
the two of them. He tried to calm his nerves and find enough saliva to
speak.

"Do you know what this man has done to me?" He whispered.
"He put something in my head while I was in a prison camp in
Sudan."

"I know." The woman lowered her hand. "My former, uh,
associate was there to make certain the surgery was done properly."

Steel felt the world tilt again. He glanced at his father. "I just
want you to tell me why."

The Captain stepped toward him and put his hat back on his

head. "You have no idea who and what you are. You have no idea about the plans that are unfolding around you. All you have to do is to be patient, son. In time, these plans will manifest themselves, and you will understand." He glanced furtively at the woman. "And, when that happens, you will see me in a new light."

Steel shook his head. "I don't think so. You've hated me ever since I became a Christian. You hated me all this time because you can't understand what it is like to be faithful to God. Instead, you pledge your allegiance to Satan and his white-eyed ghouls." He gestured toward the woman. "Does she control you? Huh?"

The Captain blinked, and he looked away. "Of course not."

Steel smiled. "That's it, isn't it? She's in charge. Not you. And, you can't stand it. What does it feel like to be the one in subjugation, Dad? What does it feel like to have someone else pull your strings?"

The Captain's face reddened, and he lurched forward. He struck out with the back of his right hand and caught Steel on the cheek. The strength behind the blow was incredible, and Steel tumbled backward onto the floor. The Captain towered over him as he rubbed his stinging face.

"Sir, is there a problem?" The speaker hissed.

"Just a family dispute, young man. This is my son, and we're having a bit of a discussion." The Captain said toward the speaker. He glanced at the woman. "Can't you do something about that?"

The woman nodded and gestured toward the speaker. Smoke hissed from the grill. "They will think it malfunctioned." She said.

Steel pushed up into a sitting position. "It's true, then."

The Captain leaned toward him. "You have no idea how much danger you are in, son. I am the only thing keeping you alive."

"Are you going to send Raven after me?" Steel said.

The Captain gasped and glanced toward the woman. She lifted an eyebrow.

"He knows too much." Her voice was melodious and musical.

"He knows nothing." The Captain said through gritted teeth. "He was unlucky enough to be there the night Raven took that man.

That's all. He can prove nothing. And, we both know that Raven will never talk."

The woman stepped toward them, and her shadow fell across Steel's stinging face. "Raven is unreliable. She hesitated and should have taken out the girl, too. She has a weakness. She is unreliable. We should soon take her out of the equation. Her usefulness is drawing to a close."

The Captain straightened and looked away. "How should we handle it?"

The woman's lifeless white eyes turned in Steel's direction. "Your son will kill her for us. It is ironically fitting. And, you know how much I love irony." The woman's hand played along the Captain's arm. He stiffened for a moment and then seemed to relax.

"Very well. Son, you will kill Raven for me." He whispered.

Steel snorted. "Right!" The Captain stepped closer, and his turquoise eyes gleamed with malice.

"Listen very closely, son. I am about to say something. It is a phrase. When you hear it, you will be, uh, indisposed for a while, and when you come to yourself, you will not remember what has happened in the interim. So, let me explain something to you very clearly." He drew a deep breath and blinked.

"Find Raven. She is a danger to you and to everyone you care for. It is true that, at times, she has worked for me. But, there are times Raven has a weakness; a failing in her judgment. I believe it is the soft, whispering voice of your God she hears, calling her back from the precipice." The Captain frowned. "But, she is too far gone. You, on the other hand, still have a chance. I want you to remember what I am about to say. Stop tracking me. I am not the answer to your dilemma. First, you will kill Raven. I will make sure you find the desire and ability to complete that task."

Steel gritted his teeth. "You're talking about the thing in my head."

The Captain laughed. "It is far more than just a thing, son. Now, take care of Raven and then forget me. Then, there is another task.

After I mention this phrase, I will give you a name. You will pursue and find that person with all you might. I will be waiting for you once you have completed these two tasks."

"And, if I don't?" His mouth was dry with fear.

"You will have no choice with Raven. The matter with the other person is more complicated. If you find that person and you do not tell me, then I will hunt you down. I will find you." The Captain paused and glanced over his shoulder at the woman as if making sure she heard what he was about to say.

"I will torture you, and when I am done, despite the fact you are my son, I will kill you." The man's face was red with anger. He blinked again and stepped back. He drew a deep breath as Big Ben tolled in the distance. He opened his mouth, and he spoke.

26

"Jonathan! Jonathan!"

Steel shook his head in confusion and looked into the concerned eyes of Jason Birdsong. "Are you okay?"

Steel felt the cold iron bars of the balcony railing cut into his back. He had slumped down against them. He climbed to his feet. "Another flashback."

"Max wants to talk to us all," Birdsong said.

Raven took Steel's arm. "How bad was it?"

He looked at her. "Very. But, I might have learned something very important." He threw aside the curtains and walked through the open sliding doors into the suite. Max frowned at him from the television.

"You could have been identified," Max said.

Steel rubbed his head. The flashback had been disturbing and confusing. His father was involved with a Vitreomancer? "Sorry, Max."

"Everyone have a seat, and let's get everyone on the same page," Max said. "We don't have long before Thakkar saturates Europe with these goggles, and we still don't completely understand what her true agenda is."

"Something to do with transhumanism." Dr. Monarch said. "That is what her Corporation is all about, and that is what she is trying to achieve before she dies."

Holmes lifted a hand. "I co-authored a book on transhumanism. Transhumanists believe that with the increase in technology, human beings will one day move beyond our mortal bodies into some kind of scientifically advanced condition."

"I remember that book," Birdsong said. "My kids at church read it. It was way over my head."

"What's so wrong with downloading your brain into a cyborg?" Josh said. "Dude, you could live forever."

"Josh, we have a soul, a spirit that is something far more than just biochemical impulses coursing through neurons." Holmes said. "Transhumanists think they can achieve mind uploading by scanning and mapping critical brain features. Then, with these brain maps, there is a hope that digitally encoded data to a computer system. Once uploaded, then some type of brain simulation software would use that data to emulate the uploaded mind."

"Emulate is the keyword," Max said. "What happens to the original mind? I have read and studied some of these theories. This process seems more like neuronal cloning than actual transfer. But, these doubts disappear because people are desperate for immortality. The transhumanism element is just the hook for Thakkar to get people involved. With these goggles, she already has the video gamers. But, by emphasizing transhumanism, she gets a much broader demographic."

Dr. Monarch was studying her tablet and stood up. "I've got it!"

"What?" Max said.

"Your associate just finished the analysis of the goggles and has forwarded me the results. Thakkar is using nanotechnology with the goggles. That explains the deeper, more immersive ability of the device." Monarch glanced at Holmes. "And, you were the source, Dr. Holmes."

"Me?"

"You gave blood after your ordeal in Arizona. According to these hacked archives, Thakkar appropriated one of your blood samples and extracted some of the residual nanomemes given to you by Boone." Monarch walked over and looked down at Holmes. "Maybe you could tell us a little more about these nanomemes?"

"Something Boone injected in us before we went to, uh, our final destination," Holmes said.

Monarch looked at Olivia. "So, what Josh told Olivia is true?"

"You can tell him, Dr. Monarch. Tell Steel." Josh said. "He will NOT be happy about it."

Steel looked back and forth between Josh and Monarch. "Tell me what?"

"Bro, she's been following you for a while. She knows everything. She knows about Jerusalem. She knows about the time machine."

Steel glared at Monarch. "What is this all about?"

Monarch lifted her hands in a defensive posture. "Okay, so I've kept a close eye on you. I had to know about the long-term effects of my surgery."

Olivia stood up and came to her mother. "Mom, it's time for the truth."

Monarch closed her eyes in resignation. "Okay. The truth is, I'm scared. Someone paid Raven to assassinate my husband, and I think it might have been the Captain. And, I knew you were pursuing the Captain. Jonathan, the safest place for me, Olivia, and Steven is as close to you as possible."

Steel wanted to get mad; he wanted to rage, but his mind was so confused. "I don't know what to say."

"Bro, that's a first," Josh said.

Birdsong punched Josh in the shoulder. "Not cool."

"We can dwell on personal problems later," Max said. "What have you learned, Dr. Monarch?"

Monarch sighed and turned back to her tablet. "Dr. Holmes was injected with nanomemes."

"They were supposed to deteriorate after seventy-two hours," Holmes said.

"There were remnants of the nanomemes in his blood samples. Thakkar got those from him and fashioned a form of nanotechnology to enhance her goggles. If what Dr. Holmes says is true, then she wasn't able to create stable nanomemes. The ones associated with her goggles last only about six hours before the body destroys them."

"Well, that ruins the usefulness of the goggles, doesn't it?" Birdsong said.

"It gets worse." Monarch studied her tablet. "Turns out once the body destroys these down and dirty nanomemes, it develops antibodies to them. If you give a second dose, your risk of allergic reaction increases. Her own research estimates that after a third dose, the user will have a fatal anaphylactic reaction."

Josh laughed. "Problem solved. The goggles are useless."

"Not so fast," Olivia said. "Remember what I told you about Steven? We think he has developed some kind of nanotechnology that lasts. After all, he has been wearing his version of the goggles for days now while he is in Numinocity."

"From what I've been able to glean from some of Steven's encrypted notes." Monarch said. "Thakkar is looking for Steven. He came to Europe a couple of weeks ago with the intent of breaking into Numinocity."

"Why?" Steel asked.

Monarch sighed, glanced at Olivia, and settled onto the couch. "To find out who paid Raven to kill his father."

Raven had wandered about the room, and she froze. "I don't know who paid me on that one case."

"Could it be in your dossier?" Max asked.

"Possibly," Raven said. "There a few cases for which I cannot recall who hired me."

"Why does Steven think Thakkar would know?"

Monarch paused and glanced at Steel. "Well, most of you in this room know that Jonathan Steel's father hired me to perform surgery on his own son. I've often wondered what his motives were." She stood up and crossed to sit by Steel. "Jonathan, do you know that your father is a member of the Dark Council?"

Steel felt like a knife pierced his chest. He stiffened. "What?"

"I'm sorry to tell you, but the Captain is a member of the Council."

"Dude, that means he has a demon," Josh said.

The television image wavered and suddenly split into two screens. The right-hand screen was filled with static and slowly cleared. "I think I can clear this up." Vivian D'Arbonne's face appeared on the screen.

Max stiffened on her side of the screen and spoke to someone off-screen. Vivian waved a hand. "Don't bother Maxie, baby. I've overridden your controls thanks to some of Thakkar's own technology. And, before we go any further, let it be known I'm here to take down the bestie, okay? So, we are technically on the same side."

Steel stood up and strode over to the screen. "Vivian, what do you know?"

"Sorry, baby, but remember I told you I didn't know the Captain was your father. Here's a sad fact. He's on the Council. And, he is numero uno. He told me he was the number one demon. But, I'm not so sure he is the one telling me the truth." Vivian sighed. "He also said he could assume multiple identities. Either way, your father is dangerous even if he is not on the council. And if he isn't, then we know that number one can assume anyone's identity."

Gasps filled the air from the rest of the room, and Steel shook his head. "I'm afraid it is worse than that."

Raven came over to him and put a hand on his arm. "You're awfully calm."

"I had a couple of flashbacks since arriving in London." He turned and looked at Raven. His gaze drifted to Monarch and Olivia. "I was there when Raven shot your father. I was the man on the sidewalk. I had been stalking my father."

Olivia stood up and came to her mother's side. Monarch hugged her. "You?"

Steel nodded. "There was another flashback just a moment ago. I followed my father onto the London Eye. He was meeting with a woman." Steel turned and looked at the image of Max. "Max, she had white eyes. And, she seemed to be in control of my father."

Max put a hand to her mouth. Vivian swore.

"He is working with the Vitreomancers." Steel said.

"Thakkar told me she had nothing to do with hiring Raven and nothing to do with chasing Josh and his girlfriend. Don't you get it? The Vitreomancers are after the goggles too. They are the ones who tried to kill Josh." Vivian said.

Olivia pushed away from her mother. "And, they hired Raven to kill my father? Why?"

Monarch collapsed onto the couch. "Oh my!"

Olivia glanced at her. "What?"

"Your father's research in South America. The protovirus."

"What are you talking about?"

Monarch pointed a finger at Max. "You have the files, I bet. Check them out. The protovirus he was researching dates back centuries, possibly thousands of years. In the Amazon basin.

Hidden away in caves untouched by human hands. He often told me the protovirus was the most efficient machine on the planet. He once said it was God's nanotechnology."

"Boone never said where he got the nanomemes from. I bet if we check, we'll find a connection with Boone and—"

"Dr. Sno." Max said triumphantly. "Just found the connection. Steel, you mentioned in your conversations you recalled Sno."

"What conversations?"

Max shrugged. "The ones I monitored. Back home."

Steel raised an eyebrow. "You and Monarch? We'll talk about this later. Yes, Dr. Sno was present when Dr. Monarch operated on me. He was blind." Steel drew a deep breath. "Of course, he wasn't! He was a Vitreomancer."

"And he is married to this woman." An image filled Max's screen. It was the same woman in Steel's flashback.

"That's the one that met with my father." Steel said. "Who is she?"

"Dr. Sno's wife is all we know. Very secretive. Seldom seen in public. But, I would bet we are looking at a high ranking member of the Vitreomancers."

Birdsong stopped pacing. "So, let me get this straight. There are two demon councils? The regular bad demons and the ones with white eyes?"

"Yes," Vivian said. "And the fact that the Captain is involved with both factions shouldn't be a surprise. He's been playing us all."

Monarch sniffed. "They killed my husband so they could steal his research? Research he had never shared with me?"

"It would seem so," Max said. "And young Steven must have found some of his father's research and developed his own version of the nanomemes."

Steel raised a hand and walked in front of the television.

"Stop! My head is about to explode with all of these new revelations. My pursuit of my father can wait. I can sort out all of these implications later. Right now, we have the problem of Thakkar's launch of these new interfaces. If these new goggles get into the hands of thousands,"

"Millions is more like it," Vivian said.

"Okay, millions, then what? What is her ultimate goal?" Steel turned and stared at Vivian's image.

"Imagine pulling a human being into a virtual world that is real because of the ability of these nanomemes to create an out of body experience. So real, you can no longer tell the difference between reality and Numinocity. What happens to you in the real world? You starve. You die. And sweet old number eight harvests the soul." Vivian said. "And, there is more. Thakkar can share her brain with a solid 'body.'"

"What?" Monarch said. "Solid body? What do you mean?"

"She is using an advanced form of nanotechnology to form a solid avatar into which she can project her spirit? I'm not much of a scientist."

"But, that would require enormous levels of power!" Monarch said.

"Sunstones." Steel said. "Cobalt used sunstones to power his portal. They were of supernatural origin."

"And, Boone used sunstones to power his time machine," Vivian said.

"What?" Steel glanced up in surprise. "That explains a lot."

"Power and principalities," Holmes said. "*For our struggle is not against flesh and blood, but against the rulers, against the authorities, against the powers of this dark world and against the spiritual forces of evil in the heavenly realms.* That's from Ephesians. All of these supposed technological advances rely on nothing more than supernatural powers that create the illusion of progress. Once again, the promise of transhumanism is bankrupt in the hands of Thakkar."

"Then, Numinocity is one big fake-out?" Birdsong said.

"Oh, no." Monarch said. "There is science behind Numinocity all right. These goggles directly stimulate the brain to help create the illusion of reality. The real question is, how do these goggles create a shared illusion? It's like pulling all of us into the same dream. There is something there that smacks of a metaphysical construct."

"You mean supernatural," Holmes said.

Monarch frowned. "I don't believe in the supernatural, Dr. Holmes."

"Well, you better change your mind quickly, Dr. Monarch, because the supernatural influence is staring us right in the face." Steel pointed to Vivian. "This Council of Darkness is real, and the pain and suffering they cause are real. I'm just now getting a glimpse of the inside workings, and, frankly, it scares me to death."

"Okay, enough of the philosophical arguments." Vivian interrupted. "This situation is for more complex than you think. Thakkar wants Raven's dossier."

"What?" Max said. "Why?"

"Imagine how this technology could influence certain people of power? Imagine the leverage Thakkar would have over anyone who has hired Raven for assassinations?"

"She wouldn't even need my dossier for that," Raven said. "If these goggles work as well as we fear, all she has to do is trap someone in Numinocity and make it appear to be the real world. She could manipulate circumstances prompting them to make the choices she chooses. Her ability to manipulate key powerful people would be fearsome."

"Then, we have to stop her." Steel said. "Number one priority no matter who else is involved, including the Vitreomancers."

"I agree," Vivian said. "I have a mission to stop her. We are on the same side here. Although, I must admit, I have ulterior motives as you would suspect. But, for now, our goals are the same. I have a connection with one of Thakkar's inside people. I believe you met her, Jonathan. Red hair. Snake tattoos?"

"Snake?" Steel hissed. "Vivian, she is more dangerous than you!"

"Honey child, I doubt that," Vivian said. She pouted her lips. "Oh, is little ole Jonathan afraid something will happen to me?"

Steel fought to control his breathing. "Vivian, you had a chance to turn away from your lifestyle. I don't know what demons you are associated with right now, but you know what it was like to be free of their influence. You saw the Savior. You were there. You remember, don't you? You have a chance to make things right."

Vivian froze, and for a moment, her features were soft and almost yielding. "What did Festus say to Paul? Almost I am persuaded? Jonathan, if I give up my source of power, then Thakkar and her personal assassin will take me out in a heart-beat. For my own protection and the sake of our conjoined efforts, I have to keep the status quo." She raised an eyebrow. "I understand your father better now. Sorry, but I have to run. I have things to do and places to be. I'll work things on my end to slow down Thakkar, but taking her down is up to Team Steel. Ta ta!" The image disappeared.

Steel's closed fists thudded against his thighs. "I am so tired of all of this!" He screamed. His head pounded, and his face grew warm. He felt a hand on his arm.

"Bro, Jonathan, chill," Josh said. "We've been in worse situations before, haven't we?"

Steel turned to his adopted son. Tears filled his eyes. "Josh, I try, and I try, and I try, and still they come. I don't know how much longer I can go on like this."

Josh nodded and pulled Steel close. He wrapped his arms

around Steel's shoulders, and Steel surrendered to the inevitable.

Olivia felt her phone vibrate in her pocket. It was one of the retail phones her mother kept for emergencies. She had activated it once she had arrived at her mother's lab. She glanced at the screen. It was a text message.

"Reaching out. Steven." It said. Her eyes grew large with excitement, and another message came across. "Don't tell Mom. Just come to this address and get me."

Olivia texted back. "Why not tell Mom?"

"She's busy. I know what is going on. Following you around. Sending Mom some information to hack into Numinocity. Need you to come get me now!"

Olivia glanced at the address in the text and copied it into her map program. She slipped out of the living room into the foyer and grabbed her backpack. One-touch to the forehead of the guards and she could be out of the building in less than five minutes. She had to save her brother!

Max suggested they take an hour's break and let everyone calm down. Steel's stomach growled, and he realized he hadn't eaten any breakfast. He chewed listlessly on a dry smoked salmon sandwich. Raven sat across from him next to Josh. Jason sat beside him. Holmes sat on the other side.

"I am fine." He said through a mouth full of sandwich.

"Dude, you had an emotional breakdown," Josh said.

Steel glared at him. "I don't do that."

"Wait a minute," Birdsong said. "You had an emotion?

Other than fury?" Birdsong crossed his arms and sat back. "I'm disappointed. That means you're only human."

Steel glanced at him and chugged some water. "Okay, that's enough!"

Raven leaned forward across the table. "We'll figure this out together, Jonathan. We'll find out what is going on with your father and the Vitreomancers and the Dark Council once we stop Thakkar." She leaned back. "I have an ax or two to grind with the Captain."

Steel finished his sandwich as Monarch walked up to the table. "Has anyone seen Olivia? I thought maybe she had taken a nap. She does that sometimes to keep her seizures under control, but she is not in any of the bedrooms."

One of the guards sitting by the front door stood up and looked around. "What happened?"

Monarch crossed to the man. "You okay?"

"She touched my forehead and told me to take a nap." He rubbed his forehead.

Steel bolted up from the table. "The foyer!"

Monarch opened the doors. Both guards were tucked in fetal positions asleep in front of the elevator. "No! Olivia, what did you do?"

The television squawked, and Birdsong stood up slowly. "Guys, I think we may have an answer." He pointed to the face filling the screen.

Dr. Sultana Thakkar, at least her avatar, smiled warmly from the screen. "May I speak to Dr. Monarch?"

Monarch ran over to the television. She motioned for everyone else to stay out of sight of the camera. "How did you?"

"Oh, really?" Thakkar chuckled. "Max is nothing compared to Numinous Corporation. Let me show you something."

Her face faded away, revealing a bizarre scene. Tall monolithic slabs of stone stood in a circle around two slabs on the ground. "New Stonehenge," Thakkar said.

The image zoomed in, and six figures reclined in alcoves in the upright stones. One woman and five men dressed in dark jumpsuits each wore a metallic helmet encompassing their entire head. The image shifted and revealed a figure clothed in mummy-like wrappings reclining on one of the central slabs. On the adjacent slab, Dr. Sultana Thakkar propped herself up into a seductive pose. She wore a silky top and matching pants.

"I have six warrior-priests ready to enter Numinocity to search for your son, Dr. Monarch." She gestured to the upright figures.

"Of course, what you are seeing is the stylized version of my reality. Let me show you the real images."

The image swiveled to focus on one of the warrior priests and faded into a very mundane image of six men and women clad in surgical scrubs leaning into recessed alcoves in upright towers similar to the monoliths. Each person wore a pair of Thakkar's goggles.

"We also have a visitor."

The image turned back to the center. In place of the Thakkar avatar, the crumpled, vulnerable body of Dr. Sultana Thakkar lay on one of the stones. As the image moved to the other stone, Monarch gasped. Olivia lay on the other stone, rigid, and unmoving.

"I have accessed your daughter's implants, Dr. Monarch." Thakkar's face reappeared in place of the images. "She is currently paralyzed as we wait for her seizure medication to diminish. I believe her next dose will be due in six hours. Six hours, Dr. Monarch, until your daughter develops status epilepticus. Six hours for you to locate your son and have him turn over his secrets within Numinocity. Six warrior-priests are hunting him now. All he has to do is to reveal himself, and I'll see that Olivia gets her next dose. Right now, I've deactivated her stimulator, and reset it to its lowest settings. That won't be enough to keep her from having seizures. When you get ready to tell me how to find your son, just give me a call on your cell phone."

Monarch's phone dinged. "I just texted you my phone number. Oh, and another little thing I need. Raven's dossier. I think Max may be able to help with that." The screen went blank.

———

27

S teel paused before the window and wiped away the grime. His vantage point was west up the Thames River toward the Shard. The building glittered and gleamed in the setting sun just beyond Tower Bridge. After the call from Thakkar, Ishido had silenced everyone. He had led them through the kitchen to a servant's entrance, never once notifying the now alert guards posted in the foyer. They descended in a raggedy service elevator to the underground garage. Ishido motioned to a dilapidated old produce truck. They all climbed inside and never spoke a word. Ishido huddled briefly with Monarch and then locked them all in the back of the truck motioning for them to be completely silent. Steel sat in the dark confines of the produce truck listening to the quiet sobbing of Dr. Monarch. Of all people, Raven sat next to her with an arm around her shoulders. What a strange world they had arrived in!

The truck had ground to a halt, and Ishido had hustled them out of the truck. They found themselves in a dank, underground tunnel that led away into darkness. Dr. Monarch took the lead, and they marched quietly behind her. She led the way up a rickety set of rusty stairs into a brick-lined basement. Up more stairs until they arrived in an open chamber with windows looking out over the Thames. A sign along the river listed the property for sale with a phone number.

Dr. Monarch pulled Steel away from the window and pointed to a far rusted metal door. She opened the door with a press of her palm on a tarnished brass plate. It popped open and cool, antiseptic tainted air blew over them. Monarch led them down another set of clean, metal stairs and into a large, spacious room. Lights came on illuminating her extensive laboratory filled with gleaming equipment and a wall covered in computer monitors. She motioned to Ishido, and he pulled out his cell phone and the tiny attachment for sensing any monitoring bugs. He smiled and nodded.

"You are still clean, Dr. Monarch. We can talk now."

Monarch slumped into a chair. "Okay, sorry for the deception. There must be a mole in Max's operations, and Ishido and I agreed we had to get away from the hotel. Not even Max knows the location of my laboratory."

"I was here earlier, and you never told me where we were," Raven said.

"It's an old grain warehouse on the Thames. People are converting these old warehouses into homes. I listed it for sale but never answer the calls. I converted the basement into my laboratory. The tunnel runs parallel to Thames Link to Surrey Water in the Rotherhithe area. Now, we get to work."

She turned to her computer monitors. "We have to do two things. One, we have to locate Thakkar's 'New Stonehenge.' From the images, it is a real place mirroring the virtual site in Numinocity. That's where Olivia will be. Second, we have to find my son. I've been looking for him for weeks, and so far, no luck."

Josh stood beside her. "How did Olivia get duped into this?"

"Good question. She had one of our retail phones. She must

have gotten a text because I never heard it ring." Monarch's fingers played over the keyboard and lines of code scrolled through a terminal window.

"Her stimulator generator," Josh said. "She communicated with you through it."

"That's right." She began typing furiously. "If I can access that connection and it has to be tenuous at best, I might locate her."

"But, Thakkar said she had turned off her stimulator," Holmes said.

"She turned off the programming. You can't shut down the simulator. It's battery-driven. If I can just find the location." A set of numbers appeared in the window. "Got it!"

Monarch copied the numbers and pasted them into a mapping program. The images of the globe appeared, spun, and zoomed in. "Paris, France?" Monarch stood up. "That's impossible!"

Monarch tapped on the keyboard, and the map turned into a street-level image. They were looking at a typical three-story French house on a typical French street in Paris. "I don't get it," Josh said. "She didn't have time to take her to France."

Monarch gasped. "Oh my!" She went back to her terminal program and scrolled through the programming. She sobbed and put a hand to her mouth. "Oh, Olivia! Why?"

Steel put a hand on Monarch's shoulder. "What is it?"

"She copied over her location with a new code. She must have gotten it from the phone. From a real message from Steven. What are the chances she got both a fake message from Thakkar and a real message from her brother?"

"What are you talking about?"

Monarch pointed to the image of the Parisian house. "That's where Steven is. She sacrificed her location to tell me his."

Dr. Monarch started rushing, packing up equipment into a portable storage container. She pointed to a cabinet. "Raven, get goggles from that cabinet over there."

Raven crossed to the cabinet and opened it. A dozen goggles hung in charging cradles. "What are we doing?"

Monarch closed her equipment case. "I'm going after Steven. Ishido, can you get me to Paris in the next six hours without notifying Max?"

Ishido blinked and sighed. "I have some contacts here in the UK. I have to be careful because some of them are looking for me. There are some commercial trains through the Chunnel I can get us on."

"Wait a minute." Steel said. "What about Thakkar?"

"That's where you come in." Monarch took the goggles from Raven. "We have to find Olivia from within Numinocity."

Raven handed Steel a pair of goggles, and he looked at like it was a scorpion. "Wait a minute!"

Monarch paused and took him by the arm. "Steel, look at me. We don't have much time. Less than five hours. Olivia gave up, giving us her location so I can find Steven. No one can remove Steven from his goggles safely but me. Believe me, I would rather go into that virtual world and find Olivia. But, if Thakkar gets those nanomemes, it's over. You know that."

Steel glared at her. "You've always been able to make the tough choice with ease."

Monarch looked away. "I have to choose between my son and my daughter, Jonathan. It's never easy."

Josh took a pair of goggles. "Tell us what we need to look for."

Steel jerked the goggles out of his hands. "Oh, no! You're not putting those things on."

Josh tilted his head. "Dude, when's the last time you played a video game? Like ever?"

Birdsong took a pair of goggles. "He's right, Jonathan. Much as I hate to tell you, we need his expertise. But, he's not going alone."

Josh glanced at Birdsong. "You've played video games?"

"Bro, I'm only 28. I grew up on PS2! Ever heard of a Macintosh game called Marathon?"

Josh gasped. "You played Marathon?"

"All three versions from beginning to end."

"Now, hold on." Steel said. "This is dangerous, right Monarch?"

"Only if you take the goggles off in the real world. You can't die in the virtual world. You can't be killed. I have a feeling you will 'feel' quite a bit, but it's not real. But, if you take off the goggles while in the virtual world, it would mess up your brain. Maybe kill you."

Raven nodded. "And what about our implants." She pointed to Steel.

Monarch nodded. "That's what I'm counting on. If these limited nanomemes work as I think they should, they will interface with your implants and give you an extra advantage."

"I think that already happened." Steel said.

"What?"

"On the train when I used the goggles to talk to Thakkar, I unconsciously summoned some kind of red wave of death, I guess you could call it. It shut her down."

Monarch's mouth fell open. "That set of goggles didn't have nanomemes, Jonathan. You did that on your own."

"But how?"

"If what Thakkar says is true about the out of body experience." Holmes stepped up to them. "Then we may be in some weird territory. Scientists also think that area is the seat of the soul. Studies done by a cardiologist in Scandinavian countries led him to suggest there is a kind of 'receiver' for the soul in the brain. Like a receiver for a radio wave inside a radio. The soul is attached to an area of the brain, and when it is dormant, the soul is free to, well, wander about."

"Oh, great," Raven said. "Sounds like a bad séance."

"Or bad science," Birdsong said.

"If it is true." Holmes went on. "Then there may be a spiritual component to all of this. Which is why Thakkar is so interested. Imagine souls floating around, waiting to be plucked by demons. If that is so, then Steel's soul, his connection to God, may have been the source of his defense against Thakkar."

"Or, one of my guardian angels?" Steel said.

"Exactly!" Holmes exclaimed. "That could be your advantage. If the Lord is on our side, and I believe He is, then we have an advantage Thakkar is unaware of."

"If, bro," Josh said. "That's a big if."

Holmes chuckled. "Look who is doubting now. Weren't you the one that was saved by an angel in green surgical scrubs named Dude?"

Josh nodded. "Point taken."

"Okay, Holmes, you and Ishido look in that storage room. There are some collapsible cots. Lay them out in a circle with one end pointing toward the center of the circle. If all of you go in, then you will have a team. You can make your way through Numinocity."

"And what are we looking for?"

"New Stonehenge." Monarch said.

Ishido and Holmes appeared pushing a cart loaded with collapsed cots. "Who will be in the lab?"

"You will." Monarch folded a laptop and slid it into a backpack. "You've been exposed to nanomemes. These are my goggle prototypes. But, after I found out about the nanomeme connection, I interfaced these goggles with Boone's nanomemes."

Steel put a hand on Monarch's arm. "Where did you get those nanomemes?"

Monarch's face paled. "Okay, I made them for Boone. Technically, I adapted them from nanotechnology from the Manning Institute of Nanotechnology. I had no idea what he was going to do with them! I used his financing to try and come up with nanomemes that might save my daughter."

"You just keep digging yourself deeper and deeper, don't you?" Steel said.

"Oh, and what would you do to save Josh? What did you do to try and save Theophilus Nosmo King? Don't judge me, you hypocrite!"

"Okay, enough of this." Holmes stepped between them. "We can point fingers later. Right now, Dr. Monarch, why can't I go in with Steel?"

Monarch stepped back and drew a deep calming breath. "You might have a fatal allergic reaction, Dr. Holmes. These are the same nanomemes from Boone. Unlike Thakkar's, they will last seventy-two hours. In theory. And someone has to stay here and monitor their actions."

Holmes opened his mouth, and his phone warbled. Everyone froze. Monarch's eyes widened. "You have a cell phone?"

Holmes pulled the phone out of his pants' pocket. "I forgot about this phone. If it's Max, no problem. I have a security app."

"That doesn't mean the signal can't be detected!" Monarch said.

Holmes glanced at the phone screen. "It's Nigel Hampton."

Monarch pushed him back across the room into a phone booth sized metal cage. "Get in here and answer it. It's a type of Ferriday cage. It will let the signal in and out but will disguise the location."

She shut him into the cage, and he answered the phone by putting it on the speaker. "Dr. Holmes."

"Dr. Holmes, this is Dr. Nigel Hampton. I'm growing quite

impatient, my young friend." A rich British accent came over the speaker.

"I'm sorry, sir. But, the security at the airport refused to release the crates."

"Oh, pish posh, Holmes. I have the crates. They were delivered this afternoon. Finally. What I need is access to the crates, my boy."

"Oh." Holmes rubbed his face. "I have to key the locks with my palm print, sir."

"Well, hurry up, my boy. I'm waiting." He chuckled. "Can't wait to put my hands on old Cephas' prizes!"

"I'll be on my way, sir." Holmes closed the phone.

Monarch pointed to a metal bin on the side of the cage. "Put it in that cage. It will block any signal."

"Will Thakkar know where we are?" Steel asked.

"Unlikely. The only way cell phone signals can get into this room is through a cellular router in the ceiling." She pointed to a saucer-shaped device on the ceiling. "You step into the cage, and no one can trace it. We should be safe. But, I recommend all of you check for phones and put them in the cage before you put on the goggles. And, Holmes, come here, and I'll get you into the monitoring program."

Holmes stepped out of the cage, and Monarch pointed to a seat. She pulled up images on the computer monitors and typed commands. Five windows filled the two screens before him. They were labeled one through five. She matched the numbers on the goggles with their respective owners and typed names into each window.

"Now, once they enter Numinocity, you will see what they see and hear what they hear. You can speak to them through these headsets." She handed him a headset with a microphone. "That's all you have to know, Holmes. Help them stay coordinated. And, this sixth window here," she pointed to a window now filling with static. "Will hack into Numinocity itself. You'll have a kind of overview. As my program infiltrates Thakkar's program, you can guide them around. Hopefully, you'll find New Stonehenge and tell them how to get there."

Monarch turned away from the computer keyboard and faces everyone. "I have put together an infiltration program. It is untested. When you place the goggles on your head, they will contain a basic generic set of body language correlates. Normally, Thakkar's 3EI takes you through a training session, but if I do that, it will alert her you have entered her realm."

"So, exactly what does that mean?" Birdsong asked.

"You will feel very awkward at first. Sort of like a baby learning to walk. Run through as many physical routines as possible once you get into the realm, and my program will adapt the generic profiles to match yours. Also, I have no idea where your goggles will take you upon entry. Thakkar has an entry routine giving an overview of Numinocity. I don't have access to that, so I have no idea what you are going to face in there."

"Great!" Steel said.

"Hey, Jonathan. You've already been inside." Josh said.

"It was just a conversation with Thakkar. I had no idea of where she was or what surrounded her."

"Bro, don't worry. I'll take you through the layout. Most games have a similar layout of lands. So, Dr. Monarch, will we have weapons and lives and bitcoins?" Josh said.

"I have no idea. The basis of Numinocity is using your imagination to create your own environment and its 'tools.' Unfortunately, that is also a sub-routine I do not have access to."

"So we have no weapons? No tools?" Birdsong said.

"Dude, I played ten levels of BioShock with only my fists," Josh said.

"Who will we face?" Raven asked.

"Well, we know that Thakkar has at least six 'warrior-priests' as she called them looking for Steven. I can't rule out other participants she may have added elsewhere. There could be only six, or there could be six thousand."

"And, all of them will be hostile to us?" Steel asked.

"Probably not unless they are directed by Thakkar to hunt you down. Remember, she has no idea you have entered Numinocity. From what I understand, Numinocity can be as violent as all-out war or as peaceful as you sitting on a front porch overlooking a lake in the mountains while sipping ice tea and reading a book. The user determines the environment and experience. That is the allure. A perfect escape from reality."

"We must go, Dr. Monarch," Ishido said after having put all of the cots together. "We will have a very tight window to reach Paris within the next five hours."

Monarch nodded and paused to look around at them. "Thank you for helping find Olivia. Once you locate her, Holmes, you can press that red button on the corner of the keyboard. It will notify me through a low-level cellular link to my bracelet. It will give me the location. By then, I hope to have Steven safely removed from Numinocity, and I can contact Max to swoop in and save Olivia. That's the best we can hope for."

Holmes raised a hand. "Before you swoop out of here, it might be best we pause and say a simple prayer."

Monarch blinked and nodded. "Okay, so I might be open to the supernatural if that helps us find Olivia. We can use all the help we can get."

Holmes stood up from his chair, and they made a circle. Steel placed his hands in Josh's and Raven's grip. His mind was reeling with the mission ahead, and he never heard the words of the prayer.

STEEL AND JOSH sat on the edge of their cots, watching Birdsong and Raven place their goggles over their eyes. They had both been there before. Holmes watched as the goggles activated on their users. The windows showed Raven and Birdsong standing in an empty, dark room.

"What do you see?" Holmes asked in his headphone microphone.

"Darkness. It feels very real like I'm standing in a closet." Birdsong said. "What do I do now?"

"Do you see Raven?"

"No. I'm alone," Birdsong said.

"Me, too," Raven said.

"Well, hopefully, once Jonathan and Josh enter the four of you can find the door to the room and exit into a common area. Think of something all four of you have experienced together as a meeting place." Holmes said.

"The hotel room." Steel said.

"Good idea."

Steel nodded to Josh, laid back on the cot, and pulled the goggles over his eyes. He was in total darkness.

NUMINOCITY

"*Technology will never lead to our salvation as human beings—because no matter how much strength we gain, or how much our cognitive capacity increases, we will never be satisfied. . . .The irony is that the human enhancements designed to help us overcome our biological shortcomings— thereby alleviating pain and suffering—will never truly end our misery because we will always crave more strength, more intelligence. Our insatiable demands on human enhancement technology will prevent humanity from ever attaining utopia.*"

Fazale R. Rana and Kenneth R. Samples, "Humans 2.0"

"*Transhumanists don't take into account that we will never be at peace, no matter what we have. We will never be satisfied no matter how much health, safety, security, and wealth we enjoy. Even as superhumans, we would always be unfulfilled; we would never arrive at utopia.*"

Fazale R. Rana and Kenneth R. Samples, "Humans 2.0"

"If humans pursue the transhumanist vision with the hope that we will save ourselves from extinction by creating posthuman species that transcend our biological limits, we will actually initiate the demise of our species. Transhumanists seek to save humanity by creating a posthuman world. But what we end up saving won't be us."

Fazale R. Rana and Kenneth R. Samples, "Humans 2.0"

28

J OSHUA KNIGHT

JOSH FELT the now-familiar wave of disorientation fall over him as he found himself standing alone in a dark room. He glanced down at his hands and his body. The room had some faint light that leaked in from under the bottom of a door before him. He was wearing a plated, white suit of metal that reminded him of the stormtroopers in Star Wars. Only he had no helmet. He wore shiny white articulated gloves.

"What is going on?" He asked himself. Where had this come from? "Oh! My last video game was Galactic Whirlpool!"

"You okay?" Holmes spoke in his ear. Josh touched his head and realized he wore an earpiece with a tiny microphone.

"Yeah, just wondering why I'm wearing this white exo-suit. I designed it for Galactic Whirlpool, the last game I played before all of this happened."

"Then, it seems Monarch is right. You mind can change your environment." Holmes said.

"Yeah, so where are my weapons?"

Something clicked on his left hip, and he glanced down. A holster hung from his utility belt. He pulled out a Phase IV Beta Plasma Blaster. "Cool! My preferred weapon!"

"And, I wonder what happens when you use it?" Holmes said. "If you kill someone in the game, what happens to them in the real world?"

"I hope they don't die," Josh said. "Bro, I hope WE don't die! Probably you reset or return to your last saved level. Unlimited lives."

"As long as your living body lasts, right?" Holmes said.

"Bro, don't be a killjoy. So, where is everyone else?"

"I don't know. So far, you are the only one to show up in the windows. Maybe because you have already been through the system?"

"Yeah, right. So, what do I do? Wait? Or go through the door?"

"Wait!" He heard Steel's voice in his ear. "I'm standing in a dark room. Just like when I met Thakkar."

"What are you wearing?" Josh asked.

"Clothes." Steel said. "A tee shirt and jeans."

"Dude, you have no imagination," Josh said. "Weapons?"

"Josh, you know I don't like guns." Steel said.

"I have my preferred pistols." Birdsong chimed in. "This is unbelievable! I feel like I'm really in a dark room somewhere. And, for the record, I'm wearing my Tucson police uniform with all the SWAT attachments."

"Good, something you're familiar with." Raven's voice joined in. "I'm in a jumpsuit with an assortment of my knives and, ahem, other deadly devices. I don't always trust a gun."

"Okay, I've got a visual from all of you. I see the room and the door from your visual point of view. So, now what?" Holmes said.

"We step through the looking glass," Birdsong said.

"Plan!" Steel said. "If we get separated, we meet back at the hotel."

"Agreed," Raven said. "On three?"

"One. Two. Three." Holmes counted down.

THE DOOR CLOSED BEHIND JOSH, and he found himself in a dark, dank alley. Rain misted down upon him, and he glanced around in surprise. "Jonathan? Jason? Raven? Anybody?"

He was alone. "Monty?"

No reply. What had happened? Josh turned around, and the door was gone, only a long stretch of a shadowy alleyway. Where was he? Instead of his exo-suit, he wore a long, black coat over a black tee-shirt and black jeans. He felt something sting on his face and touched his lip. His lip bead was back! His other piercings were back!

"Monty? I've changed. I'm wearing clothes from when I was in that vampire cult. This is not what I wanted!"

"Well, well, hello there, little mouse."

Josh whirled. A tall, willowy shape moved toward him from the end of the alleyway. "Who is it?"

"Just a friend. No need to be afraid." The voice was male, and from what little light backlit the approaching figure, it had long white hair. Josh backed along the alleyway, his gloved hands sliding on the wet brickwork coming away with a thick, sticky slime. If only there were somewhere to hide.

A light suddenly blossomed above him, and he glanced up at a hovering sphere of pale, yellow light. The brick wall behind him opened up, and he fell backward onto a hard rocky floor.

He scuttled on his backside away from the opening as the figure in the alleyway stepped into the light from the hovering sphere. The man was over six feet tall and very thin, dressed in a high necked black coat with a red ascot. His eyes were pale blue and his skin completely white. The man paused in the doorway.

"Just who are you, may I ask?" His voice had a lilt to it, an upward drift almost hypnotic.

Should he say his name? Definitely not. "Clark Savage. Jr." He blurted out.

The man smiled and revealed fanged teeth. "And, Clark Savage, Jr., what planet are you from? Based on your accent, I'd say Creole?"

Josh had come up against a solid wall in his crawling. "Sounds good. And you?"

"From here."

"Where is here?"

The man reached into his pocket and pulled out a red, gleaming cigarette holder. He retrieved a cigarette from his other inner pocket and tucked it into the holder. He clamped the holder in his teeth and inhaled. The tip of the cigarette lit up with the inhalation. He exhaled purple-tinted smoke.

"Nicstick?" He pointed to the cigarette.

"Bro, I don't smoke."

The man lifted an eyebrow and frowned as he drew on the 'nicstick.' "You are lost, aren't you? You are on the planet Wereland, the city of Transyl."

Josh shook his head, glancing around at the dark shadows around him for any escape. "I don't know Wereland."

"In the Grand Brittania system?" He exhaled purple-tinted smoke. "Oh, you humans are all alike. You think you are so superior to us, Weren. Chased us away from your world because of your groundless superstition, and yet, we were the champions of the night; the dark dwellers." He motioned to the sky, and for the first time, Josh realized the rain was not touching the creature. "Here on Wereland, we found the perfect alternative." He inhaled more smoke. "May I come in?"

Josh's forehead wrinkled. "What?"

"May I come into your presence?"

Josh thought furiously. Why was this thing asking him? He sighed. He had to have permission to come in. This was a game, after all. But, a game in which each person controlled their reality. Josh realized he had conjured up the doorway through the bricks, and now he sat in a shapeless, formless room created by his mind.

"If I were to allow you to come in." Josh slowly stood up. "What would you do to me?"

The Weren laughed and flicked ashes from his nicstick. "I just want to talk. You are a new addition, uh, visitor to Transyl. I always try and greet new visitors."

Josh nodded. "By drinking their blood?"

The man's face twisted in anger, and he balled up his fists and let forth an ear-splitting screech. Josh put his hands over his ears. "Why is it you humans always think we are vampires? Huh? Your bias; your racial hatred of my kind led to our exile from Earth!" He fought for control and smoothed his jacket. "Sorry. That always makes me angry." He stoked his nicstick and blew smoke toward the doorway. It flattened against a transparent surface and did not go through.

"In that case, no, you cannot enter," Josh said.

The man lifted an eyebrow and shrugged. "Well, you can't stay in there forever. You'll starve to death. Or, die of thirst."

The Weren walked away, and the hovering light followed him, throwing Josh into darkness. "Okay, so I can create things from my own imagination. But I didn't create that. Let's see, shut the door."

Bricks rattled and closed off the makeshift door closing off what little light leaked in. "Now, a stairway to the roof of this building."

The wall behind him disappeared, and he fell backward. Looking up, he saw a spiral staircase winding its way around a cylindrical stairwell to an opening not far above. Rain hit him in the forehead. He scrambled to his feet and started up the spiral staircase. What was unbelievable was the absolute real nature of his climb. He couldn't feel his real body on the cot. Was he moving in the real world, or was all of this just in his mind? His heartbeat increased, and he broke out in a sweat by the time he reached the last rung of the stairs. He emerged onto a flat, stone-covered rooftop and gasped.

Despite the constant rain, the city around him was amazing. Tall, spindly towers reached into the night sky composed of brick and mortar and gleaming yellow-lit windows. Copper-colored domes topped many of the towers. The towers were slightly askew as if made of melted candle wax, almost organic in their appearance.

He walked to the roof edge and looked down into the alley he had just traversed. The Weren was gone. At the end of the alley, a street yawned filled with bustling carriages drawn by steaming metal engines.

"Steampunk." He thought. What game had he seen this in? Was that memory the source of this world's architecture? Or, was it constructed by the Weren, whoever he was. He was probably one of Thakkar's warrior-priests as she called them. Or, he could have been a construct of Numinocity.

An arm draped around his shoulder, and he jerked away from a figure standing beside him. The man was slightly taller than Josh and dressed in a flowing Victorian cape with a gleaming, black top hat. Josh stepped away.

"Who are you? I didn't invite you in."

The man turned his face into the meager light from a nearby tower. Robert Ketrick smiled at him, exposing his fangs.

"That's because I'm not a player, Josh," Ketrick said.

Josh backed away and stumbled to the shallow edge of the roof. "You're dead."

Ketrick smiled and removed his top hat. His hair was short now, unlike the long, serpentine braid he had last worn in the ritual underneath the church in Lakeside. "Actually, I'm not exactly the biological Robert Ketrick. I'm more like his memory. His demonic memory."

Josh turned and ran across the rooftop toward the stairway, and the roof opened up beneath him. He fell forward onto a rain-slick surface and slid into darkness. He scrambled for a handhold, but the brick just skittered beneath his grasp.

"Monty, are you there? Anyone?" He screamed.

∼

BIRDSONG

THE DOOR OPENED ONTO HARSH, biting sunlight and stifling heat. Birdsong blinked in the sudden light. This was too surreal. He felt like he was really here. Wherever here was. He wore his dark assault vest and black uniform and a helmet with polarized lenses shaded his eyes from the sun. He looked around him. Scrub brush sprouted from dusty sand and rolling hills. He knew this place.

"No!" He said and turned back to find the door was gone. He whirled again, and from over the rise of a nearby hill, he caught the echo of a woman's scream. He shook his head and covered his eyes. When he took his hand away, nothing had changed.

"Holmes? Holmes!" He hissed. Silence. Where the man? If this is what Numinocity took from his thoughts and memories, it wasn't a game. It was a descent into a private hell!

The droning of an ATV sounded from behind him, and he

instinctively crouched behind a boulder. From behind him, the ATV rocked over the hill and ground its way past him. One of his sister's kidnappers drove the ATV.

"This can't be. I'm not doing this again whoever is controlling this. I'm not doing it again, you hear?" He whispered to the air. No one answered. What had Monarch said? She could not predict where or how they would enter Numinocity. This was some kind of unauthorized backdoor entry all right. He had dropped into his worst memory.

The woman's scream came again more intense than before. He closed his eyes and tried to bring his mind under control. This was NOT real. It was NOT happening again. He did NOT have to be a part of this.

When he opened his eyes, he crouched against the rough, aging metal wall of a camper trailer. This was wrong! They had come at night, not in the heat of the day. But, the screams from within were unmistakably his sister, Kristen.

If he went in, would he find what he had seen that night? Would Kristen be lying in a pool of sweat and blood? She had been tortured and had sweat blood! Even now, years after the incident, his anger grew, and a red wave of rage came over his vision. He should have killed the men outright instead of shooting both in their legs and then tying them to a cactus. He had left them to die in the desert but had hastened their death. He had left a cell phone for them to use but unknown to the two men, he had called their boss, Julio, first and had told him his men had betrayed them. Julio did his work of revenge for him. But, Birdsong was no less guilty for being removed one person from the deed.

He closed his eyes and visualized the hotel room. When he opened his eyes, the desert was still there, and so were the screams of his sister!

29

R AVEN

R AVEN CLOSED the door behind her and looked around at the empty, dilapidated kitchen. Grime covered the windows. Dirty dishes filled the sink. Petrified food stuck to plates piled on the kitchen table.

"Jonathan? Dr. Holmes?" No one answered. She was alone. She glanced down and realized she wore a short, pink dress with filly lace around the hem. Her knives were gone!

"No! NO!" She said out loud and turned back to the door. It opened onto a living room. She recognized the sweat-stained recliner and cigarette butts piled in an ashtray. The odors of stale beer and cigarette smoke filled the air. What was happening? This was supposed to be some kind of game. She had expected to step into a cityscape and had even been prepared to defend herself, but she had no weapons.

A bleating sound came from behind her, and she turned

back toward the kitchen. A tiny, spotless lamb stood in the middle of the floor. It looked at her with pleading, panic-filled eyes.

"No!" Raven pressed her hands against her mouth. Nausea gripped her. What would happen if she vomited and drowned in her own vomit on the cot in Monarch's lab? She fought down nausea and backed against the wall. Something dangled down in front of her.

She focused on a red thread. It writhed like a snake and suddenly wrapped itself around her right wrist. A blue thread followed, and then an entire shower of multicolored threads fell around her. They trapped her in a growing mesh, and she struggled while the lamb bleated endlessly. But, the strings were too strong and bound her tightly. She lifted off the floor and dangled prone in the air. The lamb came underneath her and looked up at her.

"Why did you let me die?" It said in a tiny, squeaky voice.

"No!" The door to the living room opened, and she looked down from her dangling position as a figure lurched into the kitchen. The legs were loose and moved with jerking, uncoordinated movement. It was a man in torn jeans and an undershirt stained with vomit and beer. The head lolled loosely, and then the face turned up at her. Her stepfather glared at her with cloudy eyes and a toothless maw.

"Welcome home, sweetheart." He slurred.

STEEL

STEEL STEPPED through the door and was hit in the face by wind-blown rain. Out of the darkness around him, a storm raged. In the distance, he could hear waves crashing along the surf. Where was he? Was this Numinocity?

"Monty? Are you there?" Nobody answered.

Steel looked down at his broken hands, and lightning flashed, illuminating his body. Pain gripped him as he looked down at his naked torso. Bruises and gaping wounds covered his skin. He was back on the night he awoke on the beach. How could this be?

He tried to see into the raging storm, but the darkness was too vast. He turned painfully and looked for the door back to the room, but instead, he found a set of wooden stairs leading up to the deck of a beach house. Painfully, he made his way up the stairs by feel with occasional aid from a flash of lightning.

"Monty, where am I?" He asked as loud as he could shout. His throat ached with the effort.

He arrived on the deck windswept with lashing rain. The wind had tumbled chairs and a table on their side. A broken umbrella whipped in the wind. Through flashes from lightning, he made his way across the deck to a screened-in porch at the back of a two-story house. He jerked open the storm door against the wind and fell through the opening onto the cold concrete of the back porch.

He screamed in pain from his broken ribs as he hit the hard floor. He held up his hands and stared at his fingers broken during his torture. Without the rain washing over his face, a red wave came over his vision, and he touched his bloody face with his good fingers.

"Oh, God!" He whispered. "What is happening?"

A shadow fell over him, and someone bent over him, placing hands beneath his shoulders and dragging him over the hard floor. He screamed again in pain and felt the flashing along the inner door scrape his bareback. The figure had dragged him into a dark living room and leaned him up against a couch.

The figure moved away and sat in a chair opposite him. Steel wiped blood and rain from his face, wincing as his crooked fingers strayed against the bruises on his cheeks. He blinked and tried to clear his vision. Lightning flashed and illuminated the face of the person in the chair.

Bright turquoise eyes glared at him. Reddish blonde hair. High cheekbones. He was looking at himself!

"Hello there. Welcome to my hell." He said to himself.

HOLMES

"One," Holmes said. The lights went out, plunging him into total darkness. He looked around the completely blackened room.

"What? No! NO!" He pounded on the keyboard before him. Nothing happened. Just a sudden abrupt silence. He sat still and heard the breathing of his friends on their cots. He stood up slowly and turned toward the cots. The faint gleam of blue light leaked around the edges of their goggles. What should he do? The goggles were still powered. Did Monarch's program still work? Should he pull their goggles off?

No! Monarch said it would drive them insane or possibly kill them. A clicking sound came from somewhere above, and Holmes jerked in fright as emergency lights came on in the corners illuminating the lab in blood-red light. The computer screen in front of him came back on, and he heard the churning of computer fans and hard drives. Coding began to stream across the monitor in front of him and stopped. A blinking cursor demanded his attention.

What now? He had no idea what to type on the keyboard. He had to find Monarch. Slowly, he made his way around chairs and tables to the cots. All four of his friends were lying serenely on their cots, their chests rising and falling. They seemed fine.

He leaned over Steel. "Jonathan? Can you hear me?"

Steel did not respond. He glanced around hopelessly. What to do? His gaze fell on the Ferriday cage. He hurried over and pulled open the door and stepped inside. He flipped open the metal box on the far wall and pulled out his phone. Would it work? Could he call someone? But who? He didn't have Monarch's number.

He touched the screen, and it came to life. A lock screen stared at him, and he hesitated to put in his code. The phone rang, and he dropped it in shock.

He fished around on the floor of the Ferriday cage until he found his phone. He answered the call.

"Hello?"

"Dr. Holmes, my good man, my patience is wearing thin!" Dr. Hampton's voice came over the phone. "When are you coming to open these crates, my boy?"

Holmes sighed. "I've had a bit of a problem, Dr. Hampton. Where I am staying, the power just went out, and until it comes back on, I can't leave the top floor of my hotel. I'm sure it will be back on soon."

"Oh, yes. I heard a bit about that on the telly. Seems like portions of London along the south shore of the Thames are affected. I'm sure it will all be spit spot soon. Very well, Holmes. As soon as you can, come my way and be so kind as to drop me a call." The call ended.

Holmes looked at the screen, and his mind worked furiously. Was he paranoid, or had Thakkar guessed at the general location of Monarch's lab? Putting a quarter of the city of London out of power was a frightening display of power if she had indeed done so. Frightening being the key word. What should he do? He dialed the number for Monarch's phone and it went straight to a prerecorded voicemail. "Monarch, the power went out. I need the password to get back. Into the computer." He ended the call. "Okay, God, I could use some help here." He said to the red-tinged ceiling.

A man stood just outside the cage, and Holmes jerked with fear and dropped the phone again. The man wore a three-piece white suit with a red carnation in his lapel. He smiled and bowed.

"Dr. Holmes, you have no need to worry any further. I have a solution for you."

"Who are you? Where did you come from?"

"You may call me Miguel. I am a friend of Mr. Steel. A friend from, shall we say, on high, mi amigo."

Holmes opened the door to the cage and stepped out. "An angel? Really? First, an angel shows up on the airplane in scrubs. Then a reject from Fantasy Island. You guys are getting on my nerves. Why can't you be here when we really need you?"

Miguel raised an eyebrow. "I believe now would be that time?"

Holmes sighed. "Yes. Of course, you are right."

"Now, it would seem the power outage is an attempt to stop you. I don't believe your enemy has a real idea of what you have planned, but she narrowed your little phone signal a while ago to this general area."

"Unless you know how to reboot that program, there's not a lot you can do to help," Holmes said.

"Oh, there is." He held up a pair of goggles. "You must go into Numinocity and find your friends and tell them to ask for help. It is as simple as that."

Holmes glanced at the goggles. "But, Monarch said the nanomemes might cause me to have a fatal anaphylactic reaction."

"This is true." Miguel held the goggles closer. "No greater

love has any man than this that he would be willing to lay down his life for his friends."

Holmes sighed and took the goggles. "You would have to quote scripture."

Miguel smiled. "My friend, have faith. All will work out as it should. The Father has assured it. Once you get inside, find your friends. Reassure them. Encourage them. They are in a prison of their own minds trapped by their own fears. When the power went out, Dr. Monarch's program ceased to operate, and your friends are on the own."

Holmes stepped around Miguel and retrieved a cot. He unfolded it while muttering under his breath and stretched it out next to the other cots. "As if I'm not afraid."

"My friend, you must remember one thing," Miguel said as Holmes settled on to the cot.

"What's that?"

"In Numinocity, you can control your own fate. Do not give in to fear. And remember, to be successful in battle, you must have the right armor." Miguel actually clicked his heels and disappeared.

"Armor! What do I know about armor? Old knights in armor, maybe. But, this is a modern virtual reality, right?" He muttered as he pulled the goggles over his head. He hesitated before tugging them down over his eyes. "Lord, protect me and let me help my friends. And, please, don't let me have a reaction." He dropped the goggles into place.

THE SMELL CAUGHT him first as a wind filled with the odor of rotting flesh wafted over him. Holmes blinked in the twilight of a setting sun and glanced around. He stood on the edge of a precipice overlooking a valley. Smoke and fire churned and bubbled beneath him. In the fires, he made out bones and rotting corpses. Scattered about the human corpses were the bodies of animals.

The rattle of a cart caught his attention, and he looked off to the left. Two men dressed in dirty robes pushed a cart to the edge of the precipice not far from Holmes. They tilted the cart over the edge, and three bodies fell out of the cart. The limbs spun akimbo in lifeless motion as the bodies of two dead men tumbled down the rocky slope and into the fire. Smoke gushed up, carrying a new wave of carrion odor over Holmes.

"Ah, the smell of death in the evening. Could anything be any better?" A hoarse voice sounded from behind him.

Holmes whirled. The figure lurching toward him was someone out of the deepest seated nightmare. The man's face was livid and puffed up from blood that had pooled under his skin. His eyes were bloodshot and bulged from their orbits. A noose hung around his neck, and the rope trailed behind him. He stumbled toward Holmes, and his thick tongue made his speech almost unintelligible. Holmes started to back away and remembered the precipice behind him.

"Judas?"

"Don't worry. My guts haven't burst out yet. I'm saving that for later."

Holmes shook his head. "No. This can't be happening."

Judas paused and planted his hands on his hips. "You let me kill myself. You could have stopped me. You could have told me he was going to rise from the dead. That would have given me hope. Hope! But, no, you wallowed in your own self-pity." Judas leaned toward him, and his eyes leaked blood and tears. "Did you enjoy watching me die? Did it ease your self-loathing? After all, who in all of humankind's history is more to be pitied than Judas Iscariot?"

Holmes tried to walk past him, and Judas moved to block his path. If this was the essence of Numinocity, the world was in danger. "I have to find and help my friends. I don't have time for self-pity. You made your choices. I made my choices, and I have to put the past behind me and move on. So, get out of my way!"

Judas straightened, shuddered, and disappeared. Holmes blinked and glanced around him. Had it been that simple? All he had to do was to stop listening to these lies and focus on the truth.

Like a lightbulb from heaven, the answer hit him. He gasped. Truth. Armor. "Oh, my Lord, how sweet you are! Armor!" He paced and fought his racing thoughts. He had once mastered scripture memorization, but it had been a few years since. His career had interfered with the memorization program developed by his old friend, Kenny.

"But, do I focus on memorizing and studying scripture?" He said to himself. "No! Instead, as an apologist, I argue philosophical arguments and archeological findings. I focus on minutia and ignore the most important thing, the Word of God." He closed his eyes and blocked out the odor and the harrowing wind. He chased the image of Judas from his mind. He imagined himself sitting at the table in the coffee shop of Brookwood Church with Westley and Daniel and Kenny and JT and Marcus. He summoned up the fragrance of his favorite flavor of latte at Easter time, King Cake Latte. He licked his lips in anticipation and sat back and felt the chair beneath him.

"Monty. Monty?"

He opened his eyes. His friends sat around him at the table in the Well, the coffee shop. Westley wore his ever-present paisley patterned shirt; his dark hair combed back from his rounded spectacles. Daniel sipped at a frozen Chai Tea Latte and wore one of his Hawaiian shirts. Kenny sat forward, hunched over his well-worn index cards mumbling to himself. JT leaned on the table and tapped a card. Marcus stood behind JT.

"Okay, Kenny, you've got to tell me. We're waiting."

"Don't disappoint us, Kenny." Marcus crossed his arms over his chest.

Kenny looked up with his bright blue eyes filled with mischief. "*Order the buckler and shield, And draw near to battle! Harness the horses, and mount up, you horsemen! Stand forth with your helmets, polish the spears, put on the armor! Why have I seen them dismayed and turned back? Their mighty ones are beaten down; they have speedily fled, and did not look back, for fear was all around, says the Lord.* Jeremiah 46:3-5. Sorry, it took a bit. I was trying to decide which translation to quote. I like the New King James Version for that verse."

JT shook his head. "I thought I had you on that one."

"Put on the armor!" Holmes said. "Put on the armor! That is the key! Ephesians. The whole armor of God."

They all looked at him. "Wait your turn," Daniel said.

"No, I need to remember it now." Holmes patted the table impatiently. The windows of the welcome center behind them allowed light to fill the gathering area of the church. The light levels suddenly fell, and thunder rattled the windows. The men looked toward the door to the Well. "Looks like a storm is brewing," Westley said. "I better go roll up my car windows."

"Yeah, I got to go check on my daughter," Daniel said.

"Time to get to work." JT stood up.

"Yeah, me too." Marcus turned toward the door.

Kenny shrugged. "Well, I'm retired. I've got nothing to do, but if you guys are done, I'm leaving. My eyesight isn't so good when it gets dark like this."

"No!" Holmes slapped the table. "Sit down and help me recall the exact wording."

"Monty, you know these verses," Marcus said.

"I'm a little rattled right now. People could die." Lightning flashed outside, and a wave of thunder shook the building. "The enemy is coming, and I have to stop him. Or, in this case, her. Help me think, guys. Please!"

Holmes felt a hand on his shoulder and looked up into the face of his pastor, Davey. "Suck it up, buttercup. You can do this." He smiled.

Holmes nodded and closed his eyes. "I can do this. I can remember the words. You've preached them. The guys have recited them. I can see them on the page. The Holy Spirit can help me."

"Finally, my brethren, be strong in the Lord and in the power of His might," Holmes said.

"Put on the whole armor of God, that you may be able to stand against the wiles of the devil." Kenny joined in with his voice.

"For we do not wrestle against flesh and blood, but against principalities, against powers, against the rulers of the darkness of this age, against spiritual hosts of wickedness in the heavenly places." Westley joined in.

"Therefore take up the whole armor of God, that you may be able to withstand in the evil day, and having done all, to stand." Daniel joined in.

"Stand therefore, having girded your waist with truth, having put on the breastplate of righteousness, and having shod your feet with the preparation of the gospel of peace." JT joined in.

"Above all, taking the shield of faith with which you will be able to quench all the fiery darts of the wicked one." Pastor Davey joined in.

"And take the helmet of salvation, and the sword of the Spirit, which is the word of God; praying always with all prayer and supplication in the Spirit, being watchful to this end with all perseverance and supplication for all the saints. Ephesians 6:10-18." Marcus finished.

"Got it!" Holmes stood up and ran into the waiting area. He glanced out the huge windows at the approaching storm. Clouds churned in the sky, and rain pelted the windows. Out of the mist, a lone figure appeared holding an umbrella against the wind and rain. Miguel smiled at him and motioned with a hand for Holmes to leave the building. Holmes pushed the door open with difficulty against the wind and rain. He was instantly soaked as he walked the ten feet to the shelter of Miguel's umbrella. He stepped into the shelter of the umbrella, and everything around them froze as if time had stopped.

"You realize that this reality in which you find yourself can be controlled by your mind, mi amigo?" Miguel said.

"I'm beginning to figure that out," Holmes said.

"Ah, but there is something significant, and it has to do with my presence."

Holmes nodded. "There is a supernatural element to this scenario."

"Yes! The purveyor of this reality chose to utilize the spiritual element of humanity to make all of this seem so real."

"Which means you are here as well as any of your fallen brothers."

Miguel nodded. "Unfortunately, you find yourself on a, shall we say, quasi-spiritual plane of conflict."

"Powers and principalities. Yeah, I get it now." Holmes said. "Why don't you end this?"

Miguel shook his head and rubbed his pencil-thin mustache with his free hand. "I am afraid this battle is the result of human choice, mi amigo. I can help when my Master allows, and that is only when you have asked for it, and it is appropriate for me to intervene. Even though you are in an altered reality, it is still part of God's reality. So, have you decided on a strategy?"

"The whole armor of God."

Miguel smiled, and his face lit up with mirth and joy. "Finally! Mi amigo, time is of the essence. Already, your body is beginning to react against its microscopic invaders. You must put on the whole armor of God and help your friends. And, when the time comes, remember what I said about the nature of friendship." Miguel nodded and disappeared along with the rain-drenched afternoon.

HOLMES FOUND himself standing in a dark room with meager light coming from beneath the seal of a door. He was no longer soaked to the bone but wore armor from head to foot. He turned away from the door as a faint light illuminated the room around him. He stood in a janitor's closet filled with brooms and mops and cleaning solutions stacked on metal shelves. Behind him, a full-length mirror captured his reflection. He wore a simple gold helmet without any fancy plume or adornment. A silver and copper etched breastplate covered his chest. A belt of woven bronze filaments held his tunic in place. He wore simple leather sandals. In his left hand, he held a shield. He lifted the surprisingly light shield up to the mirror. It was round and covered with green etchings of leaves and branches on a silver background. In his right hand, he carried a sword. He raised the sword and marveled at the sight of its translucent, crystalline structure. This was not a sword to strike against metal. No, it was something far different. For, as he gazed into the light blue, glowing crystalline surface words began to appear. He mouthed the words as he read them.

"*For the word of God is living and active, sharper than any two-edged sword, piercing to the division of soul and of spirit, of joints and of marrow, and discerning the thoughts and intentions of the heart. Hebrews 4:12.* The sword is the word of God!" He smiled. Suddenly a sharp pain doubled him over, and he gasped with nausea. "No! Not now!" It was the nanomemes. He was having a reaction! He hyperventilated, and the pain and nausea slowly subsided. What had Miguel said? Time was running out.

The sword glittered, and words came to the surface. "*Be not wise in your own eyes; fear the Lord, and turn away from evil. It will be healing to your flesh and refreshment to your bones. Proverbs 3:7-8."*

Holmes slowed his breathing. Was the sword responding to his condition, or were these verses he had memorized in the past now coming to his memory thanks to the enhancements of the 3EI? It didn't matter. "Lord, no matter what happens to me, I am ready to help my friends face against this evil, and I ask for your strength and healing power."

A sudden pain lanced into his chest like a spike that hurt from under his breastbone to the tip of his scapula. He gasped, and as quickly as the pain came, relief flooded over him. Nausea and abdominal pain were gone. His breathing became easier. Strength flowed through his muscles, and his mind cleared. "Woohoo! Thanks for that jolt!"

A voice echoed in his mind. "Did that help?"

"Who is this? God?"

"Hardly!" The female voice continued. "The power is back on, and I think I managed to reboot the program."

"Monarch?"

"No, sweetheart. Vivian. It took me a while, but I narrowed down the site for the lab based on the power outage and the nice, red glow of emergency lighting through the windows. I've been cruising up and down the Thames in a horrendous little surrey for an hour."

"Wait, Vivian, why are you helping us?"

"Fulfilling my duty. Like I said earlier. Stopping Thakkar. The enemy of my enemy is my friend. Right now, I'm your best friend. Oh, by the way, that little pain in your chest was me giving you a shot of epinephrine and steroids for the nanomeme reaction. You were going down pretty fast."

"And I thought it was an answered prayer."

"I would NEVER be the answer to a prayer," Vivian said cryptically. "Well, I can't get the observation windows back up.

Not sure where the others are in the program, but at least I can talk to you. So, I'm putting on a pair of goggles, and I'm coming in. I have a pretty good idea of how to find Olivia."

"Why?"

"My truce with the Crimson Snake. She's hedging her bets, and she's helping me in case Thakkar loses this one. We have a tentative partnership. Snake thinks she knows where Olivia is being held along with some kind of warrior priests? Says if she can get to the real location, Thakkar's real body is right next to Olivia, and she can shut down Thakkar's goggles. No Thakkar, no big bad evil queen to fight in Numinocity. Okay, I'm coming in."

The air sparkled in front of Holmes, and Vivian materialized. She wore a loose, black leather one-piece jumpsuit and combat boots. Her hair was pulled up into a knot on top of her head, and she looked around at the room.

"Well, this is boring." She studied Holmes. "Nice armor. Very shiny. Are we going to one of those medieval all-you-can-eats?"

"No, Vivian. I'm going to help my friends."

"And, I am going to find Thakkar and stop her." She turned and opened the door to the dark room and disappeared, closing the door behind her.

30

"Wait!" Holmes opened the door and followed her. Darkness swallowed him, and he stood perfectly still. "Vivian?"

Something skittered close by. A caress across his cheek startled him. "Vivian! Where are we?"

In the distance, a pale, green light began to grow, and Holmes squinted to try and make out just what he was seeing. As the light grew, it illuminated the chamber in which he stood. Huge, fleshy vines ran across the ground and over low lying structures. He reached out and touched the nearest structure with the tip of his sword. It glowed a bright blue, and the vines disintegrated and fell away in black dust. The structure beneath was a church pew.

"What?" He turned and held up the glowing sword. He was in a church sanctuary. Row after row of church pews stretched ahead and behind him covered with the leafless vines. The vines climbed up the walls and onto the ceiling far above. The ceiling moved, writhed, and suddenly dropped toward him. No, it wasn't the ceiling itself falling but something from the ceiling.

A huge, black spider, the size of a cat, landed on the vines just a meter from him. It had glowing red eyes and pulsing pincers. Others appeared all around him. His heart raced, and his mouth grew dry. What was this? He brandished the glowing sword toward the spiders, and they drew back. But, behind him, the spiders advanced. He whirled and waved the sword. Slowly the spiders were advancing from all around. Something dripped on his arm and he glanced up in time to see a dozen spiders descending on him. He waved the sword, and they pulled back up their webs. What was he to do? He had to get rid of the spiders.

"Okay, Holmes, think. This is not real. These creatures are virtual." His arm began to burn, and he grimaced in pain. He glanced at his arm, where a drop of spider venom was bubbling away on his skin. He wiped it away against a nearby vine. The pain was real. Excruciating. His eyes watered. He grew nauseous. This was too real. Not at all virtual. The pain continued, and then he saw words appear on the surface of the sword.

"*If you listen carefully to the Lord your God and do what is right in his eyes, if you pay attention to his commands and keep all his decrees, I will not bring on you any of the diseases I brought on the Egyptians, for I am the Lord, who heals you. Exodus 15:26.*" He read out loud and then touched the sword flatly against the venom. The pain stopped immediately.

He closed his eyes and tried to recall a verse. "Psalms 118:11." He said out loud. Words appeared on the surface of the sword. "*They surrounded me on every side, but in the name of the Lord, I cut them down.*"

Holmes stepped forward and brought the sword through the nearest line of spiders. They exploded in red ichor. The other spiders tried to pull back, but Holmes waded into them, swinging his sword right and left and up and down killing spiders and reducing them to crimson goo. The spiders receded into the dark shadows of the sanctuary. Holmes turned toward the glowing light.

The green light came from the baptistry. It moved and danced, reminding Holmes of the aurora borealis. He stepped over vines and slogged through dead spider goo. He hopped over a choir railing and made his way across the choir loft to the front edge of the baptistry. He stood in a chair and leaned over the edge. A swirling, sparkling whirlpool of energy filled the baptistry. Suddenly, he lost his balance and tipped forward. He fell headfirst into the pool of energy.

With a thud, he landed on his back on a hard, stone floor. The fall knocked the air out of him, and he gasped for breath, reeling under the very real pain that lanced across his back and down his legs. He looked upward at the stone ceiling of the chamber he had fallen into and watched the whirlpool of energy dissipate, leaving behind dark rock.

Holmes sat up and held up the sword to illuminate his surroundings. A tunnel led away from him toward a distant stone wall that seemed to be bathed in orange and yellow light. He stood up and caught his breath, and the pain in his back subsided but did not go away. This "virtual" world was all too real! He headed down the tunnel.

JOSH

Josh landed on wet stone and jumped to his feet. Where was he? More Weren? The chamber was dark, and the walls were rough stone. He looked up at a huge, black funnel-shaped metal structure.

"No!" He said out loud. Light flared across the chamber, and Ketrick emerged holding a flaming torch. He wore the all too familiar Aztec tunic Josh barely remembered from his time under the church. Josh couldn't remember everything that had transpired while the thirteenth demon possessed him.

Beneath the funnel-shaped metal tube lay the open mouth of the old church furnace. In the center of the chamber, Ketrick's guttering torch illuminated a low, stone slab, the altar of the spiral eye.

"Josh, you don't remember much of this, do you?" Ketrick smiled, revealing his all too perfect white teeth.

"No, I was possessed by the thirteenth demon." Josh hissed.

"Oh, and you're blaming me for that? Josh, you chose to invite the demon in. You embraced a dark covenant. And, things did not turn out the way I wanted. But, now, we get to replay it MY way!"

"Hello, Josh."

Josh whirled. A young woman stood just inside the circle of light. Her yellow hair gleamed, and her sunflower covered dress hung to her knees. The last time he saw her was in Lakeside. "Summer?"

Summer smiled and reached out to him with her bare arms. The skin of the arms rupture, revealing coarse, root-like tendrils that shot toward him and wrapped themselves around Josh's arms. He was jerked across the floor by the girl's incredible strength. Her mouth unhinged, and her jaw fell to the level of her chest, revealing a deep, black maw from which crimson roots burst forth. The roots encircled his head, and her toes exploded into limbs that surrounded his legs. Josh tried to scream and found his mouth filled with tiny sprouting rootlets.

Summer's transforming body became a walking nightmare of plant parts as she lifted him and placed him on the altar. The roots tightened and bound him to the cold stone. He fought for breath, and finally, the rootlets left his mouth and exposed his face.

Ketrick leaned over him. The war paints of the Aztec covered the man's face. He touched Josh's lip.

"Nice lip bead." He grabbed it and ripped it from Josh's lip. The pain was incredible and very, very real. Josh howled with pain and tasted blood as it ran into his mouth.

Ketrick inspected the golden lip bead and then tossed it over his shoulder. "That pain was nothing compared to what you are about to feel." He held up a knife in his hands. Josh recognized the knife that had once been in Ketrick's office. It was an ancient artifact, a knife used to remove the heart of human sacrifices. The last time he had seen it was in Cephas' collection in the basement of the Ketrick's old lakeside home.

"I must admit this knife's structure is rather primitive." Ketrick turned the knife in the guttering torchlight. "A chiseled stone shaft and a leather-wrapped handle. Ah, the blood soaked into the leather! It has seen the death of thousands, and it will see one more."

"This is not real!" Josh screamed. "You can't kill me."

Ketrick laughed. "Oh, I'm not going to kill you. I can't do that, Josh. You are one of Them. You belong to the Other side. But, you came into this realm willingly, and now, you are at the disposal of my power. No, we do not want to kill."

Ketrick's eyes widened. "We want to cause unrelenting, indescribable pain. Imagine exciting every pain fiber in your body at one time? Of course, you would pass out. So, we have to be selective. I can cut and maim and even amputate, and you will feel the real sensation of pain from that experience." Ketrick leaned even closer, and the spit from his words showered Josh's face.

"No, I will bring you to such a level of pain and suffering you will beg to die. You will want to die. And, you can. When the time comes, all you have to do is reach up to your head, and you will feel your goggles even though you cannot see them in this realm. And, with one swift motion." Ketrick jerked the knife across Josh's vision. "Tear them from your head. You will experience total neuronal disruption. It will only take a second, and your brain will shut down completely. You will die but by your own hand." Ketrick smiled. "It is the way of Numinocity."

"You're one of the warrior priests things Thakkar talked about. You're not really Ketrick."

"I am more than that, Josh." Ketrick giggled, actually giggled!

∾

HOLMES

HOLMES EMERGED from the tunnel into a huge stone chamber. In the center of the chamber, Josh lay constricted by vines and roots on what appeared to be a stone altar. Roots and tendrils led away from Josh's feet and merged into a humanoid shape standing at the end of the altar. But, what took his breath away was the figure hunched over Josh. Holmes had looked through many of Cephas' artifacts in the short time he had been in charge of them. He recognized the Aztec knife in the man's hand. The man's black hair and facial features matched a photograph of Robert Ketrick.

But, what was strange about the entire scene was the lack of motion. Everything around him seemed frozen in time. He walked over to the plant girl and waved the shield in front of her strange, fibrous eyes. No reaction. He leaned over Josh, and the boy did not acknowledge his presence. The kid wore a long, black coat, and his hair was dyed black. Blood had run down his chin and neck from a tear in his lip. What was happening?

Words sprang to the surface of the sword. "*So the sun stood still, And the moon stopped, Till the people had revenge upon their enemies. Is this not written in the Book of Jasher? So the sun stood still in the midst of heaven, and did not hasten to go down for about a whole day. Joshua 10:13.*"

Holmes smiled. "I was thinking about that verse just now. So, I can make things stand still until I can figure out what to do. But, like the verse says, there is a limit to making time stand still even here in this realm. So, what should I do to save Josh? What verse can I bring to bear?"

Try as he might, he couldn't think offhand of a verse that applied to a plant girl entrapping a human being on an altar on which an Aztec priest was about to offer a pagan sacrifice. If time moved forward, Ketrick would bring the knife down onto Josh and cause great damage. How to block that? He looked at his shield.

"Ah, the shield of faith. It can block the knife. Faith is trusting in something for which you have seen the evidence. Faith is certainty in what you believe." He leaned over Josh. "I don't know if you can hear me, Josh. But, you are the newest Christian of our group. I know you have faith. You had to have faith to receive Christ. So, now, I want to remind you of that faith." Holmes saw movement at the corner of his vision. The knife in Ketrick's hand had moved slightly. Time was moving again. Holmes tore away at the vines and freed Josh's right hand. He took the shield and worked Josh's hand into the hand-hold on the back of the shield. Then, he placed the shield over Josh's chest between his heart and the knife.

"The shield of faith will protect you, Josh." He whispered. When Holmes stood up, the air swam around him, and he was somewhere else.

JOSH

JOSH BLINKED as Dr. Holmes appeared and disappeared in a matter of seconds. He felt the shield across his chest. Ketrick brought down the knife, and it shattered against the metal surface of the shield. Ketrick's eyes widened, and he stepped back.

"Where did you get that?"

Josh recalled only one thing Holmes had said. "This shield of faith will protect me." He whispered. He concentrated on the vines holding him down. What was real? What did you believe? Faith was the substance of things hoped for, right? He hoped the vines were fragile and would yield. He flexed his arms, and they burst like rotten paper. He sat up and swiped the shield across the vines gripping his feet.

Summer hissed, and Josh slid off the altar and swung the shield through the girl's fibrous torso. "You're not real." He shouted. She disintegrated into dust. Josh turned toward Ketrick and held up the shield. "You're dead. You're not the real Ketrick. So, who are you?"

"An old friend." Ketrick smiled, and his face elongated, and his body grew behind him. Legs sprouted from his side, and a huge, segmented tail sprung from his own legs. Ketrick *became* the thirteenth demon in the form of a huge scorpion. The scorpion reared up on its legs and pointed giant pincers at Josh. "I am the thirteenth demon! I am here. Really here within this world. I inhabit the spiritual spaces of Numinocity and travel its ways as easily as air flows through the trees! And, your pain will be unending, shield, or no shield. Because I was in YOU!"

Josh stepped back as the memories returned. He was trapped once again in his own mind held captive by the thirteenth demon, powerless, hopeless, at its mercy. No, he couldn't go there again. He was different now. When the thirteenth demon had entered him, he was not a follower of Christ. But, since that time, he had committed his life to the one and only true Son of God. The shield he held represented his faith; his belief in the power and truth of that commitment. This creature was all lies and deceptions and deceit.

A pincer closed around his waist, and he was lifted from the ground. The pain was excruciating, and he screamed in agony. "See what I can do? Your real body is now wracked with pain, and I will not let up until you beg for release."

Josh fought against the pain and tried to bring the shield up, but it slipped from his hand and landed on the altar. He tried to call upon the name of God; to use the name of Christ to combat this creature, but the pain was too much. He hovered on the edge of unconsciousness, and his mouth grew raw from screaming. "Help!" He managed to whisper.

"Release my son!"

Josh blinked through eyes filled with tears of pain. A man stood on the altar holding the shield. He wore an odd-looking robe and around his neck dangled a gold chain and the Bloodstone. It was his father!

"Dad?" He whispered. "How?"

Arthur Knight lifted the shield and held it before him. "I demand you release my son, you daemon! Do so, or I will unleash the power of the Bloodstone!"

The Scorpion convulsed and drew back in fear. Josh felt something grow warm at this chest. The bloodstone! Yes! He reached up with his right hand into his shirt and clenched the shard of the Bloodstone. "Help me, God." He managed over the unrelenting pain.

A ruby wave of light burst forth from his father's jewel and caught the creature in the torso. A beam of red light cut through Josh's shirt from his own bloodstone and bisected the scorpion pincer. He fell back, and someone caught him. He looked up into the eyes of his father.

The scorpion began to whirl in the assault from the ruby light and disappeared. The room faded to black, and they were back in the entry room. Knight lowered his son to the floor and handed him the shield.

"How?" Josh said. And then, he launched himself at his father. The man wrapped his arms around Josh.

"I do not know. But, I sense I don't have much time, Josh." Knight pushed him away and looked down at his son.

"I always knew you were still alive."

"You had faith that God would take care of me," Knight said. "Just as I had faith when I risked my life for you that God would take care of you."

"What happened?"

"I was pulled through a portal to the same world on which Renee and the Children of the Bloodstone went. And, your Uncle Cephas is there. We are battling evil and doing our best to keep Earth safe from Darksyn."

Josh rubbed tears from his face. "Is this real, or are you part of the game?"

"What game?" Knight said. "Josh, the portal activated, and I stepped through. But, I already feel it tugging me back. My coming to rescue you, wherever this place is, was a God thing."

Josh reached for him, but already he was fading away. "Don't leave."

"I will see you again, Josh. I promise. Do not lose faith." Knight said as he faded from sight. Josh gasped and sat down on the cold floor. How cruel could life be? He had lost his father, regained him, lost him again, and now, he appeared abruptly and talked of a far world.

Legs clad in green surgery scrubs appeared before him. He looked up into the face of Dude, his guardian angel.

"Well, that went great, Josh. You now have part of the whole armor of God."

"My Dad was here." Josh slowly climbed to his feet and groaned in pain. The thirteenth demon had really hurt him.

"So, I understand." Dude scrunched up his face. "Although, I don't understand. Our Master doesn't tell us everything. But, it seems you have triumphed because of your faith. Now, your friends need your help. You must follow Holmes and find Olivia."

Dude disappeared, and Josh sighed. "Wait! What about my father? Where is he? Hey, Dude, answer me!"

The room was empty. "Great!" He looked down at the shard of the bloodstone glowing faintly inside his shirt. It glowed with life. There was a power at his disposal if he only believed; had faith. He had always believed his father was alive, and he had been right.

Josh groaned in pain again and noticed the blood soaking into the bottom of his shirt. He pulled up his shirt. Where the thirteenth demon had gripped him, a long, serrated laceration leaked blood. He stumbled back as weakness overcame him. He reached to his back and felt warm blood on his hand. He had been so excited to see his father, he had forgotten about his injuries. What was going to happen? Could he bleed out in this realm? He ran a hand over his face making sure he had no other cuts. His piercings were gone! He had returned to his normal appearance. But he still wore the black clothing. He shrugged out of the black overcoat and tossed it aside. Right now, he needed to find help. Gripping the shield, he opened the door and walked through.

31

B IRDSONG

BIRDSONG FELT the wall of the dilapidated trailer tremble behind him. Once again, he heard the screams of his sister from inside. He did not want to do this. He did not want to see this. He did not want to relive this memory. He closed his eyes and tried to imagine being somewhere else. When he opened his eyes, the stark, sun-blasted landscape assaulted his senses. He licked drying lips. He was still here, still experiencing that day. He pushed the tinted shield from his eyes. More excruciating light!

He had found Kristen and he could have taken her and run away. But, no, he wanted to look her captors in the eye. He wanted revenge!

Birdsong stood up and opened the door to the camper, dreading what he would find. Stifling heat came from inside, along with the odors of unwashed bodies and excrement. He stepped into a living area darkened from the foil covering the windows. Through the trashed kitchen, he made his way until he reached the bedroom. Kristen lay tied to the bed by her arms and her legs. She wore a dirty flimsy nightgown. Bloodstains dotted the garment.

"Kristen." He said.

She shook her head back and forth, and he said her name louder. She paused and opened swollen, bruised eyes. Her vision seemed unfocused as she searched the room for the source of the sound.

"Jason, is that you?"

"Yes. I've come to save you." He took his utility knife from his pocket and cut the ropes. He sat beside her and lifted her listless body. At first, she resisted him anticipating more torture.

"Shh! It's me. Jason. You're safe now." He pulled the helmet from his head.

Her eyes focused on his face, and she raised her hands still trailing the ropes. She touched his cheeks as tears poured from his eyes. "Jason. You came for me."

"Yes."

"I'm so sorry. I should never have—"

"No time for regrets. We have to go."

From outside, he heard the sound of the ATVs. He had forgotten them, or had this realm given him the time to decide to rescue her? What was the game Numinocity was playing with him?

"Stay here." He stood up, and she grabbed for him.

"No, don't leave me!"

He turned back to her and took her hands in his. "I have to stop them so we can get to safety. You must stay here."

She fell back onto the bed; her hands pressed to her bruised mouth as her tousled, matted black hair fell over her face. She began to mumble incoherently. Birdsong swallowed hard and went to the door. He cracked it open and looked out.

In the real version of these events, he had had the element of surprise. Did he still have it? The sound of the approaching ATVs grew louder, and they rolled over the hill and stopped just a few meters away from the camper. They were driverless. Where were the two men?

He stepped out of the trailer and into the shadow cast by the afternoon sun. From his left, a shadow shambled its way from around the camper. He pressed his back against the camper. Two shadows!

What came from around the corner was unspeakable, impossible. The basic body of the two things was an articulated cactus with long, blood tipped spines. It had a torso and arms and legs. Sitting atop the torso of each cactus thing were the severed heads of the two men he had left for dead that day. Their eyes roved back and forth, looking for him.

Birdsong pressed his hand against his mouth to stifle a scream. Terror seized his heart. He edged along the wall of the camper and slipped around the other end. The cactus things lurched and dragged their legs through the sand with a scratching sound. He smelled the odor of decay as they came closer to him. He reached for his pistol. His holster was empty! He had left the knife inside. The two cactus men stopped and faced the door.

"Mi amigo, you can come out now." One of the men's voice said hoarsely.

"We want to play some more with you." The other more high pitched voice said.

"Hola? Como esta?"

Birdsong swallowed. What to do?

"You know you did us wrong, mi amigo." The second voice said. "You left us to die. You lied to us. What kind of forgiveness is that, eh?"

"You are a hypocrite, a murderer no better than we are." The first voice said.

"It is time for you to feel the pain we felt when Julio tortured us."

Birdsong felt nauseous. Guilt gripped his heart. In the years since that day in the desert, he had relived the nightmare of tying them to the cacti and leaving them to die. He should have brought them in for justice. But, he had been judge and executioner and had left them to their fate.

"You deserved what you got." He screamed.

"Oh, we did?"

"Who made you a god?"

Who indeed, Birdsong thought. He was about to step from the end of the trailer when Dr. Holmes appeared in front of him. Birdsong gasped, and Holmes looked around. He wore the strangest thing, a set of armor.

"Jason?" Holmes said. "Where are we?"

Birdsong nodded toward the clearing. "In the desert."

"Ah, your sister?" Holmes said. He leaned to the side and glanced around the corner of the trailer. "Well, that is gruesome."

"I can't do this again, Monty. I can't live with this guilt."

"Yeah, I just had an encounter sort of like that."

"What?"

Holmes looked back at him. "Judas Iscariot. Trailing his noose."

Birdsong took a deep breath. "That's cold, Monty. But, you didn't kill Judas. I left those men to die. I knew what I was doing."

Holmes nodded. "What you were doing was what you *wanted* to do. But Jason, what you did, was it the *right* thing to do?"

Birdsong looked at him. "What? Look, at the time, I thought it was."

"And, after you thought about it? And, maybe, prayed about it?"

Birdsong looked away. "The guilt has eaten me alive. Yes. I should never have done it. I should have brought them to authorities. I should have done the right thing."

Holmes touched Birdsong on the shoulder. "I have just the solution." He sheathed his sword in a scabbard and shrugged out of the breastplate. He handed it to Birdsong.

"Go ahead. Put it on. The breastplate of righteousness."

Birdsong glanced at the armor piece and pulled it over his head. It settled on his chest and seemed to mold itself to his torso. He felt a jolt of power and assurance. "I get it! The whole armor of God?"

"Yeah. I just got through helping Josh. Now you. I guess this is my purpose, my right thing to do to help all of my friends." Holmes said.

"What now?" Birdsong said.

"You do the next right thing," Holmes said. His eyes widened, and he laughed. "Here I go again." He disappeared.

"Holmes? Where did you go? Do the next right thing?" Birdsong asked. "What is that?" Pain shot across his back and down his legs. It was as if a thousand fire ants had bitten him at once. He whirled, and the cacti men were right behind him. He glanced over his shoulder. Dozens of cacti needles protruded from his back and his legs. The pain was overwhelming and growing. He gritted his teeth to keep from screaming.

"Now you have a taste of what we felt." One of the cactus things said.

"Then, it is what I deserve. I should have taken you in for the legal authorities to deal with. I am not the judge and jury." He groaned in pain, and tears formed in his eyes. "For that, I am sorry. For what Julio did to you, he is answerable for that. I did not put your heads on cacti. He did. So go away and leave me alone!"

The cacti men stepped back and their mouths opened

amazement. They looked at each other. "You don't want to kill us?"

"Again?"

"No. Just being who you are is punishment enough. I know you are not real. I'm guessing you're two of Thakkar's 'warrior-priests.' But, I also suspect you're some kind of demonic manifestation of my memories. Is that how you enter Numinocity? Do you have to be hosted by a human mind?"

The cacti men looked at each other. Birdsong moaned again as another wave of pain poured over him from the cactus needles. "You know, there is one happy thought for me. You see, I am human. I am mortal. And God has allowed me to realize I cannot be righteous all of the time. And, in those failings, I feel my humanity. I sense my mortality, and I want to make things right."

Birdsong took a painful step toward them. The cactus men stepped back. "I have the opportunity for forgiveness. But, as fallen angels, I would say your punishment is more than anything I could inflict." He stepped toward them again. They retreated another step. The two things looked at each other and lifted their grotesque cactus hands. They unleashed a shower of the blood tipped cactus needles. Birdsong bared his chest, and they bounced harmlessly off of the breastplate.

"You cannot face a righteous God because of your own unrighteousness. You can never be forgiven because of your eternal choices. Hear that word, eternal? You're stuck because you can never die; never pass from your physical form into a spiritual existence with God. I'd say that's punishment enough.

He stepped closer, and both cactus men found themselves backed against the camper trailer. "But, I am forgiven, and nothing you can do to me will ever separate me from God. Go do your evil deeds. Wallow in your eternal punishment. In the name of my Savior, Jesus Christ, go away now and let me get on with doing the right thing!"

Both men put their cactus hands up to their heads, and before Birdsong could stop them, they tore away something ethereal, something nonexistent in Numinocity. With a wail of incredible pain, both things disappeared. They had torn off their goggles!

"Well done, son."

Birdsong turned painfully, and standing against the setting sun was an aging, small woman with tight salt and pepper hair and a face etched with wrinkles. It was his grandmother, his Hu'ul. But, she was younger than when he had last seen her.

"Grandmother?" Birdsong ran to her, and she put up a restraining hand. "How are you here?"

"I was on my pilgrimage walk and stopped for some air and heard you speak. Why are you here? You are so much older than the last time we talked." Her wrinkled, weathered face twisted in surprise.

"I am here, but you are not, Hu'ul. I am in your future. But this place is not real."

His grandmother motioned for him to turn around. "Let me see your back."

Birdsong turned his back to her, and he felt the pain as she pulled the spines from his skin. "Oh, Jason, what evil men have done this to you?"

"It is what I deserve, Grandmother. I made a poor decision. Now, I am paying for it with this terrible pain. How are you here?"

"My son, all I know is I am here. There. They are gone. But, I do not have the healing salve for your wounds."

Birdsong turned around and reached out and touched her cheek. "You have given me a salve for my soul, Hu'ul. Thank you. I have to walk this journey alone now just as you must walk the pilgrimage."

She nodded. "I do not know how God is allowing me to speak to you, but whatever pain you are feeling, you must move past it. The task God has placed before you must be completed." She reached out with a gnarled hand and touched his chest.

"I see you are wearing the breastplate of righteousness. Know that you are justified and cleansed by God's forgiveness and go and do what you must. One day I will share a very special poem with you written by our people, Jaybird."

Birdsong smiled. "You already have. I like the last two lines the best. 'We are complete with this light.'"

"*This is the way we begin and end things.*" Hu'ul smiled and patted his cheek. "With love. I love you, Jaybird." She turned and walked toward the setting sun. Birdsong blinked, and she was gone. The world around him fell into darkness, and he found himself in the entry room again. Warmth trickled down his legs. He glanced at the back of his legs. The cacti spines were gone, but he was still bleeding, and the pain was still there.

"Good work, Jason."

He looked up into the face of a small, thin man with short, black hair and bright eyes. "Alar?" It was the pilot who had flown them to Boone's island and who had later turned out to be an angel.

"Time is short now, Jason. You must go and help Jonathan. Just walk through the door."

The pain from the cacti wounds burned up and down his back and legs, and a puddle of blood had formed around his feet. "Am I going to die?"

"Not if you find Jonathan and the girl before the time runs out," Alar said. "Now, go!"

Birdsong drew a deep, painful breath and walked through the door.

32

R AVEN

RAVEN HUNG in the threads and dangled above the figure of her stepfather. His gaunt form was all too familiar as well as his stained, chipped teeth. He held the knife from *that* day in his hand, and he pointed it at her.

"It's your fault I'm dead, Raven. It's all your fault."

Raven felt tears form in her eyes. "No! You had a heart attack. You were already dead."

"When you stabbed me a dozen times? Does it matter? If I had not been dead, you still wanted to kill me! You still wanted to murder your own father." His face twisted in anger.

"Stepfather. My father died in the war." Raven felt the strings tighten around her arms, her wrists, her waist, her legs. She was growing numb from the lack of circulation.

Her stepfather walked directly underneath her, and his face was only a foot from hers. "You know it was your fault your mother died, don't you? She blamed you for your father's death. He was such a hero, and he promised his little girl he would fight for his country to keep her safe. Remember?"

Raven shook her head. "I can't remember. My mind is so jumbled. So many mixed memories all colliding and bouncing off each other. I don't know what to believe anymore."

"Well, then end it." Her stepfather offered the knife to her. "You can end all of this madness right now. Take the knife. Reach behind your head and sever the strap that holds your goggles to your face. One flash of pain and it will all be over."

Raven felt the threads release from her right hand, and she could bend her forearm just enough to reach the knife. Could she end it all? Would it finally all be over? She remembered those moments after the fall in the cavern when she had caught a fleeting glimpse of her Savior. She could return to him!

Her fingers opened, and her palm almost touched the hilt of the knife. She recalled the knife being held in the air above her lamb shaped cake in which her stepfather had put parts of her murdered pet lamb. She glanced around at the floor. Where had the lamb gone?

The small, perfectly white lamb came up to her stepfather and bleated. He glanced down at the lamb.

"No, don't do it again." Raven pleaded.

"It's you or the lamb." Her stepfather looked back at her.

White lamb, white skin. A memory surfaced clear and sharp, and she saw the tall, ghostly figure of Satan's assistant, Lucas, with his pale skin covered with living tattoos and his crimson eyes. Lucas had tried to seduce her into taking a demon, but when he touched her, it had hurt him. Why? Because she belonged to the Son of God. That forgiveness flooded over her as she recalled the day she had accepted it as a ten-year-old girl. It was the same forgiveness she had recalled when she chose to sacrifice herself to stop Rudolph Wulf, the twelfth demon. What had Monarch said about her and Steel?

They were different because of their implants. They could operate differently in this realm.

Raven stopped reaching for the knife and looked into the eyes of her stepfather. "You're not real. You're a demon."

"Does it matter? I lived inside your stepfather, almost his entire life. I motivated him. I dominated him. I made him do bad things ." He leaned closer. "But, here is a little secret. He enjoyed it! When we harvested his soul, it was so sweet! You see, we weren't after you that day. No, we wanted him. And, the bonus was, it ruined your childhood. It tainted your soul. Oh, the disappointment that must have brought to your master."

Raven tried to recoil, but the threads tightened. "No! Don't say that."

"Good! I feel your self-loathing growing, your anger. Stoke it. Use it. Here." He handed her the knife and pressed the hilt into her hand. "Kill me again. It is what you do, isn't it? You kill! Kill or be killed, right?"

A figure materialized in the doorway to the kitchen. Dr. Montana Holmes looked around the kitchen, and his eyes met her gaze. Her stepfather seemed frozen before her.

"Raven? What is going on?"

"Dr. Holmes? I wondered what happened to you? Are you here? Are you in Numinocity?"

"Yes. And I'm here to help." Holmes lifted a glowing sword in his right hand. Words appeared on the surface of the sword, and he said them out loud.

"If you abide in my word, you are truly my disciples, and you will know the truth, and the truth will set you free. John 8:31-32." He tossed the sword into the air in a spiraling motion. It sliced through the threads, and Raven fell to the floor. The sword boomeranged back into Holmes' hand. Holmes came over to her and helped her sit up.

"He had me so confused. My mind is so messed up, Dr. Holmes. All those confusing memories." She held the knife before her and glanced at the figure of her stepfather frozen in time. "He almost convinced me to end it all."

"Your mind? Ah, that's the key to you getting out of this mess. With all you've been through, it's a wonder you have a mind at all. I think this might help." Holmes took the helmet from his head. He slid it over Raven's head. "The helmet of salvation. It will give you the certainty of your salvation against the lies and the insanity of the enemy. Embrace your salvation again, Raven. Find the mind of Christ."

Raven felt the helmet settle over her head. Instantly one thought burned its way through the fog. She was a child of God. She had found forgiveness when she was a child and had rediscovered it in the caverns of Romania.

"Dr. Holmes, how can God possibly forgive me for all I have done?" She felt tears fill her eyes.

Holmes lifted his sword, and it gleamed. "*For as high as the heavens are above the earth, so great is his love for those who fear him; as far as the east is from the west, so far has he removed our transgressions from us. Psalm 103:11-12.* There's your answer, Raven. Grace. Unmerited favor. Unconditional love."

Raven felt the truth settle on her thinking, and a peace calmed the troubled water of her myriad of confused memories. "Yes."

Holmes looked her in the eyes. "Cling to the only true and important event in your life that matters, the moment He came into your life; the moment He introduced you to the real Father. Not this false, demonic puppet."

Raven stood up, and Holmes nodded. He stepped back and disappeared. Her stepfather lurched into motion again and looked around the room in confusion. "How did you?"

Raven held up the knife. "You gave me a knife, remember? I cut those strings. I've severed myself from the past you want me to remember."

Her stepfather frowned and, in a sudden blur, tore the knife from her hand. He reached for the lamb, and Raven threw herself between her stepfather and the lamb.

The knife blow caught her in the abdomen. The lamb looked at her with moist eyes and ran out of the room.

"So noble, aren't you. You took the penalty for the lamb. Is this ironic or what?" Her stepfather's face was right next to hers as he twisted the knife in her abdomen.

Pain shot through her midsection, taking her breath away. He stepped back, holding the bloody knife. Raven staggered, trying to catch her breath. This pain was all too real. The blood running down her abdomen was hot and sticky. This is what the helmet had told her. In her mind, she knew the truth that Jesus of Nazareth had taken the penalty for her. He was truly the Lamb of God. And, in that realization, she knew what she now had the power to do. She looked at the demon and gasped for breath as she said, "In the name of Jesus, go to your eternal punishment!"

Her stepfather's eyes widened in shock, and he raised his hands in defense as something bright and gleaming appeared between them. The angel was not a stranger to Raven. He had caught her on her fall in the cavern. She knew him as Raffle.

Raffle held out his closed fist and opened his palm. Bright lightning skittered over the demon posing as her stepfather, and for a second, she saw his true form all twisted, gnarled limbs and yellow eyes and red fangs before he screamed in agony and disappeared. The knife clattered to the kitchen floor, and the room faded into darkness.

Raven stood in the entry room again, her hands clasped to her abdomen. She felt the weight of the helmet on her head. Her true salvation had sent one of Satan's minions to hell! She groaned in pain. Raffle turned toward her, his dark skin and bright eyes gleaming.

"Good work, daughter. But time is running out, and you must help your friends."

She held out her hands, covered with blood. "Am I dying?"

"Only if you choose to die."

She shook her head in disbelief. "This is all too real."

"But it is from your mind. Control it. Use it. Now, hurry." He motioned to the door behind her. Raven nodded and imagined the blood vessels closing off in her abdomen. She imagined the nerve endings not firing, and soon, the pain and the bleeding lessened. Maybe she could control other things in this realm. All she needed was practice and imagination. She stood tall and rubbed the blood from her hands on her pink dress and walked through the door.

OLIVIA

OLIVIA FLOATED in a sea of confusion. She tried to move her arms and legs, and they did not respond. Was this what it was like when she had an absence seizure? Every part of her body totally unresponsive? She was thankful she did not remember what happened during those seizures. She could still blink her eyes, and she could still breathe, but drool had dribbled down her cheek. She couldn't move her eyes, and she could only stare at the bleak, black ceiling of the warehouse in which she had arrived to meet her brother. How stupid of me, she thought. This was Josh's fault for filling her mind with the sentiment of hope. It had blinded her to the possibility of a trap. He had given her false hope she could find her brother. And, now, she had fallen into Thakkar's trap. All his talk of God. Where was God now? Why didn't he help her? She slowly blinked, and the tears ran down her cheeks. Could Josh be right? Did God really exist? To be honest, she had no one to blame for her situation but herself.

Something clanged to the side of her. Olivia had no problem with her hearing. At the periphery of her vision, she had made out tall, black monoliths arranged in a circle, and she felt the hard scratchy wood surface of the slab beneath her. Thakkar's new nanomeme enhanced physical form had appeared in the periphery several times, talking to at least six individuals leaning into the monoliths. They all wore goggles.

"No! No!" Thakkar screamed. "Alastair, talk to me. Alastair!" Thakkar's shadow fell over her, and Olivia saw the distress on Thakkar's beautiful face. "That's four of them taken out in the last two hours." Thakkar leaned over Olivia. "It's your brother, isn't it? He's taking on my warrior priests, and he is destroying them. How I don't know? You can't be killed in Numinocity unless your tear off your goggles in the real world! How is he doing it? Do you know? Blink once for yes and twice for no."

Olivia tried to smile and blinked three times. Thakkar swore and seemed to blur as she moved quickly out of Olivia's field of vision. The air seemed to ripple as if something were moving through slowly undulating waves. The ripples blurred the image of the far ceiling, and for a microsecond, something filled her vision. Olivia caught a glimpse of something beyond the ceiling, another world of gleaming towers and rolling mountains. What was happening? The vision faded, and the dark ceiling returned.

Thakkar's voice slowed and changed in timber and quality. Colors began to ripple through the air in translucent ribbons of light, and everything seemed to freeze.

She felt the tickle of an electric current along the senses at the surface of her brain. It was nothing like the beginnings of a seizure. It was just a tiny caress of current, and then, deep within her mind, she felt a new sensation build and begin to swell inside her head.

What was happening? She wasn't wearing goggles. And yet, it seemed as if she were somehow in contact with the altered reality of Numinocity. Thakkar had bent over her. No, the *image* of Thakkar had bent over her, and it seemed solid as if composed of what? Nanomemes! What if some of those nanomemes had been attracted to her brain interface? Could it be that some stray nanomemes had now entered her system? But, without the goggles, how would that connect her to Numinocity?

Concentrate! Imagine being in that world with Steven. Imagine passing through this barrier of unreality into that realm. She blinked and saw a cave, and then it was gone. Yes! The nanomemes were adapting to her implants! After all, these nanomemes that Thakkar had designed were not as clean as they should be. She had heard Thakkar talking about a six-hour limit when she had called her mother. Steven must have perfected his nanomemes because he had been in Numinocity for days. But, if Thakkar's nanomemes were imperfect, then they might stray from their basic programming. My implants, she thought. Access my implants.

If she could have shaken her head, she would have. It was ridiculous trying to will the nanomemes, if they were there, to adapt to her implants and take her into Numinocity. She felt something twitch at the corner of her eyes, and she blinked again. Slowly. For the second time, she saw the cave as she closed her eyes in a slow blink. A blue glow came from deep within and a shadowy figure.

Her eyes opened again, completing the blink. Could she close her eyes? Did she now have more control? If she could block out Thakkar and this room, she could concentrate on the cave and the blue glow. She blinked again, and this time willed her eyelids to stay shut. The cave returned, and this time she was inside nearing the shadowy figure. It turned, and the blue glow from something in the figure's hand illuminated his face. Steven!

Her eyes opened, and tears began to leak down her cheeks.

Had she found Steven? If so, she couldn't let Thakkar know. But she could join him. What she needed was an out of body experience. Rarely, when one of her seizures hit her particularly hard, she could for a short period look down upon herself. She often remembered the experience poorly, but it had happened. Of course, Josh had talked about her soul, her spirit. More talk about his God and her eternal soul. Was it her soul that had temporarily left her body? If that was so, there was truly more to her existence than biochemistry and firing neurons. If she could induce a seizure, would that help? Thakkar would think she was having an absence seizure and wouldn't notice the importance of her closed eyes.

Emotions often produced the conditions that brought on a seizure. She imagined her mother standing in the alleyway outside the theater in London. She pictured her brother and her father standing over the homeless man sprawled on the sidewalk. It had been Jonathan Steel, a fact her mother had hidden from her. Steel said her mother had operated on his brain! If that was true, then what else had her mother done? Did she deserve the attempted assassination? Was the bullet that killed her father and crippled her brother's hands and caused her brain damage really intended for her mother? If so, what kind of monster was her mother?

Her heart raced, and her breathing quickened. Thakkar's face appeared in her vision.

"Seizure coming on, dear?" She asked. "Well, there will be more, and more often, if your mother doesn't tell me how to find your brother. And soon."

The darkness came on like it always did, and this time, Olivia hovered above her body. The warehouse was massive, but the Stonehenge like construction was all that mattered. Six people were leaning into alcoves built into the surrounding monoliths.

But, the most disturbing sight was her body laid out on one

of the central slabs. And, next to her on the other slab was the twisted, paralyzed body of Sultana Thakkar.

Olivia looked above her at the ceiling. For a second, she saw a man hovering there. He wore green scrubs and a smile. He beckoned to her with a hand gesture.

"Hurry. Josh needs your help." He said.

"Who are you?"

"Dude. Josh's guardian angel." He waved at her again and disappeared. Before she could open her ethereal mouth to comment, pinpoints of light began to form, and she felt it happen in her brain. Only this time, she did not fall into amnesia and confusion. This time she was totally aware of the world around her and the new world that opened up before her. As she soared upward toward the warehouse ceiling and into an opening portal into Numinocity, she caught sight of a figure crouching in the rafters. The woman with red hair and an artificial arm never saw her as she left reality behind for the world of Numinocity.

33

S TEEL

"WHO ARE YOU?" Steel mumbled through his bruised, swollen lips. Lightning flashed outside the beach house and illuminated the image of himself sitting in the chair.

"I'm you." The other Steel leaned forward. "I'm the one you deny. I'm the one you've forgotten."

"No!"

"Oh, yes." The other Steel stood up and paced around Steel's fallen body. Lightning played across the man's face, and his bright, turquoise eyes flashed with insanity. "I've hidden away too long. It's time for you to become who you really are."

"I'm just fine." Steel tried to sit up, and the pain of so many broken bones and bruised flesh brought stars before his eyes. He felt dizzy and light-headed and crashed back to the floor.

The other Steel stood at his side, crossed his arms, and tilted his head. "Look at you. How the mighty have fallen. All you had to do was tell Father what he wanted to know. But, no, your stubbornness led you to this." He opened his hands and moved them to take in Steel's body. "Broken, defeated, no memory."

The other Steel knelt beside Steel. "But, I can bring all of this to an end. You can become the man you were meant to be. I can open the doors of your memory. I can restore it all with the utterance of one phrase." The other Steel held up a finger. "All I have to do is say it."

Steel shook his head. "I do not want to be you."

The other Steel frowned and stood up again. "Well, you are me. Maybe if we relive a few select memories, it might help."

Steel shook his head and winced at the pain. "No. Just leave. Go."

The other Steel laughed. "I'm not going anywhere. We belong together. Let's see. Do you remember the demon?"

Steel shook his head and tried once again to roll away, but the pain brought nausea. He retched.

"Oh, you don't want to vomit." The other Steel said. "In your real body, you would aspirate it into your lungs, and you would die." He reached down and rolled Steel onto his back. The other Steel took a pillow from the couch and tucked it under his head.

"Now, do you remember the Major?" The other Steel sat on the floor beside Steel. "I believe he might have told you something about your demon. You know, our father introduced the Major to the ninth demon. Grandfather's diary introduced you to the third demon. Oh, what fun we had together. Don't you remember?"

Hot tears ran from Steel's eyes. "Please, no."

"Oh, the things we've done! Obscene. Corrupt. Destructive. We would have been the apple of grandfather's eye. Until." The other Steel paused and looked away. Lightning played across his face.

Steel swallowed blood and spit. He couldn't take the bait. He couldn't ask. But, he had to know. "Until what?"

The other Steel looked away from the beach and back toward Steel, and for a moment, a flash of lightning froze the tears trickling down his face. "What do you remember about mother?"

Steel gasped, and pain shot through his chest. "No. Not now."

The other Steel leaned over him, and his tears dripped onto Steel's chest. "Surely, you have a memory. Tell me about it."

Steel looked away, and his head throbbed with pain. "I can't."

"Sure, you can. Look, I know you're hurting. But, remember, you heal quickly." The other Steel said. "Why, some of those broken bones are already straightening out." The other Steel took Steel's arm and lifted it into Steel's sight. Steel cringed, but the pain was less than he imagined. He focused his vision on his hand. The twisted, broken bones were straight. "You see. The more you remember about who you really are, the faster you will heal."

Steel swallowed and glared at the other Steel. "I would rather die in agony than be you."

The other Steel dropped his arm, and Steel winced in pain. "Too late. You ARE me, remember? It's only a matter of time until it all comes back to you. Isn't that what you are after? Aren't you chasing father so you can recapture your memory?"

Steel looked away again. Was it true? Did he want to become this heinous thing that claimed to be him? Maybe amnesia was preferable.

The other Steel walked away to the window, and lightning flashed only softer as the storm receded. "This is not working. Maybe if you were somewhere, that might trigger your memories. Like, at the hospital."

The beach house living room faded, and Steel found

himself on the floor of a conference room. The pain had mostly subsided, and he looked down at his hospital scrubs. He was in April Pierce's group therapy room. "No! Don't do this."

He slowly climbed to his feet. The other Steel stood behind a chair, and sitting in the chair was a small, bony man with a spiral tattoo around his right eye.

"Braxton!" Steel hissed. "I'm not doing this."

"Sure you are, man of steel." Braxton giggled. "You had some good memories come back. Don't you remember what happened in this room?"

Steel closed his eyes, and he was pushed back by some kind of force into a chair. The memory came, and it would not stop as the room faded into a scene from his recent past.

Five other patients drifted in. Mr. Sanora was an elderly man suffering from obsessive-compulsive disorder wearing spotless pajamas with sharp creases. Chuck came in next, chewing on his nails, his eyes focused on the floor. He was a teenager with a serious neurosis. Mr. McCoy, the manic-depressive, came next. He carried a box of donuts in his right hand and a bag of cookies in the other. Suicidal Mr. Watson peeked around the corner and hurried to one of the free chairs. And last, came Rocky Braxton. Braxton was short and extremely thin with a shock of black hair that stood on end and a tattoo around his right eye, a dark spiral that wound its way from just under his lower eyelid out toward his cheek, back up under his eyebrow, down the line of his nose and ended just above his eyebrow. Every time Steel saw it, something itched in the back of his mind. But when he tried to pin it down, the thought skittered away like an insect. And then, the memory returned with a vengeance.

Steel opened his eyes, and he knelt in a pool of blood from his swollen, bloody nose. He had been in some kind of fight. He wore tattered jeans and a tank top. He was 15 years old. His head pounded, and his body racked with spasms of pain. He glanced up, and a man stood in front of him. He was short and balding. But his eyes held a love as deep as the sea.

"Hey, man, we've come to get you. You need to come on home." Steel looked at the man. His name was Kevin. "You know we all love you. It's time to walk away from all of this. Would you like for me to help you?"

Down the alley in which he stood, a shadowy figure glanced over his shoulder as he disappeared around a corner. He felt a pang of fear and hatred and turned his gaze back to Kevin. He held hope in his hands. "I don't want to go on like this. Will you help me?"

"I promise," Kevin said.

"I was a teenager in an alley. Kevin prayed with me. Whoever he is," Steel said. "I was transformed into something new. Something forgiven. But I can't remember what I was like before that."

Dr. Richard Pierce nodded. "Without the framework of your past, you will have difficulty determining who you became. But you have taken a big first step, Jonathan. You have remembered a life-changing occurrence that is so profound even amnesia can't erase it."

THE MEN FADED AWAY, leaving only the empty room. The other Steel sat in Braxton's chair.

"You were in some kind of fight, right?"

Steel's head pulsed with pain. "Yes."

"The mysterious figure, do you know who it was?"

Steel looked away, and the memory still lingered. "No."

"Could it be the figure was not human?" The other Steel said gently. "Could it be your friend, what was his name, Kevin, drove the demon away? The demon that was inside of you?"

Steel looked back at the other Steel. Was it possible? Had he been possessed? "All I know is that memory is of when I changed. It was when I became a Christian. I cherish that memory."

The other Steel nodded and stood up. He placed a hand under Steel's chin. "Where did the blood come from?"

"What blood?"

"All over you." The other Steel paused. "If the other figure was spiritual, how did you get blood on you?"

Steel blinked in confusion. "It was my blood?"

The other Steel smiled. "No. It came from somewhere else. Tell me again about your memory of Mother."

Steel tried to push the memory away, but it surfaced from the dark shadows of his mind. Only once in the past few years had a single memory of his mother surfaced. He saw her now; beautiful eyes fixed on his. Her red hair clustered around her pale features. He was cradled in her lap.

The other Steel shook his head. "No. Look again."

Steel glanced up and realized his memory had been projected on the wall like some kind of movie. He stood up and walked over to the wall. "How is this possible?"

"Numinocity can access your memories if you let it." The other Steel stood beside him. "I remember this differently. I remember the truth."

"What?" Steel said.

The other Steel waved a hand, and the image pulled back from Steel's mother's face. As it did the world titled upside down. Steel's mother was not cradling Steel. A young, teenage Steel was cradling his mother's head in his lap. Her body was covered in blood. Blood was all over Steel. He was crying, and the image went to black.

Steel stumbled backward. "No."

The other Steel advanced on him. "She wasn't holding you.

You were holding her body. The blood wasn't yours. It was hers."

Steel was shaking, and he collapsed onto the floor. He pulled his knees up and his arms down to fend off the truth. In the fetal position, he could not see the other Steel as he bent over Steel and whispered in his ear.

"You killed Mother."

34

H OLMES

HOLMES WALKED through the door from his dark room into a raging thunderstorm. Rain lashed at him and soaked him to the skin. He looked around into the darkness, interrupted by flashes of lightning, and heard the roar of the surf above the thunder. He was on a beach. Why had Miguel sent him to a beach, and who was here? Vivian? Steel? Olivia? He heard a distant scream and whirled to face the beach house rising from the dunes. It was over three stories high with staircases leading up to the second level. A light flickered from a second-story window.

A set of wooden stairs led over the dunes to the lower deck. He mounted the wide stairs leading up to a large deck coming from the second level. Sliding doors led into a dark living area. Where had the scream come from? Who was screaming? At the back of the living area, a large kitchen with hanging pots gleamed in the lightning. He made out an inner stairway leading up to the next level. Holmes made his way carefully across the floor, dripping water from his tunic. His sandals squished, and he stopped at the foot of the stairs. He realized the house actually had four levels. No doubt, the lower level was a garage underneath the kitchen. The stairs led up to another landing and then past that to the highest level.

He gasped when he looked down, and a slash of lightning illuminated bloody footprints on the stairs. From the middle level, he heard a groaning sound that sent shivers up his spine. Slowly, he made his way up the stairs avoiding the bloody footprints. He reached the next level, and the footprints led to a closed door. Bedroom maybe? Media room? He had no idea, but the handle on the door dripped with a dark material that proved to be blood when the next flash of lightning came. From the other side of the door came the scream again. It was male and filled with such agony and pain it drove Holmes back away from the door. He almost fell down the stairs.

He approached the door again, and taking the edge of his tunic wiped away the blood. He twisted the door handle and slowly opened the door. The flickering light he had seen in the window came from a dozen or so candles scattered around a large bedroom. Lightning illuminated a chamber of horror.

Holmes froze, bile rising in his throat. On the right-hand wall, a man hung with arms and legs outstretched. In the flickering light, Holmes made out dozens of nails driven through the man's hands, arms, legs, and feet. Blood had run down the wall and coagulated. His hair was white, and he had been stripped down to his underwear.

The man's head hung at an angle, and his chest did not move. He was quite dead. Something dark moved around the body, and the next flash froze flies in mid-flight in a strobe infested second of horror.

The man's blood had trickled down over letters and words

written all over the wall up to a man's normal reach, but the man's head almost touched the ceiling. The words and letters were indecipherable, and flies landing on the letters confirmed Holmes's fears. They were written in the man's blood! In the center of the room, something moved, and Holmes jerked back in fear. The candles stood in a circle on the floor, and the furniture pushed back away from a figure folded in upon itself. The figure wore hospital scrubs. Blood covered his bare feet, and bloody smears marred the otherwise white clothing.

The figure moaned again and pulled in on itself in its fetal position. Holmes stepped closer and recognized the man's head.

"Jonathan?" He croaked in a breathless whisper. Holmes hurried through the candles and crouched beside Steel. The man's eyes were closed, and he was mumbling to himself.

"No! Please, no. Why did I do it? Why?" And, then, his mouth opened in one of those throaty screams, a wail of despair and pain, unlike anything Holmes had heard.

Holmes reached out gingerly and took Steel's hands and tried to pull them away from the man's face. Steel resisted, and his turquoise eyes flew open illuminated by the flickering candlelight.

"No! Kill me. Let me die." He screamed.

Holmes lay down on his side, so his eyes lined up with Steel's. "Jonathan, it's me. Monty. Your friend. Look at me. I'm here to help."

Steel's eyes opened, and he tried to focus on Holmes. Holmes pointed to the wall. "Who is that?"

"Richard Pierce. Braxton killed him. Maybe. Or, did I? I don't know anymore. I'm a murderer." Steel moaned and began to sob. Holmes swallowed hard and drew a deep breath.

"Jonathan, you are not a murderer. I know you."

"No, you don't!" Steel screeched, and he pushed himself up

off the floor. His eyes were wild. "I killed her, Holmes. I killed my own mother! If I did that, who else did I kill? Huh? At the gun range, I found out I was a sharpshooter. Every bullet right through the forehead." He poked himself hard in the forehead and crusted, dried blood stayed behind.

Holmes sat up and faced Steel. Thunder rattled the windows. "Jonathan, listen to me. This place we are in is not real. This is not real. It's plucked from your worst memories, but it is made worse by your guilt. I know you. We were in Jerusalem together. Who put this memory in your head? Who told you that you killed your mother?"

Steel leaned toward him. "I did."

Holmes sat back, and blue light gleamed from the sword in its sheath. He pulled it from the sheath and held it up.

"You can kill me with that." Steel said. Blue light played across his face.

"No, Jonathan. But, I can liberate you in another way." Words appeared on the sword, and Holmes read them. "*Why do you not understand what I say? It is because you cannot bear to hear my word. You are of your father, the devil, and your will is to do your father's desires. He was a murderer from the beginning, and does not stand in the truth, because there is no truth in him. When he lies, he speaks out of his own character, for he is a liar and the father of lies. John 8:43-44.* Jonathan, Satan is the father of lies. You have bought into his lies. Ask yourself, 'what is the lie?'"

Steel jerked his head and closed his eyes. "What?"

Holmes looked down and gasped. "The belt! Every time a piece of the armor was perfect for each one of you." He loosened the belt. He placed the golden belt around Steel's waist and pulled it around him. He tightened it around Steel's waist.

"Jonathan, you are wearing the belt of truth. It girds you. It encircles you. Use the truth to defeat the lies. Know the truth and know that Satan is the father of lies."

Jonathan blinked and looked down at the belt. "But what if it is true?" He whispered.

"You are forgiven."

"How can God ever forgive me?"

Holmes lifted the sword, and it glowed with blue light, and he read out loud the words that formed above him in the dark air. "*And giving joyful thanks to the Father, who has qualified you to share in the inheritance of his holy people in the kingdom of light. For he has rescued us from the dominion of darkness and brought us into the kingdom of the Son he loves, in whom we have redemption, the forgiveness of sins. The Son is the image of the invisible God, the firstborn over all creation. For in him, all things were created: things in heaven and on earth, visible and invisible, whether thrones or powers or rulers or authorities; all things have been created through him and for him. He is before all things, and in him, all things hold together. And he is the head of the body, the church; he is the beginning and the firstborn from among the dead so that in everything he might have the supremacy. For God was pleased to have all his fullness dwell in him, and through him to reconcile to himself all things, whether things on earth or things in heaven, by making peace through his blood, shed on the cross.* Colossians 1:12-20. Did you get that, Jonathan? The truth is not this place. This realm is the creation of the mind of a human being. Truth is transcendent. The only thing we can create is a falsehood. Don't buy into the lies in this place. Thakkar may hold this realm together with her demonic power, but that power is nothing compared to the power of the Son of God who holds all of reality together. Even here in this realm, Jonathan, we can know truth, and to know truth, all we have to know is Jesus!" Holmes said hoarsely.

A sudden bolt of lightning hit just outside the windows of the beach house. White-hot light filled the room, burning away the bloody words and letters and extinguishing the candles. Holmes put his hands over his eyes, and Steel gasped as the light filled the room. The figure hanging on the wall transformed from the body of Richard Pierce. The outstretched hands and bent legs glowed with light, and someone else hung on the wall, nailed to a bloody cross. Only the body slowly moved away from the cross, and the figure hovered in the air. Eyes that held the structure of the universe in place looked down from the thorn pierced brow. Hands that had once leaked holy blood reached out toward them.

"I am the way, and the truth, and the life. No one comes to the Father except through me." A voice deeper than thunder and more powerful than an earthquake and yet as gentle as falling snow filled the room. The figure vanished, and Steel and Holmes found themselves back in the dark room.

Two ghostly figures appeared from the now blank wall. They shimmered into focus, and Steel gasped.

"Cephas? Theo?"

Cephas Lawrence wore a long purple robe, and standing next to him was a much older Theo in a black robe.

"Chief? What is happening?" Theo said.

Cephas glanced around the room and then at Monty. "Monty? You are here, too? Wherever here is."

"Inside a virtual reality world." Steel said. "So, I assume the two of you are not real."

Cephas poked his belly and then turned poked Theo. Theo grunted. "Watch it, Papaw."

"We are quite real, Jonathan. And, we are both alive in a faraway world transported here by God for purposes we are only now beginning to learn. And so, I must assume we are now speaking to you for the same reason. God has a purpose for our appearance; however, brief or spectral."

"Chief, if you are in trouble, remember God will always put someone there to have your back," Theo said. Theo! His friend. His partner! He was alive!

"But how?" Steel said.

"Not now." Cephas looked down at his hands. They were fading. "Time is running out. You must overcome whatever this is you're involved in. A time is coming when we will need your help."

"That's right, Chief. Worlds are at stake, and only you and Josh can help us." Theo said.

Steel ran forward and waved his hand through their wispy forms. "No! I want you to be real. I need you."

Cephas pointed to the wall above him. "We saw what just happened. You have all you need Jonathan in the face of Satan's lies."

"That's right, Chief. Focus on the reality of Jesus. He is the truth. Use truth to kick old Lucifer in the butt."

Steel smiled and felt tears on his cheeks. "That's my Theo."

"Told you, I was real." Theo chuckled.

"Where are you?" Steel asked.

Cephas and Theo faded quickly from view, and only a few words were audible. "The Node of God."

Steel felt Holmes's hands on his arm. "Jonathan, I don't know what is going on here, but only God could have kept them alive, and only God could have let us hear from them. We have to discern the lie from the truth."

"You and Theo both said it. Jesus is Truth." Steel said.

Holmes squeezed his arm. "You are forgiven, no matter what you've done. You cannot change the past." Holmes sniffed and wiped at tears on his cheeks. He fell to his knees, and his eyes widened. "Jonathan, just now He let me see Him. I did not see Him in Jerusalem."

"You remember Jerusalem now?"

Holmes gasped, and tears poured down his cheeks. "Yes! I remember it all. I saw the veil torn from top to bottom. It was all real. It is all real. Not like this pale reflection of a virtual world."

Steel touched the belt at his waist. "We know the truth, Monty. I will not be deceived again."

Holmes slowly stood up and turned to the door. "Time is running out. We have to find Olivia."

Steel tightened the belt and reached for the doorknob. "Let's go."

35

IVIAN

VIVIAN CLOSED the door behind her and gasped. The hotel room was spotless. Bright sunshine streamed in through open windows on a sitting room with a couch, a comfortable chair, and a desk built into the wall. A large screen television dominated one wall. She walked across the incredibly plush carpet to the window.

The hotel room looked out over downtown Shreveport, Louisiana. She was on the penthouse level and gazed down on the Red River, winding its way between the sister cities of Shreveport and Bossier City. Casino hotels towered along the Red River. It seemed to be a warm spring day with trees along the Red River Entertainment district dotted with colorful flowers. To her right, an open park on the river bank sat across from the Sci-Port Science Center. She squinted in the afternoon sunlight. Towering monoliths sat in the center of the park. New Stonehenge! Could it be this simple?

"Hello?" A voice echoed from the door leading into what she presumed was the bedroom. Vivian tensed. Who was here? The hotel room was not familiar. She had never been here before. The last time she had stayed in a hotel room in Shreveport was? No! It couldn't be!

She quietly slipped across the carpet and peeked through the open door into a spacious bedroom illuminated by sunlight. The man lay under the covers. His incredibly handsome face held that stunning smile, and she knew behind the high forehead was a brain not quite as nimble as hers. It was the deputy sheriff she had dallied with when she was trying to stop the eleventh demon. What was his name? Westley? Cheston? Weston!

"Hi, ma'am. I've been waiting for you." He said gently in his deep Southern accent.

Vivian drew a deep breath. She stepped into the bedroom and instantly recalled the memory of the touch of his slightly calloused hands, the brush of his lips against hers. She closed her eyes and bathed herself in those memories because this creature that lay before her was not real. She opened her eyes, and he was standing right in front of her now wearing his deputy uniform. He smelled faintly of cologne, sweat, and hay. She looked around, and they were no longer in the hotel room. They were in a barn surrounded by hay. It was here she had fought with the deputy over a rifle and a tripod set up to kill the governor of Louisiana who would appear at an outside campaign rally.

Vivian stepped back, and he grinned. "Thought you had killed me, didn't you?" He pulled his shirt open to reveal the punctures in his chest from the tripod he had landed on. She looked back at his face, and blood poured from a hole in his chest. Blood pulsed from the tear in his neck. The blood hit her in the face, blinding her. She gasped and stepped back and fell, tumbling through the air and landed on a soft, cold surface. She wiped the blood from her eyes, and she was surrounded by frigid air. She was back in that memory, the one memory she wished she could eliminate forever.

"Hurry, we don't want to miss the meteor shower."

Daddy spread out an old blanket on the ground. It was cold, and there was frost already over the grass. We settled right by the fence that separated our yard from the pasture. I looked through the barbed wire at the pasture for Ludie. But, the old heifer was nowhere in sight.

"Now, we put down the blanket." Daddy said. "Then we lay down and cover up with the other blankets and we wait." Daddy took off his jacket and made a pillow out of it. He patted the blanket next to him and I lay down. I settled onto the old blanket. It smelled like fried chicken and butter. The smell made me feel good. It was like being in our kitchen when Daddy would fry chicken. Momma would sometimes eat some but mostly she screamed at Daddy and drank her stuff.

Daddy pulled the blanket over his chest and settled down beside me and pointed to the sky. I had never seen anything so beautiful. I guess I had never just stopped playing or running from Momma and hiding to look up at the sky at night. Millions of stars twinkled in the cold, clear air like jewels spilled out of a jeweler's bag onto a sea of black velvet.

"See that cloudy looking bar across the sky?" Daddy pointed.

"Yeah."

"That's the milky way." He said.

"Can we get milk from it," I asked in wonder.

"No, honey. That's not milk. That's the rest of our galaxy filled with billions of stars."

I smiled and scooted over until I could feel my Daddy all warm next to me. He made me feel safe. He made me feel loved. Momma didn't make me feel that way. She made me feel ugly and stupid and cold and afraid. But, tonight was our night, just my Daddy and me. Suddenly, a white light flashed deep in the sky and streaked across the heavens leaving behind a trail of brilliant luster.

"Oh, Daddy! Did you see that?"

"That's a shooting star. Make a wish."

I closed my eyes real tight, and I wished that my Momma would go far, far away, and leave Daddy and me alone. I opened my eyes, and they were filled with tears. The tears ran down my cheeks and got real cold in the night air. More shooting stars filled the sky until there were dozens and dozens that filled the night sky with magic.

"Oh, Daddy, they're so beautiful. Just look!"

He patted my hand, and it was the most perfect moment in my short eight years of life.

"What you two doing?"

I heard the coarse voice in the darkness and sat up. Momma was lumbering towards us with an old flashlight. The light was dancing like crazy around the bushes. She ran into a tree and fell down. Daddy swore next to me, and I felt him go tense.

Momma got up, and blood was running down from a cut on her head. She touched the blood and swore out loud. She swore and swore and swore until her face was as white as a sheet, and the blood was running down her cheeks.

Daddy got up and went to her and brought her over to the blanket. "Sybil, you should have stayed in bed. You're drunk."

"I'm always drunk!" She screamed, and the flashlight danced around the sky like a sick searchlight. My stomach began to hurt, and I wanted to crawl down under the blanket or float up into the beautiful stars and get away from her.

Something snorted loud in the darkness. I looked through the barbed wire, and Ludie lumbered up. Her single huge, curled horn glistened with dew. Her eyes glowed from the reflected flashlight. She stopped at the fence and eyed Momma. She probably thought Momma had an apple.

"Well, at least the cow is glad to see me," Momma screamed. "You sneaking off into the night with our girl. You gonna kidnap her and run off like you threatened to last week? Huh? You worthless shell of a man!" Momma said. She jerked out of Daddy's grasp and fell onto her backside on the blanket. She turned her reddened eyes on me and behind her, stars fell from the sky.

"What you looking at pumpkin? Huh? Look hard, cause this is what you'll be someday. Marry Prince Charming and then find out life is hell. That's all you got to look forward to. The only thing happy to see me is a cow! My own daughter and husband don't want to be around me!"

She struggled to her feet and went for the fence. Ludie backed away, I guess cause she realized Momma didn't have an apple. That's when Daddy tried to stop Momma. He grabbed her shoulders and Momma shoved him to the side up against the barbed wire. I saw Daddy grimace in pain. He turned his back to me and blood was running down his shirt from the cuts from the barbed wire. I picked up his jacket and stood up to hand it to him. Momma cussed me and shoved me back down on the blanket. And that was when heaven fell.

The blinding ball of light came out of nowhere, streaking across the sky toward the pasture, burning like a flare from hell, etching itself onto my eyeballs. A loud roar passed overhead in its wake and it hit the ground. The explosion rocked the trees and the pasture and echoed into the distance and the light rushed over us.

Ludie reared up on her back legs and rushed the fence. Her right horn exited out through Daddy's back. She picked him up, impaled on her horn and ran off into the darkness. Momma stood there in the sickening whirling flashlight and I couldn't speak. I couldn't breathe.

She looked down at me. "Now look what you've done."

≈

VIVIAN TORE herself up from the blanket and backed away from the lurching form of her mother. She was no longer in the memory. The woman lumbered as she walked, and her eyes were the dead white of an attacking shark. She held a pair of scissors in her hand.

"You took away the only thing that ever mattered to me." She slurred the words. "I'm going to cut you out of my life." She held up the scissors like a knife.

Hands closed on Vivian's arms, and she looked up into the white eyes of Weston. "Want me to arrest her, little darling?"

Vivian tried to jerk out of his grip but couldn't. Blood had poured from the wounds in his face and neck and joined the blood from his chest wound. His bright, blue eyes so reminiscent of those of Jonathan Steel were now the milky white of a Vitreomancer. "I can put the two of you in the same cell."

The pasture and cold night faded, and they stood in a jail cell. Weston released her and backed through the open cell door and slammed it shut. "Have a nice family reunion."

The first blow knocked Vivian to her feet, and she gasped with pain. She looked over her shoulder at the scissors protruding from her left shoulder. She whirled, and her mother was no longer there. In her place, another incredibly handsome man smiled at her. His long hair caressed his shoulders. He wore a knee-length waistcoat and a silk shirt open to his chest. It was Armando from her encounter with the twelfth demon.

"My sweet, sweet Vivian." He said quietly. "Having a bad day?"

Vivian reached over her shoulder and jerked the scissors painfully from her shoulder. She held the bloody scissors before her and felt hot blood run down her back.

"Stay back."

Armando smiled and held up a goblet filled with crimson liquid. "I only wanted to offer you a drink like you did me." He snapped his fingers, and Vivian was thrown back against the bars. Hands gripped her arms and legs and pulled her painfully up against the cold metal bars. She looked over her shoulders into the eyes of a group of vampires, the ones she had left in the caverns of Transylvania. They all had fangs, and she felt the teeth sink into the skin of her arms and legs. She screamed in agony, and Armando drew closer. He grabbed her chin and opened her mouth. She dropped the scissors as the pain took her.

"Just a sip, right?" Armando leaned in close to her and touched her lips with his. "All the men you have met you destroyed, Vivian. Now, it's our turn."

He squeezed her cheeks and forced her mouth open. He poured the coppery flavored fluid into her mouth. She choked on the hot blood, and it sprayed all over Armando's face.

He licked the dribbles away from his lips. "Just a little bit more." He forced more into her mouth. She swallowed involuntarily. The blood filled her stomach, and she retched.

Armando stepped back. "Now, be careful. In the real world, you are lying on your back. You'll aspirate, my dear."

Vivian felt the blood burn through her gut and she could feel the prions enter her bloodstream. Fever took her, and the hands released her. She fell forward onto her face while a hundred puncture wounds drained her life away, and the prion laden blood pumping through her veins.

"Help me." She mumbled.

Armando knelt beside her. "Help you? Do you think there is anyone who cares enough about you to help you? How many did you help, Vivian? You are the destroyer of men and women. You leave bodies in your wake and souls left to rot in hell. There is no mercy for you."

"Step aside." Someone said.

Vivian rolled over onto her back, and another figure loomed over her. His white skin was covered with scars and open wounds. His red eyes gleamed with hatred. Lucas! The last time she had seen him, the Master had punished him and exiled him to a never-ending torment.

"Look what the cat dragged in." He knelt beside her. Armando and the vampires were gone, and she was back in the abandoned castle at the center of the macabre theme park, where she first met the Council of Darkness. She looked around and found herself on a stone slab surrounded by the circular table of the Dark Council. Voices murmured behind the curtains that hid all twelve chairs around the circle.

"They told you to be careful. They told you they would prevail." Lucas laughed and licked his red lips with a long tongue. His perfectly white teeth gleamed in candlelight from the table.

"What do you want?" She croaked painfully.

"I want you to die," Lucas said. "All you have to do to end this is pull off your goggles. Rip them away like a bandage, and the pain will not last long."

"Someone help me." She said.

"Help you?" Lucas stood up. "There is no one to help you, Vivian. You are beyond hope, beyond help. Your enemies surround you, and you will find no mercy here."

Vivian looked up at the far ceiling of the castle. It had been built in a failed theme park based on horror, death, and the occult. But, high up in the dome of this banquet room was something so bizarre, so out of place, it caught her eye. A tiny cross carved into the apex of the ceiling. Placed there perhaps by a zealous worker who prayed for those who would come to such a place? A tiny, quiet protest by someone who was forced to work to bring this hell on earth? A cross? Was that the only source of her hope?

"God, help me." She whispered.

The room faded along with Lucas and the Council of darkness as she passed out. She opened her eyes into darkness again. Someone moved beside her, and a faint blue light fell over her face.

"Vivian?"

She looked up into the eyes of Olivia. "Olivia?"

"Yes. You just showed up out of nowhere."

"Not nowhere." A young man stepped around Olivia. A gleaming blue stone hung from a golden necklace. His hair was dark, and a Maori tattoo covered his cheeks with squiggly lines. His chest was bare and covered with more dark tattoos. He wore a kind of loincloth.

Vivian sat up slowly and looked around. "Who saved me from Lucas?" She looked at the young man. "Tarzan?"

"In this realm, I am Roland1143, but you can call me Steven," Steven said. "I embraced my father's heritage. It has brought me strength, although not for long. Olivia found me in a cave, and we found ourselves transported here."

Vivian stood up, and more blood trickled from the wounds in her limbs and the stab wound in her back. "How are you here, Olivia?"

"Nanomemes," Steven said. "She was in the warehouse with Thakkar and the other six warrior priests. Somehow, the nanomemes have interfaced with her brain implant."

"Without goggles?"

"Yes," Olivia said. "Thakkar has no idea I am here."

"And, that is our ace in the hole," Steven said.

Vivian felt around her face, and although it could not be seen, she felt the straps of her goggles. "Lucas told me to tear off my goggles."

"And, you would have died," Steven said. He stepped forward and stumbled. Olivia held him up. "I have been in Numinocity for days without a break. In the real world, my body is weakening, and I cannot get out of here unless I stop Thakkar. I could take off my goggles if I had strength enough, but I would die or at the least go insane."

"How do we stop Thakkar?"

"We find New Stonehenge, and then you let me handle it," Steven said.

Vivian stumbled across the dark room toward the door. "I know where it is. Follow me."

36

S TEEL

STEEL STEPPED through the door into a sweltering jungle filled with heat and humidity. He was not sure of anything in this strange land. But, the moment spent in the presence of absolute Truth had given him the strength to move past the bad memories, real or imagined, and face the threat before him. He had to find Olivia and stop Thakkar.

Holmes stood beside him. "Jonathan, I've shown up with everyone so far, but Vivian."

Steel glanced at him. "She's here?"

"Saved my life," Holmes said. "I was reacting to the nanomemes, and she gave me drugs. She said she was going to come into Numinocity to stop Thakkar."

Steel nodded. "For once, we are on the same page. And the others?"

Holmes sighed. "They were all injured and in impossible situations. I gave them part of my armor."

Steel looked down at his belt. "The belt of truth."

"The whole armor of God." Holmes held up the sword. "I've given some pieces away. I've got the sword and the sandals of the preparation of the good news of the Gospel."

"A firm foundation to walk on?" Steel said.

"Now, you're thinking the right way," Holmes said. "Where are we?"

Steel moved forward through dense foliage, and birds and animals scampered away through the vines. The air smiled of decay, underscoring the rich fragrance of vegetation and flowers. He stepped from the jungle into a vast clearing and gasped at the sight of the pyramid before him.

Holmes joined him and stiffened. "An Aztec pyramid."

"Human sacrifices." Steel said. "This is where it all began for me with Ketrick and his Aztec heritage."

"What do we do?"

Steel pointed to the pyramid. "We climb and scope out the area. We find New Stonehenge."

He started toward the pyramid. Holmes followed. "This is Teotihuacan." He said as they made their way down a broad passageway toward the pyramid. "This is the Avenue of the Dead leading toward the Pyramid of the Sun, site of human and animal sacrifices. And, Jonathan?"

"Yes."

"This is not how it looks now. This is how it was then." Holmes said. "These are my memories of a virtual reconstruction of this city."

Along the way, they passed shorter versions of the bigger pyramid. The air was still and hot, and they walked in total silence. No people. No animals. The city was deserted. They arrived at the plaza before the dominant structure, the pyramid of the sun. Steel didn't pause and hurried up the stone stairs to the top of the pyramid.

"248 steps." Holmes wiped the sweat from his brow as they arrived on the open top of the pyramid. "Jonathan, I can't get over how real this experience is. Thakkar's system must access our autonomic nervous system to change our pulse and make us sweat. I feel like I've been running up steps in a real, sweltering jungle heat."

"My thoughts and actions count just as much as the structure of this program, right? We use that to our advantage." Steel turned slowly, examining the short, squatty homes clustered on the periphery. "I don't see anything resembling New Stonehenge."

"Now what?"

"Pyramids have hidden chambers, right?" Steel asked hopefully.

Holmes smiled and clapped his hands. "Now, you're thinking. There is a man-made tunnel under this pyramid. It leads to a chamber six meters down that was believed to be the source of human life by the Aztecs. It was named Chicomoztoc."

"See Monty, you're thinking like an archeologist. Lead on."

Holmes led them back down the stairs and along the periphery until he found an open doorway leading down into cool darkness. "This is it, Jonathan."

Steel looked down at his blood-soaked hospital scrubs and his bare feet now covered with dirt and blood. "We need to leave some kind of sign for the others. If they also make here, we need to let them know where we went." He shrugged out of his scrub top and wedged it under a rocky outcropping at the top of the open doorway. If flapped in the breeze and the blood-soaked stains stood out sharply against the white fabric. He wiped the sweat from his bare chest and felt the belt of truth bite into his skin. "Monarch said my implants give me some advantage. I want this to be a sign for our friends to follow." He motioned to the dark tunnel. "After you, Indiana."

JOSH

JOSH WAS HIT by the sweltering heat and humidity and crumpled to his knees. He looked around at the huge, gray pyramid that towered over him. No! It couldn't be. He had left Ketrick behind with the altar of the spiral eye, and here he was right in the middle of the Aztec empire. He stood shakily as more blood trickled from the lacerations on his back and abdomen. He looked around at the empty avenue and spied something fluttering in the breeze. He stumbled across the hard, hot stone and stood before the tunnel entrance. A white shirt with blood on it fluttered in the breeze. Who had worn it? It didn't matter. It was oddly out of place in this hot wasteland. It was a sign to follow. He mumbled a prayer; it would lead him to his friends. Gripping his bloodstone for strength and holding the shield before him, he stumbled into the darkness.

BIRDSONG

BIRDSONG STEPPED from the dark room into more darkness. Light fluttered in the distance. He was in a tunnel leading to bright sunlight. He hobbled toward the light as the bleeding wounds on his back continue to leak blood. The cool of the tunnel transitioned to stifling heat, and sweat poured beneath his breastplate. He stepped out of a tunnel into harsh light and glanced around at the landscape. Low lying squatty pyramids stretched away from his, and the largest pyramid was behind and above him. He turned and there, fluttering in the breeze was a white shirt with blood on it. It had been wedged on the outside of the tunnel. Someone wanted him to follow them into the tunnel. It was then he noticed the trail of dried blood spatters leading into the tunnel. Whose was it? Some fresh blood spatters were his own. The shirt was out of place in this world. A sign? He shifted his breastplate to make it more comfortable and went back into the tunnel.

RAVEN

RAVEN STOOD in the harsh sunlight gasping in pain. She tore the pink dress from her waist and watched it tumbled away in the hot wind. She wore a pair of white tights and a body-hugging shirt beneath the dress. They were both stained with the blood that leaked from her wound. She looked around at the pyramids and the wide-open stone avenue. Where was she? Mexico? Mayan or Aztec pyramids?

She had to find her friends, and she had to find help before she bled to death. The helmet was hot, and sweat poured down her neck, but it afforded her reassurance. She was not losing her mind in this unreal realm. Because in the distance, she saw something white and red ripple in the breeze, a burst of color in this gray, stony landscape. A sign? She saw the tunnel entrance. At least it would be cool inside. She set off toward the tunnel.

37

H olmes and Steel stepped out of the end of the tunnel into a vast, stone chamber. It towered into the darkness above them. Around the periphery of the chamber, dozens of other tunnels emptied into the vast chamber. The floor sloped downward away from them. Hovering globes of yellow light illuminated a vast open plain of green grass. In its center, towering black monoliths encircled two stone slabs. New Stonehenge.

"Why, Stonehenge?" Stone asked.

"Stonehenge is the best-known site of pagan rituals, Jonathan. Everything we have seen reeks of ancient pagan rituals. It points to the ascension of man, the ultimate evolution of man into some kind of divine being."

"Transhumanism again?"

"At least Thakkar's version," Holmes said. "So, what is the plan?"

"Find Olivia. She was tied to one of those slabs in Thakkar's real location. But, those slabs look empty from here."

"That is true for this reality. We have to find out where those slabs are located in the real world."

"How?" Steel asked.

"We find and defeat Thakkar. We force the answer from her." Holmes said, holding up his sword. "She cannot resist the Word of God."

Steel touched his belt. "Or the belt of truth. We will make her tell us the truth."

"Because we have the Truth," Holmes said quietly.

Looking down the slope toward New Stonehenge Steel noticed the bowl-shaped depression was actually a series of wide step-like plateaus each subsequent level lower than the outer level. Steel paused at the next downward step and nodded to Holmes.

"Be prepared for anything." He stepped onto the next level, and everything around them changed. A path led straight ahead, illuminated by the light of two moons. The landscape before them was painted in muted dark blues and grays. The wind whipped at them cold and dry. Around them, tall trees with no leaves reached toward the sky covered in black, crenelated bark. The limbs rattled like clacking bones. Steel glanced once at Holmes, and Holmes held up the sword. The meager blue light illuminated the path before them.

As Steel walked down the path, more of this "world" came into view. To their right and left tall, snowcapped mountains gleamed in the silvery moonlight. And eclipsing the base of those mountains were stone walls, stone towers all stretching in both directions from the wall that had appeared behind them. In the distance, a high pitched series of howls more frightening than that of wolves echoed off the walls.

"Where are we?" Holmes said.

A figure appeared ahead of them at the base of the trees. He was hunched over his abdomen and hobbling toward them.

"Wereland." He shouted. "We are in Wereland."

Steel recognized the voice and started running toward the figure. "Josh!"

Before he had covered twenty feet, the ground before him began to crack open, throwing up clods of black earth and showers of stones. Things popped out of the ground into the air and landed on the path before them. A dozen dark warriors lined up. Their white hair was pulled back in a long tail. Black eyes stared at them from ghostly white faces. One figure separated from the group and stepped forward.

"You are not allowed passage through the Great Vailyard of the Weren King of Transyl." The figure said in a deep, resonant voice. He halted a meter from Steel and Holmes. He towered almost seven feet tall and glared down at them with red eyes. His white skin was marred with etchings of gray scars. He wore a helmet that fanned out over his shoulders. He unsheathed a gleaming, black sword from its sheath.

"You shall not pass."

Steel looked past him and saw the distant figure of Josh fade slowly back into the tree line. They had not seen him. Good.

"I am Jonathan Steel. I guess I'm talking to one of Thakkar's warrior priests."

The Weren warlord laughed and revealed his fangs. "You are such amateurs. Did you actually think you would escape the notice of our queen?"

"We had hoped we could surprise her, yes," Holmes said.

"Well, she now knows of your presence, and the element of surprise was your only advantage. When I unleash my twelve Weren warlocks, you will experience a level of pain and suffering hitherto unknown."

"Hitherto?" Steel said. "You actually said hitherto?"

Holmes held up the sword, and words appeared on the surface. He shouted them into the dark, windy night. "*The wicked plots against the righteous and gnashes his teeth at him, but the Lord laughs at the wicked, for he sees that his day is coming. Psalm 37:12-13.*"

The Weren warrior-priest launched himself at Steel. Holmes stepped in front of Steel and held up the sword. "My sword is not an offensive weapon but a weapon of defense."

The Warrior priest brought down the black, gleaming sword against the bright blue sword. The resounding clash shook the air, and Steel fell to the ground. The Weren sword bounced back and pierced the Weren warrior priest's chest. He screamed in agony and fell back into his twelve warlocks and disappeared.

"*The wicked draw the sword and bend their bows to bring down the poor and needy, to slay those whose way is upright; their sword shall enter their own heart, and their bows shall be broken. Psalm 37:14-15.*" Holmes said loudly.

The assembled warlocks looked at each other, and then another voice came from behind them. "Basically, bros, run," Josh shouted as he crashed into the center of their line. The warlocks scattered running off toward the tree lines.

Steel stood up and ran to Josh. "Josh!" He grabbed him and tried to hug him, but Josh winced. He held a shield at his side.

"Sorry, Jonathan, I had a run-in with a certain giant scorpion. Bro, that was your shirt in the tunnel? I thought so. When I stepped into the clearing, I found myself in those trees. I think we had them pinned between us."

Holmes joined them. "Good job, Josh. The shield of faith took care of the rest of the demon hoard. How much pain are you in?"

"I'd say seven out of ten. I'm not hurting enough to end it all if that is what you are asking."

"What is this place?" Steel resisted the urge to grab the young man again in a hug.

"When I stepped off the upper level and found myself in those trees, I heard howling wolf things, and when I saw the Weren, I knew I was on Wereland."

"Wereland?"

Josh shrugged and groaned in pain. "We've met before when I first entered Numinocity. Bro, they can have this reality. In video games, you don't really feel the pain."

Holmes looked around at the eerie landscape. "Let's keep moving down the path toward New Stonehenge. The sooner we get out of this place, the better."

Josh limped alongside Steel as they passed through the tall, wind-tossed trees until they came to a wall with a doorway opening onto darkness. The threshold of the door led downward in another step-down. Steel put out a hand and halted them. "Okay, I guess we can expect something new."

"A new level," Josh said. "It's like a video game in the sense we will have to pass through several levels to get to the goal."

"Thakkar had six warrior princes," Holmes said. "So, we have at least five levels left, right?"

"I would think so," Josh said. He groaned again in pain and sat on the ground. "Give me a minute, bro."

"Monty, you go on without us. I'm staying here with Josh."

"No!" Josh said as he stood up. "I just needed a rest. We are stronger together. You should know that by now, Jonathan."

Steel looked into Josh's eyes. He had come so far since the day they had met in Lakeside. He reached over and pulled Josh's head into a hug. "You are right, Josh."

"Dude, the pain," Josh said. Steel released him, and Josh glanced at Holmes. "You're my witness."

"For what?" Holmes said. "The fact he hugged you?"

"No, bro. He admitted I was right about something. Now, let's get on with this. Time is running out." He stepped forward.

The heat hit them like a blast furnace. Smoke choked Steel as he looked around. The stood on a rugged path leading through towering rocks. Ahead, smoke and soot swirled into the air.

"What is that smell?" Holmes retched.

"Rotten flesh." Steel said. "Burning flesh. Sulfur?"

Holmes looked down the path and moved ahead to an opening. "No!"

"What is it?" Josh followed him.

"The Valley of Hinnom," Holmes said. "It's where we get the name Gehenna. You know, Hades, Hell. It was here children were sacrificed to Baal and Molech." The sword gleamed, and words appeared. Holmes read them. *"Ahaz was twenty years old when he became king, and he reigned in Jerusalem sixteen years. Unlike David, his father, he did not do what was right in the eyes of the Lord. He followed the ways of the kings of Israel and also made idols for worshiping the Baals. He burned sacrifices in the Valley of Ben Hinnom and sacrificed his children in the fire, engaging in the detestable practices of the nations the Lord had driven out before the Israelites. 2 Chronicles 28:1-3."*

Steel joined them and looked ahead at a glimpse into "hell." Ragged rocks towered toward a sky filled with churning gray clouds. Caves pocked the stone walls and from their opening sparks, and flames appeared.

"Gross!" Josh stepped back into Steel. A flowing sludge of putrid ichor wormed across the path. Imbedded in the yellowish-green sludge were broken, burned bones, and writhing maggots. "What is this place?"

Holmes coughed as more smoke poured around them. "As I said, it was once a place of human sacrifice. Children were sacrificed to Baal. They were tossed into the flames. Over the centuries, trash was dumped here from Jerusalem. Bodies were thrown into the ravine from crucifixions. This valley is the image Jesus evoked when he spoke of a place of eternal punishment. Although, there is a distinction from the use of the word Gehenna and the use of Hades in the book of Revelation." Holmes paused. "Sorry, once a professor always a professor."

"What you're saying is we have to walk through hell." Steel said. A shadow passed over them, and Steel whirled in a defensive posture. Someone dropped from the rock behind them and landed before Steel. Arms grabbed him in a tight grasp. Steel fought against the tightening grip until the voice pierced his shock.

"Jonathan, stop! It's me. It's Jason." Birdsong pushed Steel away at arm's length. His face was covered in soot, but his smile lit up the dark cloudy day.

"Jason! You scared me half out of my wits." Steel said.

Birdsong dropped his arms. "Sorry. I've been climbing around this dreadful place after taking the wrong step."

Josh tapped his breastplate. "Cool armor, dude."

"Hey, little fellow," Birdsong said. "Monty. Thanks for the breastplate."

Steel noticed droplets of blood on the stone behind Birdsong. "Jason, you're bleeding."

"Yeah, I ran into a cactus creature thing. Two of them, in fact. It hurts, but I've got to keep moving. Time, you know."

Holmes motioned to the stream of decaying matter. "We have to pass through the Valley of Hinnom."

"Oh, great," Birdsong said. "Baal, Molech, and all of their demonic ilk. Isn't that lovely." He shrugged and walked through the shallow stream. "Come on. We have the Lord on our side, and He is bigger than any of these false gods."

Steel let Holmes and Josh precede him and glanced behind once more to make sure no other surprises waited for them. They made their way deeper into a maze of rocky pinnacles and yawning chasms filled with the screams of dying humans. The smoke grew so dense in places they had to hold their breath. The path led through two tall, jagged rocks, and they paused at the edge of a flat plateau. A pyre of roaring logs filled a central pit. Twelve priests in red, flowing robes stood around the pit. They each held a bundle in their arms. One figure separated herself from the other men. She was tall and willowy, and her flowing red robes were diaphanous and translucent, revealing all of her anatomy.

"Hello, Josh," Lusensa said. "You finally came to see me."

Steel stepped protectively in front of Josh. "Josh, who is this?"

"She spoke to me when I first used the goggles," Josh said hoarsely.

Lusensa paused and planted her hands on her hips. "And, did you honestly think you could continue to withstand my overtures, young man. Can't you feel the hormones surging, the lust springing up in your mind?" She motioned to the priests behind her. "You no longer have to worry about the consequences of giving in to your sexual desires. We have taken care of the offal."

"Offal?" Holmes said. "Those are children!"

"No, Dr. Holmes. They are just lumps of meat. Protein and fat and carbohydrates. They will burn just like wood. They are nothing." She stepped closer, and her alluring eyes sparkled with desire. "Can't you feel the call? Can't you feel a growing desire? Throw away all cares. Put aside the guilt and shame of your petty conscience. Toss them into the fire with the unwanted and unloved."

Birdsong gently pushed Steel aside and stepped forward. His breastplate reflected back the red flames of the fire pit. "I am not a righteous man. I have made many mistakes in my life. I have done more things wrong than I have done things right."

Lusensa smiled. "Well, finally, a man I can appreciate." She stepped toward him.

"But." Birdsong held up his hands to ward her off. "There is a difference between you and me. I am forgiven by the Son of God; God made flesh in the person of Jesus Christ, and in His name, I call down the cleansing fire of righteousness on you and YOUR offal!"

The skies cracked with thunder, and red and orange lightning spiked down into the midst of the fire pit. The bundles disappeared from the hands levitated into the sky on beams of light as the lightning bifurcated and struck each priest in the chest. The fire from the pit reached out with tentacles of orange and red and wrapped themselves around the priests. One giant tentacle encircled Lusensa. She screamed as her skin bubbled and smoked, and she reached toward Birdsong. Her hands brushed against his breastplate, and she screamed even louder as her hands burst in blisters from the contact. She was dragged back into the fire along with her priests until they disappeared, screaming into the flames. The lightning dissipated, and the fire sunk into the earth. The stones surrounding the pit tumbled inward, and all was quiet. The clouds split, and a gentle rain fell, dousing the remaining embers in the pit. Between two stones on the far side of the area, the path led to another step.

Birdsong sank to his feet and groaned in pain. Steel knelt beside him. "Jason, that took so much out of you, didn't it?"

"Yes," Birdsong said. "Every good deed comes with a cost." He held out his hand, and Steel took and helped him to his feet. "Let's move on before this rain turns into Noah's flood because this land needs cleansing."

38

S teel stepped into a hospital hallway filled with chaos. Nurses, doctors, aides ran back and forth as the four of them flattened against a wall. A doctor paused near them and spoke to her nurse.

"It's the woman in 666. She's gone ballistic. Call security."

The two hustled off in opposite directions. Three security men ran by with their hands on holstered pistols.

"Bro, I say we go to that room," Josh said.

"No, Josh. The last thing we should do is run into the fray." Birdsong said.

"Did you just say 'fray'?" Josh said.

A woman dressed in a black security uniform stopped in front of them. Her hair was pulled behind her head, and she wore a pair of mirrored sunglasses. For a second, Steel missed his pair of sunglasses.

She took off her sunglasses and ran her gaze over all of them. "Now, you are a bunch of shady characters if I ever saw any. Either you're lost and should have gone to the children's ward. Or, you escaped from the behavior unit. Either way, you're coming with me."

"But, what about the patient in 666?" Josh said.

The woman smiled. "You can't help her. She's on her own."

Birdsong's hand shot through the air, and he snagged the woman's club. With one swift blow, he caught her at the nape of the neck. The eyes rolled up in her head, and she crumpled into the hallway. Health care professionals merely stepped over her body and continued their to and fro motion.

"Jason, what did you do that for?" Steel asked.

"I wanted to cut to the chase. She's stalling us. That means we have to go to that room." Birdsong bent over and pulled the pistol from the officer's holster. He glanced at it and mumbled under his breath.

Holmes put a hand on Birdsong's arm. "Jason, we won't need that."

Birdsong tucked the pistol into the waistband of his pants. "Let's hope so." He barreled down the hallway. Steel glanced at the pool of blood Birdsong had left on the floor. They followed Birdsong.

Steel jostled and shoved people out of the way as they made their way down the corridor and around the corner. He almost ran into Birdsong. He had stopped behind a laundry cabinet.

"What is it?"

"Two of them. Standing guard in front of that door."

Josh peeked around Steel. "Dude, who is in that room?"

"Three guesses and the first two don't count," Holmes said. "Olivia!"

Josh started forward, and Birdsong put an arm out to stop him. "Wait! We don't know that. It's probably a trap."

"Of course, it is." Steel said.

Colored bands were painted along the wall, each leading to separate areas in the hospital. Suddenly, the bands seemed to come off the wall and writhed in the air like iridescent tentacles. People hurrying down the corridor ran in the oppo-site direction. The colored bands became ropes, and they hung in the air, pointing toward the security guards like poised snakes.

One of the guards pulled out a taser and shot it at the closest rope. The rope recoiled, wound through the air and caught the taser wires, and tossed them back toward the guard. They hit their mark, and he fell to the floor.

Two of the ropes wound themselves around the other guard and lifted him off the floor. The guard struggled against the rope. A third rope picked up the now unconscious guard and slammed both of them together. Then, lifting both guards high in the air, a fourth rope opened a trash chute in the wall, and the other three ropes tossed the men down the chute.

"What is going on?" Birdsong asked.

"I am going on." A voice said behind them. Raven walked around the corner. The four colored ropes emanated from her like tentacles. She wore her one-piece underclothing from the dress. Blood marred the white material.

The ropes retracted and took their place on the wall. Raven relaxed and tapped the helmet on her head. "Sometimes our minds can be very useful when confronting evil, right, Dr. Holmes? Especially with our implants. I just imagined what Jesus must have been like when he drove the money changers out of the temple area. Only, I didn't have a cat of nine tails, so I used something else instead."

Steel ran to her and almost embraced her. She managed a smile, and then her eyes rolled back into her head, and she collapsed. He caught her, and blood ran across his forearms from a puncture wound on her abdomen. "She's been stabbed!"

"We've all been hurt in some way. Josh from a giant scorpion's pincers. Jason from a cactus monster."

"Who did this to Raven?" Steel growled.

"Her stepfather."

Steel glanced down at the face of the woman he no longer recognized. She had been everything from his one-time love interest to an enemy assassin. For a moment, he saw a lamb shaped cake with a knife protruding from its bloody icing. She had told him about that cake somewhere in their past. What kind of father had forced such an innocent young girl to become an assassin? A father like his own? He pulled her to him and pressed his face against hers.

"Jonathan, we don't have time for sorrow. Before our enemy can retaliate, we need to get into that hospital room." Holmes said.

Birdsong charged ahead and threw open the door to the room. Steel followed along with Josh and Holmes. The room was like any other hospital room. A lone occupant lay in one bed. The other was empty, and Steel hurried to it and placed Raven on the bed.

"Olivia?" Josh said.

Steel whirled. Olivia lay beneath the sheet. Her eyes were closed, and her chest moved up and down erratically. Josh reached for her, and Holmes grabbed his hand.

"I've seen enough movies to know you don't just automatically touch something."

"Good idea." A rough voice came from behind them. Steel whirled, and a figure moved out of the bathroom. Black cloth-covered him from head to foot. A black mask hid his face. "Don't be alarmed. I think you know who I am. I cannot reveal my identity because someone is looking for me."

Josh almost said "Steven," and Holmes clasped his hand over his mouth. Holmes raised an eyebrow.

"We have no idea who you are, good sir. What are your intentions regarding Olivia?"

The man walked across the room and placed a hand on Olivia's arm. "I am her guardian. She is here in this realm by means I do not understand." He pulled back the sheets, and a blue stone glowed at Olivia's chest. He touched the stone, and a bubble of pale blue light swelled to encompass them all. Steel felt his palm pulse and looked down at the glowing light in the center of his hand.

"Now, we can speak for a short period." The man said. "Olivia is here by a fluke, a glitch in the system. She was never attached physically through the goggles, but I found her like this and imagined this hospital room to care for her."

"The warrior-priests outside were not guarding you," Birdsong said.

"No, they were trying to get in." The figure motioned to Raven. "She took them out. Now, there are no more warrior-priests left. You've taken out all six in your journeys here to New Stonehenge."

"Good. For once, I'm glad I took someone out." Raven sat up groggily. Steel sat beside her.

"Hey, take it easy."

Raven put a hand on his. "I'm okay. Just weak from the pain. Remember, they can't physically harm us, just hurt us."

"What do we do now?" Holmes asked.

"For now, within this bubble, we are protected, but it will not last long. When you open that door, we will be at the last level. We will be on the plains of New Stonehenge and the final confrontation. I will possibly grow weak and paralyzed in the coming hour because my body is weak in the real world. If I do, you must protect Olivia."

"Why?" Josh asked and groaned in pain.

"There is a plan." The black clad figure said. "I cannot say more."

"And you?"

"I will not be captured by Thakkar. The secret must not fall into her hands. Someone has preceded us onto the plain and is hiding and biding her time."

"Her time?" Steel said.

"Vivian." The man said. The edges of the blue bubble

began to ripple. "Our time is running out. We must step through the door now."

Steel helped Raven to her feet, and she leaned against him. The man motioned for Birdsong.

"Can you carry Olivia?"

"Of course." He picked up Olivia. The man motioned for Josh to open the door. Josh lifted the handle and opened the door. They stepped through to the final level.

39

They huddled in a cold, shallow tunnel lined with lichen and moss. Raven leaned against a wall, and Steel moved to the entrance of the tunnel. Before them stretched the final level, and in the distance, New Stonehenge seemed dwarfed by the towering mountains encircling them. Perhaps it was the level plain of deep grass stretching away from them that made the structures seem so small and distant. The sky was a dark purple with rolling gray clouds churning above them. Lightning illuminated the clouds from above, and thunder rolled across the open plains. The wind carried the fragrance of ozone, and the grass undulated like dark green waves in an endless ocean.

It seemed so real, and Steel recoiled at the thought of how easily he had accepted the seeming reality of this place. No wonder someone could get addicted to this reality, especially if they could alter and control their surroundings. He closed his eyes and tried his best to concentrate on making his surroundings change. For a moment, his thoughts were interrupted by the memories of his alternate self and the accusation that Steel had killed his own mother. Had he? He could not recall much about his life, and only one brief memory of his mother now forever altered by the version of Steel that had appeared in the beach house. And, had he been possessed by a demon? The memory of the alleyway and his conversion was striking and an anchor in the storm of his shattered mind.

He shook his head in frustration. How could he concentrate on changing anything in this reality when these thoughts would not go away? He felt a touch on his shoulder and glanced at Jason.

"What now?"

"I don't know." Steel looked down at the blood pooling at Birdsong's feet. "Some of us are hurt. Bleeding."

"I know." Josh bent over in pain. "But it isn't real."

"It feels real," Raven said as she stumbled up beside them.

"Yes, but we aren't losing blood in real life. Thakkar can't kill us. She can only hurt us. And, make us want to die." The dark hooded figure said quietly. "I've been in pains for days." He groaned and slumped to the ground. Steel knelt beside him and felt his pulse. It was strong.

"What's wrong?" Birdsong asked.

"His body is growing weak in the real world." Steel said. The boy's body stirred and he slowly stood up.

"I'm back." He whispered.

Steel wanted to call out the boy's name, Steven. But, to do so would alert Thakkar. He glanced at Olivia's inert body cradled in Birdsong's arms. "We have to find the real Olivia and save her. Not here, but in the real world."

Static hissed behind his right eye, and Steel doubled over in pain. He grabbed his head as the pain paralyzed him. He opened his eyes, and Raven stood right in front of him, her hands on her head. The others were frozen.

"Do not react." Olivia's voice said in his head. "I am communicating to both of you over your implants. Don't ask me how. I don't have time to explain. Using this form of communication will bypass Thakkar's system. It is direct from my brain stimulator to your implants. You must get me to New Stonehenge and put my body on one of the slabs. Then, I will take it from there."

Steel gasped as moving time kicked in again. He looked at Raven. Holmes glanced at them. "You two, okay?"

Raven blinked and grabbed the wound in her abdomen. "I'm in pain. That's all." She nodded at Steel as a tear trickled down his cheek. He nodded back at her and turned to the boy. "The rest of you stay here. I'll take Olivia."

And, before the boy could stop him, Steel had taken Olivia's body from Birdsong. He hugged the surprisingly light body to his chest. The blue stone glowed beneath the fabric of her shirt, and his palm burned with light. He turned and ran out into the coming storm. Behind him, he heard Josh scream for him to stop and glanced once over his shoulder. Raven was blocking the group from leaving the tunnel entrance.

The grass moved like waves. As he hurried through the knee-deep grass, the direction of the waves changed. In what seemed like the reversal of a normal outward moving wave, the grass tilted and undulated toward him, converging on his legs. The grass wound its way around his ankles and slowed him down. It was like running through sand.

Rain swirled from the sky and bent by the wind, dove directly toward him. The pellets of water lashed at him, stung his skin, and pelted his open eyes. His stomach churned with pain. It had been hours since he had eaten, and his body back in Monarch's lab was growing weak. How had Steven lasted this long?

He was a third of the way to New Stonehenge when the giant scorpion reared up out of the grass. It was golden-hued with a carapace that glistened in the lightning. Rain ran down its legs, and its giant tail curled up over its head, ready to impale Steel.

Steel slid to a halt. "You!"

The head of the scorpion grew transparent, and within, he saw the face of Vivian. "Hello, sweetie." It's mandible's clacked.

"Vivian! You're working with thirteen?"

"Oh, I have been for a while. I learned its name in Jerusalem, and now I control it. It no longer controls me. Now, give me Olivia, and I'll take it from here."

Steel placed Olivia in the tall grass and stepped over her to bar the scorpion's way. "Over my dead body."

The scorpion's tail flicked, and the stinger caught Steel in the shoulder. The pain was greater than anything he had ever experienced. It dwarfed the pain from his torture. He fell to his knees in the grass and screamed.

"That was just a small droplet of venom," Vivian said. "Now, move aside, Jonathan, and let me do what needs to be done."

Someone moved through the tall grass and stood between Steel and the scorpion. Holmes held up the gleaming blue sword and words poured from the sword into the very air. Holmes's voice pierced the roar of the storm. *"May those who seek my life be disgraced and put to shame; may those who plot my ruin be turned back in dismay. May they be like chaff before the wind, with the angel of the Lord driving them away; may their path be dark and slippery, with the angel of the Lord pursuing them. Psalm 35:4-6."*

Lightning shot down from the sky and struck the ground just in front of the thirteenth demon. The grass and dirt showered up in the air and threw the scorpion back toward New Stonehenge. A strong wind caught the scorpion's body, and no matter how it tore at the ground with its feet, the wind pushed it backward. It opened its mandibles, and something shot forward, and Vivian tumbled into the grass. The scorpion turned and ran toward New Stonehenge.

The wind died down, and the rain stopped. The clouds tore

apart like tissue paper revealing a hot sun. Holmes ran to Vivian, and she sat up in the grass.

"It rejected me!" She said. "You fool! All you had to do was give me Olivia! It was part of our plan!"

Steel stood up shakily and fought off the pain. "What plan?"

"I can't say." Vivian was covered from head to toe in amber goo. She wiped it from her body and groaned in pain at her wounds. "Don't worry. All I have to do is say its name."

And then, her mouth shut. Her eyes grew wide in fear and panic, and she tried to open her mouth. She screamed and frantically tore at her lips with her fingers. She turned and shook at fist toward the receding scorpion.

"In here, Thakkar controls us, it would seem," Holmes said.

"She has access to Monarch's system." The boy in the dark hood said as he joined them. "If that is so, then we have lost any possibility of control."

Steel turned as the rest of the group joined them, and Bird song knelt to pick up Olivia.

"Our element of surprise is gone. It doesn't change the outcome." The boy said.

"If she can control us, then she can stop us," Josh said.

Steel shook his head as Vivian turned to them, her face streaming with tears. Her eyes were filled with fear. She seemed defeated, deflated.

"You forget. She is not a believer. We have protection from the power of demons. Thakkar can hurt us, she can put obstacles before us, but she cannot control us." Holmes said.

Steel pointed to the boy and Olivia and didn't say a word. Holmes shrugged. "Not sure, but my guess is because they are not believers, their connection is different from ours. Maybe that is why they are unaffected."

"We need to hurry." The boy said and started walking toward New Stonehenge. The group hobbled, stumbled, moaning in pain, and moved around Vivian. Steel stopped before her, and her eyes were pleading, begging for help. "I won't leave you." Steel said. "Come with me." He reached out, and she looked at his hand as if it were itself a scorpion. Slowly, she put her hand in his. It felt real, cold, and moist with her tears. He would never have imagined he would willingly take the hand of this woman to help her. Steel led them toward New Stonehenge.

40

A bright, maroon light appeared in the sky and moved down to the center of New Stonehenge as they arrived. It settled in the air perfectly centered in the circle of monoliths. The maroon light coalesced and morphed, moving through multiple abstracts shapes until a body formed draped in golden and teal robes. Thakkar, in all of her imagined beauty, hovered in the air. Her dark eyes glittered with malice. Her hair writhed around her head like tiny snakes. The third eye glowed crimson from her forehead.

"Well, you have brought me a prize, I see." Her voice echoed across the plains around them.

The boy paused at the edge of the ring of monoliths. He looked up at her with his hidden face. "We are returning Olivia to her resting place. You have defeated her already."

Thakkar raised an eyebrow. "Yes, she is an enigma. How is she here in Numinocity? Or, is she a construct of your doing, Steven?"

The boy ignored her hovering figure as Birdsong placed Olivia on the slab to the right. He gently arranged her legs and arms and crossed her hands on her chest.

The boy moved into the circle of monoliths and stopped between the two slabs. He looked up at Thakkar. "You may have found me here in Numinocity, but you have not found me in the real world."

Thakkar lowered to the ground. "My operatives have tracked the movements of your mother. We know she is now in Paris and is going street by street looking for your hiding place. When she finds you, my operatives will be right behind her. And, don't think that weakened Ninja of hers can stop me. Soon, I will have you and your special creation."

The boy stepped back. "What are you talking about?"

"Your eternal nanomemes. They will give me the final solution for my ultimate plan. Now that I know you are here, I can access your goggles and change your reality." She gestured, and the boy groaned but not in pain. He fell back onto the grass. "Feel that pleasure? It is but a taste of what I can give you. All I need are your nanomemes, and you can have this pleasure forever."

Steel motioned to his friends, and they slowly moved into the circle of monoliths. Vivian held fast to his hand. Thakkar looked at him. "Yes, join us. It is true I cannot control you. But, I can give you pain and joy all at one time." She gestured with her hand, and Steel heard them fall on the ground behind her. He did not need to look to know they were experiencing the same fate as the boy. For some reason, Raven had also fallen. Was she pretending to be affected? But, Vivian stoically stood still beside him. Was she also unaffected?

"Oh, you wonder about dear Vivian? Now that she cannot utter his name, the thirteenth demon can have his way with her." The scorpion reared up from behind one of the monoliths and moved into the circle. Vivian's grip tightened on Steel's hand.

"You may hurt us, but you cannot kill us." Steel said.

"Oh, but I can give the world such pleasure it will fall at my

knees. Imagine millions entering Numinocity to find the ultimate escape, the ultimate pleasure. They will join me and leave
the real world behind. They will transcend. They will become
truly transhuman."

"Until they die." Steel said.

Thakkar shrugged. "If it happens, then we harvest their
souls. But, there is one thing I know about humanity because I
am one of them. We are relentlessly inventive, and once we
taste this pleasure, we will find ways to keep the physical body
alive as long as possible. And, then, one day when our imagination and our inventiveness and our progress has accom-
plished our ultimate goal, we will move beyond these mere
physical bodies and into a state of perpetual being. And, we
will owe it all to my Master. We will worship not only the
eighth demon and yours truly, of course, but we will worship
our Master."

Vivian moaned out loud and shook her head. Thakkar
moved toward them and put out a hand to touch Vivian's face.
Vivian flinched at the woman's touch.

"Poor Vivian. You thought you could stop me. True, my
plans are premature. The Dark Council and the Master wanted
me to wait until the technology was finished. But, once I
succeed, once the eighth demon succeeds, the Master will
reward me for my foresight. You see, Vivian, once you taste the
power of godhood, all of your plans will change."

VIVIAN D'ARBONNE KETRICK WULF had never been more
desperate in her life. All of her plans were failing. And now, she
clung to the only help in the world, her hated enemy Jonathan
Steel. She pulled away from Thakkar's cold touch and tried to
open her mouth. She desperately wanted to call out the name
of the thirteenth demon. But she could not.

Thakkar stepped back and gestured to the scorpion. "She's all yours."

She felt Steel stiffen at her side. She knew he already felt the pain from the first sting she had sent his way. She had meant it only as a warning shot, a tiny pain. But, now, she no longer controlled the eighth demon. Dark spirals formed around its multiple insect eyes as it lurched toward her.

Steel pulled her behind him in a quick, fluid motion, and she saw the stinger exit from his back. Steel crumpled beside her, dragging her down by his clenched hand. Blood poured from the wound in his abdomen, and she looked up at the thirteenth demon.

"Oh, how long I have wanted to do this! How long I have suffered under the nauseating control of you mortals!" It hissed. "Now, I am free to fulfill my wishes to end you, Vivian. Once, we were partners, but you betrayed me, and now you will pay."

Steel rose to his feet again as the stinger shot toward Vivian's chest. He stepped in front of her, and the stinger pierced his chest. She tried to scream, but her mouth was sealed. Behind her, the boy, Josh, tried to come to Steel but fell under his own wounds.

This was ridiculous, she told herself. Stop fighting this. Who was she to think she could stand up to the entire Dark Council? All she had to do was release Steel's hand and surrender; show that she wanted to join Thakkar in her great victory. She would live through this horrendous pain, and she would gain her special place with the Master again.

It was then she felt a burning in her palm. She looked down, and a glimmer of light leaked from their clasped hands. The embedded crystals of the Grimvox grew warm in her hand. And light came from Steel's palm even as he groaned in pain at her feet. Light. In the darkness. Beckoning to her. The memory of the cross in the castle came back to her. What had she said to free herself? No! She would never repeat it. No! She would not even think it.

The stinger caught her just below her breastbone, and the pain was like every nerve in her body had joined in one electric current. Her back arched, and her hand tightened even more on Steel's hand. She fell beside him and gasped as the pain grew and grew, burning every cell in her body.

"You can end this, you know." Thakkar knelt before her. "You can stop the pain. Just reach up and take the goggles off, Vivian. Reach up and end it all and join your other conquests in hell. No need to fight anymore."

Vivian glared at her, lips still sealed. She looked at Steel, and their eyes met. His turquoise eyes burned with something passionate and so different from anything she had ever seen in the eyes of the deputy or Ketrick or Wulf. They burned with something deeper, a caring, a trust she did not deserve. He knew. Somehow, he knew she had called out for help. She wanted to curse him. She closed her eyes and felt the pain searing through every fiber of her being. She could do this, but it would change everything.

When she opened her eyes, a distant figure stood in a shaft of light in the midst of the grassy field. The grass reacted to his presence and surged toward him. He held out scarred hands and spoke quietly. The grass collapsed in upon itself. One of those hands reached toward her, beckoning, welcoming. He looked directly at her and His eyes! She only thought she had seen concern, empathy, maybe even love in the eyes of Jonathan Steel. But His eyes! Such love, such forgiveness. How could He even look at her much less care for her? How could He ever forgive her for all that she had done?

She looked back at Jonathan Steel, writhing in pain beside her. Her hand was still clasped to his. Why had he been hurt by the thirteenth demon? He was protected by his allegiance to the Son. Then, like a wave of cold water, she realized what Steel had done. He had willingly taken the punishment meant for her. He had willingly allowed the stinger to pierce his body even though he could have easily rejected it. He had taken it all for her!

Vivian looked out over the grassy plain. In the air, an open portal showed the dark, dusty day in Jerusalem. The man now hung naked and bloody on a cross. She had been there! She had seen this! For the first time, it sunk in that this man, this Son of God had died for those He loved. Like Steel, only on a cosmic scale, He had taken the punishment all humanity deserved. In fact, He had taken her punishment!

Something tore within her. It wasn't the pain that drove her; it wasn't the desire to destroy the thirteenth demon. Instead, it was something so simple, so benign, and yet, so deep she had seen in Steel's eyes. Hope. Fine, she thought. I will say it. There are no demons in here with me anymore. I am on my own. She mouthed the words as she thought them.

"God, help me." And her lips flew open, and the words flew out of her on a powerfully expelled breath. The thirteenth demon moved back, and Thakkar stepped away in shock.

"What did you say?" Thakkar said.

Vivian turned to face Thakkar as the waves of pain poured over her body. She felt the light from Steel's grip. She felt the crystals from the Grimvox slowly fading away under the onslaught of that light. She drew a deep breath. "I said, 'God, help me.'" She shouted out loud. And then, she shouted thirteen's name screaming every obscene syllable. Then, she paused, gasping for breath against the pain and glared at the pulsing spirals around the thing's eyes. "Go to hell!"

Lightning flashed from the sky and caught the thirteenth demon in the upraised tail. It coruscated over its body, and Steel stood up beside Vivian, his body growing stronger as the venom began to subside.

"In the name of my savior, Jesus Christ, I command you."

And Steel said the name of the thirteenth demon perfectly, flawlessly. "to the depths of Tartarus."

The scorpion screeched as the lightning crackled over his body and constricted in a net of lighted fibers until it shrunk to a pinpoint of darkness and disappeared. Steel jerked Vivian around and stared into her eyes.

"Vivian, you did it!"

Vivian shook her head as the conflicting feelings flowed within her. "No! I did not want this. I can't be forgiven, Jonathan. I don't deserve this." She knew what she had to do. It was what she deserved so much more than forgiveness. She leaned into him and, for a moment, almost touched her lips to his. Then sliding her face along his cheek, she whispered something in his ear. Then, she pulled away, and her eyes riveted to his she reached up in the real world and pulled the goggles from her face.

41

"No!" Steel screamed as Vivian faded away into nothing.

Laughter echoed around the circle of monoliths. "Thank you for eliminating two of my biggest problems, Jonathan Steel," Thakkar said. "And, don't think you will use that tactic on me like you did on thirteen."

Thakkar gestured, and behind her, Josh, Jason, Raven, and Holmes flew through the air. Each one of them was pressed against adjacent monoliths. Steel whirled. "What are you doing?"

"Biding my time, Mr. Steel," Thakkar said. "You open your mouth again, even just a tiny crack, and I will bring such pain on your companions they will be driven mad. When, and if, they leave Numinocity, they will no longer be sane."

Steel raised his hands and nodded, closing his mouth. Thakkar paused as if listening. "It seems my operatives are almost there, Steven." She glanced at the boy. "It will soon be over for all of you but will only just be beginning for me. So, Steven, why fight me? Why try and stop me? With your genius and your inventive nature, you could join me, and we could make Numinocity fill up this world. You could rule by my side."

The boy nodded. "I'll think about it." And then, he fell to his knees. "I'm growing so weak."

"I can save you, Steven. I can make you a king." Thakkar stepped closer to the boy, and her gilded robes rustled around her.

Steel backed away from Thakkar and turned to his friends. Holmes motioned him over to him. He was plastered against the monolith. "Jonathan, I know what you have to do. Vivian had the missing ingredient. She completed the whole armor of God when she called to God. Prayer."

Steel glanced over his shoulder at Thakkar hovering over Steven. He couldn't say anything, and they were running out of time. Holmes groaned in pain and fought for control of his voice.

"I can't talk, but you can read. The sword. Take the sword."

Steel reached forward and took the sword carefully from Holmes's hand, hiding it from Thakkar. Words began to form on the gleaming blue surface.

"*Put on the full armor of God so that you can take your stand against the devil's schemes. For our struggle is not against flesh and blood, but against the rulers, against the authorities, against the powers of this dark world and against the spiritual forces of evil in the heavenly realms.*" Holmes said quietly. Steel looked up at Holmes, and he nodded. "We are fighting those powers in this spiritual realm, Jonathan."

Steel looked back at the sword. "*Therefore put on the full armor of God, so that when the day of evil comes, you may be able to stand your ground, and after you have done everything, to stand. Stand firm then, with the belt of truth buckled around your waist, with the breastplate of righteousness in place, and with your feet fitted with the readiness that comes from the gospel of peace. In addition to all this, take up the shield of faith, with which you can extinguish all the flaming arrows of the evil one. Take the helmet of salvation and the sword of the Spirit, which is the word of God."*

"And here was the verse that had given Vivian a vision of the power that was available when she called out to God. '*And pray in the Spirit on all occasions with all kinds of prayers and requests. Ephesians, 6:11-18.'"*

All kinds of prayers and requests. Vivian's plea was a prayer, a desperate prayer. It had been the prayer of a lost soul seeking peace and hope from the only source: God. Jonathan knew that feeling. In his one memory of the alleyway with his youth pastor, Kevin, he had called out with the same kind of prayer. And, he had been saved. Now he knew it had cast out a demon from his young soul. That meant there was hope for Vivian even as she had pulled off the goggles. What had been her fate? He couldn't think about that right now. He had to free his friends.

The palm of his other hand began to glow again, and he recalled the encounter on the train with Thakkar. He had the power of that Spirit within him. He had the power of the Holy Spirit to tap into. Holmes' feet were level with his face, and Holmes held out his sandals.

"Put them on. I give them to you."

Steel took the sandals off Holmes' feet and slid his bare feet into them.

"Jonathan," Birdsong said from the monolith next to him. "Take my breastplate."

Steel glanced over his shoulder, but Thakkar was preoccupied with Steven. He went to Birdsong and pulled the breastplate from his friend's chest and fitted over his bare chest. Already, the pain from the sting was subsiding, and he felt strength returning. He moved to Raven. She held her helmet in her hands.

"I would never pass as Magneto, Jonathan. Protect your

mind from Thakkar's mind games. And, I can come down from here whenever you need me." She whispered.

Steel slid the helmet over his head, and his thoughts instantly sharpened. He drew a deep breath and turned to Josh. Josh hung from the monolith, blood leaking from the lacerations on his abdomen.

"Bro, you can do this. This one time, dude, please save us all. Save everyone, and I'll never tell you not to save anyone ever again." He handed the shield to Steel.

Steel hefted the surprisingly lightweight shield. He turned to face Thakkar. The light in his palm began to spread up his arm and across his shoulder. Soon, he was bathed in the glowing, warm light of love. He felt it seep into his very being chasing away the bitter thoughts from his "other" self. The pain disappeared.

"Jonathan, remember, this armor is defensive. All you have to do is to stand." Holmes said.

Steel glanced at the sword, and words filled the air before him. *"The people of the land have practiced extortion and committed robbery. They have oppressed the poor and needy, and have extorted from the sojourner without justice. And I sought for a man among them who should build up the wall and stand in the breach before me for the land, that I should not destroy it, but I found none. Therefore I have poured out my indignation upon them. I have consumed them with the fire of my wrath. I have returned their way upon their heads, declares the Lord God. Ezekiel 22:29-31."*

Steel mouthed the words without speaking. Was he that man? Was he willing to stand in the gap? He had fought against that purpose for so long, waffling back and forth, even calling himself a reluctant draftee. But, here on these quasi-spiritual plains where all of reality was morphed and twisted by the enemy, he knew that he had to finally and without reservation accept his role. He looked up at Thakkar.

"I want to see the eighth demon." Steel said out loud.

Thakkar looked up from Steven. "What did I say about opening your mouth?" She opened her hand, and fiery darts shot forth from her fingertips. Steel held up his shield, and the darts were drawn from their course and collided harmlessly with the metal surface. He lowered his shield. "I will protect them. Now, I want to speak to the eighth demon. I demand it."

Thakkar laughed but suddenly stiffened and began to shake. Something moved around inside her image, distorting her skin and features in a Picasso type nightmare. Thakkar's skin burst asunder, and the eighth demon emerged. It was human in form only with eight arms, each holding items of royalty such as scepters and crowns. The head was that of a lion with a huge mouth opened to expose its ghastly teeth. Behind the head reared a collar of flesh that ended in a semicircular membrane, and from the edge, eight cobra heads emerged. Thakkar's virtual image fell into a heap onto the other slab, and for a moment, the façade of Numinocity grew translucent. Steel saw the real body of Thakkar hunched in a fetal position on one slab and Olivia on the other slab. He saw the fake monoliths surrounding him as what they were, plywood constructs with wires and tubing running into the lifeless bodies of the six warrior-priests shackled to the monoliths. Around the monoliths, clear plastic curtains hung from the ceiling of what appeared to be a warehouse. And, far up in the rafters, something moved; something reflected light off of a copper-hued mechanical arm. Snake!

Steel glanced back at the eighth demon. It moved toward him, and its hands dropped the implements of royalty and filled with darts, knives, spears. It began to hurl them at Steel. Steel hopped up onto the end of one of the slabs and moved around Thakkar's body to the end opposite the direction of his friends. The shield deflected each of the implements. The eighth demon now had his back to his friends. Good, it was distracted.

"I'll finish up your friends when I finish with you. What is this armor you have constructed with your imagination?" The eighth demon's voice thundered.

Steel held up the shield. "This armor did not come from a computer program. Nor did it come from my imagination. It came from the Word of God." He thrust the gleaming blue sword into the air, and bright, blue light shot outward in a circle. A voice echoed from the heavens, shattering the monoliths and cracking open the ground.

"*Humble yourselves, therefore, under the mighty hand of God so that at the proper time, he may exalt you, casting all your anxieties on him, because he cares for you. Be sober-minded; be watchful. Your adversary, the devil, prowls around like a roaring lion, seeking someone to devour. Resist him, firm in your faith, knowing that the same kinds of suffering are being experienced by your brotherhood throughout the world. 1 Peter 5:6-9.*"

The eighth demon actually looked stunned, and his lionlike face filled with fear. "What is this?"

"Your end." Steel said. He recalled the words Vivian had whispered in his ear, the true name of the eighth demon. "Hiranyakashipu, by the power of the savior of this realm, this real universe, Jesus Christ, Lord of all, I commend you to your eternal suffering in Tartarus."

The eighth demon convulsed. The cobra heads hissed and writhed in pain. The eight arms gyrated. Above the eighth demon, Miguel appeared in his flawless white suit. He nodded at Steel and took the red carnation from his pocket. He dropped the red flower, and it expanded into an all-encompassing shroud that wrapped around the figure of the eighth demon. The demon screamed in an unholy wail of pain as the shroud curled in upon itself into an ever-tightening scroll of red that disappeared in a burst of holy light. Miguel smiled and was gone.

Steel fell back off the slab and landed on the hard ground.

He was weak as a kitten now. Thakkar's deformed body lay on the slab next to him. Things began to crawl and move along her body. The real world began to fade from around him. The swarming, crawling bits coalesced into the virtual form of Thakkar standing at the end of the slab. Her shadow loomed over him, and he looked once again into the face of Sultana Thakkar.

"Well, you may have taken my demon from me, Steel, but you are still here in Numinocity. You have not stopped ME, and I will find another demon to give me the spiritual edge I need to keep Numinocity running."

"No, I will stop you." The boy said.

Thakkar turned and laughed. "Oh, you think I forgot about you? You were mulling it over in your mind about joining me. It's not too late."

The boy moved toward Olivia on the slab. "I gave Olivia my gift. She has it in her hands."

Thakkar turned to the body of Olivia on the slab and reached forward and gently uncrossed her hands. Against her chest, a blue stone glowed. "What is this?"

"First, you tell me who ordered the death of my father." The boy said.

Thakkar smiled. "The death of your father? My boy, you are quite mistaken. I or my factions did not orchestrate the assassination of your father. The Dark Council had nothing to do with it. Nor was it ordered by our rivals those white-eyed idiots, the Vitreomancers." She stepped toward the boy and rubbed her hands together. "I guess it doesn't hurt for you to know the truth. The bullet that killed your father was never intended for him. It was meant for your mother. And, it was ordered by a traitor to the Dark Council who has his own agenda."

"Who?" The boy said and then crumpled, falling forward onto the slab. "I can't hold much longer." A totally new voice came from within the all-encompassing facial mask. "You're growing too weak."

Thakkar looked back at the slab as the image of Olivia changed, fading into the image of a dark-haired teenage boy. In his hands, the boy held the blue stone. "I'm sorry, Olivia. I am near death now. I cannot hold the illusion much longer."

Thakkar reached over and pulled the mask from the other figure's face. Olivia stared back at her. "Fooled you."

"What?" Thakkar said. She snatched the blue stone from Steven's hands. "It doesn't matter. I now have the nanomemes."

Olivia stood up, shakily. "You have no control over me, Thakkar. I entered Numinocity on my own. Your faulty nanomemes have filled the warehouse, and they interfaced with my brain stimulator. I had a few absence seizures while pretending to be Steven, but the bottom line is you cannot control me. I didn't even feel a flicker of that pleasure you boasted of. Just acting."

"That doesn't matter." Thakkar held up the blue stone. "This is what I came for."

"Really?" Olivia said and motioned with her hand. The air seemed to shudder, and the image of New Stonehenge grew translucent again. Thakkar turned and studied her body, lying on the other slab. "What is this?"

The Crimson Snake stepped from behind a monolith. She walked over and looked down at the sleeping figure of Olivia. She then walked over to Thakkar and reached to her back and pulled out her walking cane. She pressed a button, and the ceramic blade popped out.

"Good, Snake," Thakkar said and looked back at Olivia. "End her."

"No!" Steel tried to stand up and collapsed again in weakness.

Snake laughed and looked back across the ethereal air from her real world into the virtual reality of Numinocity. "I've already had a little conversation with the girl, Thakkar. And, someone else! I have a new boss, Thakkar."

Snake raised the cane's blade and plunged it into Thakkar's neck.

"No!" She screeched as her real body spasmed on the slab. Blood poured onto the slab, and the virtual Thakkar convulsed. She seemed to expand, to swell as her virtual image recoiled from the dying embers of her real mind. Thakkar's body moved again, and then the chest ceased to move. Snake wiped the blood from her cane.

"Snake, this was not what I agreed on." Olivia whispered.

Snake smiled and wiped the blade clean of blood against the hem of Thakkar's garment. "Like I said, I have a new boss."

Thakkar's image almost faded. Her face twisted in concentration, and her lips moved as she spoke aloud a language only machines could understand. Bits and bytes and zeroes and ones spewed from her lips and disappeared in the air. Her fading image stabilized. Her features grew clearer.

Thakkar laughed out loud, and her laughter cascaded throughout Numinocity. "I did it! I have ascended! I am no longer confined to that body." She whirled, and her eyes grew crimson. "I am more than mortal. I am more than spiritual. I am human 6.66! The world will bow before me. Numinocity will replace your reality. With this." She held up the blue stone, and it pulsed once and then opened like the petals of a flower. Tiny blue particles floated into the air.

"Yes, my new nanomemes. Flow into the life blood of Numinocity! Ignite the flame that destroys the real world!"

A particle landed on the third eye and burst into flame. Thakkar looked at it cross-eyed and screamed as the flame spread across her skin. "What is this?" More particles landed on her skin and ignited it. She tried to drop the stone, but it melted into the palm of her hand. She screamed again as fire bubbled her skin.

"My final revenge." Steven opened his eyes and said tiredly from the slab. "A virus that will destroy your creation. You will be deleted." He gasped in pain and faded from view.

Olivia screamed and threw herself onto the empty slab, where now her real body seemed to float ghost-like back in the warehouse. Thakkar was aflame, and her screams were inhuman, the screech of machine language and shattering diodes. The monoliths in the real warehouse burst into flame around Snake.

Steel felt his armor fade away, and as Thakkar dwindled away into formless smoke, the last thing he saw was the body of the real Olivia on the slab in the burning warehouse. And then, there was darkness.

42

Olivia opened her eyes and instantly began to choke on the smoke. She tried to move, and her arms and legs responded sluggishly. The effects of the nanomemes should be gone by now, but the real problem was her brain stimulator. Thakkar had turned it off, and she could tell it was now active and rebooting. She coughed again as smoke eddied around the slab, and she tried in vain to sit up. She fell back on the wood surface of the slab, and tears poured from her irritated eyes. She had to get up! She had to find out about Steven!

He had disappeared, which meant either he had removed his goggles or he had died! Either prospect was dire. A shadow fell over her, and the Crimson Snake looked down on her. She held a finger of her good hand to her ear. She coughed and nodded.

"So, you want me to save the girl? Got it." Snake leaned over her and scooped her off the slab. The monoliths were burning around them, and the flammable plastic curtains were falling all around, filling the air with toxic fumes.

Snake hopped over a flaming pile of plastic and into the

cooler air of the warehouse periphery. She came to sliding doors and glanced once at Olivia.

"Good thing you're still useful to someone." She said and tore open the door with her mechanical arm. She stepped outside and placed Olivia on the cool concrete of the parking lot.

"Got to go, girl. They'll find you. Tootles!" She disappeared, and Olivia stared into the night sky as smoke and flames grew behind her. She coughed some more expelling the smoke from her lungs and hoped that her brother had made it. An unfamiliar patch of stars appeared in an opening in the smoke, and for a second, a random assortment of stars assumed the shape of a cross. Should she place her hope in some Being that ruled this universe that was filled with pain and suffering? Did she dare to hope?

"God, if you're there, help my brother." She whispered before an absent seizure gripped her and took her under.

Monarch raced up the rickety stairs. She was looking at her phone at the tracker app she had installed after receiving the location of her son. She paused on the top stair landing and looked right and left. Four apartments sat off the hallway. Which room was it?

Below her, she heard the commotion in the stairwell. Ishido had stayed behind, and she heard the dull thump of hands on flesh and the groan of pain. She had to hurry. Thakkar's operatives were right behind her. Which room? She ran down the hallway and paused in front of each door. Kick it in? Knock? No, this wasn't the one. How she knew was beyond her. She arrived at the last door and smelled the odor of body excrement. Yes, Steven would have been under for days and unable to take care of his basic needs.

Monarch hurled herself against the door and bounced painfully off. She pounded her fists against the decaying wood and splinters tore into her flesh. Ishido appeared beside her, his neck leaking blood. His pale features were covered in sweat.

"Three men. They were fighting me and then just stopped and looked at each other in confusion. That's all the break I needed. Allow me." Ishido kicked the doorframe at the handle, and the door flew inward. The odor was overwhelming, and they both gagged.

Monarch ran into the room and spotted her son instantly. He was laid out on a couch in an adult diaper and tee shirt. A feeding tube came from his nose and was attached to an automatic feeding apparatus. The bag of liquid nourishment was empty. He was thin and emaciated and white as a sheet. A pair of bulky goggles covered his eyes. Should she remove them?

Monarch ran across the room. "Get medical help, Ishido!" She screamed as she knelt beside the couch. Her hand went to her son's neck. No pulse! His chest was not moving.

"No!" She screamed as she pulled him off of the couch and onto the firmer surface of the floor. She started chest compressions and then pressed her lips against her son's mouth, blowing air into his lungs.

"Come on, Steven. Don't do this to me." If his heart had stopped, then chances were it was safe to remove the goggles. She tore them from his face and hurled them across the room. Steven's eyes were empty and lifeless. Monarch pressed on, and Ishido put a hand on her shoulder.

"Max is sending someone she knows here in Paris. They will be here in five minutes."

Monarch kept the chest compressions going. Five minutes was long enough for his brain to be starved. She continued to work and found herself breathing a silent prayer. On the ledge outside the open window, a bird fluttered away into the night.

~

STEEL PULLED the goggles off of his eyes and tried to sit up. He was in Monarch's lab on the cot. He was weak, hungry, and thirsty. But, he was alive. He touched his chest. No scorpion stinger wound.

Beside him, Josh sat up and tossed his goggles across the room. "Bro, we got to check on Olivia! That fire!"

"I know." Steel said. He stood up shakily, and Josh helped the others with their goggles. One cot was empty. Vivian? Where was she? He glanced at Holmes.

"Vivian was here?"

"Yes. Said she found the place. She saved me from an anaphylactic reaction with this." He held up a syringe he had found on the cot beside him. "But where is she?"

Birdsong rubbed his neck and shook his head. "Where are her goggles? No Vivian. No goggles."

Raven stretched, and her back cracked. "Good riddance."

Steel glared at her. "She saved us all."

"By praying," Holmes added.

"Dude, I never thought Vivian would ever pray to anyone but Satan," Josh said. "Now, can we please check on Olivia?"

"How do we know where the warehouse is?" Holmes asked as he turned to the computer screens. They had come back on and revealed multiple windows filled with static. "Is Numinocity really gone?"

"Let's hope so," Raven said. She came over and put a hand on Steel's arm. "Sorry about Vivian. I didn't know why she disappeared like that. Everything was so chaotic."

Steel patted her hand. "Yeah, I know. Thanks for the helmet."

Josh joined Holmes at the console and began tapping on keys. An image came up in one of the windows. Dr. Monarch's face filled the screen.

"You're back!" She was obviously video chatting from her phone. Behind her, the swaying interior of an ambulance could be seen. "We've got Steven stabilized, and I'm heading for one of Max's private clinics. What about Olivia?"

"We are working on it." Steel said. "She's at the warehouse where Thakkar had her New Stonehenge set."

Monarch looked down at her phone. "Just got a message from Max. There is a fire at a warehouse in south London, and they found Olivia!" Monarch pressed her hand against her mouth. "She's alive, and she is heading for this hospital." Monarch touched the screen, and the address showed up in the window. "Jonathan, please go check on her."

Steel nodded. "We are heading there now. What about Thakkar?"

Monarch smiled. "Max said Steven released some kind of virus into Thakkar's system. Her entire network is gone!"

Steel sighed. At least something was going right for a change. He felt a tug on his arm.

"Bro, let's go," Josh said.

"I'll stay here in case Monarch needs anything," Raven said. Steel glanced at her, and a strange expression came over her face. He wanted to ask, to talk, but there was no time. As usual. He followed the others out of the room.

43

J osh paced back and forth across the living room floor of their hotel suite. He stopped and rechecked his watch. "Bro, they should be here by now."

Steel sat at the kitchen table and tried to remain calm. "Dr. Monarch had to come from Paris, Josh."

"Yeah, and she should have been here by midnight. It's 9 in the morning!"

Dr. Montana Holmes came out of his bedroom and brushed back his hair. "You can still go with me to see Dr. Hampton."

Josh shook his head. "No, Olivia, first."

"Dr. Monarch said she was fine. Just some burns from the warehouse." Steel said. "She's picking her up at the hospital and bringing her here. You got to see her in the hospital."

"Yeah, all covered in burns and under from her pain medicine," Josh said.

"Why are you so anxious? Are the two of you an item?" Steel said.

Josh paused and raised an eyebrow. "Did you just use the word 'item' to describe my friendship with Olivia? Dude, sometimes I forget you are an old man in a young body."

Steel shrugged. "Fine then." He turned back to the table. "Then go with Monty, and I'll call you when they get here and tell you she's okay."

"Oh, no," Josh said. "I want to see her with my own eyes."

Jason Birdsong stepped from his bedroom, pulling a piece of luggage. "Well, my flight is less than 12 hours to Houston. Then, a few hours' drive to New Orleans."

"And you'll be meeting Steel's friend, the FBI guy?" Holmes said.

Steel stood up. "Ross is not my, uh, friend." But the statement wasn't even convincing to himself.

"Methinks he doth protest too much. Bro." Josh said.

"I've already spoken to Ross. He is waiting in Shreveport and will let me ride with him to New Orleans." Birdsong came over to Josh. "Little brother of mine since we now share, what is in your case a new great-grandmother, I need a hug."

Josh smiled, and Birdsong pulled him into a tight hug. "Bro, I forgot about Hu'ul. I want to meet her someday. After all, now that she has adopted Jonathan as her grandson and since Jonathan adopted me, we are all one big family."

Steel nodded. There was a time such a thought had bothered him. But, now an unfamiliar warm feeling filled his chest. "True. Jason, be careful, and thank you for taking care of Josh."

Birdsong stood in front of Steel, and his eyes moistened. "You're a good man, Jonathan, no matter what your memories tell you. Remember that. And, that is why I am proud to be your partner." Before Steel could protest, Birdsong had embraced him in a tight, painful hug. Birdsong pushed away and turned to Holmes.

"You get just a handshake, my friend," Birdsong said.

"Why?" Holmes shook his hand.

"Because I can't let the man of steel see me cry. Ishido has a ride waiting for me, so I'm getting out of here." He paused at the door and looked back at Josh. "Call me when you get home,

Josh. I need to mentor you in the proper way a young Christian man should date."

Josh opened his mouth to protest, and Birdsong hurried through the door. Steel dabbed at his eye. This emotional stuff was getting ridiculous. No sooner had the door closed than it reopened, and Raven walked in. She wore a pair of jeans and a maroon tee-shirt underneath a brown leather jacket. She closed the door behind her and nodded to Steel.

"Max told me to come here so we could talk." She said.

Steel glanced at Holmes and then at Josh. "Talk?"

Raven rolled her eyes and sat at the table. "Not you and me. Us." She motioned to them all. The television sprang to life. No doubt, Max was always watching.

"My young, impatient man, Josh." Max smiled. "Olivia and her mother are only 5 minutes out."

Holmes settled at the table, and Josh joined him. Max looked at them from the television. "Well, that was an interesting diversion from our original mission." She brushed at her white hair and her eyes burned with passion. "Now, what is this I hear about Cephas being alive?"

Steel cleared his throat. "I don't know, Max. In Numinocity, I had a hard time telling fantasy from reality. I saw Cephas. And, Theo. They said they were alive on some foreign world."

"And I haven't told Jonathan this yet." Josh looked at him. "I saw my father. In a robe. He said he was alive with Uncle Cephas."

"What?" Steel said.

"Dude, we've been kinda busy."

"I don't know what to think," Max said. "If they are alive on this other world, the question is why?"

"I think Cephas called it the 'Node of God'." Steel said. "Ring a bell?"

"No." Max shook her head. "But, it gives me something to look for."

"Like my father," Josh said. "And my uncle. Although," he put a hand on Steel's arm. "Bro, I gotta say it. Don't go all emo on me. But I have a father now."

Steel stiffened and looked down at Josh's hand. He still was not used to being called that. He blinked at moisture. Again. "Thanks, Josh." He said hoarsely. Josh looked away, but Steel would have sworn he saw a tear in the boy's eye.

"Be that as it may," Max said. "Raven, I am pleased you are alive and back to your real self."

"Mostly." She said. "I'm still trying to sort through the memories."

"So, what about your amulet?" Steel reached into his shirt and pulled out the necklace.

"Keep it for now," Raven said. "When the two of us get back to Max, then give it back to me. A lot can happen between now and then."

"Like getting Josh home." Steel said.

"Bro, I'm not leaving you. If I gotta go to Switzerland with you, then I'll make the sacrifice. After all, we will soon be on Thanksgiving break back home. And, I saw a Facebook post Buck is home from the hospital. I don't want to hurry back into the nest of hornets. Or, in his case, wasps." He sat back and closed one eye. "I wonder if Olivia has ever seen Switzerland?"

"I have made arrangements for the three of you to fly back to Zurich tomorrow morning," Max said. "We will finish Raven's business so the two of you can get back to the states."

The door opened, and Olivia stepped through. Max smiled and winked at Steel as the television went to black. Josh stood up, his eyes filled with eager anticipation. Olivia's head was covered in a wraparound bandage, and her right arm was in a sling. Her mother stepped in behind her.

"Olivia!" Josh's voice squeaked. He cleared his throat and started walking toward her and ran the last few feet. He brought himself up with a stop; his hands outstretched as he looked over Olivia's bandages.

Olivia smiled and hugged him with her good arm. "Hey, demon boy. Good to see you."

Josh's hug lingered, and then he stepped back and seemed antsy. "Uh, yeah, good to see you. Uh, cyborg girl. Nice hairband. Mandy would love it." He cleared his throat. "Are you okay?"

"Just some second-degree burns and smoke inhalation. My implants are back to their normal settings." She motioned to her mother. "Tell them about Steven."

"Yeah, Steven," Josh said sheepishly. "How is he?"

"Alive and recovering in an ICU. Max had him transferred to a private clinic in London. He's getting stronger by the hour. He was terribly malnourished and weak, but he'll make a full recovery." Monarch said.

"Tell them about his hands," Olivia said.

"His hands?" Steel asked.

"Steven's hands were damaged by the, uh, bullet." She glanced at Raven. "He's had trouble since then, but somehow, his version of the nanomemes have repaired most of the damage. He has gotten the full use of his hands back."

Olivia nodded. "Not so lucky for me. Thakkar's nanomemes merely hijacked my implant generator and pulled me into Numinocity. Still got seizures!"

Josh reached out and touched her good arm and then pulled his hand back. "I'm sorry, Olivia."

Olivia sighed. "Josh, it's okay. I'm not completely convinced about this God of yours, but I did see some things in Numinocity I can't explain. Things that transcended the virtual world."

Olivia dropped her hand and closed it around Josh's hand. Josh stiffened and then grinned from ear to ear. Dr. Monarch walked over to Raven and sat beside her.

"Raven, I know you had no choice when you, uh, killed my husband. But, I hear I was the target all along. Do you have any memories of who hired you?"

Raven shook her head. "No. But, we will get my dossier in the next day or so, and we will know for sure."

Monarch nodded. "Well, there is something I wanted to talk to you about. You may not have to wait that long. The nanomemes Steven developed are amazing. I've been going over his notes, and I believe I can use them to reverse your surgery."

Raven stood up abruptly. "What?"

Monarch nodded and turned slowly to face Steel. "And, yours, too, Jonathan."

Steel blinked, and his face grew cold. The memory of his mother's face flashed in his memory. So much had changed in the last few days. His father was a member of the Council of Darkness AND in league with the Vitreomancers. A demon had once possessed his own soul. And, his mother had been killed? Perhaps by him? "Wait! I don't, I mean, I might not want to know about my past."

Raven glared at him. "Is it because we once had a thing?"

"You two had a thing?" Josh said.

Steel jerked out of his reverie, and his face turned red and warm. "I, uh, might have a memory of us talking about it. But, no, I don't remember the details of a 'thing.'"

Raven nodded. "I don't blame you, Jonathan. I wouldn't try to recover my memory unless it would help with two things. Finding who ordered Dr. Monarch's assassination." Raven leaned over the table. "And how to find your father."

"Well, I'm not so sure about Jonathan just yet." Monarch said. "I have brain mapping of Raven's mind from the time she was in the goggles and connected to my system. Her surgery was much less invasive than yours, Jonathan. Performed by Dr. Sno."

Steel recalled the white-haired Asian surgeon in the African prison. Was the man a Vitreomancer? The memory was all too real, as was the memory of his other self in Numinocity.

"I am very confident I can help Raven, but I need some more time before we would try to restore your memory."

Steel nodded. "Take your time."

Raven nodded. "When do we start?

44

Monarch's lab was mostly back to normal. Steel and Raven sat before one of her consoles. Josh and Olivia had accompanied Holmes to Dr. Hampton's museum to open the crates. On the computer screen, Monarch pulled up an image of a brain. Red, branching lines blossomed from the bottom of the image of the brain and made their way into the center of the brain. The image rotated.

"The original implants were in the cerebellum, or base of the brain back here." Monarch patted the bottom back of her head. "Then, tendrils of carbon nanotubes branched up along the nerve tracts into the hippocampus and basal ganglia." She pointed to the center of the brain. "Just know that these areas can control memory and emotion. I am still processing the data I collected on Jonathan, but his implants are a different type of carbon nanotubes with a much more sophisticated implant module."

Raven glanced at Steel. "You got the upgraded version."

"Which explains your confusion, Raven. Your implants are much less effective, much messier, and dangerous." Monarch looked at Raven. "If we don't remove them or at least deactivate them, you will suffer permanent brain damage. Now, being carbon nanotubes, I think these nanomemes can break down the filaments, and then I can go in later surgically and remove the module without permanent damage. Ready?"

Steel felt warmth and a squeeze. He looked down. Raven had taken his hand. "Yes."

Raven clung to his hand as they followed Monarch through an inner door and into a sterile, white room. An operating table occupied the center of the room. On a metal stand sitting next to the operating table, a small glass vial actually glowed with an amber light. Raven released Steel's hand, and he wiped his own sweat on his jeans. Raven leaned over the vial. "Are these the babies?"

"Yes. If you lay down on the table, I'll hook up your EEG leads." It took about ten minutes to attach all the leads to Raven's scalp. Monarch then took a pair of the goggles from a nearby table. "New goggles. I'm using them mainly to monitor your brain activity. It's attached to my computer program and will give us a real-time map of your brain and the nanotubes."

Raven took the goggles and looked back at Steel. "One last thing, Jonathan, in case this all goes south."

"What?"

"You said you met yourself in Numinocity."

"My bad self." Steel said.

"I keep recalling there was another you. A weird memory that keeps floating around."

"You said something about me being the *other*." Steel said. "Right before you, uh, died in the cavern. I wondered what you meant."

"I meant this other 'bad' you. If that is what you were like before, then don't do what I'm doing. You have a fresh, clean slate. Put that other 'you' out of your mind. He doesn't exist anymore."

Steel knelt beside the bed and met her gaze with his. "And what about you? Don't you risk just as many bad memories?"

Raven sighed. "My memories are well earned, Jonathan. I wasn't a good girl like you were a good boy."

"How do you know?"

"You are looking for your father because you wanted answers to why he has turned into a monster. Why would you look for a monster other than to kill him?"

Steel's forehead furrowed. "I don't follow."

Raven put a hand on his cheek. "Jonathan, the real reason you are looking for your father is not to kill him. It is to forgive him."

Steel blinked and stood up. "No."

Raven nodded and winced as Monarch pressed an intravenous angiocath into her other arm. "Sorry, but we need to move on. You two can reminisce and discuss this at length when you've gotten all of your memory back."

Raven nodded, reached out, and squeezed Steel's hand one more time. "You have to forgive him, Jonathan. Because I'm not going to forgive him. I'm going to kill him."

She released his hand, and Steel stepped away. This was the real Raven, the murderous Raven, the dark heart that, although forgiven by God, still found it impossible to forgive people. Would that be his fate? Could he truly every forgive his father?

Monarch nodded at Raven, and she pulled the goggles over her eyes. On the nearby console, two large monitors sprang to life with squiggly lines. A three-dimensional image of Raven's brain appeared drawn in tiny, thin lines. The red branching tendrils of her implant glowed and pulsed as the image rotated.

Monarch inserted a needle and syringe into the nanomeme vial and filled the barrel of the syringe with glowing, amber fluid.

"Dr. Monarch beginning treatment on Raven. Computer, mark time." The monitor beeped. Monarch attached the syringe to the I.V. line and slowly injected the liquid. She turned and watched the monitors. For a moment, nothing happened, and then the nanotubes changed color from a pulsing crimson to a glowing amber. The color change began at the back of Raven's brain and moved upward and forward along the tendrils.

"Raven?" Monarch asked. "How do you feel?"

"Funny." Raven slurred. "Silly. Balloons. Lambs. Strings." Her voice grew softer and more juvenile sounding. Monarch detached the syringe and ran to the monitor.

"No, no, no!"

Steel bolted over to stand beside her. "What?"

The EEG squiggles were changing, losing their spiky appearance. The tendrils faded from the image. "Everything is going. Everything!"

Monarch turned back to Raven. "Raven, talk to me."

"Daisy, Daisy, give me your answer do." She sang in a tiny, thin voice. "Hi, my name is, my name is, uh." Raven rolled on the table onto her side and pulled her legs up to her chest. She pushed her thumb into her mouth. Monarch turned back to the monitor again.

"What is happening, Dr. Monarch?" Steel hissed.

"It took out the tendrils, Jonathan. But, it took out everything else." She looked at Raven as the woman began to coo. "She wanted a clean slate."

Steel's eyes widened. "What?"

"She's essentially a baby, Jonathan." Monarch looked at him and turned back to the monitor. She hit a button on the keyboard, and a window popped up in the corner. Max's face appeared.

"I know you're monitoring me, Max." Monarch said.

"What have you done?" Max barked. "Raven is now like an infant?"

"Yes. Every memory is gone. She'll have to be retrained

completely." Monarch looked at Jonathan, and he felt her eyes on his face. He was still looking Raven as horror gripped his heart. Tears filled his eyes.

"Jonathan, we can't even begin to try this on you." Monarch said.

"I'm sending Ishido. He will bring Raven to me. We will take care of her from now on." Max said.

"But I have to do testing. I, uh," Monarch began.

"You have done quite enough!" Max said as her image faded.

Monarch looked at Steel and then down at Raven and crumpled onto the floor. Steel merely stood there, no compassion, no mercy left in his heart for Monarch. Only an undying and now unrequited love for Raven.

EPILOGUE

Josh wandered through the dark hallways. Doorways opened to his right and left, but he was drawn straight ahead by the light at the end of the hall. He stepped through the opening at the end of the hallway onto a balcony filled with dust-covered theater seats. Three rows of seats encompassed a round gallery. He moved down the three steps to the railing and looked down.

It must have once been an old medical theater for observing surgery or dissection. Below, more rows of seats in concentric circles overlooked a circular "theater" in the center of the chamber. Dr. Holmes and another man stood by one of the three crates from Uncle Cephas. Dr. Montana Holmes lifted his hand from one of the three crates. The top popped open, releasing a plume of gas.

"That's the second one. Sorry for the delay, Dr. Hampton."

Dr. Hampton was a tall, frumpy figure of a man with a ring of white hair around his balding head. He wore tiny reading glasses perched on the tip of his nose. His rumpled jacket matched his rumpled pants, and a red bowtie sat crookedly at his neck.

"My good boy, I was beginning to wonder if you were ever coming. I am afraid I was looking for a decent pry bar." Hampton glanced up at Josh. "Oh, young man, good of you to come. Where is your friend?"

"She's upstairs. Her burns are hurting, so she's waiting for us. Monty, how much longer?"

Holmes looked wistfully at the crates. "Just one last crate. Give me a minute." Holmes went to the last crate. Unlike the other two wood crates, this one was of burnished metal with a glass screen in the lid. Holmes passed his hand over the screen, and it came to life. He placed his palm on the screen, and it gleamed with a green light. A small buzzing sound came from the screen. Holmes pulled away his hand and leaned over the lid.

"There's a message. It seems I do not have the authority to open this crate." Holmes shook his head in confusion. "I don't understand. Dr. Washington assured me that each crate's locking mechanism was keyed to my palm print."

Hampton crossed his arms, and a cross look came over his face. "This is a most unfortunate development, Dr. Holmes. Whatever shall I do?"

"Well, you have two crates to work on while I contact Dr. Washington and see what we can do to get this crate open. I wasn't planning on returning to the states just yet. I was hoping to see the contents of the crates."

"Well, let me give you some powerful incentive. Open the third crate, and I will share the contents of all three with you. Until then, I will rummage through the crates on my own. Sorry, old boy. But, you've delayed me enough."

Holmes nodded. "You're going to make me wait like I did you."

Hampton smiled. "Yes, my dear boy. Now, off you go. Find out how to open this last crate quickly, please. Oh, and stop by the office on the way out. I think there are at least 42 forms to be filled out and notarized."

Holmes shook his head and moved past Josh toward the top of the theater. "This may take a while."

"Now, my good lad!" Hampton looked up at Josh. "I was hoping you would come by before you left. Come on down here to the amphitheater."

Josh found a spiral staircase and hurried down to the amphitheater floor. Hampton clapped him on the shoulder and motioned to the first crate to open. "I wanted to ask you about this crate. Dr. Holmes told me you found something of interest in this crate, and it was removed. As you know, I am cataloging all of Dr. Lawrence's gifts to me for an exhibit on evil, pain, and suffering. Perhaps you could enlighten me as to what was removed?" He tilted his head, and his bright, pale blue eyes focused on Josh. "Hmm?"

Josh swallowed nervously. What should he say? How could he explain to Dr. Hampton that Theophilus Nosmo King had traveled back in time and had left them a message?

"Uh, we found a box containing a coin with an inscription from a person named Theophilus. Monty believes it is the same Theophilus referred to by Luke in his gospel and in the book of Acts."

Hampton raised an eyebrow in surprise. "Really? Excellent! I wish I could have seen it."

Josh shrugged. "I guess Monty took it and forgot to put it back into the crate."

"Perhaps you could look in the crate and make sure nothing else is missing? Hmmm?"

Josh shook his head. "I don't remember what was in the crate."

Hampton put a hand on his shoulder and gently pushed him toward the crate. "Just a peek. It might jog your memory. Hmmm?"

Josh hesitated and then moved toward the crate just to get away from the man's hand. He gingerly leaned over the crate. Its contents were starkly outlined in the cone of harsh light from the theater's ceiling. Straw like packing material cradled several items. His gaze ran over them.

"I don't remember what was in here that day other than the box with the coin."

Hampton moved around to the opposite side of the crate. He smiled and pointed into the crate. "What about that box? Was it in the crate?"

Hampton pointed to a wooden box etched with golden filigree. It was roughly the size of a shoebox.

"I don't remember, Dr. Hampton. I really must go."

"Wait, my dear lad. I can't reach that box from here. Could you retrieve it for me?"

Hampton smiled, and for a second, his tongue darted across his lips. Josh shivered. "Sure." Hampton was getting creepy!

Josh leaned over the edge of the crate and slid his hands beneath the bottom of the box. It was surprisingly heavy. He lifted it straight up and leaned back.

Hampton gasped. "Just a moment! I forgot to get my white gloves. Just hold it for me while I get my examining gloves."

Hampton hurried across the room and out through a doorway. Josh stood still with the box, weighing heavily in his hands. He shifted his grip, and the index finger of his left hand brushed against something sharp on the underside of the box. A stabbing pain shot into his finger, and he almost dropped the box. He cried out in pain and whirled.

Hampton was standing a foot behind him with white gloves on. "Are you okay, lad?"

Josh shoved the box into the man's hands. "Something stuck me."

He looked at his left hand. A drop of blood oozed from a puncture in the pad of his index finger.

"Sorry, Josh," Hampton said. "These old boxes have all kinds of metal edges to them. Have you had a recent tetanus shot?"

Josh sucked on his finger. The blood had a distinct copper taste. "I'll check with Jonathan. It's just a scratch."

Hampton frowned. "Well, we must be sure. I'd have it checked out."

Josh motioned to the box. "Just what is that box?"

Hampton's eyes lit up as he studied the box. "If Dr. Lawrence's theory is correct, you are looking at Pandora's box. You know the legend?"

Before Josh could open his mouth, Hampton continued. "According to Hesiod, when Prometheus stole fire from heaven, Zeus, the king of the gods, took vengeance by presenting Pandora to Prometheus' brother Epimetheus." Hampton's eyes widened in excitement. "Pandora opened a box left in his care containing sickness, death, and many other unspecified evils which were then released into the world. Though she hastened to close the container, only one thing was left behind." Hampton leaned closet to Josh. "Now, here is where it gets very interesting and where most people who have heard the legend of Pandora's Box get it all wrong. You see, the one thing left in the box was represented by a single word. Have any idea what that word would be, my dear boy?"

Josh looked again at his finger. It was still stinging. "I don't know, bro. Death. Decay. Disease. Evil. Demons. Am I getting warm because if I'm not, I really need to get out of here."

Hampton smiled and chuckled. "Well, the word was usually translated as Hope." Hampton tapped the box in glee. He raised an eyebrow. "But, the word can have another translation, a rather pessimistic meaning of 'deceptive expectation.' How about that?"

Josh shook his head. "I don't get it."

Hampton ignored him. "Of course, the original Greek word referred to a jar, not a box, but one can always hope."

Josh felt the puncture site sting some more, and he shoved his hand into his pocket. "Well, I wouldn't open it if I were you. I have to go."

Josh hurried up the spiral staircase and paused at the top of the balcony. He walked quietly to the front of the gallery and glanced down into the theater. Dr. Hampton was standing deathly still with his eyes turned up toward the balcony. And, the smile on his face was far from happy — no, it was almost a rictor of death. Josh stumbled away from the balcony edge and hurried down the hallway to find Jonathan Steel.

Dr. Hampton carried Pandora's box across the room and entered the hallway leading from the first-floor operating theater. He stepped through the first open door into a room illuminated by a candle chandelier. Around the periphery of the room, shelves held arcane artifacts of varying types. Hampton sat the box on the table in the center of the room. He smiled as he ran a gloved finger along the closed edge of the box. Oh, how he wanted to open the box! To see what evil lay within!

"What are you doing?"

He froze and stood stiffly. "Just admiring your handiwork."

"It is not time to open the box." The voice of a woman came through the door.

Hampton turned and rubbed his hands together as someone moved into the room. She was short and diminutive, almost a pixie, he thought. Her features hinted at an Asian ethnicity. She wore a bright yellow pantsuit and a matching hat on her short, black hair. To Hampton, she could have been a go-go dancer from the 1960s. The woman had no sense of style.

Hampton moved away from the table as she approached, her gaze fixed on the box.

"We do not know what has evolved within the box. We do not know how magnified and distorted the evil has become that lives within." She reached out a tiny hand and placed it on the lid. She closed her eyes and smiled.

"Yes, they are almost ready."

She spun deftly and crossed her arms, and smiled at Hampton. "Tell me you inoculated the boy."

"It is done. What will happen to him?" Hampton said.

"That is not your concern right now. You have fulfilled your side of the bargain. You will be rewarded."

Hampton motioned to the artifacts around the room. "I am already richly rewarded. But, there is the matter of the last crate."

The woman frowned. "You have not opened it yet?"

"No." Hampton pushed his glasses back up his nose with a gloved finger. "Dr. Holmes' palm print would not open it. Dr. Lawrence may have deceived me."

"Did you tip him off?"

"Heavens, no. I barely spoke to the man weeks before he disappeared. We only met once long ago, and he was more than willing to lend the three crates for my Museum of Misery display."

"If the final artifact is in that crate, we could have finished this business much sooner. Events have already been set into motion with the boy. I can use that leverage for my own purposes. But, the others will want the contents of that crate. Who can open it?"

"Dr. Elizabeth Washington, perhaps? Or, maybe Dr. Lawrence's other associate who is alive and was just here in London." Hamilton said. "And, the boy is his adopted son. Perhaps I could use the box as leverage?"

The woman gestured with her bare left hand, and Hampton

felt a vise-like grip close on his throat. Slowly, his body elevated off the floor, and the grip tightened. He gasped for breath, fumbling at his neck for a pair of hands he could not seize.

"You will not interfere with our plan. I will attend to Jonathan Steel." The grip released, and Hampton fell backward onto the floor. He looked up at the small woman. She raised her hands and snapped her fingers. The air sizzled with static electricity, and two more women materialized on either side of her. They were the same size as the first woman and, as Hampton studied their identical faces while gasping for his returning breath. The only difference was the color of their clothing. The two new women wore scarlet and blue pantsuits.

"Numbers six and five, I presume." Hampton managed hoarsely. "Together with you, seven, I understand you are named the Unholy Triad."

"The Council is compromised." The first woman said to her companions. "There is a Vitreomancer among us. We cannot wait for the entire Council to be replenished and to find unity. The three of us must handle this situation. Agreed?"

"Yes, sister." The red one said.

"Yes, sister." The blue one said.

The first woman turned and stared at Hampton. "If Dr. Washington cannot open this crate, then Jonathan Steel will open this crate. And we have two other tasks for him."

They popped out of sight, leaving Hampton to stumble to his feet, his bruised neck aching. Hampton returned to the back room. Inside, he brushed past cluttered counters and tables covered with moldy, dusty artifacts. He slid aside an ancient curtain and revealed a metal door. He pressed his hand on a glass plate next to the door. The door slid aside.

Hampton made his way down a set of metal steps into a room that illuminated with light at his presence. The room was smaller than the one above and round, just like the theater. In fact, the room had an old operating table sitting in the center.

Hampton paused and studied the figure on the table. A shadow passed behind him. The Crimson Snake stepped up beside him. Hampton lashed out at her and slapped her across the cheek. She gasped, and blood trickled from her split lip.

"Where were you just now? The triplets almost killed me!" Hampton hissed.

The Crimson Snake pushed her unruly red hair back from her face. "If you weren't paying me so much, I would crush your throat. You told me to guard her."

Hampton slowed his breathing and massaged his aching hand. "Go. Keep an eye on the boy."

Snake wiped the blood from her lip with her artificial hand. "You sign the check." She left the room.

Hampton massaged his sore neck and turned to study the figure on the table in the center of the ancient room. "Well, my dear, my eyes are quite dry. It is a shame that as we age, we can't stand wearing contacts. If you'll excuse me for a moment." Hampton moved over to a counter and opened an old porcelain cabinet and withdrew a leather bag. From inside the bag, he took out a holder for contact lenses. He teased the lenses from each eye and placed the blue irises into their receptacles.

He turned back to the table and rubbed his ghostly white eyes devoid of pupils. He leaned over the figure on the table and stared into the empty eyes. He ran a finger along the woman's pale cheek. She did not flinch.

"My poor, sweet Vivian. Trapped inside your own mind. What will I do with you?"

AFTERWORD

"Transhumanism" by Julian Huxley (1957)
   In New Bottles for New Wine, London: Chatto & Windus,
1957.

"Humans 2.0: Scientific, Philosophical, and Theological
Perspectives on Transhumanism
   Fazale R. Rana with Kenneth R. Samples

These are the sources for quotes in this novel.

All scripture comes from New King James Version of the Bible,
English Standard Version of the Bible, and New International
Version of the Bible.
   Also, to learn more about The Manning Institute of
Nanotechnology check out my book, Shadow Merchant. Infor-
mation can be found at hopeagainbooks.com.

ACKNOWLEDGMENTS

With my daughter's permission, I would like to tell my readers that she is the bravest person in the world. She has suffered from epilepsy since the age of 8 and now is 33. Her journey has been tumultuous and filled with medical procedures and diagnostic procedures and still she battles this disease. For most of her day, she is completely normal but inevitably, she will have one or two seizures each day. Most of the time, these are minor but occasionally, they are major seizures. I chose to feature a major character with epilepsy in this story to raise the awareness of epilepsy in the world.

About 1.2 percent of U.S. people have active epilepsy, about 3.4 million people nationwide, and more than 65 million globally. Estimates are that 1 in 26 people will develop epilepsy at some point during their lifetime. We need your prayers and your support. One of the most irritating issues is the prevalence of flashing lights and strobe like effects in movies. More people need to understand these flashing lights can trigger a seizure. We love to go to Walt Disney World, but we have had to stop visiting the parks after dark since the vendors in the parks sell thousands of flashing necklaces and light swords.

Be aware of the presence of those around you who may suffer from epilepsy and give us your support by visiting the Epilepsy Foundation's website at www.epilepsy.com.

ALSO BY BRUCE HENNIGAN

Fiction:

The 13th Demon: Altar of the Spiral Eye

The 12th Demon: Mark of the Wolf Dragon

The 11th Demon: The Ark of Chaos

The 10th Demon: Children of the Bloodstone

The 9th Demon: Time of the Cross

Death By Darwin (Featuring the first appearance of Jonathan Steel)

The Homecoming Tree

Upcoming:

The 7th Demon: The Unholy Triad

Non-Fiction:

Hope Again: A Lifetime Plan for Conquering Depression